Books published by The Random House Publishing Group
are available at quantity discounts on bulk purchases for
premium, educational, fund-raising, and special sales use.
For details, please call 1-800-733-3000.

THE BETRAYAL

PATI NAGLE

BALLANTINE BOOKS • NEW YORK

A Del Rey Books Mass Market Original

Copyright © 2009 by Patricia G. Nagle

Published in the United States by Del Rey Books, an imprint of The Random House Publishing Group, a division of Random House, Inc., New York.

DEL REY is a registered trademark and the Del Rey colophon is a trademark of Random House, Inc.

ISBN 978-0-345-50385-5

Printed in the United States of America

www.delreybooks.com

OPM   9   8   7   6   5   4   3   2   1

To Peggy, Beau, and Loui—my soul sisters.

Acknowledgments

Warmest thanks to those who helped bring this story, which is very dear to me, to publication: my editor, Liz Scheier, and Betsy Mitchell at Del Rey; Jane Lindskold and Peggy Whitmore for their encouragement and insight; and my husband, Chris Krohn, for his endless patience. Thanks also to Kris Rusch, Dean Smith, Laura Resnick, Pat McLaughlin, Mary Jo Putney, Plotbusters, the OWN gang, and the many other friends whose support has kept me going through dark times.

Walk many paths, leaving no mark behind but of beauty.

Honor the ældar and spirits who watch over all.

Serve in good faith, with true heart, those who share the bright journey.

Live in the world, giving thanks, speaking truth, harming none.

—*Creed of the Ælven,* first stave

✠ Alpinon ✠

A footfall on the forest floor below brought Eliani's head up sharply. The scroll in her hands curled back into itself. She had not been reading it—her thoughts had drifted long since. The Lay of the Battle of West-gard had failed to entrance her this day.

She leaned out from the branch where she sat and peered down between the leaves of her favorite oak, seeking the sound's source. A shadow of movement below, the edge of a cloak curling out of sight. Not a kobalen, then. Nor could it be a guardian, for Alpinon's patrols were always at least three strong.

Eliani laid a hand against the oak's trunk—slender there, near its top—and closed her eyes. The tree's khi was slow and deep. She sent her own khi through it and out into the forest: roots running strong into the earth, whisper-fine grasses moving with each light breeze, small creatures dwelling in branch or under root. A much brighter, stronger pulse of khi reverber-ated through the wood, one that could only be ælven. Eliani drew back from it, as the ælven did not trespass upon one another's khi.

She opened her eyes and carefully set her scroll in a notch of two branches where she had stored little trea-sures since childhood. She loved the old ballad—heroic mindspeakers and soul-consuming alben warlords still thrilled her despite her inattention this day—but her curiosity about the intruder was more immediate.

She moved stealthily down to the oak's lowest limbs, making no sound at all, for she could have climbed the tree blindfolded in any direction. Pausing on a lower branch, she saw a solitary figure walking away north-ward: tall, male, pale-haired.

She caught her breath, thinking for an instant that it was an alben. Fear set her heart pulsing before reason reminded her that an alben would not be walking in daylight even if he dared to cross the mountains into Alpinon.

No, it was a Greenglen, his hair not white but pale blond, as was common to his clan. He wore a cloak of Clan Greenglen's colors—sage lined with silver—and carried a long bow slung over one shoulder.

Greenglens rarely were seen in Alpinon, though their homeland of Southfæld shared a nearby border. Eliani had met only a handful of them in her short fifty years, and none recently.

She smiled a hunter's silent pleasure. She would track this foreigner, try to glimpse his face, see how long she could follow him unnoticed. It was the sort of game she most enjoyed, and she was good at it, having spent the last two decades in Alpinon's Guard. She felt a moment's wistfulness, reminded that soon she would be-come the Guard's commander. The other guardians would call her "Warden" instead of "Kestrel," the nick-name they had given her.

Tomorrow, on Autumn Evennight, she would be confirmed in her majority and formally named heir and designated successor to her father, Felisan, gover-nor of Alpinon. The command of the Guard would pass to her as well. This was her last day of youth and irresponsibility. A little mischief might be forgiven her this last time.

Grinning, she turned her attention to her quarry. She tensed her thighs, balanced carefully, and sprang to the forest floor, making no more sound than the falling of a leaf.

⁜

Turisan walked at his ease, enjoying the rich earthen smell and myriad colors of autumn leaves, only mildly curious at first about his pursuer. He was not quite certain how long he had been followed.

He was not averse to meeting a patrol from Alpinon's Guard. In fact, he half hoped to encounter one, for he had not been in this realm previously and did not know the way to Highstone. His pursuer, however, though certainly ælven, was evidently not a guardian. Such a one would have challenged him, not stalked him. He therefore continued to stride through Alpinon's fair woodlands, which were full of life and untouched by ælven hands, as unlike as could be to his home in Glenhallow.

Pausing to examine a spray of scarlet leaves, he saw a flicker of movement above. His brow creased in a slight frown. It was impolite to treat a visitor so, whether or not they knew who he was. He began to tire of the game.

And now he could hear his father berating him for not bringing along an escort suitable to his dignity. Had he been accompanied by ten of Southfæld's Guard, as Lord Jharan had wished, no zealous Stonereach would have dared to stalk him. In Jharan's view, a member of Southfæld's governing house should never travel unattended though he walk through the most benign lands. Indeed, he should not walk. He should ride a finely caparisoned steed or, better yet, take his ease in a chariot emblazoned with marks of state, surrounded by a mounted escort.

It was such excess of ceremony that made Turisan

long so often to be gone from the court at Glenhallow. The more he learned of the intricacies of governance, the more he yearned for the simplicity of a wild wood, a clear stream, and the flicker of stars through leafy branches.

This journey was in part an escape from court formalities, though at the end of it they awaited him again. His father had sent him here on a visit of ceremony, to pay respects and carry messages to Lord Felisan, the governor of Alpinon, and to witness the confirmation of his heir.

Turisan had made no objection to this errand, for he knew it to be his duty as his father's nextkin. Lord Jharan's eyes, so often stern, grew soft with fondness whenever he spoke of Felisan, and that alone made Turisan curious to know him. He also expected the visit to Alpinon's woodlands to satisfy his longing for wildness. Yet even here in the forest he was to have no peace, it seemed. Annoyed all at once, he turned in midstride and nocked an arrow to his bow, aiming it amidst the branches overhead.

"You have followed me half the afternoon. Come down and declare your business with me or begone."

A moment's silence. Then a rustle in the branches, and a lanky ælven female in worn and dusky hunting leathers emerged, landing softly before him. She brushed a strand of nut-brown hair from her green eyes and stood gazing at him.

"Peace to you, friend. I meant no harm. We seldom have visitors from the south."

Turisan lowered his bow. "And who are you?"

The little chin went up, then a corner of her mouth curled. "I am called Kestrel. I am kin to Lord Felisan."

Surprised, Turisan paused to return arrow to quiver while he reevaluated her status. No rustic this, whatever her appearance. Even a lesser relative of Lord Felisan deserved his respect, though she had not given her true name. He bowed.

"It is to bring messages to Lord Felisan that I have come. Will you honor me by guiding me to his house?"

The green eyes lit. "Messages? From Southfæld?"

Turisan smiled. "From Glenhallow."

He had thought that mention of Southfæld's seat of government would thrill her. She drew a breath, as of deep pleasure, then surprised him by replying with quiet dignity.

"It will be my honor to guide you."

She turned and, with a friendly glance over her shoulder, started northward. Turisan hastened to come up with her. Though not as tall as he, she had a guardian's purposeful stride. She looked at him sidelong as they walked apace.

"Forgive my discourtesy, I pray. What visitors we do receive from Southfæld generally come by the trade road."

Turisan smiled to show he held no grievance. "I prefer the woodlands."

"So do I. You have no horse? Glenhallow sends its messengers on foot?"

"I have a horse. I left it with the guardians at Midrange, thinking to enjoy a walk. I believe it is not far from here to Highstone?"

"No, not far." She smiled, her mouth twisting with private amusement.

Not a rustic, and not quite so young as he had first thought. Turisan observed her while she answered his polite questions about the land through which they walked.

She was fair of face and form, her coloring middle dark as was common in the Stonereach clan, her figure well enough though leaner than the gently bred maidens of Glenhallow's court. Turisan, being accustomed to receive the open admiration of every maid he met, was intrigued and somewhat abashed to realize that this female seemed more interested in his messages than in himself.

It would be a lesson to him, he acknowledged silently. He had indeed dwelt too long at court.

The woodlands, all ablaze with autumn, grew denser. Turisan's legs told him they were climbing, though at first the slope was scarcely noticeable. It became a true hill before long and led to numberless others increasing in size, greenleaf trees giving way to tall pines as they proceeded from foothills into the mountains proper. Though he would have enjoyed a rest, his guide seemed unweary, and he followed her onward, reflecting that the day he could not outmarch a slip of a Stonereach girl was the day he should renounce his heritage and become a magehall acolyte.

The mountain air took on a chill as evening fell, and warm glints of light had for some time been showing through the trees when they reached a road that sloped upward along one side of a pine-filled valley. It led to a town centered on a level shelf of rock where houses spread out from an open public circle and clung to the steep, rocky walls above and below. A pale river cascaded through the chasm to the north, and he heard the distant roar of a waterfall.

His guide paused at the edge of the circle. "Welcome to Highstone."

This was Alpinon's chief city, then. Smaller than Turisan had expected. The houses were built of stone with steep slated roofs to shed snow. Their ornamentation was minimal and rough compared with that of Glenhallow's graceful buildings, but after the long walk, the glow of their lighted windows in the blue-shadowed dusk was especially welcoming.

The grandest structure was a long hall situated on an outcrop commanding the valley a little way above the public circle. Its roof timbers were carved with stag's heads, the token of Clan Stonereach. A row of tall arched windows gave a muted glow through tapestries already drawn for the night.

"Felisanin Hall. Come, they will be at table. We are in time to join the meal."

"I would not intrude on Lord Felisan. Will you show me to a place where I can await his leisure?"

She grinned. "We are not so formal here. He would berate me for keeping an honored guest waiting. Surely you are tired and hungry?"

"Ah—yes."

"Come, then."

She led the way across the circle with a backward glance to see that he followed, and started up the steep stone stair beyond that led up to the governor's hall. Reflecting that a lack of formality did not necessarily imply a poor table, Turisan hastened after his guide.

⁂

Eliani could not wait to see the faces of the household when she introduced their exotic guest. She was certain now that he was high-ranking. Elusive, too; he had said little about himself and had turned aside a probing question or two with practiced ease.

She had longed to question the visitor about his homeland and what was happening outside Alpinon, but as he clearly had not wished to discuss such things with her, she had refrained. When asked the same questions by her father, he could scarcely refuse to answer, and so she would hear the news all the same.

Pausing in the hearthroom that served as the entrance

to Felisanin Hall, Eliani warmed her hands by the welcoming hearth and looked more closely at the stranger while he gave his cloak, bow, and small pack into the keeping of the attendants who came forward to welcome him.

He was tall and slim, though his firm shoulders told of strength with bow and sword. The hunting clothes he wore were of fine soft leather, dyed in subtle shades of green and richly embroidered. The silver clasp that pinned his cloak was intricate in design and bore a large glinting white stone. He left it in the cloak as it was taken away, as if its possible loss would mean little to him, though it was finer than any jewel Eliani possessed.

How rich his life must be! How simple he must think what she deemed grand and fine. She felt as if she were watching a creature out of another world entirely, one to which hers bore no comparison. Even his person was of rare and unusual beauty: fine features, long graceful fingers, hair of rich gold, eyes like dark pools of shadow.

Abruptly he glanced up at her and smiled. Caught in her curiosity, she returned the smile and stepped forward.

"May I know your name so that I may give you a proper introduction?"

He seemed to hesitate for an eyeblink, then answered quietly. "It is Turisan."

"I have heard that name." Eliani gazed at him, frowning slightly, certain they had never met. "I do not remember when."

His lips twitched. "It matters not. I am ready, if you will lead me in."

She started into the hall, pushing the tapestry aside. No doubt he was used to much grander feast halls, but at least she need not be ashamed of her house's hospitality.

Torches burned brightly, musicians played in a corner of the hall—for Lord Felisan was very fond of music—and the household talked merrily around the long table. Eliani was glad to see that the meal had not progressed very far. Her father looked up and beckoned to her, but instead of taking her place beside him, she strode up to his chair, bowed formally, and stepped to one side. The conversation fell away as the household became aware of the stranger she had brought with her; thus, it was to the accompaniment of music alone that she made her announcement.

"Lord Felisan, I bring you a visitor from afar. May it please you to welcome Turisan, who bears tidings from Glenhallow."

The murmur that followed confirmed the importance of their guest. Her father rose, and she was pleased to see that he wore one of his better robes of deep blue velvet broidered with gilt thread and pinned at the neck with a large violet stone.

Felisan glanced at Eliani, his eyes glinting mischief. The next moment it was gone as he turned to greet Turisan.

"Welcome indeed!" Lord Felisan smiled broadly as he offered his arm. "I was present at your naming day, but you will not remember that, of course. Lord Jharan does me honor to send his own son with his tidings."

Eliani drew a sharp breath. She hoped it would go unnoticed and quickly assumed a disinterested smile. As Turisan clasped arms with her father, she thought his glance flicked to her.

Lord Jharan's son, was he? Heir to the governance of Southfæld, the second oldest and second largest ælven realm. She closed her eyes briefly, silently chiding herself for not remembering where she had heard his name.

"I thank you, Lord Felisan, and crave pardon for arriving unheralded."

Felisan waved dismissal. "Jharan and I have been friends for centuries. There is no need of ceremony between our houses. Come, sit beside me and give me news of your father! These are all my household; I will not trouble you with their names just now. And two of my theyns, Luruthin and Gharinan, there at the end. My daughter you have met."

Eliani, standing beside her chair, was gratified to see Lord Turisan glance up at her in surprise. Her suspicion was correct, then: He had thought her of little importance. She returned a sweet smile, and he acknowledged her with a bow before taking his seat. That appeased her somewhat. Even more so did the kind thanks he made to the cousin who gave place to him.

Eliani helped herself to warm bread from the basket before her, listening to the pleasantries that passed between her father and his guest. Lord Jharan's messages would be given later and in private. She intended to be present, and Lord Turisan might make of that what he would.

"Your mountains are beautiful. I have seldom seen such richly timbered woods, and some of the prospects are breathtaking."

Felisan looked pleased. "You have yet to see the best of them, having arrived from the south. Ask Eliani to show you the Three Shades. It is a high fall of water not far from here, a very pretty spot with some interesting legends attached to it."

Turisan's gaze shifted to Eliani, and he gave a solemn nod. "I would be honored if Lady Eliani would show it me."

Eliani felt color rising to her cheeks. No one had called her "lady" before. That honorific was reserved for governors and their heirs, the masters of guildhalls, and other persons of high responsibility. She was not yet formally her father's nextkin.

She returned Turisan's nod, then glanced away and took a sip of wine. She did not know why she should find Lord Jharan's son any more disconcerting than she had found a nameless high-ranking Greenglen, but so it was. Perhaps because she had always thought of House Jharanin as stately and dignified, dwelling in luxurious palaces and occupied with lofty concerns of governance.

Turisan did not fit that picture at all. What governor-elect of any self-importance would undertake a journey on foot and alone?

She would. She laughed and choked a little on her wine.

Her father raised an eyebrow at her. "I hope you will stay with us some few days, Turisan. We are to celebrate a handfasting soon. Your presence would grace the occasion."

"A handfasting?" Turisan's gaze shifted briefly to Eliani, then back. "It would be my honor to attend. Are both parties from your household?"

"No, only Beryloni. She is the daughter of my departed lady's brother. She sits just there, in the blue gown, and beside her is her partner to be, Gemaron, who is of the Steppegard clan."

Turisan turned to the couple and smiled warmly at them as he raised his goblet. "I wish you great happiness together."

Others took up the toast. "Great happiness!"

Eliani raised her cup, smiling, and sipped. She, too, wished them great happiness, though her feelings were shadowed with reserve. Handfastings were rare among the ælven, for it was a lifelong pledge, and the breaking of a promise was unthinkable. Part of the creed, to keep good faith and to speak truth.

Eliani had witnessed only one other handfasting, that of her father's sister, Davhri, many years earlier when she herself was still a child. Her most vivid memory was of the ribbons: blue and violet for Stonereach, orange and gray for Clan Sunriding, and the mage-wrought handfasting ribbon woven with images and blessings— all tied into a complicated braid about the joined hands of the couple who were to be forever bound, body and spirit.

Davhri, whom Eliani had loved fondly but whom she now scarce remembered, had gone north to her new partner's home in Fireshore. Gifts and messages had come from time to time, brought by traders, but Davhri had never revisited Alpinon. Thus, Eliani tended to associate handfastings with loss.

Cup-bonds were much more common than handfastings. A promise to be true for a year and a day was no less serious a pledge, but one more easily kept.

Eliani had cup-bonded once herself, though she had regretted it halfway through the year. She was not an easy partner, it seemed. She and Kelevon had fallen into disagreement and dissolved their bond the day after its year at last had concluded. She had gone immediately into the Guard, and Kelevon had departed for his home in the Steppe Wilds and not been heard from again.

The minstrels struck up "The Battle of Westgard," and Eliani glanced toward them, feeling a tingle of foreboding. She tried to shake it off. It was not unusual for them to perform the lay, for the tale of how the Bitter Wars had ended, how mindspeakers had helped the ælven conquer the alben and drive them westward across the mountains, was a favorite of her father's. Eliani remembered hearing it at his knee, begging him to tell how he had fought in the battle, and his answer that it was at Midrange and Skyruach that he had fought, not at Westgard. The Bitter Wars had ended many centuries before his birth.

The meal drew to a close, and the householders gradually took their leave. Many paused to exchange greetings with Lord Turisan. His courtesy was flawless, his voice soft, and he seemed never at a loss for a kind word, even to Eliani's youngest kin, Curunan, who at twenty summers was just old enough to sit with the household.

Felisan rose from the table. "Well, then, Lord Turisan, come into my chamber and give me Lord Jharan's news. Good night, yes, good night." He waved to the last few guests as he started toward the back of the hall.

Eliani followed her father, shoulders-on with Lord Turisan, who glanced toward her and yielded the way. In turn she held aside the tapestry for him to enter the governor's private quarters. Only she and her father dwelt here now. Others of the household lived in their own homes in the city.

Lord Felisan led the way into his study. Scattered scrolls of music and tomes thick with history lent the chamber a comfortable air. Eliani banished a worry that Lord Turisan would think the place unkempt and held her chin high as she fetched mead and chalices from a cupboard. If Lord Jharan's son disliked his surroundings, he could take his leave.

⁂

Luruthin gazed at the tapestry long after Eliani had let it fall. The minstrels finished their final tune and began to pack away their instruments, the governor's departure having signaled the end of their duty.

Though Luruthin enjoyed music, he was content to have the hall fall silent. He had sensed Eliani's tension and thought she was not entirely pleased with their visitor. A stirring beside him made him look at Gharinan, kin to Eliani and himself, though closer to Felisan in age. His gaze also was fixed on the curtain.

"Eliani was at her most courteous tonight. I wonder what put her in a dangerous mood?"

Luruthin could guess but refrained from doing so aloud. Gharinan did not know Eliani as well as he, dwelling farther from Highstone in the village of Heahrued, of which he was theyn. Apart from their mutual service in Alpinon's Guard, Gharinan had spent little time in Eliani's company, though enough to conceive a futile ardor for her.

That was not at all uncommon. Since her ill-fated cup-bond, Eliani wanted no lover and took pains to express this in her dress and behavior, with the result that full half the Guard had lost their hearts to her.

Luruthin, whose village of Clerestone was but a day's ride from Highstone, had been somewhat luckier than most, for he had known Eliani since her childhood. They had even enjoyed a brief and blissful intimacy a little more than two decades past, but it had ended abruptly when Kelevon had swept into Highstone, and since that disastrous alliance Eliani had held Luruthin at a distance. He knew her better than did many of her kin, and knew that her maddening ability to wrap herself in blind solitude was her way of avoiding the attentions of those who were attracted to her.

Possibly Lord Turisan had made the mistake of flirting too overtly. Luruthin's lips curved in a small, grim smile. If that were so, Eliani would be sure to punish him.

He made himself look away from the tapestry, turning to Gharinan instead. "How many recruits do you expect to provide to the Guard this winter? Is Iliron old enough yet?"

Gharinan shook his head, his face hardening with worry. "Not for another few summers. I will not place mere children in harm's way. We are not yet so desperate."

Luruthin's gaze strayed to the tapestry once more as he agreed. "Not yet."

⁜

Eliani offered Turisan a chalice of mead and watched as he held it up to admire it. Light from the hearth danced off the golden liquid within, sparking along the patterns cut into the cup.

"These are exquisite. They are carved of crystal?"

Lord Felisan nodded. "Each from a single flawless stone. It is one of our finest crafts."

"I have never seen their like."

"Your father has a pair. No doubt they were tucked away safe when you became old enough to roam the palace and never brought out again."

Turisan laughed. "I shall ask him."

Lord Felisan smiled as he raised his chalice. "To Lord Jharan's health."

Eliani and Turisan echoed him together. The honey wine was cool and sweet on Eliani's tongue. She relaxed into her chair, stretching her booted feet out to the fire. None too ladylike, she reflected. Ah, well. Ladylike remained in her chamber wardrobe, along with her seldom-worn gowns.

Felisan gave a sigh of pleasure, then turned to Turisan. "Now, what is this message you bring?"

Turisan reached into his tunic and withdrew two letters, each sealed with pale green and silver ribbons. He handed one to Felisan.

"My father sends you this. He charged me also to say it is not his fault that I come before you without a respectable escort."

Felisan chuckled. "Ah, dear Jharan. Always concerned with appearances."

Turisan's dark eyes gleamed with laughter, then

went grave as he turned to Eliani. He bowed in his seat as he offered her the second letter.

"To you, Lady Eliani, my father sends this greeting on the occasion of your majority. I offer my personal congratulation as well, and hope that I may have the honor of being present at your confirmation."

A pretty speech, and so earnestly spoken. Even his voice was beautiful. Eliani felt a sensation of breathlessness, as if she were standing at the edge of a precipice from which a gust of wind might send her tumbling. She had felt so before and had fallen, with unhappy result. She blinked and looked away, swallowing a sudden tightness in her throat as she opened the letter.

> *To Lady Eliani of Felisanin,*
> *Greeting from Lord Jharan of Jharanin*
>
> *Pray accept my felicitations upon the occasion of your confirmation as nextkin to Lord Felisan and governor-elect of Alpinon. May your life be filled with blessings, may the ældar honor you with their wisdom, and may spirits guard your path. Should that path at any time bring you to Glenhallow, I would be most honored to greet you at Hallowhall, and beg you to accept the welcome of my house.*
>
> *Jharan, Governor of Southfæld*

A formal missive. Eliani folded it again, wondering if Jharan was so oppressively polite in person. Setting the letter aside, she leaned toward the fire, cupping her chalice in her hands, and turned to Turisan.

"What news from your western borders? We have had kobalen coming across our passes in greater numbers."

He sipped his wine. "We have seen an increase as well, especially in our northernmost reaches. We are considering augmenting our guard at Midrange Pass."

"At High Holding?"

He shook his head. "That would take at least fifty guardians, and the fortress is in disrepair." He set down his chalice and turned toward her. "We keep an outpost to the east of there, by the Silverwash. Our patrols report an increase of kobalen in the area, both on the main pass and on the harder trails."

"And farther south?"

"No—they do not like the cold overmuch."

Eliani smiled grimly and gazed at the fire. "They are venturing into our higher passes now—colder paths where they never roamed before. They have begun to raid some of our more remote settlements, and their numbers are increasing every year. They have become a serious concern." She finished her wine and set her chalice on the table between them, then met his gaze. "Also, we have heard report of an alben seen in the far north of our realm."

Turisan looked appalled. "An alben, east of the mountains?"

"Close to our border with the Steppe Wilds."

Turisan frowned. Eliani looked into the flames.

"Have you ever seen an alben?"

"No, and I hope I never may!"

She glanced at him, and his eyes flashed as he met her gaze, though his face remained reserved. An interesting reaction. Perhaps, as a Greenglen, he bore a prejudice against those who had once, long ago, been of his clan.

The alben were now considered a separate race, but they had begun as ælven. Few had been seen since the Bitter Wars, when many of them had been slain and the rest driven west across the Ebons. Eliani remembered her father telling her the history, making a story of it so that she would remember it the better, with shining heroes—the mindspeakers Dironen and Dejharan, who could converse in thought though leagues might separate them—and the white-haired, black-eyed alben, so evil that they seemed to breathe darkness. The Lay of the Battle of Westgard told of the end of the Bitter Wars, but there were no songs of how the alben had come to be.

Originally, Clan Darkshore had cleaved from Clan Greenglen and journeyed north to settle Fireshore, where the forests were rich in darkwood. A few centuries later the Ælven Council had determined that Clan Darkshore had broken the creed in the most vile and brutal way, practicing evil cruelty upon kobalen, keeping them in captivity and even drinking their blood. When Darkshore had refused to desist, the Council had cast them out of ælvenkind, naming them alben and launching the Bitter Wars to drive them from ælven lands. All this had happened long ago, centuries upon centuries ago. Long enough to have become legend, so that the truth of it was fading amidst the many tellings.

Felisan folded his letter. "Lord Jharan has summoned the Council of Governors to meet at Glenhallow on the first of winter to discuss this increase of kobalen."

Eliani looked from him to Turisan. "The Ælven Council? Does he fear another attack at Midrange?"

Turisan nodded. "My father would rather we not be caught off guard, as we were in the Midrange War."

"A sentiment with which I am in complete agreement." Felisan drained his glass and set it down. "Jharan shall host a Council at Glenhallow the like of which has not been seen in many centuries, and it will be well for the ælven. Our clans have become too scattered." He arose, and Eliani and Turisan followed suit.

"You are welcome to bide with us as long as you choose, Turisan. A guesthouse has been prepared for you"—Felisan glanced at Eliani, who nodded—"and my daughter will show you the way."

"I thank you for your kind hospitality."

Felisan clasped his arm. "Good night, son of my shield-brother. Rest well."

Eliani watched her father go out, then turned to their guest, feeling a return of her previous awkwardness. She should say something pleasant, but nothing came to mind. She led him out through the feast hall, where a few of her kin lingered, to the hearthroom, where they paused while an attendant fetched his cloak.

Outside the air was chill with approaching autumn. Lights burned in most windows, for the night-biders were about their business. The ælven could see almost as well at night as in the day, though darkness robbed the world of color. Many loved moon and stars better than daylight. Night-biders often shared tools and workrooms with their sun-dwelling counterparts, who retired to rest and meditate during the hours of darkness. Between them, the day-biders and night-biders populated ælven towns with activity and music at all times.

Turisan paused in the circle to gaze up at the night sky. "The stars are far more brilliant here than at Glenhallow. Saharis is like a beacon!"

"It is the mountain air. No doubt the skies above your southern peaks are similar."

"True. I have seen just such a sky on a winter's hunt." He looked at her, smiling. "Tell me of the Three Shades. Are they best viewed by daylight or starlight?"

"Either. They are quite different by night. I would view them both ways while you are here."

"That would please me, if you will again be my guide."

Was that meant to rebuke her for not telling him her name at once? She gazed at him but could not read his face. Subtle, this Greenglen lord. She made a formal bow.

"Of course. I recommend daylight first."

She led him to the guesthouse and bade him good night, then returned to the hall and invaded the kitchen, which was warm with the heat of newly fed fires and smelled of flour and yeast. Gathering a handful of small cakes left over from the evening meal into a napkin, Eliani thanked the cook and went out again into the night.

She climbed a steep stair that led above Felisanin Hall to a solitary house, the oldest in Highstone. It was the original governor's hall, so ancient that its stone walls were covered deep in moss and lichen, making it seem a part of the cliff rather than a hand-built structure. A light burned inside, sending a faint glow through the dark blue tapestries that screened the windows. Eliani paused in the hearthroom, rang the guest chime, and, when bidden, entered the house.

The front room ran the width of the old hall and would have accommodated a feast table for twenty, but held only some chairs, shelves, a table that would seat ten at most, and an even smaller worktable. Two draped doorways stood on either side of a large low hearth. A freshly kindled fire glowed there, and nearby sat a dark-haired lady with eyes of twilight blue, tall and beautiful with the grace of many years on her smooth brow.

On the table before her, a branch of candles illuminated a small loom on which she was weaving an elaborate ribbon. Spools of floss lay neatly together: blue, violet, russet, and pine green, along with fine-spun silver thread. The weaver looked up, smiled a welcome, and set her work aside.

Eliani bowed. "Lady Heléri, bid you good even. I have brought you some pinenut cakes."

Heléri answered in a soft, rich voice. "Thoughtful child. I have not tasted one since the harvest."

"Because you will not join us at table." Eliani grinned. "We miss you, Eldermother."

"There is no help for it. You break your last bread before I arise. Come, sit by the fire. Tea is brewing."

"And you have set out two cups. Did you know I was coming?"

"I thought you might. When Misani came to lay the fire, she told me you have an important visitor."

"Ah." Eliani settled into a chair. "Word is all over Highstone, no doubt."

"Oh, yes. The governor of Southfæld's son? We have not had such a visitor in decades."

Heléri rose to retrieve a steaming ewer from the hearth. Eliani spread the napkin full of cakes on the table between them, moving the floss aside to make room.

"How well these colors go together."

She lifted the finished end of the ribbon to admire the twining images of river, cloud, sand, and wood. Silver letters in ælven script began just short of the loom.

"This is for the handfasting."

"Yes. Beryloni is much excited."

"Oh, I know. I have listened to her raptures every day. I hope she truly knows her heart."

Heléri poured tea into two tall pottery cups. "They have cup-bonded twice. They must know their hearts by now. You are thinking of your own disappointment."

"Perhaps so."

Eliani accepted a slender flared teacup and wrapped her hands around it, savoring the fragrance of burnt honey that arose from within. She sipped the tea, which had a flavor entirely different from its scent—warm, dark, and slightly pungent.

"Tell me about our visitor."

Eliani took a larger swallow, feeling the tea's warmth spread through her. "Lord Turisan, son of Lord Jharan."

Heléri smiled. "I remember Jharan well. He and Felisan were inseparable in their youth. They were always hunting or exploring, here or in the south, until the Midrange War redirected their fates."

Eliani nodded. She had heard many tales of their adventures together, both at Heléri's knee and at her father's. Some, from the time of the war, had been wrought into song.

"What is Lord Turisan like?"

"Well . . . he has Greenglen coloring, is tall and comely, and is very gracious." Eliani glanced up at Heléri. "It is clear he was bred in the high court. No doubt he finds our humble hall quite rustic."

"Has he said so?"

"He would never be so uncouth. He does not have to say it; it is in his eyes."

"Ah." Heléri smiled. "So you have mastered the art of reading the soul through the eyes."

Eliani felt her cheeks warm. "No."

"Then do not be hasty to judge." Heléri put down her cup and gazed at Eliani, who had to make an effort not to look away. "What is it that troubles you?"

"Nothing."

"Has Lord Turisan brought bad news?"

"None we did not guess. He tells us the kobalen are increasing along Southfæld's borders, especially near

Midrange Pass. Lord Jharan is summoning the Ælven Council to Glenhallow."

"Ah. You will enjoy visiting Southfæld."

Eliani thought of Lord Jharan's letter to her. Had he meant to encourage her to attend the Council?

She frowned. Even that morning she would have greeted an invitation to visit the south, or indeed any ælven realm, with unabated pleasure. She wanted to know of the world beyond her homeland. Why, then, did she now feel hesitation? She looked up at her elder-mother.

"I fear change. I can feel it coming, and I do not want it."

Heléri's brows rose slightly. She set aside her cake and took Eliani's chin in one hand, gazing long into her eyes, making her feel that the light words about reading souls had masked a deeper truth. Through Heléri's hand, Eliani felt the resonance of her khi, a silvery tickle against her own energy. Heléri's eyes held hers, the blue glowing like dusk in the firelight, filling all Eliani's being until at last they closed and she was released.

The fire snapped, and Eliani started at the sudden sound. She looked up to see Heléri sipping from her cup.

"You would remain forever as you are?"

"N-no. But I would not lose what I have."

"We do not always have the choice of that."

Eliani had no answer. She had expected words of sympathy from Heléri, assurances that her feelings were merely nervousness about her coming majority. Instead, Heléri drew her loom toward her and began again to weave.

Eliani looked at the spools of color on the table. Blue and violet were her favorites—Stonereach colors—and she wanted never to give them up. Beryloni would carry them away with her, in this very ribbon that Heléri wove for her, but henceforth she would align with clan Steppegard and wear their colors as her own.

Eliani glanced up at the handfasting ribbon that hung above Heléri's door: white and gold entwined with the violet and blue. White and gold for Ælvanen, oldest of the ælven clans, governors of Eastfæld, of which she knew but little.

Heléri seldom spoke of her homeland. Eliani had never met any other from that realm and had seen Ælvanen's colors only in this ribbon. Letters of silver were woven through it, commemorating the joining of Heléri and her Stonereach lord, Davharin, who once had governed Alpinon and who long since had crossed the gray border into the spirit realm. The ribbon was all that remained of their union in the physical world.

More than a little magecraft went into such ribbons, for the ceremony of handfasting was also a binding of the couple's khi, and the ribbon not only an artistic masterpiece but a focus for its resonance. Heléri's ribbon was centuries old, yet the silver script gleamed as if it were new. Davharin's ribbon, the mate to it, was tied around the conce that marked where he had died, ambushed by kobalen. Eliani had seen it while riding patrol high in the mountain passes. That ribbon was every bit as fair and bright as this one. She had always felt a little in awe that such a delicate thing could last so long.

Heléri picked up the silver thread. "I would like to meet Lord Turisan."

Eliani watched her fingers ease the fine strand into the weaving, then shifted her gaze to the fire. "He is certain to pay his respects."

"Is he? Not every visitor to Highstone thinks to call on me. Some are never aware that I am here, and others are day-biders and only leave messages while I am at rest."

"That would be unlike him. He will come."

Eliani sensed Heléri watching her. She looked up at her eldermother, who smiled and silently returned to her weaving.

✤ Nightsand ✤

A sliver of red sunlight slipped through draperies that were not quite fully drawn, spilling across the stone floor of Shalár's audience chamber. She frowned at the intruding light and lifted her head to command its removal. A glance was all that was needed to send an attendant scurrying to adjust the heavy drape. No one cared to court Shalár's displeasure.

She shifted in the massive darkwood chair from which she held audience, uncomfortable despite its deep cushions. She was not usually in the chamber so early, but this night she had a decision to make and wanted to give it due consideration. She had called an audience just after sundown so that lesser matters could be settled quickly and put out of her way.

Two oil lanterns on pedestals, so recently lit that she could still smell the sharp smoke of their kindling, gave the chamber its only light. Their flames flickered against the ceiling of black volcanic stone and glinted in the metal threads of the one ælven tapestry that had been brought across the mountains when she and her people had been forced to abandon Fireshore.

Shalár stared at the weaving, her frown deepening. It depicted a simple scene on the wooded seashore near Hollirued, the first ælven city, capital of Eastfæld. The weaver's work was merely competent, though superior to anything that had yet been achieved by Shalár's people. Clan Darkshore had neither the techniques nor the resources for making such colors—bright colors that lasted for many decades—nor had they yet succeeded in crafting metal thread that would hold its shine. So many skills had been lost to her people when they were driven west.

Someday we will reclaim all that was taken from us.

Shaking her head slightly, she straightened and glanced around the chamber. Only a handful of petitioners had come this evening. She looked to Dareth, her steward and consort, who stood beside her chair. He was lean and handsome, pale-skinned as were all her folk, his silver hair almost as bright as her own. His tunic was of black linen, supple in weave, the finest to be had in the Westerlands. She liked the way it clung to him.

He felt her gaze and met it, black eyes waiting for her command. Shalár nodded, and he called forth the first supplicant, a thin-faced female cloaked in homespun cloth who put back her hood and knelt before Shalár.

"Bright Lady, I come to ask your aid for my family. The kobalen we had for our use has died, and my partner is not strong enough to capture another."

"So you wish me to give you one?"

Hollow eyes were raised in a furtive glance at Shalár, then quickly hidden. "Bright Lady, you have many kobalen—"

"They are reserved for the use of my household and the city guard."

The female bowed her head. "Nightsand has great need, I know. I hoped you might spare but one."

"And if I spare but one kobalen to you, then what can I say to the next who begs to be given what she cannot get for herself?" Shalár leaned forward in her chair, fixing the petitioner's gaze with her own. "Are you unable to hunt? Or merely unwilling?"

"I have tried, Bright Lady. There are few kobalen to be had near my home."

"Go into the hills, then."

"My partner is ill—I cannot leave him—"

Shalár tossed her head to get her hair out of her eyes. She was losing patience with this fretful female. "Put him in a neighbor's care."

"But I . . ."

The petitioner's khi darkened with fear. There was something else, and she did not wish to tell it. Shalár looked at her with renewed interest, waiting.

"Bright Lady, you are wise and just."

And strong, and cruel. Shalár said nothing, knowing the thought had been finished in the mind of everyone present. Her reputation was deserved, and she took pride in it. Those qualities—all of them, particularly cruelty when needed—had preserved her people.

The supplicant's shoulders sagged in defeat. "I have a child, too young to be left behind."

"A child?" Shalár leaned forward. "How young?"

"Fifteen summers."

Shalár glanced at Dareth, whose face remained impassive. She drew herself up in her chair.

"Fifteen summers. Too young to be left, yes, but not too young to be of use. Pledge your child to my service and I will give you your kobalen."

The female looked up sharply, fright widening her eyes. Her lips formed the word "no," though she did not speak it. Did not dare, Shalár knew.

"Under my care, your child will live as well as any in Nightsand. Better than most in the Westerlands. And it will have the advantage of being near other children. Thirty years' service."

"She would be nearly of age by then!"

"Yes, and raised in better circumstances than you can give her. Do you not wish this for your child?"

The supplicant stared at the stone floor, looking thoroughly miserable. Shalár understood the female's reluctance but was not about to encourage others to implore her aid by granting this one her wish for no return. Charity belonged to the ælven. Clan Darkshore, who struggled to survive in the Westerlands—still struggled after centuries—could not afford it.

"Thirty years, then she is free to return to you. During that time you shall have your kobalen, and if it dies and you can show the death was not malicious or careless, it will be replaced. In addition, I will send a healer at once to attend to your partner. Perhaps he will regain his strength enough for you to conceive another child."

Shalár gentled her voice for this last, intending to give the petitioner both hope and praise for having achieved conception. Few could do so. Shalár, to her infinite frustration, had not.

A female who had conceived and survived childbirth had a fair chance to conceive again, a better chance than the childless. Shalár knew the importance of every birth to her people's survival and honored this female for her accomplishment even while she envied it.

They had been so few, those who had reached the haven of Nightsand Bay. Eleven hundreds, no more. Their numbers had grown with painful slowness to a mere three thousand souls and of late, to Shalár's great dismay, had begun to diminish again. Hardship, the despair of having lost Fireshore, grief for those who had fallen at Westgard—all had taken their toll on the survivors. And hunger, always hunger—the hunger that had cost them everything.

Shalár turned away from such useless thoughts.
Finding that her gaze had strayed to the tapestry, she
looked back at the petitioner. The female was sitting
on her heels, staring blankly at the floor.

"Take a night to consider my offer. You will be received when you return."

Shalár signaled to an attendant, who came forward
to help the female to her feet and lead her away.
Dareth waited until she was gone from the room before calling the next.

The rest of the petitions were commonplace, and
Shalár dealt with them swiftly. She could have entrusted them to Dareth or even to an underling, but
she preferred to keep an eye on her people as much as
she could.

When the last supplicant had been ushered from the
chamber, Shalár stood up and stretched, the pointed
sleeves of her dark red tunic brushing about her legs. An
attendant brought forward a tray of fruit and roasted
nuts. Shalár took a morsel, though she hungered for another kind of sustenance.

All her people hungered so. It was the single thing
that bound them to her more than any other. That
wretched female who had lost her kobalen hungered
desperately, no doubt.

She would return to accept Shalár's offer. Shalár
wished to help her, but it must be at a price. Clan
Darkshore could not afford that she should give away
their resources. The pens held kobalen, yes, but fewer
than most knew. The numbers remaining had dwin-
dled dangerously low. Shalár knew she must take action soon or her people would face a cruel winter.

It was to her they looked, and not only because she
provided kobalen to ease their hunger. It was she who
had gathered the straggling, starving remnants of
Clan Darkshore after they had been driven across the

mountains by the combined armies of the other ælven realms. She had been young then but determined to survive. Because of that determination and because she had carried her father's sword, they had followed her.

Morshalan had been head of Clan Darkshore and governor of Fireshore. Shalár had collected what remained of his people and had led them westward, away from the danger of ælven pursuit, until at last they had arrived at Nightsand. They had no love of the ocean, but the black sands of the bay reminded them of the shore at the foot of Firethroat, north of Ghlanhras, the city that had been the governor's home. It was both strange and familiar, and in their exhaustion Clan Darkshore had halted there to rest. They had never left.

She turned to Dareth, who stood patiently waiting. Constant Dareth, ever watchful. One of the few left from Fireshore.

Many of the original refugees had given up the fight, unwilling to face the cost of survival. Dareth himself had wished to return to spirit at one time. She had persuaded him against it by seducing him, and he had been her chief companion ever since.

She reached out a hand to him now. He bowed as he took it, deferential as always. His khi tingled against her flesh, waking her hunger. She fought back a craving to draw upon him. Dareth was too important to be used so.

"To the pens."

Dareth escorted her from the chamber, outside to the stone shelf that gave access to the Cliff Hollows, her home overlooking the city of Nightsand. They paused there to gaze out over the bay.

The sun was down now, and the dusk swiftly rising. Westward a ruddy smudge hung over the ocean horizon. To the south Nightsand Bay sprawled inland, its waters black in the growing darkness, stretching southward to lap at the feet of Blackheart, that restless mountain whose rumblings and belchings of smoke also reminded her people of home. Small points of firelight gleamed here and there along the bay's eastern shore, marking lesser villages and homesteads outside the city. Nightsand itself was brighter, the more so as folk stirred and opened their windows to the night.

Across the bay there were no lights. Kobalen sometimes roamed there, but though Shalár's people never crossed the bay to gain that shore, the kobalen rarely showed themselves. They knew they were hunted, though perhaps they did not know that her people would not cross the water to reach them. It mattered not. They would reach them in any case, though it meant a long trek around Blackheart.

"I must summon a hunt soon."

Dareth nodded, his smile fading. "You will excuse me, I hope."

"It would please me to have you along."

"But the governance of Nightsand would suffer. Remember the last time I hunted with you."

She nodded, sighing. It had been many decades since, several hunts since. True, the chaos of petitioners and problems that had met their return had annoyed her, but she would accept that gladly as the cost of hunting with Dareth at her side.

He stood gazing at the last blur of light on the horizon. She watched him, wishing for the boldness he had once shown. He turned to her, a wan smile on his lips. "I used to watch the sunset every day. Do you ever miss it, Shalári?"

Anger flared in her. She turned cold eyes upon him.

"Never call me that! I have no ælven name, nor have you, Dareth!"

She gathered her khi, focusing it in a spot in the center of her torso, then sent a hot pulse forth toward Dareth and saw him wince as it penetrated his own khi. She sent her khi flowing through him, around him, tightening her hold on him. Her hunger sharpened at the exertion, and again she was tempted to draw on his khi, but she resisted. Only once had she done that, and had nearly lost him for it.

He bowed his head, squeezing his eyes shut. "Forgive me, Bright Lady."

She held him for a long moment. "Say my name, Dareth."

He stood breathing shallowly, eyes closed. At last he opened them and glanced up at her beneath white brows.

"Shalár."

She released him, then held out her hand, allowing him to take it once more. They turned southward along the broad stone ledge.

The black volcanic cliffs above Nightsand were riddled with natural caves worn from the hard rock by water and wind. One series of them, overlooking a broad view of the bay, had been enlarged and carved into the graceful rooms of the Cliff Hollows. Others, smaller yet more numerous, served as holding pens for kobalen and captives. They were reached from the same ledge that fronted the Cliff Hollows but were far enough away that no khi from those kept there could disturb her.

A network of tunnels connected the pens. At the near end a cave had been enlarged for the use of the keepers, and at its entrance two guards in Darkshore red and black yielded the way to Shalár and Dareth.

Shalár noted that the scarlet trim to their tunics was wearing thin. It was difficult to keep her guards in clan colors. The red, especially, was precious, for it could not be made so bright in the Westerlands. It had to be salvaged from cloth brought from Fireshore. All that the original survivors had carried with them was long gone, returned to dust. From time to time fresh supplies had been captured, but the most recent of those, too, was nearly gone.

Perhaps it was time to gather more.

Shalár frowned slightly, pondering whether her people had the strength for the larger undertaking she was contemplating. The last attempt, though partly successful, had taken a severe toll.

She led Dareth into the wind-worn passage, grimacing slightly at the dank smell of the pens. Kobalen were unclean creatures, and although their keepers were under orders to keep the pens in a tolerable state, the caves were far from comfortable by her people's standards.

She need not stay long, though. She never tarried long there. Only long enough to collect what she wanted most times.

From the keepers' antechamber, two passages led deeper into the cliff, one emitting the sharp stink of kobalen and the other leading back to the deepest of the holding caves. The head keeper, a thin, pale female of bitter aspect, rose from behind a small table to greet them. She wore a dark tunic and a black hood trimmed with a narrow band of scarlet. Shalár nodded to her.

"Greetings, Nihlan. How fare your charges?"

"As usual, Bright Lady."

"Have any of the female captives quickened?"

"No, Bright Lady."

Shalár was disappointed but not surprised. "Perhaps we will soon correct that."

Dareth glanced at her but said nothing. Shalár held her gaze upon the keeper, who gestured toward a shelf carved into the stone wall behind her. On it rested a finely wrought silver chalice and a small curved knife. Both had come from Fireshore; both belonged to Shalár and were reserved for her exclusive use. She left them there, on display, to remind all who saw them of her power.

She nodded to the keeper, who took down the cup and knife and set them on the table.

Nihlan glanced up at her. "Shall you choose for yourself, Bright Lady?"

"No. Bring the strongest."

Shalár ran a finger around the rim of the chalice. Her hunger flared, but she kept a tight rein on her impatience while Nihlan took a ring of keys from a hook on the wall and went into the kobalen pens.

Shalár watched Dareth, noting the trouble on his brow. Even now, after centuries, he had not reconciled himself fully to this necessity. From time to time she argued with him about it, but she had no temper for it this night. She had greater matters to consider, and she needed his cooperation.

A rattling of chains heralded the keeper's return. The scent of kobalen increased, and Nihlan entered the chamber, leading a large shackled male.

If this was the strongest, it was most definitely time to hunt more. Kobalen were thickset and heavy-limbed, but this one's flesh had gone slack over its large bones, and its skin showed through thin patches in the fine black fur that covered its body.

Its eyes, dull and heavy, sharpened with fear when it saw Shalár. It jerked against its shackles, surprising Nihlan. The keeper had the strength to control it, but Shalár was out of patience and took pleasure in seizing the creature's khi. She consumed a little of it—only a breath's worth, enough to ease the edge of her hunger.

The kobalen went limp, eyes fixed unseeing as Shalár took complete hold of its limited mind. Nihlan fastened its shackled wrists to a high ring on the wall. The kobalen's legs buckled, and it hung heavily from its arms.

Shalár picked up the knife and cup, glancing at Dareth. "Do you care to harvest?" He shook his head, looking away. She could feel his hunger in the air, so sharp it was, yet still he resisted. Poor tormented Dareth. He would never find his full strength so long as he indulged in sentiment in this way.

Shalár stepped up to the kobalen, releasing its mind, waiting for it to see her again. Fear would spice the creature's khi. The kobalen's eyes cleared, and it spat obscenities in its own coarse language. Shalár smiled and set the knife to the underside of its arm, where dozens of scars attested to the creature's prior use.

Blood welled bright red and ran down the inside of the chalice as she held it against the wound. The kobalen howled and struggled feebly. Shalár retook its mind and stilled it to prevent any of the blood from being lost. Khi alone was sustenance, but khi in fresh blood was the richest and best food for her and her people.

This kobalen had been used many times before. They all had been used, carefully, sparingly. Only enough was taken at a feeding to slake the hunger of Nightsand's guard and Shalár's household. Over time, though, and even with the most careful keeping, the kobalen weakened. Their lives were brief even when they roamed free. In captivity, each was good for no more than a decade or two.

The chalice was full. Shalár stepped back, nodding to Nihlar to stanch the wound. The keeper moved to do so, setting a large wooden spoon to it to claim her rightful share before pressing dryleaf to the cut. Shalár handed her the knife and turned away.

She looked down into her cup, inhaling the scent of

the blood, savoring the heavy khi that rose from it. Glancing at Dareth, she lifted the chalice slightly in a silent salute, then drank deeply of the salty-hot draught.

She paused to breathe, feeling the weighty flow of khi throughout her flesh, the surge of strength through her veins. A little over half the cup was gone. She offered the rest to Dareth.

He hesitated, waging the same self-battle as always. As always, he yielded to the demands of his flesh. He offered her the cup with the last swallow in its base. She shook her head and watched Dareth finish it, then hand the cup to Nihlani, who received it with a slight bow.

"How else may I serve you, Bright Lady?" Even as she spoke, the keeper's eyes did not leave the chalice. Her hunger was palpable despite the share she had taken. Shalár knew that she would lick the cup and knife clean before washing and restoring them to their place.

"I wish to look over the captives, but you need not accompany us." Shalár glanced toward the kobalen. "Do not let that one give you trouble."

"Never, Bright Lady." Nihlan bowed again, cradling the chalice against her.

Shalár turned to Dareth, who offered his wrist. She laid her hand on it, and they went into the second passage. Here the air was close but did not have the pungency of kobalen. The few captives who were kept here had the desire and were given the means to keep themselves clean. Shalár wanted them healthy, as healthy as they could be, but captivity inevitably told on any living creature.

The passage wound deep into the cliff. Now and then a beam of feeble starlight slid down through a wind-carved chimney to splash against the dark rock wall. These channels to the cliff's surface above gave more air than light, but little light was needed. Shalár could see in darkness, as could her captives. Khi flowed thinly here—a finer khi but weaker even than that of the kobalen. The condition of her captives had worsened to the point where they no longer were useful, or so Shalár suspected.

She and Dareth reached the holding chambers, which were unlike the large caves where kobalen were kept, breeding away as they so easily did. Here each captive was isolated in a small chamber behind a heavy door, all of them opening off a larger cave. Grated windows in the doors allowed the keepers to watch over their charges. Shalár stepped up to the first door.

The chamber contained a pallet, a small wooden basin and pitcher of water, and a covered slop bucket. A tunic of good cloth—unused by its appearance—hung on a peg on the wall, and in the far corner lay what looked like a bundle of rags. Shalár gathered her khi and sent a pulse into the chamber, commanding attention. The rags stirred, and a head arose from them. The face was thin, pinched, and endlessly sorrowful yet defiant. An ælven female.

Dareth moved restlessly beside her. Shalár had sent him to breed to this one, numerous times. She had hoped the female's strength of will portended strength of flesh, but no child had been conceived. None of the ælven captives had bred successfully in over a century.

She glanced at Dareth. "Will you try again?"

He closed his eyes, gave a tiny shake of his head. Unsurprised, Shalár spoke to the female.

"Come here."

She could order Dareth to breed her, and he would obey, but the ælven was in poor health, even less likely than usual to conceive. That was one curse the ælven and her people shared—the rarity of conception. Compelling Dareth to try yet again with this failing female was useless. Better to reserve his strength.

The female arose and listlessly approached the door, the tatters of her ælven garments hanging from her thin frame. Fear had long since given way to resignation, though she still showed a streak of stubbornness.

Shalár nodded toward the tunic hanging on the wall. "You have not put on your new clothing."

The ælven glanced at the tunic, then looked down at her feet, saying nothing, giving Shalár no argument. Nothing to push against, no way to fight. "I have provided the best available for you. My own attendants do not wear as good."

The female did not respond. Feeling a stab of impatience, Shalár stepped closer to the door.

"Shall I send all my guard in to you? Perhaps one of them will light a spark in your belly."

The ælven did not move, but Shalár felt cold fear flood through her khi.

"Put it on if you wish to live."

She knew even as the words left her lips that the female had no such wish. Disgusted, Shalár turned away and strode down the passage, glancing into each of the other chambers. Five ælven females and three males, all in dismal condition. One—a male who had been quite young when captured—stared out at her with fierce hunger in his eyes.

It happened now and then. An ælven captive would manifest the hunger that plagued Clan Darkshore. Shalár once had made it her practice to offer them freedom and a home in Nightsand in exchange for a term of service, but the few who had accepted had not survived, and she no longer bothered. They could never reconcile themselves to their changed state. They would not embrace the hunger. Some had refused to shelter from the daylight and had sickened and died. One had tried to flee to Fireshore. His bones had been found some years later in the forest near Westgard, picked clean and overgrown with a tangle of verdure.

Shalár looked at the hungry one, considering whether to try him. His flesh might yet have the strength to sire a child. His eyes, still green like a Stonereach's, sharpened under her gaze. Hair that once had been the color of good oak was now streaked with white. Hunger licked at her thoughts as, probably without his awareness, he sought to draw strength from her khi.

She repulsed him with a vicious thrust of khi that sent him reeling back from the door. No captive might presume to draw upon her, or on any of her people. He should have known better, and would know better in the future.

She turned and was surprised to find that Dareth was not beside her. He had remained by the first door, gazing in at the female in rags. Shalár strode up the passage to stand before him. Her boots were of a height to bring her eyes just above level with his. She stared a hard silent warning, which he acknowledged with a downward glance. Appeased, she touched a finger to his jaw.

"Come away. We are finished here."

She led him back out to the antechamber, conscious of his rejuvenated khi at her back. She would have him now, she decided. They were both fed, it would be the most likely time for them to conceive, and she wanted him. She also wanted to drive from his thoughts any female but herself.

As they emerged into a cool night breeze off the ocean, she glanced back at the pens. The two guards posted at the entrance saluted her. She debated whether to carry out her threat and send them and ten or twenty of their comrades to the ælven in rags as the price of her stubbornness.

Perhaps later. Just now she was impatient to be in her bed, alone with her lover.

She looked at Dareth, and he sensed her gaze, withdrawing his own from the ocean to smile hesitantly at her. His khi tingled against her palm and up her arm, sparking a longing in her loins. Shalár laughed and pulled at his hand, leading him at a run along the ledge toward the Cliff Hollows.

⁜

Her hair, still damp from washing, lay heavily across her shoulders as she paced alone in her private sitting room. She had left Dareth in her bed, and for all she knew he was still there, mourning, perhaps, that he had failed to conceive with her yet again.

The polished stone was cool against her bare feet. Her robe, richly cut of Eastfæld silk in an exquisite ruby red, brushed long about her ankles. A touch of magecraft had gone into its making, for it was painted with shimmering white flowers that seemed to tremble on their long stems with her every movement. One of the many useless products of magecraft, she thought bitterly. The ælven mages indulged their gifts in creating such fanciful gauds while her own people suffered from lack of the simplest mage blessings.

Few with mage talent had survived to cross the Ebons, and most of those had died since. Of the new folk born to her people in the west, almost none had exhibited such gifts. None could fashion blessings to strengthen their weapons or add protection to their garb. It was one of the reasons she continued to encourage breeding to ælven captives, hoping to restore the gifts of magecraft to her people. Meanwhile, she felt an odd resentment for the ælven's indulgent magemade fripperies, enchanting though they were. She brushed a hand over the painted flowers, making them sway as if caught by a breeze. This was the last such robe she had, and it was beginning to wear. Secretly, in her heart, she wanted more.

It was not the time, however, to pursue such luxuries. She must mount a grand hunt for kobalen now, before winter arrived. A blood moon was coming. The time was right. The only question in her mind was whether to hunt for more than sustenance for her people.

Already she had initiated the gathering of information. She had three trusted watchers who spent their nights roving the borders between the Westerlands and the ælven lands to the east of the Ebons. Their usual task was to keep her informed of any intrusions of ælven across the mountains, but that was not enough for the plans she was contemplating.

Shalár felt her shoulders tensing and made an effort to relax them. She hated having anything to do with the ælven and yearned for the day when she would be entirely free of them, but that day was far distant as yet. Until her people could create all that they needed themselves, until their numbers rose beyond the threat of extinction, they would be bound to the ælven.

For survival. Even now. It enraged her, and she fed the anger, knowing it would serve her in the coming effort. She stopped pacing before the hearth and crouched to drink in its warmth.

Already the flush of strength from the kobalen's blood she had consumed was beginning to wane. She needed more, always more.

She closed her eyes, indulging in a moment's bitterness. The hunger was none of her choosing. She would be rid of it if she could. She had no choice but to feed upon kobalen; none of them had a choice.

The ælven had refused to accept that. Instead of trying to understand, trying to help, the ælven had cast all of Clan Darkshore out and made war on them because of the bane suffered by a few. Because of something they could not control.

Hypocrites. Did not their precious creed command them to be of service to others? Yet they had done nothing to aid their afflicted brethren of Clan Darkshore. Nothing.

She felt a tear slide down her cheek and hastened to brush it away. No weakness; she could not afford weakness. Abruptly she stood and summoned the nearest attendant. Galir, recently entered into her service, was yet a child, as evidenced by the darkness of his hair. Perhaps thirty summers of age and surely never bedded from his look of startled surprise at finding her so lightly clad.

She let him take in her appearance, watching with amusement as his wide gaze traveled her form and finally arrived at her face. A moment later he ducked his head.

"How may I serve you, Bright Lady?"

"Summon Ciris to me."

"Ciris?" The youth looked up at her, uncertain.

"Ciris the watcher. He has just returned to the city. Try the hunters' lodge."

"As you will, Bright Lady." He bowed low and moved to leave.

"And Galir—"

He stopped, still as a startled buck, wary eyes turned to her. Shalár smiled.

"Tell the steward I wish to see you clad in clan colors. I think they would suit you."

His chest rose and fell with quick, frightened breaths. At last he found the presence to bow again.

"Thank you, Bright Lady."

She watched him flee the chamber, never meeting her eyes again. Amused, she smiled. He showed promise, this one. When he reached maturity, she would try him. Perhaps his young strength could give her the child she desired.

While she waited for Ciris, she dressed in a heavier robe of supple linen, dyed as close to black as Nightsand's drapers could manage. The hem and sleeves were broidered with twining vines of night-blooming jasmine, the pale flowers standing out against dark green leaves. They did not shimmer or move.

Shalár ran her fingers over the vines on one sleeve. The artist who had done the needlework had died recently, giving in to weariness and despair. That left but one broiderer in the city, an apprentice. Another would have to be trained. Perhaps the child of the petitioner who had lost her kobalen would prove handy with the needle.

A gentle knock on the door heralded the arrival of an attendant—not Galir—who informed her that Ciris was waiting in her audience chamber. She sent him away with orders to bring bread and ale to them, then went out to her public room.

The heavy draperies had been drawn back from the west side of the chamber to reveal a broad opening. Formerly a cave mouth, it had been widened into a vast gallery with pillars carved from the black stone at either side, framing a sweeping view of the ocean and Nightsand Bay. Starlight glistened on the dark waters, all silver, blue, and black. Warmer lights twinkled in the city below as her people went about their night's business.

Standing at one side of the gallery, looking down, was a tall male clad in hunter's leathers. His hair was long and stark white, a few wiry strands escaping the braid. He turned, regarding her with piercing black eyes.

"Ciris. You are well fed, I trust?"

He nodded. "You have work for me?"

"Yes. Come and sit with me while we discuss it."

She led him to a small table at the side of the chamber, laid with a platter of bread and cheeses, two pottery cups, and a jug of ale. The meal was more a symbol of hospitality than a practical gift, for her folk no longer could survive on such foods alone, and Ciris would have fed well in the wilds. That was one advantage of being a watcher: One could catch one's own feeders from the kobalen who roamed the plains.

Old customs had their uses, however, and such simple foods aided digestion. With a gesture Shalár invited Ciris to help himself to the meal, and he at once reached for the jug.

"You are weary of watching."

Ciris shrugged as he poured ale for both of them. "Little changes. I saw a large band of kobalen cross into the Steppe Wilds, near Coldwater Lake."

Shalár sipped her ale. "Hunting mountain geese for feathers to fletch their darts."

He nodded. "There are more such forays than usual this autumn. The kobalen have gone into the mountains in greater numbers."

"Food must be scarce on the plains."

"And the kobalen more plentiful than ever. Their numbers have increased rapidly of late."

Shalár nodded. She had observed the same, with some bitterness at the ease with which the kobalen multiplied.

"Good, for I want a grand hunt."

Ciris's eyes lit with fire. "A grand hunt? Soon?"

"Soon, yes." She set down her cup. "Send word to every village. All who are fit and willing may join the hunt."

She rose and went to the gallery to look out over the bay. A night bird glided by below the cliff's edge, white and silent, seeking some small prey.

"Have the hunters assemble here two tendays hence."

"As you will." Ciris stood.

She turned to look at him. "I want enough hunters to fill the pens twice over with their catch."

He nodded, his harsh mouth curving in a satisfied smile. "You shall have them, Bright Lady."

✠ Evennight ✠

Eliani had her best gown, a misty blue dress with long pointed sleeves and a pleasant drape, halfway over her head when a knock fell upon her chamber door.

"Who comes?"

"Misani. My lady sent me to your assistance."

Assistance? To dress? Eliani laughed and shrugged into the gown, letting it fall heavily about her bare ankles, then went to open the door.

"Too late!" She grinned, then stared in wonder at what Misani was carrying.

Misani, who was Lady Heléri's attendant, smiled. In her arms were fabrics of the richest blue and violet Eliani had ever seen.

"From your father. A new gown for your confirmation."

Eliani opened the door wider to let Misani enter. Misani carried the gown to the curtained alcove at the back of Eliani's chamber that served as her tiring room and hung it up to shake out the folds.

It moved like clouds. The underdress was of pure blue, rich and glowing like the sky just at twilight, with full sleeves caught into long cuffs that were broidered with gold. A sleeveless overdress accompanied it, violet with narrow gilt embroidery at the neck and along all the edges. The neckline was deep and pointed and would show off the underdress. It was caught below the bosom with a sash of golden leaves.

Elaini reached out a hand to touch the violet. It was softer than any fabric she had ever felt, and featherlight.

"Eastfæld silk. Your father loves you well."

Eliani looked up at Misani in awe. "I have never owned anything so fine."

"Come, let me help you out of that."

Eliani suffered her to pull the mist-colored dress, which suddenly seemed heavy and coarse, back over her head. Misani also took away her linen shift, bringing out a silken one in its stead that slid over Eliani's shoulders like a summer breeze, cool at first, then warm as it settled upon her. Eliani wriggled her arms, delighting in the feel of the silk against her skin.

Misani brushed out Eliani's hair and braided it back, then garbed her in the blue underdress, fastening the long cuffs about her forearms with loops of ribbon that slid over round glowing pearls. She lifted the violet overdress over Eliani's head and lowered it to settle on her shoulders, tying the sash underneath, which left the back hanging free, capelike.

Eliani caught an edge of the drape, then let it fall. It just brushed the floor behind her. She took a step backward, and the gown floated lightly out of her way.

"Oh, it is beautiful! How did they know to make it just the right length?"

"Your father got your measure from the leathermaker."

Eliani glanced up at Misani, who affected to be grave but could not keep her amusement from showing in her eyes. It was true that Eliani had commissioned a new set of hunting leathers, for her old ones were worn almost beyond service. She laughed at the thought that her measure for leathers had gone to the maker of this gown.

Misani brought forth another length of silk. "Lady Heléri hopes it will please you to wear this as well."

She opened it out, and Eliani saw that it was a long veil, its color shifting from blue to violet as it moved in the light. It was beaded along its curving edges with tiny Clerestone crystals caught trembling on golden threads.

"Her own work."

"Yes."

She let Misani drape the veil around her shoulders and cast it over her brow, the crystal beads weighting it just enough to prevent its slipping from her head. Eliani stood before the mirror in her tiring room, gazing at herself in wonder. The female looking back seemed taller and more graceful than she had ever hoped to be, a stranger but oddly familiar.

"I look like my mother's picture." Her voice caught as she thought of the portrait that hung in her father's private room.

Misani gave her an appraising look. "So you do. She is sure to be watching over you this day."

Eliani swallowed a pang of grief for the mother who had crossed long ago. Belani's father, Elmoran, had been killed by kobalen in the mountains. In her grief, Belani had followed, leaving Eliani motherless at an early age. Heléri had taught her what her father could not, but she still wished she had known Belani.

Eliani coughed to clear the tightness in her throat. "Thank you, Misani."

"It was my pleasure. Blessings to you."

Eliani smiled, then with silent thanks to the spirits who walked with her, her mother and all the others, went out into the great hall. The silk swirled around her ankles, making her wish to dance. She was glad it was a feast day, for indeed there would be dancing this night.

As she entered the hall, all those within it turned to her, and she had the gratification of seeing surprise on the faces of a number of old friends. It had been many days since she had worn a gown at all—since Midsummer, if she recalled correctly—and she had never worn a veil. A lady's veil, as she had always thought of them. She remembered Misani scolding her for playing with Heléri's, long ago.

Heléri was there, she saw, hooded and veiled against the last of the daylight. Torches already burned in the sconces, though light still glowed through the windows on the west side of the hall, setting fire to the colored glass.

Beside Heléri stood Lord Turisan, a pale gleam in the darkening hall. He was garbed in a soft sage-colored tunic, his hair loose about his shoulders and caught back from his face by a silver circlet with a white moonstone at the brow. He looked up at Eliani's approach, then smiled and bowed.

Eliani could not help smiling in response, though she glanced away. She was pleased, if only because she wished Lord Turisan to know that the heir of Alpinon's governor was not a complete savage.

"Ah, my daughter!"

Lord Felisan came forward with open arms, and Eliani walked into his embrace. "Thank you for the gown, Father. It is beautiful."

"Not near as beautiful as you." He held her at arm's length and beamed as he gazed at her. "You shine, my child! Come, let us give you your rightful place."

He offered her his arm, and she laid her hand along

it as he led her through the hall. The governor's chair had been set against the back wall where it stood on audience days, and young Curunan stood nearby to wait upon him. Eliani saw that her own chair had been placed beside her father's, and her heart gave a small frightened thump. This was new.

Confirmation of majority was a simple acknowledgment and required no ceremony beyond a formal declaration of nextkin relationships before at least two witnesses, usually members of the same household. Eliani had been present at a number of such occasions, and they were often little more than a toast to the honoree's majority.

Since she was to be governor-elect, however, her naming as Felisan's nextkin required the acknowledgment of Alpinon's theyns. Save for Mirithan, they were all gathered there.

Her father led her to the two chairs, then turned and stood before them, facing the hall. The others drew near.

"Welcome, theyns of Alpinon. Welcome, noble visitors." He nodded toward Turisan and Heléri. "Thank you for your presence on this doubly joyous evening. I call on you to witness the majority of my daughter, Eliani of House Felisanin."

He gestured to Curunan, who brought forward a cushion bearing a narrow circlet of hammered bronze set with a small blue stone. Another gift from her father; this one she had known about, for as governor-elect, she would now be entitled to wear a circlet. Her father placed it on her brow, then stepped behind her and laid his hands on her shoulders.

"Eliani, from this day forth you are my nextkin, to stand in my place should I be absent, to bear my burdens and inherit my holdings should I choose to return to spirit."

"Hail, Eliani of Felisanin, governor-elect of Alpinon!"

It was Luruthin who had called out. Eliani shot him a glance as the others repeated the cheer. He grinned back.

Heléri stepped forward, her face hidden by her heavy veil. "Who do you name as your nextkin, to follow in your own place, Lady Eliani?"

"I name Gharinan, theyn of Heahrued."

Heléri turned toward the theyns. "Let him come forward."

Gharinan strode toward them, tall and grave, though his eyes lit with pleasure when they met Eliani's. Like her father, he was the son of a son of Lady Heléri, and his descent from her showed in the bluish cast to his eyes. Sea-green more than leaf-green, Heléri called them. Eliani had never seen the sea.

As theyn of Heahrued, one of Alpinon's larger villages, Gharinan was seldom at Highstone. Eliani had not known him well until she had joined the Guard and begun to ride patrols near his village. She had grown to like him despite his gravity and considered him a dear friend as well as kin.

Now he knelt before her, and she laid her fingertips on his shoulders. "Gharinan, from this day hence I name you my nextkin, to stand in my place should I be absent, to bear my burdens and inherit my holdings should I choose to return to spirit."

He bowed his head. "You honor me, Lady Eliani."

Lord Felisan squeezed Eliani's shoulders. "Bear you all witness of nextkin to nextkin. This day Lady Eliani takes her rightful place among us, to serve and be true so long as she walks in flesh."

Heléri nodded. "May spirits walk beside her and bless her path."

"So may it be."

The others repeated her father's words. Felisan released her shoulders, and Gharinan stood, bowed, and returned to the gathering while her father led Eliani to her chair. They sat and prepared to receive each guest, for the theyns had brought customary gifts of welcome to the new governor-elect.

Heléri stepped up before Eliani, being of higher rank than the theyns. Curunan slipped forward to place a cushion for her to kneel upon. She held out her arms, and Eliani clasped them.

"Thank you for the veil, Eldermother."

"I am glad it becomes you so well. Blessings on you, child." Heléri leaned forward to kiss her cheek. "Come and visit with me later."

"I will."

Heléri arose, giving her place to Lord Turisan. His tunic seemed to glisten as he moved, and when he came near, Eliani saw that it was covered all over with silver embroidery, a tracery of delicate leaves. He bowed first to Felisan and then to her before kneeling upon the cushion.

"Southfæld offers felicitations to you, Lady Eliani. Please accept this gift from Lord Jharan and all his house in honor of your majority."

He proffered a small box of pale-hued wood—whitewood from the forests of Southfæld—carved with intricate interlacing vines and flowers. Eliani opened it and caught her breath at what lay inside: a round gilt brooch in the shape of two stag's heads, their eyes great blue stones. Many smaller stones of violet and blue glinted among the tines of their antlers. She had never seen its like. She swallowed, humbled by the richness of the gift.

"My thanks to Lord Jharan and his house. I shall treasure it."

Turisan nodded, then reached to his belt. "I hope you will accept this small gift from me as well."

He held out his hands toward her with a flute lying across them. Eliani gazed at it for a moment. It had been long since she had any heart for making music, save for the sort of songs guardians enjoyed around their campfires.

She closed the box with the brooch and set it in her lap, then took up the flute. It was simple, carved of a single river reed. She ran her fingers along it, then put them over the holes and set it to her lips, and hesitantly played three notes. She looked up at Turisan, feeling shy.

"It has a sweet voice."

He smiled. "I am glad it pleases you. Many blessings to you, my lady."

He rose and made way for the next guest. Eliani laid the flute in her lap and smiled up at the first of the theyns.

Before long she had too many gifts to hold, and Curunan discreetly relieved her of some of them. Luruthin's gift was a crystal carved in the shape of a stooping kestrel, hung from a fine golden chain. She grinned up at him, and he smiled back.

"A memento of younger days, O Esteemed and Wise Lady."

Eliani refrained from punching his arm as she was inclined to do. Instead she cast a demure glance at him.

"I will give you the benefit of my wisdom later."

"I tremble at the prospect." Luruthin glanced around the hall. "A pity Mirithan could not be here."

Eliani managed not to laugh aloud, though she could not repress a grin. Every theyn in Alpinon save one had come to Highstone for her confirmation. Mirithan, theyn of the village of Althill, the smallest and northernmost settlement in the realm, had sent messages of congratulation and regret that he would not be present.

A decade since, Eliani, Luruthin, and three other guardians had patrolled up to Althill and earned Mirithan's disapproval by running buck races in the meadow above the village one fine autumn afternoon. It had been a day of riotous fun, and absolutely nothing had been accomplished by the villagers during the impromptu festival, which had continued past sundown. That night everyone in Althill, even the theyn, had supped on cold cheese and apples, for there had been no time to build back the cook fires. Mirithan had yet to forgive them.

Luruthin grinned back at Eliani, obviously aware of her thoughts. He bowed just a little too deeply as he left.

By the time she had received the compliments and gifts of every theyn, the light was beginning to fade from the western windows. Her father rose, glancing at Curunan.

"Relieve the lady of those gifts, if you will. There is one more awaits her."

Baffled, Eliani handed the contents of her lap to Curunan and accepted her father's assistance to rise. Gharinan came forward again, bearing across his arms a length of folded velvet, deep violet in hue.

Felisan threw back the cloth, revealing a sword. Eliani gasped as he picked it up, its golden-hued blade flashing in the fading daylight.

"This day you become warden of Alpinon's Guard. May this sword serve you well, even as you serve your realm."

"Mountain-forged!"

Eliani glanced at Gharinan, who was smiling. His village was high in the Ebons, on the slopes of a peak whose fiery heart was the crafthall of mage-smiths.

The blades they made there were infused with fire-khi, the molten power of the mountains. They were stronger, sharper, more perfectly balanced than normal blades. As Eliani accepted the sword from her father, she felt a whisper of the smith's khi, and an echo of fire, running through it.

"Thank you, Father! Oh, thank you!"

Felisan smiled, then began to usher the theyns out to the public circle for the Evennight celebration. Luruthin came up to admire the blade until Felisan shooed him away.

"Time enough for that later. The sun is about to set."

Eliani gave the sword into Curunan's keeping and glanced at the large basket where he had stored her other gifts. She wanted to wear either House Jharanan's brooch or the crystal kestrel. It would be a politic gesture to wear the brooch, but it was large and heavy, and she feared it would weigh down her gown. She opened the box to look at it again. The gilded stag's heads gleamed, and torchlight glinted on the stones.

It was almost too fine. She remembered her thoughts about the clasp of Turisan's cloak: how it was finer than anything Alpinon could produce, how he seemed unconscious of its worth. Closing the box, she put it back in the basket.

She unfastened the kestrel's chain and put it about her neck. The little crystal bird lay atop the silken veil just at the hollow of her throat. She smiled. This was a burden she could bear.

Getting up from her chair, she found Luruthin hovering nearby. He offered her his arm.

"I thought my father had chased you away."

"I am not so easily got rid of. May I escort you to the circle?"

"Thank you."

She laughed, glad to be finished with courtesies,

slightly giddy with her new gown flowing about her and an evening of celebration ahead. As they stepped out of the hall, she drew a deep breath of the cool autumn night, smelling wood smoke and roasting apples on the breeze.

All Highstone was gathered in the circle, the theyns mingling with the populace. Stonereach blue and violet flashed everywhere, accompanied by the colors of lesser kin-clans and autumn colors bright in the evening twilight.

The circle was decorated with flowers and harvest bounty: sheaves of ripe grain from the valley farms to the east, baskets of apples and grapes from mountain holdings. Minstrels played softly from the dais at the eastern side of the circle. They ceased as Lord Felisan stepped toward them, with Curunan bearing the Alpinon banner before him.

The governor walked to the easternmost point of the circle and raised his hands skyward. All fell silent.

"Ældar of the east, guardians of the air, we bid you welcome. Be with us this Evennight and watch over our celebrations."

Solemnly he paced the perimeter of the circle, pausing again at the south to greet the ældar guardians of fire, the west to greet the guardians of water, and the north to greet the guardians of earth. Eliani watched and listened, knowing that someday, as governor, this would be her duty. Strange to think of herself addressing the high ældar. Those brightest of the spirits, guardians of the physical world, seemed remote to her.

Returning to the east, Felisan stepped onto the dais and raised his outspread arms. "Citizens of Highstone, friends, neighbors, and honored guests, welcome to this joyous celebration of Evennight. From now to Midwinter, each night grows longer."

The setting sun touched the Ebons as he spoke, and

all paused to give honor to the west. Eliani did not look at the sun for fear of hurting her eyes but fixed her gaze on the mountains a little to the side. As the sun dipped below the horizon, golden rays streamed upward around the mountain peaks.

Felisan's voice broke the silence. "May we rejoice in the bounty of our harvest, may we welcome the repose of the coming winter, and may we all keep the creed in our hearts and in our deeds. Blessings to you all. Let the celebration begin!"

Music sailed forth, bright and lively. The throng in the public circle resolved itself into rings, one within the other, for the dance of greeting that opened every feast day celebration. Luruthin led Eliani into the dance.

"Thank you for wearing my gift."

"I thought it would go well with Heléri's handiwork."

"It does indeed."

Beryloni and Gemaron were beside them and clasped hands for the turns; Eliani and Luruthin merely crossed wrists. Most found touching hands too intense, for the palm was the strongest locus of khi. In some places, such as the high court in Eastfæld, Eliani had heard that dancers did not touch at all but held their wrists a handspan apart in the air. She thought it would be difficult to dance so, without the aid of a partner to balance.

As they made the final turn of the dance, Luruthin's wrist slid against hers and his fingers brushed her palm, leaving it tingling. She looked at him, and his smile told her it had been deliberate. She smiled back, but only slightly. She had fond memories of their time together, but there had been pain in the meantime, and she was not ready to try again.

The rings shifted and brought them to face new partners. The revolution of the dance began anew. Twilight glowed blue now, above the mountain peaks, and the first stars were beginning to shine.

A flash of pale hair caught her eye. Turisan was dancing past in the outermost ring. He moved like a catamount, smooth as silk yet with strength beneath the surface.

"—beautiful this evening, my lady."

Eliani looked back at her partner with a hasty smile. "Thank you, Firthan. You look very well yourself."

"You are too fine to be warden of the Guard."

"Say that again at the next sword practice."

He smiled. He was kin to her, and also a friend from the Guard. She liked him but feared that he liked her too well. She felt a sudden wish to shed her lovely new gown and return to her leathers. She was more at home in them, and safer in the saddle than in this dance.

⬥

Turisan was breaking fast the morning after Evennight, recalling the previous evening's festivities, when a knock on the door disturbed his reflections. He took a sip of tea spiced with sunfruit and clove to clear his throat.

"Come."

The door opened, and a Stonereach—the theyn who had been named Eliani's nextkin—looked in. "Good morrow, Lord Turisan. Forgive the intrusion."

"Theyn Gharinan, yes? Will you join me?"

The Stonereach entered and closed the door. "Thank you, but I have already broken fast."

"Have some tea, then. It is excellently spiced."

"That I will accept. By its scent, that is Heléri's special festival blend."

"Lady Heléri makes teas?"

"She is an herbalist of high repute. Her teas are prized as far away as Eastfæld, where she could name any price if she chose to trade them. She does not, though. She prefers to make small quantities of high quality and for the most part shares them only with her kin."

Turisan glanced at the cup in his hand. "I am honored."

"As well you should be."

Turisan raised an eyebrow. Gharinan grinned and sipped his tea.

"I called to invite you to join us riding out today, if you are so inclined."

"I was hoping to see more of Alpinon. Thank you, I accept."

"You came on foot, I believe. Lord Felisan's stables can lend you a mount."

From what he had seen of Alpinon's horses, the mount would be humbler than what he was used to, but he smiled his thanks nonetheless. To show disappointment in Felisan's hospitality was unthinkable, not to mention that his father would consider it unforgivable.

He liked these folk. Their realm might have little grandeur that was not made by nature, but the people of Alpinon had few pretensions, and he valued their open friendliness more than any elaborate arts.

Gharinan stayed for as long as it took to drink two cups of tea, then took his leave, bidding Turisan to meet them in the public circle. Turisan wasted no time getting into his leathers. As he walked out to the circle, he was gratified to see that the party would include Eliani.

The half-wild forest girl he had met two days previously was back, looking far more at ease in her worn leathers than she had in her silks. Turisan could not help smiling at the difference.

The mount he was given was small but sturdily built. He had brought his hunting bow and saw that the others carried bows as well. In Southfæld, all guardians went armed whenever they rode. Apparently it was so in Alpinon as well.

Eliani led them northwest on a steep road out of Highstone. The morning was brisk, a sharp breeze rising from the chasm to the east and north of the city, the whisper of the river far below.

The party rounded a ridge that revealed a prospect of the long, deep chasm stretching before them into the mountains. On the opposite cliff a high waterfall cascaded around two rock outcrops, forming a treble veil of white against dark rock. Turisan halted, compelled to admire it.

Drifts of pale mist moved across the plummeting water and billowed in clouds where the three streams struck the rocks far below and became one again in a wide pool. From this the water emerged into the Asurindel, the river that flowed eastward past Highstone.

Eliani reined in her mount beside Turisan's. "The Three Shades. This is the fairest prospect of them. There are other views, but only this takes in the whole."

"Beautiful. Are they the highest falls in your mountains?"

"There are higher but lesser falls. These are the largest and best known."

Beyond her, Gharinan leaned forward to look at Turisan. "Have you heard the legend?"

"No. Will you tell it?"

"It is said that three sisters were handfasted to three

brothers of Stonereach, who then went off to the Bitter Wars and never returned. The sisters climbed the cliff beside the falls—you can see the path there—and kept watch for a year and a day. When their lords still came not, they leapt over the falls and perished on the rocks below."

Luruthin nodded. "Another version says they remained by the falls until they faded into the mists. One is supposed to be able to hear their voices in the rush of water, lamenting their lost loves."

"A sad tale. Has it any basis in truth?"

"That is doubtful"—Eliani's voice was dry—"considering that few couples are blessed with one offspring, let alone three."

"Davharin and Heléri had three." Luruthin looked at Turisan. "Our elders. My mother told me of the shades. When I was younger, I spent many nights seeking them by the falls, and though I never heard their voices, I once saw pale figures flickering in the water."

Turisan gazed across at the falls again. "That path is still in use?"

Eliani made a sound of derision. "Mostly by very young lovers in search of a trysting place who do not care how wet they become."

She turned her mount away and started up the trail. The two Stonereach males exchanged a glance, and Gharinan favored Turisan with a smiling shrug.

They fell into line again, following Eliani westward along the canyon's rim. Numerous small streams crossed the path, seeking their way down to join the river. Some steamed and left sulfurous deposits in their beds.

"You have hot springs."

"Yes." Gharinan glanced back at Turisan with a smile. "This runs from the largest of them. The

Guardian's Reward we call it, for it is customary to rest there after a tour on patrol. You might enjoy visiting it when we return."

They rode on for a league or more, then Eliani led them down a trail that branched southwestward and widened, losing its definition as the dense forest opened out. Greenleaf trees of a variety unfamiliar to Turisan began to appear among the dark blue-green pines. They were slender, white-barked and decked in round gold leaves that fluttered in the slightest breeze. Soon the party was surrounded only by the golden-white trees, restless leaves ever moving, whispering together like raindrops, making the air seem to shimmer. A steady, gentle fall of dry leaves added to the flickering of the light.

Turisan gazed up at the golden boughs, enchanted. "What trees are these?"

Luruthin answered. "We call them firespear, for they thrive where older forests have burned. They are common enough, though they will not grow in the lower regions. Do you not have them in the south?"

Turisan shook his head, gazing up at the white branches, watching the small rounded leaves tremble and dance. "I have never seen them before, there or anywhere. They should grow in Eastfæld with these colors."

"Not high enough."

He glanced at Eliani, then gazed upward at the canopy of golden leaves, inhaled their dry woody scent, and smiled. This was the sort of place he craved, blue sky crowning the glory of the gold-white trees, without a made thing in sight save what the ælven carried with them. Still smiling, he looked at the others and found Eliani watching him.

"You have come at the right season. They are merely

green for most of the year, and in another tenday they will be bare. Since they please you, let us take our meal here."

Lord Felisan's kitchen had packed cold meat, fresh cheese, bread, fruit, and nuts for them, with flasks of wine that they drained and refilled with clear water from a nearby stream. Turisan stretched out on the leaf-strewn ground and listened to the Stonereaches discussing their Guard, learning more about Alpinon from their conversation than any dry history might teach him.

On his first evening he had tended to confuse the two theyns, both of whom had classic Stonereach looks, with green eyes and hair of reddish brown that they wore braided back in hunter fashion. He now knew that Gharinan had sharper features than Luruthin, who laughed more readily than his elder. Both were friendly, Gharinan somewhat more so than Luruthin. Eliani, though courteous, remained aloof.

Turisan watched her cut slices of apple with her knife and take them daintily off the blade with small white teeth. She was pretty, he supposed. Rather wild in her leathers and windblown hair always falling across her green eyes.

He rolled onto his back and gazed up through the sea of golden leaves at the brilliant blue sky. If only he could dwell in such places all the time. At ease, he allowed the firespear wood's khi to flow through him, drinking in the sensations of life beyond the bright signs of the Stonereaches and the less cognizant ones of the horses. The firespears were all connected, he sensed, sharing khi and even roots. They were almost one tree instead of many, and there was a spark of something unusual in their khi.

Lying lazily there, he became aware of a darkness rippling through the forest's khi. He frowned, opening his eyes just as a streak of black whipped through the shimmering leaves overhead.

He was on his feet and running even as he realized what it had been—a dart of the kind thrown by kobalen raiders. The heaviness he had sensed was the kobalen's khi. He should have recognized it, but it had been some years since his last encounter with kobalen.

He vaulted onto his startled horse and urged it to turn as he freed bow and quiver, slinging the latter over his shoulder. The Stonereaches were with him, thundering down the slope, leaving the remnants of their meal scattered on the forest floor.

Turisan glanced at Eliani and saw her eyes flash back at him—not angrily but lit with the fire of the hunt—and he felt a thrill of delight as they pressed forward. Ahead, shadows moved, lumbering clumsily, noisily through the wood. They were swift but no match for the horses, and soon their number could be discerned: six kobalen on foot, crashing downhill southward and westward.

The two Stonereach males veered off to the right, leaving Turisan and Eliani to strike from the left. Turisan nocked an arrow and let it fly, missing his aim by a hairbreadth. Eliani's found its mark, and a grunting cry signaled first blood.

Bowstrings thrummed as all four ælven struck and struck again, circling their horses around the kobalen, who snarled and swore but could not save themselves. The few darts they let fly were easily avoided. It was over in moments, the raiders a huddled heap pierced with many shafts.

"Hold!"

They all halted at Eliani's cry, horses stamping until soothed back to calmness. She dismounted and approached the kobalen. The others followed.

Breathing hard, Eliani turned a scowling face toward

Gharinan. "What are these vermin doing in the South Wood?"

He frowned, matching her disgust as he gazed at the kobalen. "I know not, my lady, but they are done."

Luruthin nudged a kobalen with his foot. "This one lives yet."

The creature bled sluggishly from its wounds, dark liquid oozing into its fine black fur. Eliani stood over it and addressed it in its own tongue, a guttural language of coarse inflection. She must have learned it on patrol; what little of it Turisan knew he had acquired during his service in Southfæld's Guard.

"What brings you so far from your sandpits, rogue?"

The kobalen made no answer. Eliani touched the flights of an arrow lodged in its shoulder. It snarled but said nothing.

"There is no plunder within leagues of here. Why came you hither?"

Turisan saw its arm begin to move and loosed an arrow to pin the wrist. A knife dropped from the gnarled fingers, its blade of ebonglass, the black volcanic glass that kobalen shaped into weapons.

Belated dread washed through him as he realized how close Eliani had been to danger. She glanced at him, then picked up the knife and examined it, its evil edge glinting in the sunlight. She turned back to the kobalen.

"Tell me where you came from and why and I will end it. A clean death."

Turisan, watching closely, thought he saw a change in the kobalen's eyes. Hope seemed to lighten them, but an instant later fear chased it out.

"My lady, I think you should see this."

Eliani straightened and went to Gharinan, who had

begun collecting their arrows and searching the dead kobalen. Turisan hung back, keeping an eye on the survivor.

He watched Eliani join Gharinan beside the body of a kobalen. The theyn pointed toward its head, and Eliani crouched to peer more closely at it.

"By the spirits!"

She glanced up at her nextkin, then with the ebonglass knife sliced the ear from the dead creature's head in one swift motion. Standing, she carried it to Turisan and held it out for him to see.

Amid the black fur he saw a glint of gold. He took the severed ear, careful to avoid dripping blood on himself, and peered at the small hoop of metal that pierced it.

"No kobalen made this."

He glanced up, and his gaze met Eliani's. She nodded, then looked over her shoulder.

"Gharinan, do any of the others wear these rings?"

"I have seen no others."

"Search them all."

Turisan stared at the earring. It was finely wrought, adorned with elaborate coiling scrollwork. Even had it been plain, it could not have been made by kobalen, for they had no skill with metals.

Suddenly a pattern of seeming leaves wrought into the gold resolved into something else. Turisan's heart went cold.

"This is script."

He turned the ear over to confirm his impression, then held it toward Eliani. She took it back and squinted at the ring.

" 'Preserve.' " She looked up at him, her face gone pale. "Do you know of any reason an ælven would mark a kobalen thus?"

Turisan shook his head. She had reached the same conclusion, then. If no ælven had made it, only one other race had the skill.

"Alben."

A chill coursed through Turisan at the whispered word. He glanced up, opening to the khi of the wood. Reaching through the vast web of firespear, he extended his awareness past the chaos of the nearby slaughter from which all the woodland creatures had fled, past the edge of the grove, into the pines well beyond. Something dark lingered yet, but it was distant and he could not place it. More kobalen, perhaps. No doubt they already were fleeing westward.

Luruthin hurried to Eliani, bow still in hand. "There is nothing else. They have food and water but no plunder."

Gharinan joined them. "And no others are marked."

Turisan looked at the handful of dark bodies. "They are too few for a raid. This was a scout."

Eliani took a small leather pouch from her belt and emptied it of a spare bowstring, then put the ear into it. "They have never come this close to Highstone before. They must have crossed at Midrange and come up through the South Wood." She turned to face Turisan. "I fear I must cut short our excursion. My father should know of this at once."

"Of course."

"And we had best offer atonement."

Eliani grimaced with the words, and Turisan sympathized. It was part of the paradox of living in the flesh-bound world that the ælven creed sometimes was difficult to keep.

Slaying kobalen was part of a guardian's duty, but because doing harm was against the creed, they must ask forgiveness from the ældar who watched over the creatures, no matter how much harm the kobalen themselves had wrought. Their ældar must be honored, even as the hunter thanked the ældar of his prey, the farmer the ældar who watched over his crops.

Luruthin and Gharinan began to gather fallen wood and pile the kobalen bodies atop it in a clear space. Eliani joined them, and Turisan returned to where the surviving kobalen lay.

It breathed shallowly, close to death. Turisan leaned over it. "Why does your friend wear a ring in his ear?"

The kobalen gazed at him, eyes already seeming dull. At first he thought it had not understood, but then it drew a deep breath and spat at him.

Turisan dodged. Furious, he drew his belt knife and made one swift slash across the creature's throat. It gurgled, eyes wide with alarm, then was still.

Turisan stood and wiped his knife blade, regretting his angry impulse. It was possible he might have coaxed more information from the kobalen, but he had little patience with the creatures. No use bemoaning his action, for it was dead now. He picked it up and carried it to the pyre.

The others had gathered the rest of the kobalen. The four of them stood around the pyre, and Eliani spread her hands toward it.

"Ældar guardian of these creatures, we pray you pardon the destruction of their lives and the waste of their flesh. We honor their spirit and commit their bodies to flame."

Turisan added his silent atonement. He spread his hands, as did the others, and closed his eyes in concentration. Narrowing the focus of his khi into his palms, he sent it forth into the dry wood beneath the kobalen and placed a spark there, willing it to set the wood alight, pouring his energy into the creation of fire. He could feel the others doing the same, and soon the pyre was aflame.

Opening his eyes, he stepped back, away from the stink of burning kobalen flesh. Eliani turned from the fire, pausing as she met Turisan's gaze. She had shown no fear during the encounter, only the skill and quick response of a seasoned guardian. She had been magnificent, in fact, and he wished to compliment her, but a hardness in her eyes stayed him. She was on guard still, though against what he could not say. She dropped her gaze as she turned toward the horses.

"Let us hasten to Highstone."

⊹

Lord Felisan received the news of the kobalen intrusion with a sternness that surprised Turisan, who had formed the impression that Alpinon's governor was perpetually merry. There was nothing soft in Felisan's response, however. He ordered an immediate doubling of patrols in the South Wood.

"I will dispatch my letter to your father this day, Turisan, unless you wish to carry word to him yourself."

Turisan glanced from Felisan to Eliani, who was staring down at the kobalen's ear that lay on the table between them. He might be forgiven for returning at once to Glenhallow.

"No." He looked back at Felisan. "I am expected to attend your cousin's handfasting. If I were to depart in haste, it might further alarm your people. My father will lose nothing by receiving word from your courier, and my presence at the handfasting might give some reassurance."

Felisan nodded, slowly smiling. "Wisely said."

He went to a shelf and brought out parchment, ink, and pens. "You may add your own message if you care to."

"Thank you. I would gladly enclose a note."

Turisan wrote a brief two lines to his father, assuring Jharan of his return after the handfasting. He gave the note to Felisan, who folded it inside his own letter and bound it with ribbons of violet and blue.

The company at Lord Felisan's table was notably thinner that evening, and shadowed with worry. Gharinan and Luruthin were absent, gone to carry word of the kobalen to their villages.

Eliani had changed into a blue-gray gown; rather shapeless, but it draped nicely along the lines of her body. She seemed lost in thought and more than once returned vague answers to Turisan's attempts at conversation.

In this dampened mood, most of the company retired early. Sensing that Lord Felisan would prefer to retire as well, Turisan took his leave. Eliani glanced up and smiled an absent farewell as he left the hall.

Outside he paused to gaze up at the moon. It was nearly full, blue-white light casting strong shadows. He would take this chance to explore, for the next night he would be preparing to depart or already traveling. He felt regret that he must leave Highstone so soon, and frustration that the shadow of the day's events had spoiled the pleasure of his visit. He would visit the Shades regardless and take that memory home with him.

Two streets diverged from the public circle: the one he had taken that morning with Eliani and her kin and another leading southeast, down the valley. Looking toward the first, he considered a visit to the hot springs but instead chose the other path. There were springs near Glenhallow. This might be his only chance to view the Three Shades by night.

Eliani had said she would show the falls to him, but he thought it best to leave her be. Her mood had been dark through the evening, and he doubted a demand to be escorted to the Shades would improve it.

The road out of Highstone led to a bridge that crossed

the Asurindel. On the far side the path ran both ways along the foot of stone cliffs. He took the westbound branch, guided by the distant rumble of the falls.

Long before he reached them, the air became damp and heavy with water-scent, and the sound of the cataract increased to a roar. He felt unsettled, a sensation he knew well from the fountain court at Hallowhall, for water, especially moving water, interfered with khi. Here the effect was far more powerful than he was used to, blocking his awareness of the small creatures and the green growing things around him.

He followed the path around a sharp rock outcrop and suddenly found himself at the foot of the cascade. The roar of the falls battered at his khi, and a dark pool spread from their foaming base.

Near to the pool, half-hidden by mist, stood a trio of conces. Each small, pointed pillar of carved stone marked the spot where an ælven had died in circumstances of distress. Turisan approached the monuments, peering at them in the moonlight. They stood waist-high, their edges and carvings long since worn soft beyond reading by water and wind. Perhaps they had been placed in memory of the Three Shades themselves. Not entirely a legend, then.

With mist billowing in his face, he started up the footpath, wondering how anyone could ever hope to hear the shades' lamenting over the noise of the falls. Treacherous at first, the path soon became less slippery as he ascended. The noise of the waterfall receded. At the top of the cascade he paused to gaze out over the dizzy height. Stars glimmered faintly beyond the blazing moon.

His head was near level with the easternmost cascade. The two great rocks that split the river towered into the night. He could see the cliff wall through the water just an armspan away and was conscious of the river's silent power as it slipped over the edge. So clear was the water that he was tempted to reach through it to touch the dark stone beneath, but he knew that to do so would be fatal. Asurindel might be near silent here, but it was no less powerful than the raging maelstrom below.

A strange elation filled him as he stood at the top of the falls. He could understand why the legend had persisted. A place of such raw power inevitably must host legends.

A sound drew his attention to the footpath. He turned to see Eliani approaching, a dark cloak cast over her shoulders and her gown gathered into her hands. Surprised to see her, he smiled as he ventured a jest.

"Do you stalk me again, lady?"

"Of course not." She tossed her hair out of her eyes and glared at him. "You would not have heard me if I were stalking you. I came to be sure you were safe. The path can be dangerous even to those who know it."

"The moon is bright enough."

Whatever answer she would have made was lost as she trod on the hem of her gown.

Turisan flung out an arm to keep her from falling, his heart racing with alarm. She regained her balance without his help and gave him a rueful smile.

"I am not very graceful in gowns."

"Let others judge that."

Her smile turned bitter, and she looked away, toward the Shades. Turisan did the same, wondering how his words could have offended her. After a moment he tried again.

"The Shades are truly magnificent."

"Yes."

"Thank you, my lady, for showing me this."

She looked up at him, and this time her smile was unreserved. "You are welcome."

A warm glow sparked within his chest, and he smiled back. She did not like to hear herself praised, it seemed, but would accept praise of her homeland. He gave it to her, speaking with open enthusiasm of Alpinon's beauties, of the wonder of the Shades and his delight in the fluttering firespear wood. All the while he watched her, enjoying the quick brightness of her glance, the dark blush that came to her cheek when he expressed a wish that he might remain to see more of Alpinon, her sudden burst of laughter at a foolish jest.

They talked thus awhile, avoiding the graver subjects that hovered unvoiced in Turisan's thoughts and that he suspected were also in hers. At last they made their way down the footpath, back into the thunder and the clouds of mist that masked the stars above.

Near the bottom, Turisan glanced up at the falls, and so misstepped on the wet rock. Eliani caught his hand to steady him, and he smiled his thanks, knowing words would be lost in the roar of the water.

He kept hold of her hand and looked down at her face bathed in moonlight and mist. Her khi was warm, tingling against his flesh where they touched. She returned his gaze, her smile fading a little as her eyes widened. He thought her quite lovely, her face showing none of the calculated seductions he was used to, only sweetness and a lingering shyness.

Dare I kiss you?

Eliani's expression changed to storm. Her eyes flashed with anger and her voice rang in his mind.

What are you doing!?

Turisan reeled. He released Eliani's hand, stunned by the force of her thought, clear as words shouted into his ear. Blinking, he peered at her through the mist.

My lady?

Stop it! Stay out of my mind!

He stumbled backward and came up against the rock wall. The power of the Shades vibrated through it, relentless, as vivid as her anger. Trembling with shock, he stared at Eliani.

Mindspeech?

It was an ancient ability and very rare. He knew of only one living who claimed it—Lord Rephanin—and he himself had never witnessed it, never truly believed in it though he had heard the legends at his father's knee.

Eliani's face changed from anger to the shock of dawning realization. If they truly shared mindspeech, they held a gift that would place them among the brightest legends of their folk. Mindspeech had ended the Bitter Wars, had enabled the ælven to cast out the alben forever.

Eliani's face twisted in dismay, and she took a step backward. Gasping, Turisan reached for her, thinking she would fall into the churning water below. Instead, she turned from him and fled, running down the trail away from the falls, rounding the narrow ridge, and vanishing.

He gazed after her, trying to understand what had happened, wanting to reach out to her, to hear her voice again, to feel the vibrance of her khi. In the brief moments of their speaking, their khi had blended as intimately as he had felt with any lover. He wanted to feel that again but knew instinctively that she would resent it. Her angry thought had stung as surely as if she had slapped him.

He took a deep breath and ran a hand over his face, finding it damp with mist. He glanced at the Shades, thinking that perhaps some legends were true. Steadying himself, he started slowly back toward High-stone.

✠

"Eldermother, it is Eliani! Please, may I come in?"

Lady Heléri drew back the hearthroom tapestry, a shawl draped around her shoulders. "Child! What is it? Come in."

Eliani sank onto a chair beside the main hearth, where the fire had fallen to embers. Heléri's worktable stood nearby, with Beryloni's ribbon upon it, much longer now, with her name and Gemaron's woven in elaborate silver script, entwined with blessings. Heléri set it aside and sat facing Eliani, then reached out her hands.

"Tell me."

Eliani put her hands, shaking a little, into her eldermother's, glad of their warmth and strength. "Turisan."

"Jharan's son? Yes, what of him?"

Eliani swallowed. "He spoke—he spoke in my mind."

Heléri leaned forward, gazing at her intently. "Just now?"

"Yes."

"Are you certain? He did not speak aloud?"

"We were at the foot of the Shades. I could not have heard him."

Heléri drew a deep breath and squeezed Eliani's hands. "This is a great gift!"

"Gift?" Eliani looked up at her in dismay. "I do not want this gift!"

Heléri released her hands, only to put her arms around her. With a gasp, Eliani slid out of the chair onto her knees and clung to her eldermother.

"Gently, gently." Heléri stroked her hair. "It seems strange and frightening now, but it truly is a gift, my child. It truly is."

Eliani coughed, wiping angrily at her tears. "I do not want him in my mind. I do not want anyone in my mind!"

Heléri held her close until she was calmer, then helped her back to her chair and poured water into a cup for her. As Eliani drank, Heléri reached for the handfasting ribbon, coiling it out of the way.

"I think it is time that I had converse with Turisan. Will you ask him to come?"

"I do not know where he is. I do not want to seek him."

"You need not, do you?"

Eliani looked up sharply, her heart tightening with dread. "Please do not ask me to."

"I will not ask it after this." Heléri's voice was soft, but her eyes were hard and bright. "How else will you know if you can speak to him at a distance?"

Eliani opened her mouth, then closed it again. She stared down at the cup in her hands, noticing that she had drained it. She set it on the table, ran her hands through her hair, then leaned back and closed her eyes.

Turisan. Please come to the old hall above the circle. The stair begins to the southwest of my father's hall.

She opened her eyes quickly as if to escape, and took a shuddering breath. For a moment she sat blinking at the hearth.

"He did not answer."

"Very well." Heléri stood and reached into the wood bin, withdrawing a small log, which she gave to Eliani. "Let us build up the fire, and I will make tea."

Eliani knelt on the hearth to lay the wood, finding the task soothing, for she had always loved the building and tending of fires. She used an iron poker to gather the coals up to the fresh wood. By the time the flames licked at the log, she was steady again.

She took off her cloak, hung it on a hook by the hearthroom, and returned to watch the new flames dance within the hearth. Heléri hung a pot of water over the fire and sat at her worktable, pulling her loom toward her and taking up the strands of colored floss.

"Tell me of your day."

Eliani thought back to the morning, to setting off on horseback for an excursion of pleasure. How long ago it seemed!

"We found kobalen in the firespear wood."

She explained the encounter and the excitement that had followed when they brought the news back to Highstone. Heléri listened, her face grave.

"I will consult with your father tomorrow."

"Something dreadful is happening. Something is changing."

The visitor's chime rang, so softly it was barely audible. Eliani glanced toward the hearthroom, then looked at Heléri, who gave a small shrug.

"It may be Misani."

Eliani got up, her heart sinking. It was not Misani; Misani would not ring, and she knew who stood in the hearthroom. She pulled back the tapestry and saw Turisan there, concern in his dark eyes. A tingle went through her at the sight of him, so fair, so kind. She realized now that he had refrained from imposing his thought on her. She stepped back and gestured him in.

Heléri favored him with a smile and set her work aside. "Sit down, Lord Turisan."

He did so, taking the chair that had been Eliani's. Eliani remained standing, her heart full of unease, ready to flee at any moment.

"Tell me, my lord, what do you know of mind-speech?"

Turisan glanced toward Eliani. She paced to the window, unwilling to meet his gaze.

"Very little." His voice was quiet, controlled. "Lord Rephanin claims the skill, but I have never witnessed its use."

"Rephanin still presides over the magehall at Glenhallow?"

"Yes."

"He is able to touch the mind of anyone in his presence."

"So it is said, but if he does so now, no one tells of it."

Heléri looked thoughtful, frowning slightly. Eliani glanced at Turisan and was struck anew by the fineness of his features, frightened anew by conflicting feelings. Something had begun to burn beneath her heart.

He looked up at her, and she had to fight an impulse to turn away. She did not want to be rude to him, but neither did she want the closeness that was only a thought away.

Heléri continued. "This gift has not appeared for many centuries. It is a great boon. It gives me hope, arriving together with dark news."

Eliani could not bear to be silent. "Forgive me, and I beg your pardon, Lord Turisan, but I do not see it as a boon."

"Mindspeech ended the Bitter Wars, my child."

Turisan stirred in his chair, glancing up at Heléri. He did not look at Eliani but nodded his agreement.

"The Battle of Westgard."

Eliani frowned. "You mean the ballad? But that is just fanciful storytelling!"

"The ballad tells truth." Heléri began to sing, her voice low and rich:

*Dejharan and Dironen advanced their armies
    westward,*
*Divided by high mountains but one within their
    hearts,*
*The alben bore their blow upon sands where white
    spray crested*
In Ghlanhras by the fiery shore.

"I remember their return to Hollirued after West-gard. The warrior brothers, victorious—they were much lauded. Some of the tales about them are fanci-ful, but it is true that they shared mindspeech. I heard them speak of the battle and how it was won by their ability to communicate across the mountains."

"You knew them?"

Eliani was astonished. She had known that Heléri was the mistress of many years, but Westgard had been fought twenty-seven centuries before.

"I knew of them. I had just come to Eastfæld's court. Dejharan and Dironen were the light of the realm, and they were inseparable."

Heléri smiled softly at her memories, then seemed to brush them aside. She fixed Eliani with a stern gaze, then looked from her to Turisan.

"The choice belongs to you both, how you will use this gift. You may even choose to deny it, though those who have gone that way before have ended sadly."

She looked again at Eliani, and her voice grew softer. "Take time to understand it before you decide. Find its limits so that you may know how best it can be employed. It may be that you are able to speak to others. It may be that you must be close by to hear each other. All this should be explored."

Eliani's heart sank. The last thing she wished was to explore what she was rapidly coming to consider a curse. Turisan's expression told her he understood too clearly how she felt. She would hurt him—had already hurt him, perhaps—and there would be arguments, recriminations . . .

He gazed at her in concern. "Lady Eliani—"

"Not now." Eliani struggled to control her rising panic. "I am too tired to think of this now. Bid you good night." She hurried to the hearthroom, catching her cloak from the hook, and escaped.

⌖

Turisan gazed after her, his feelings a mixture of regret and need. The urge to call out to her in thought was strong, but he knew that to do so would only worsen the problem.

"Give her time."

He turned to look at Lady Heléri. Honored lady, elder of Stonereach, depths of wisdom in her blue gaze. She calmed him; she was still water, untroubled by the winds of change.

She returned to her work, and he watched for a while. The handfasting ribbon she wove was as intricate and delicate as any he had seen. His father's ribbon, which Turisan often had admired, was not finer.

Heléri's graceful hands managed the multiple threads with ease, blending the colors to create tiny beautiful images in the ribbon: stars and mountains for Alpinon, hills and open vistas that must represent the Steppe Wilds.

Heléri glanced toward the hearth. "Ah, the water is hot at last. Will you stay to drink tea with me?"

Turisan smiled. "Yes, thank you. May I be of help?"

"No, no. This will take but a moment, and you have much to think on."

Instead of thinking he watched her bring out ewer and cups, measure dried herbs, and pour hot water over them. Fragrant steam rose from the ewer, which she set on the hearth to steep. Here was a scene he would never have imagined: Lady Heléri, Clan Stonereach's eldest member, who claimed to know figures out of legend, was making tea for him.

She returned to her chair and smiled. "You are very like your father. A bit more serious, if that is possible."

"I am not quite my usual self tonight."

"I imagine not, indeed. A most extraordinary evening. I would apologize for my young relative except that I believe you had best sort this out for yourselves."

"Yes." He gazed at the fire. "I do not know what to do, though. I fear anything I say will only anger her."

"She is not angry. She is afraid."

Turisan gave a bitter laugh. "Am I such a monster?"

"It has nothing to do with you. She has been hurt."

He looked up at her, startled.

"And that is more than I should have told you. Here, the tea is ready."

He accepted a cup and inhaled the steam, enjoying scents of summer grass and sweet flowers. They sat in silence for some moments, sipping their tea.

"My lady, what can you tell me of mindspeech?"

"What do you wish to know?"

"Anything there is to know. What I should expect."

Heléri smiled gently. "That I cannot tell you. It is different for each soul who finds it."

Turisan rubbed the edge of his cup with a thumb. "I assume it is somehow related to khi."

"I believe that is so, though the gift is so rare that there has been little chance to study it. My perception is that it is made possible by a resonance of khi between the speakers."

"How will I know if I can speak to others?"

"By trying. Speak to me if you like." She smiled again and sipped her tea.

Turisan set down his cup and drew a breath, then

looked into her eyes. *Lady, do you hear me? Will you answer?*

Her smile did not change. He shook his head, saddened but not surprised.

"If you care to tell me, was there anything different when Eliani first heard you?"

Turisan thought back to the Shades, which could not but quicken his heart. "I was holding her hand."

Heléri extended a hand to him. He took it, a bit surprised at the firmness of her grasp. Hesitantly, for it was an intrusion, he opened himself to the powerful depth of her khi.

Now do you hear me?

They stayed thus for a moment, gazes locked and hands clasped. He knew it was useless, though. He looked away, whereupon she pressed his hand and let it go.

"Do not be disappointed. From what I have seen, those who can speak to many can rarely speak over distance. The closer, personal bonds are those which can cross leagues, and that is a powerful gift."

He smiled grimly. "I am sorry to say it, but I think we may soon have need of such a gift."

"Yes. Eliani told me of the kobalen in the wood."

"Did she tell you of the ring in its ear?"

"She did. I have been pondering the reason for doing such a thing."

"The alben. They are returning." His voice was tight with anger. The alben were hated for their betrayal of the creed, their cruel torment of kobalen.

She bent down to pick up the ewer. "It is well that your father has summoned the Council. May I fill your cup?"

Turisan straightened in his chair. "No. Thank you, I believe I should retire. I am preventing you from finishing that fine ribbon, and it will be needed tomorrow, yes?"

"It will be finished in time."

He lifted a coil of the ribbon, the silky substance sliding through his fingers. He felt a tingling of khi where it touched his skin.

"Your work is exquisite."

"Thank you. You are welcome to stay; you will not hinder me."

"That is kind, but as you said, I have much to think on." He rose and made a deep bow. "Thank you, Lady Heléri. I hope to visit you again."

"I hope you will, child. Good night."

He walked slowly down to his house, crossing the circle in starlight. The voice of the Shades was a restless whisper on the night air. He paused outside his door to gaze up at the sky, thinking of Eliani and of mindspeech.

Imagine being able to pass commands from one side of a battlefield to another with merely a thought, as Dejharan and Dironen had done! It would give the ælven commanders an enormous advantage. There had been no battles since the Midrange War, but the recent increase of kobalen activity implied that the possibility was increasing. That had been part of the reason for his coming here.

He did not wish for war, but if it came, he would stand forth and do his part. As Jharan's son he could do no less, and in fact he would be glad to prove himself.

He had no trouble picturing Eliani in the midst of battle. She would be entirely at home. A smile grew on his face at the thought. She would be magnificent!

Assuming that he could convince her to accept their gift. What a difficult creature she was. He seemed destined to reap her displeasure no matter what he did. Had he discovered he shared this gift with any maiden

of Jharan's court, that lady would have been in raptures.

Eliani was not in raptures. She was frightened, Heléri
had said. He wanted to fold her in his arms and kiss her
fears away. He had felt so ever since the moment their
thoughts had met.

⛬ Nightsand ⛬

Shalár heard a commotion outside her audience chamber. Voices of her guards challenged someone who demanded admittance. Dareth went to the entrance and a moment later returned with a tall, hard-featured male in hunter's garb, travel-weary but sharp-eyed.

"Irith!"

By the look of him, he had come to her straight from his journey. Shalár was glad, for she was eager to know the state of things east of the mountains.

"Welcome back, Watcher! What news of Fireshore?"

"I have no news of Fireshore, Bright Lady. I have something better, but your guards would not let me bring them in."

"What have you brought? Kobalen?"

"No, Bright Lady." Irith's eyes narrowed as he smiled. "Ælven."

Shalár drew a swift breath, then strode at once to the chamber entrance. A glance through the archway showed her that Irith spoke true: A small group of ælven stood huddled together under the watchful gaze of five guards.

"Bring them in."

Shalár nodded to the guards to let them pass, then returned to the chamber and mounted the step to her chair. Irith followed as his five hunters escorted the captives into the audience chamber.

"Where did you take them? In Fireshore?"

Irith shook his head. "We were on our way there and had just crossed the Ebons when we came upon these encamped near Hunter's Pass. Their horses took fright and bolted."

The ælven were somewhat battered by their journey but all in good health. Shalár could taste their khi in the air, so vital it was. Five were Greenglens and bore the gear of Southfæld Guards save for the weapons of which they had been relieved. A sixth wore simple riding leathers and had the wild hair and sun-gilt skin of a Steppegard.

Irith brought forward their swords and bowed as he presented them to Shalár. The swords alone were of high value, for none among her people could make them. She had metal-smiths but no sword-smiths, and these blades were mountain-forged.

She walked around the small cluster of ælven, observing them. "What have you learned from them?"

"Very little, Bright Lady. They are reluctant to talk, but we found this on one of them."

He handed her a folded and sealed parchment. Shalár turned it over in her hands, keeping half an eye on the captives to see their reaction. They seemed dispirited but not alarmed. Either the missive was not precious or they were resigned to its loss.

She tore open the seal and read a formal invitation from the governor of Southfæld to the governor of Fireshore to attend a meeting of the Ælven Council in Glenhallow. For a moment she was tempted to turn to her table and pen a response, sending back an acceptance under her signature as the true governor of Fireshore. She relished the thought briefly, then dismissed it. That would be a foolish waste of this interesting message.

So Southfæld was summoning a Council? That had not occurred in several centuries so far as she knew. Interesting, and possibly troublesome. She must think on how to turn it to her advantage.

Leaving the letter on the arm of her chair, she descended to inspect the captives. The Steppegard and four of the Greenglens were male. The one female was somewhat weather-worn but looked healthy. She might breed well.

"Which of them bore the letter?"

Irith indicated one of the Greenglen males. Shalár walked up to the ælven and took his chin in one hand. He pulled away, and the flash of defiance in his eyes moved her to punish him.

She struck out with khi, and the Greenglen flinched, crying out in surprise and pain. Shalár let his response ripple through the khi of the others in the chamber, then put her hand to the Greenglen male's throat and enwrapped him with her own khi, cutting him off from the others.

His eyes went wide with dismay as she began to drink of his khi, drawing it through her palm. She took her time, slowly savoring his strength, aware that the others were watching intently.

When the Greenglen's legs would no longer support him, she released him. He dropped to his knees, gasping.

Much refreshed, Shalár stepped toward the next captive, who cringed away from her. She merely smiled at him and walked on.

She would try the males, each in turn, and if they were all unsuccessful, she would give them over to the females in her guard and thereafter make them available to any female citizen of Nightsand desiring to breed out to an ælven. Perhaps she would even offer an incentive for conception, as she had just done with that poor starving farmer.

The female she would breed more selectively, sending Dareth to her before any others. Perhaps Irith would be next.

If these six all bred successfully—highly unlikely but possible—six more children would be born in the next year. Not enough to reverse Darkshore's decline, but a beginning. It would be more important as a means of inspiring hope, a herald of greater changes to come. If even one child were conceived—

"Bright Lady?"

She glanced up at the ælven who had dared to speak to her. It was the Steppegard. He tossed his head in an effort to get his wildly curling hair out of his eyes.

Shalár came toward him and reached up to push the curls behind his ears. He did not draw back. Impressive after the demonstration she had just made with his comrade, who was still on his knees. The Steppegard's skin felt warm and smooth, his curling golden-brown hair silky, his khi sharp with the tang of danger, but with only a hint of fear's bitterness. He actually leaned toward her to whisper.

"I have no allegiance with these others, nor any importance in my homeland. I can be no use to you. Let me go free."

Shalár was amused at his daring. "Why were you traveling with Southfæld Guards?"

"We fell in together by chance on the trade road."

"You were going to Fireshore?"

"Bringing horses down to winter pasture."

"Ah."

His golden eyes pleaded along with his words. "I am useless to you, but if you free me, I will act in your service."

Shalár gave a soft laugh. "Be of use to me, and perchance I *will* set you free."

A spark of hope lit his eyes, and he took a half step toward her. "How?"

"Get a child on a female of my people. I will even offer you several to choose from."

His face fell into a frown. "That is a jest in poor taste."

"It is no jest."

This new group of ælven, though small, represented the best new hope for children that her people had known in centuries. Perhaps she would try this one first, with his wild hair and desperation to be free.

She would not free him, of course, even if he did conceive. Especially if he conceived, for if he was fruitful, he would be all the more valuable to her.

A small movement at the side of the chamber drew her attention. Dareth had returned. She glanced over at him, saw the look of resignation on his face.

No doubt he guessed her intentions. He disliked her frequent attempts to conceive with anyone who might prove potent, but as he himself had failed her in that effort, he had no grounds for complaint. Silent and patient but jealous, her Dareth. She wondered how long he had been standing there.

She looked back at the captive before her. "Why should I trust you, Steppegard?"

"I have a name."

"You do not need it here."

He might never need it again. She had not bothered to learn the names of her other captives. Laughing softly at his annoyance, she turned away.

"Take them to the pens."

Shalár returned to her chair, lounging back in it as she watched the captives being taken away. The Steppegard would not move at first and continued to stare at her as the hunters pushed him ungently toward the entrance.

Yes, she would try him first, she decided. But let him have a taste of the pens before she bedded him in more comfortable circumstances. It might make him more willing to talk about Fireshore.

⁜

Some nights later, Shalár raised her head at the sound of a knock on her chamber door. She slid off her bed and flipped the folds of her robe to cover her legs.

"Enter."

Two guards came in with the Steppegard captive between them. His hands again were bound behind his back, though he had been given the freedom of them in his cell in the pens and had taken advantage of the opportunity to wash himself. He wore the legs of his leathers but only a linen shirt above them. No doubt the walk from the pens had made him cold.

"Leave him."

"As you will, Bright Lady. We shall be within call."

She watched the Steppegard from where she stood until they withdrew. He gazed back at her silently, seeming unafraid, waiting.

When the door was shut, she came toward him, looking him over appraisingly. She fingered the cloth of his shirt and found that it was finely woven, more finely than anything Nightsand's weavers could produce.

"You are not so poor a creature as you would have me think. This is no herder's clothing."

"I never claimed poverty. I did not speak of my fortunes when I told you I was insignificant."

"Speak of them now, then. What are you?"

"I raise horses."

"Ah, yes. Winter pasture."

Shalár found the air in her chamber a trifle cold. She

strolled to the hearth, added wood to the fire, and shut the screen once more. The Steppegard had not moved.

"Come over here. It is warmer."

He obeyed after the slightest hesitation. Shalár sat down in a cushioned chair and regarded him.

"Why were you traveling with Southfæld Guards?"

"We met by chance, as I told you."

"Did they tell you of their errand?"

He looked at her in surprise, then glanced downward. Deciding, no doubt, whether to answer her would be a betrayal of his chance companions.

"They were messengers to the governor of Fireshore. I do not know the nature of the message."

"And your winter pastures are in Fireshore? For your paths lay the same way."

A reluctant smile pulled at a corner of his mouth. "One of them took an interest in a horse of mine. I hoped to trade it."

"Ah. I see."

"I cannot tell you anything of their errand, Bright Lady. They did not speak of it to me."

"What can you tell me of Fireshore?"

His brow creased with confusion. "Fireshore?"

"When were you last there?"

"In the summer."

"Selling horses?"

He shook his head. "Managing a trade caravan. I provided the horses."

"You do so often?"

"Now and again. How does this help you, Bright Lady?"

"Poorly, so far." Shalár shifted in her chair, leaning back. "How fared the folk in Ghlanhras when you were there in summer?"

"We did not go to Ghlanhras. Only to Bitterfield."

Shalár suppressed impatience. "How fares Bitter-field, then?"

"Prosperously enough. We traded hides and balm-leaf for sunfruit and darkwood."

"Does the city grow?"

He tilted his head slightly as he gazed at her. "Yes. Slowly, but it grows."

Shalár stood up and moved toward the hearth, turning her back on him. It was a waste of effort, perhaps, to question him. He was unlikely to provide her with any useful knowledge. Unfortunate, for unlike the Greenglens, he seemed willing to answer questions. If he knew anything of importance, though, she guessed he would have offered to share it.

"Do you travel to all the ælven realms?"

"At one time or another, yes."

"Tell me something useful."

"Useful?"

He was silent for a moment. Shalár turned around, expecting to see him defiant, and instead saw him frowning in thought.

"One of Ælvanen's kin-clans is contemplating withdrawing from Eastfæld to create a colony on the southern coast. They are negotiating with Southfæld for a grant of land. Is that the sort of thing you mean?"

"That sort of thing, yes."

She did not know how useful this particular bit of news would be beyond its indication that Eastfæld still prospered. No surprise, that.

The Steppegard's eyes grew narrow. "The governor of Alpinon will have named his daughter his nextkin by now."

"You know Alpinon's governor?"

"Somewhat."

The Steppegard's khi darkened as he stared unseeing

toward the hearth. Shalár found this intriguing. The succession of Alpinon was of little interest to her, but it appeared to mean something to this captive. She moved up beside him, watching his face closely.

"What is Alpinon to you, Steppegard?"

His glance flicked toward her, then away again. "Nothing. Nothing at all."

Shalár's lips curved in a sly smile. "I believe that is the first falsehood you have told me. How interesting."

He held silent. Shalár decided it was time to remind him of his position. She stepped to him and took hold of his collar with both hands, feeling the softness of the linen.

"Yes, this is a very fine shirt. These are well made also."

She let her hand stray to the supple leather covering his legs. He started slightly as her fingers brushed his thighs, then drifted upward. The darkness in his khi bled away, replaced by wonder, anticipation, and a tinge of fear.

Shalár smiled and pressed her hand against him, feeling the immediate response of his flesh. With her other hand she pulled loose the tie of her robe, allowing him a glimpse of her pale bosom.

She looked up and saw his eyes widen. Sliding a hand around his elbow, she led him to her bed. There she turned him around, unlaced his leather legs, and pushed them down to his knees. Pressing her hands against his shoulders, she obliged him to sit down atop the furs.

He gazed up at her, his chest rising and falling with quick breaths. "I can better pleasure you with my hands free."

Shalár smiled as she removed her robe and set it aside. "It is not pleasure I want from you."

She pushed him onto his back and mounted him, settling herself upon him with care so as to urge her body to open completely. He squirmed beneath her, trying to make his arms comfortable.

"Be still." She set her hand to his neck to give him a warning pulse of khi.

The startled look in his eyes told her he understood, and he fell still. She moved her hand up to touch his hair, feeling it curl around her fingers. Then she leaned both hands against his shoulders as she slowly rode him, willing herself with each stroke to open, open and receive a child.

She closed her eyes, enjoying the richness and vitality of his khi, though she did not draw upon it. Nothing must interfere with her chance of conceiving.

She had desired it for centuries, both for herself and for her people. If she could conceive a child, perhaps she would inspire them to hope for the same good fortune. Attitude played a great part in success, she was convinced.

She thought of her parents, of her own conception, which she could not remember, for the soul left much of its spirit memory behind at birth when it took on flesh. She knew, though, from her mother's fond stories that their first meeting in thought had been joyous.

The spirit of the child-to-be greeted its parents at the moment of conception, the one moment when every soul in flesh experienced mindspeech—the sharing of thought as though speaking aloud. Even Shalár, who was more skilled with khi than any other in the Westerlands, ordinarily could not do this.

She ached for that moment, longed to hear her child's salutation. The sire would hear it also, of course. All at once she remembered that it was not Dareth beneath her but a stranger, an ælven.

She would share deepest thought with an ælven if she conceived of his get. The reflection startled her into opening her eyes.

The Steppegard was silent, unmoving, and had his eyes squeezed shut. A slight frown creased his brow. Shalár, curious to know if it was anger or grief, brushed her awareness against his.

Not anger or grief but concentration. He was striving to withhold his seed until she was ready to receive it. He was trying to cooperate with her.

She felt a strange rush of admiration and affection, and as she still was in close contact with his khi, he opened his eyes in surprise. Their gazes met, his mouth dropped open, then with a small gasp, he flooded her with hot seed.

Disappointed, she slid off of him and stood up, reaching for her robe and for a cloth with which she dried herself. The smell of the stranger's seed rose into the chill air of her chamber, curiously pungent.

Shalár dropped the cloth on the stone floor and walked to the hearth, her robe open to its warmth. She felt she had come close to succeeding and was annoyed with herself for interfering with the Steppegard's khi. Perhaps she would try him again in a night or two, for he was certainly strong.

A soft sliding sound made her glance back toward him. He had sat up and was watching her. She looked away.

"I tried."

Shalár turned to face him, her feelings a mix of irritation and disappointment. He sat on her bed, looking at her with his leathers down around his knees and his member softening against his thighs.

He was unafraid, unreproachful, unresentful. A strange creature, this Steppegard.

"Please, either dress me or let me use my hands."

Shalár came toward him, closing her robe against the chill as she moved away from the hearth. She set a knee on the bed next to him and looked down into his face.

"What is Alpinon to you?"

There, at last, was consternation in his eyes. He glanced away. Shalár stepped back and turned toward the door.

"Guard!"

"Wait!"

She walked away from the captive and, smiling to herself, went to the cupboard where she kept a decanter of the strong rough wine that was made in the river valley southeast of Nightsand. When she heard the door open, she turned, leaning against the cupboard and sipping her wine.

"Take him back to the pens."

The captive's face was closed now. He did not look up, nor volunteer any movement. One of the guards kept his expression schooled to stone; the other betrayed himself by a slight look of disgust as they hauled the Steppegard to his feet and pulled up his leather legs, none too gently.

"Wait," he had called. At the last he had been willing to yield, but too late. Shalár watched him leave her chamber between the guards. Let him spend some time alone, thinking about what he would tell her when next they met. That conversation might yield something, though this night's had not.

⁜

"Bright Lady, Yaras is returned to the city. He desires to speak with you. Urgently."

Galir made a nervous bow as he corrected himself. Shalár, who was seated at her worktable, was careful to conceal her excitement at the watcher's return.

"Where is he?"

"Waiting in your audience chamber, Bright Lady."

"Tell him I will be there shortly. Offer him refreshment."

Galir hesitated, mouth open as if to comment, then

hastily bowed again and left. Shalár rose and went not
to the audience hall but to her bedchamber. Dareth
glanced up at her from the table, which was covered in
scrolls of parchment, some so old that they were crum-
bling. He was carefully copying them anew.

"Why do you bother with those? They are ælven."

"Ælven history is our history. It should not be lost."

She forbore to argue, though she saw no value in
holding on to a past to which they could never return.
She kissed his cheek, then left him to his work, glad
that he was occupied, for she wanted to speak to Yaras
alone.

She found the watcher seated on the step to the dais
that held her chair. The tapestries were open, and
moonlight silvered the black stone floor and lit Yaras's
pale hair.

The youngest of her watchers, Yaras had proved
himself through many hunts and in decades of service
watching the mountains to the east. He was quiet but
capable and entirely trustworthy. That was why Shalár
had chosen him to venture east of the Ebons with a
small group of kobalen. From the frown he wore, the
venture had not gone well.

He rose at her approach and bowed deeply, then
knelt upon one knee, his head bent low. "Bright Lady,
I crave your forgiveness. The kobalen you sent with
me were slain by the ælven."

Shalár swallowed a sharp breath of disappointment.
She tried to be angry but found she was more worried.
Though glad that Yaras had escaped the kobalens'
fate, she was concerned at their loss.

"How came they to be slain?"

"I took them to a crest where we could watch the
roads into Highstone. We watched for three days, the
kobalen by day and I by night. I was bringing them

back through the woodlands and sheltered for the day in a tall pine with the kobalen resting at its feet."

"Poor shelter."

"It was all there was to be had."

Shalár nodded. Exposure to the poisonous sun was a risk all hunters and watchers took at times.

A quiet footfall made her glance up. Dareth had come into the chamber and leaned against a pillar at the far end of the gallery, his arms folded across his chest. Shalár let her gaze travel his lithe form, then returned her attention to the watcher, who still was speaking of his kobalen.

"I allowed them to hunt their own food each day, never permitting them to stray beyond my control. One day they went into a firespear wood, chasing small game."

Yaras paused, swallowed, and cast a fearful glance up at her, then looked down again. "They came upon a party of ælven in the wood, and before I could prevent it, one of the kobalen flung a dart at them."

Shalár hissed in disapproval. Kobalen were stupid and often reacted without thought. They had slain themselves, then, by alerting the ælven to their presence.

"Ælven hunters?"

Yaras shook his head. "I do not think so. It seemed a party of pleasure, but they were well armed and made quick work of my kobalen. Forgive me, Bright Lady."

"Do not dwell on it. You are not at fault. I trust the ælven did not detect your presence?"

From the tremor of fear that went through his khi, Shalár knew Yaras had been in terror of his life, alone in the ælven woodlands, with only a tree's boughs as shelter from their fury against Clan Darkshore. His voice fell to a hoarse whisper as he answered.

"No. I kept still and blended my khi with that of my tree. When they had ridden away, I ran."

"In daylight?"

Shalár took his jaw in her hand and made him raise his face. She saw the dry texture of his skin, which she had not noticed before. It was brittle beneath her touch, and it had cracked and bled in one place.

"I dared not stay for fear they would return. I found a gully and hid among its rocks until nightfall, then made my way to the pass. I—could not travel as quickly as I wished . . ."

Shalár released him, feeling horror and pity at what he had suffered. "Go to the pens and feed. Stay; I will give you my command for Nihlan."

She strode to the writing table near her chair and scrawled a note on a slip of parchment, telling the keeper of the pens to give Yaras a kobalen to feed on as much as he desired. She returned and handed it to him, putting a hand beneath his elbow to help him rise.

"Stay in the city until you have recovered your strength. Come to me a night or two hence."

"Thank you, Bright Lady." He glanced toward Dareth, then met her gaze and added softly, "It would have worked, I believe. It was going well until then."

"Yes, we shall talk of it when you are better. Go now."

Yaras bowed again, paused to steady himself, and left. Shalár watched him walk wearily out, aware of Dareth's gaze upon her. When Yaras was gone, Dareth came to her.

"So you sent him across the Ebons. Have you sent many other watchers into this danger?"

"Not yet."

"Why did you send kobalen with him? Not merely so that he could feed himself."

"Not that at all."

She turned away, not deigning to elaborate further. She would tell Dareth of her plans in time.

She paced before the gallery, musing. The ælven probably had taken note of the mark she had put on the kobalen band's leader. Well, so be it. She could not alter what had occurred, and the time was coming when her plans would be plain to all, or at least seem so.

"Shalár?"

Dareth's voice was quiet, almost entreating. She turned and saw the hurt on his face. Hurt at being excluded—he knew it was so. She might hide her plans from him but could not hide that she was making them. He knew her too well.

She reached out a hand toward him, and he hastened to kiss it. She slid her fingers across his wrist and up his arm, a tingle of khi accompanying the touch.

"I am not ready to tell you yet, but I will."

She moved closer and softly kissed him to reassure him of his place in her favor. He gave a reluctant smile and slid his hands around her waist. She leaned into him, deepening the embrace, aware of the differences that kept them both lonely no matter how closely they touched.

⁜

Dusk rose chilly and damp on the night the grand hunt was to set out from Nightsand. Shalár, garbed in leathers and her cloak of Darkshore black and red, stood upon the ledge before the Cliff Hollows, watching the hunters gather on the bay shore below.

Dareth joined her on the ledge, clad in pale robes that glowed faintly in the early starlight, eyes dark and liquid, khi humming with an undertone of desire, for she had denied him her bed these ten days. She wished her own nerves to be afire for the hunt and would satisfy her lust after the victory, perhaps with Dareth if she cared to wait so long. If not, with someone among her hunters who had distinguished himself. She would choose when the moment arrived.

She gave Dareth her hand, and he bowed low to kiss it, the touch of his lips against her flesh making her tingle. "Success to you, Bright Lady."

"Are you sure you mean that, Dareth?"

His eyes slid away from her gaze, glancing toward the pens. A slight frown creased his pale brow.

"They are intelligent creatures. They have language. They are the closest to our kindred that walk in flesh."

"Which is what makes them the best suited for our sustenance."

She had danced this argument with him many times and was ready to dance it again, but he yielded. He bowed his head and spoke in a dull voice.

"I wish you success in your hunting."

"Thank you." She pressed his fingers, then withdrew her hand. "Watch over my people."

He nodded. "As ever."

By the bay a large pale creature was being controlled by three keepers. The hunters gathering on the shore gave the animal a wide berth, and though its jaws were confined by a leather muzzle, the keepers stood well back from its powerful limbs. A catamount was never to be trusted.

Shalár smiled. Only she among her folk ever rode one of the huge cats. Only she dared to divide her attention between hunting and controlling such a dangerous creature. She had caught this one but three days earlier on a foray toward the Ebons.

She looked back at Dareth, put a hand at the back of his neck, and drew him to her for a swift, hard kiss. Releasing him, she turned to descend to the city.

Two guards fell into step behind her, along with Galir, who carried a basket of headbands for the hunters. She did not look back at Dareth, though she felt his khi follow her.

The crowds parted before her. A child skipped out toward her and was swiftly caught back by its father, who wore the badge of the Crafters' Guild. His eyes met Shalár's in one fearful glance before he bent to whisper to the child.

The hunters had gathered along the shoreline, some hundred and fifty all told. Some were experienced, some came from the ranks of her guard. Others had come to Nightsand for the first time, having left their rural homes for the hope of a kobalen or two to bring back to their families. They all fell back before Shalár, who paused to look over their ranks, a sea of silver-haired hunters with sharp, eager faces. Hungry faces.

Three captains were to command them: Ciris, Yaras, and Welir. Their brows were bound in Dark-shore colors of ælven make, brilliant and distinct.

Shalár looked closely at Yaras's face and saw no remaining sign of sun-wrought damage from his ill-fated journey across the Ebons. Yaras was among the best of her hunters; that was the reason she had chosen him as a watcher. He had gained further honor by fathering a child, conceived on a previous grand hunt.

She summoned Galir with a gesture. The youth stepped forward with his basket. The headbands it held were black tipped with red at each end, made in Nightsand, the colors not as vivid as she could wish, but they would serve. She took a handful and began walking along the ranks of the hunters, giving each a headband, nodding or saying a word to those she recognized. It would have been quicker to have others pass out the tokens, but Shalár wanted to look each of her hunters in the eye. They were to become a pack this night, and must bond together as a pack before they made their first catch.

When the last headband was given out, she returned to where the captains stood. "Divide them into three companies and follow me."

She strode along the shore to where the catamount's keepers wrestled to hold it still. The great pale cat fumed and snorted, eyes furious above the muzzle. Under starlight its fur was a warm amber-white, darker at the ears and tail.

The catamount spied her and stopped its fretting. Shalár felt dull recognition in its khi, mixed with anger and fear. It pinned back its ears and growled low in its throat.

She focused her khi, then sent it forth and took the creature's mind, coiling her will around its fury, making it her own. She went so far as to look through the cat's eyes for a moment, seeing many reedy, two-legged creatures that should have been easy to kill but were not, herself a menacing figure with pale hair.

She drew back from the catamount's perception, keeping an iron hold on its khi. Without hesitation she reached out and unstrapped the muzzle, letting it fall to the ground. The keepers' ropes attached to it fell slack. Someone behind her gasped.

The cat made a strangled, gargling sound. Shalár did not permit it to move, though its eyes flashed with rage. She climbed upon its back, taking hold of the loose skin at its shoulders, the fur warm and coarse against her fingers.

Only when she was comfortably seated did she allow the beast to let out the roar it so wanted to voice. The sound began as a growl and rose to a high scream, echoing along the cliffs of Nightsand Bay.

She smiled. If kobalen were skulking across the bay, that sound had alerted them to what was coming. She

was untroubled by this. Kobalen lived short lives and
were simpleminded. Even if any lived among them
now who were old enough to remember the last grand
hunt and warn their comrades of what the cat's cry
meant, they could not escape.

Kobalen were swift but not as swift as Shalár's people, and they saw poorly in darkness. They were no
match for a hungry pack.

Shalár made the catamount pace southward along
the shore, aware of the tension in its limbs, the rage
that seethed within it. Catamounts were large—one
beast might weigh as much as five Darkshores—and
vicious. The effort it cost her, the khi that she spent to
control the beast, was well worthwhile. Her people
would never forget seeing her thus.

Behind her the captains called their hunters to order
with whistles and bird trills. No one spoke. All had
said their farewells in the city.

She glanced up at the Cliff Hollows, saw the pale
form standing alone on the dark ledge, and smiled.
Sentimental Dareth. He would watch her out of sight
before going in. Though she would never do such a
thing herself, she liked that he did it.

Clear of the jumbled khi of the city and ahead of the
hunters' pack, she thought she sensed a whisper of
Dareth's khi reaching to her from above. It came and
went as she proceeded down the shore, like an elusive
fragrance of flowers on the fitful breeze. At last it was
lost when the path turned away from the bay, passing
inland between ridges that blocked the Cliff Hollows
from view and snapping the fragile contact between
her and her consort.

✣ Highstone ✣

The day of the handfasting dawned bright and clear, with a cool wind whispering of winter. Eliani had long since arisen, for the night had brought her no counsel and little rest. She had tried to meditate, but her thoughts had drifted and she ended imagining she was ensnared in countless ribbons that only tightened as she struggled to break free.

The public circle was decked anew with garlands of autumn flowers, its stone surface adorned by the winds with a scattering of leaves in every shade of flame. As noon approached, all of Highstone's day-biding citizens and many of the night-biders came out for the handfasting, a ceremony that rarely was performed. Ælven lives were long, so to pledge oneself to another for life was no light commitment.

Lord Felisan's minstrels were there, hard at work, their music half-lost amid the chatter of the gathering folk. Eliani lingered nearby, ready to witness the handfasting. To her dismay, she learned that her father had invited Turisan to stand witness as well. The Greenglen gave her a brief smile as he joined them, then engaged the two Steppegard witnesses in conversation.

Luruthin stepped up onto the dais beside her, freshly dressed and smiling as if he had not spent the night riding to Clerestone and back. His eyes took on a shadow of concern as he looked at her.

"What troubles you, Kestrel?"

Eliani noticed Turisan's head turn toward them, but he resumed his conversation. She raised her chin and tried to smile.

"I remember Davhri's handfasting, and how unhappy I was to have her leave us."

"Ah." Luruthin grinned and lowered his voice. "I warrant you do not feel quite the same about Beryloni."

"I am most fond of Beryloni!"

"And distance is said to increase fondness. You will be even more fond of her when she is gone to the Steppes."

Eliani smacked his arm, stifling a laugh. The two Steppegards were close by, but fortunately, they were attending to Turisan and had not heard.

A hush fell in the circle as the midday sun reached its zenith. The minstrels ceased their music, and a single clear horn note hung in the air. A tall figure in deep blue entered the circle from the north—Heléri, cloaked and veiled in the color of the midnight sky.

Eliani had seldom seen her in daylight. Within the shelter of her hooded cloak, beneath the deep blue veil, her skin glowed rose-white. Her eyes were a deep rich blue, and her dark hair fell forward from the hood in two long braids bound with the Stonereach colors: violet and blue.

Eliani watched intently, for she had been so young at the time of Davhri's handfasting that she had only a few vague memories. Heléri came before the dais and began the formal ceremony, pacing the edge of the public circle and pausing in each direction to offer greetings to the ældar, as Felisan had done on Evennight. When she returned to the east, she stepped onto the dais and gathered the witnesses around her.

"Gentle friends, kindred of Stonereach and of Steppe-gard, and honored guests, before you come two souls to be forever handfasted. Bear you all witness to their pledge."

From the north, under banners of violet and blue, came Beryloni with thirty of House Felisanin. She wore a blue and violet mantle over her pale gown and a cir-clet of autumn flowers in her hair. From the south came Gemaron, attired in a tunic of russet and green, at-tended by his kindred beneath fluttering flags in the same Steppegard colors.

Heléri stepped forward, the handfasting ribbon in her hands. Sunlight caught the interwoven colors and made the silver script flash and glisten.

"Who stands forth for Stonereach?"

Beryloni's parents, long ribbons of blue and violet in their hands, came forward with their daughter be-tween them. They led her to face Heléri.

"And who for Steppegard?"

Gemmani and Rhomiron led Gemaron to his place, bearing ribbons of russet and pine. Heléri gazed down at the couple before her.

"Gemaron and Beryloni, you stand before us to join hand and heart, never again to part in flesh or in spirit. If this is not your choice, now is the time to withdraw."

Gemaron looked at Beryloni, who stood smiling, white flowers trembling in her burnished hair. Eliani feared for a moment that he would balk, but he smiled back at Beryloni, then spoke in a clear voice that rang through the circle.

"I choose to be handfasted to Beryloni of House Fe-lisanin, never to part again."

Beryloni declared likewise. Heléri beckoned to them.

"Then join hands and be bound together by your kin before these witnesses."

Gemaron took Beryloni's hand in his, and Heléri

drew them forward. Bishani, Beryloni's mother, laid her blue ribbon across their clasped hands.

"I bind you together under Stonereach."

She crossed the ribbon once below their hands, then stepped back, retaining the ends. Gemmani placed her dark green ribbon over the blue and crossed it.

"I bind you together under Steppegard."

Likewise their fathers, Lanrhusan and Rhomiron, bound them with the violet and russet ribbons. Heléri then laid the handfasting ribbon over all.

"I bind you together in heart, body, and spirit."

She crossed the ribbon once and began to weave it with all the others. As the five traded the ribbons back and forth, Eliani watched the pattern envelop the couple's clasped hands. Heléri spoke while she guided the work.

"This union is not only of two souls but of two houses, Rhomironan and Felisanan, and of two realms, the Steppe Wilds and Alpinon. In this joining all our ties of kindred are renewed. Though many leagues separate us, though we stand under different colors, we are all of one people, the ælven who first walked this land when the stars were young. May those in spirit as well as those in flesh extend their blessings over Gemaron and Beryloni, who from this day forth shall be as one."

The woven ribbons now covered the couple's arms below their wrists. At a sign from Heléri, the ends were let fall to flutter in the breeze. Sunlight caught at the blessings woven into the ends of the handfasting ribbon.

Eliani felt a tingle of khi in the air; there was strong magecraft at work here. She saw the bliss on the couple's faces and marveled. She could not imagine doing this, pledging herself to one partner for all the centuries ahead. She had not managed even a single year despite the best intentions.

It seemed that her gentle, somewhat foolish cousin had more courage than she. Beneath the crown of white blossoms, Beryloni's face shone with confidence and happiness.

Eliani glanced at the other witnesses and saw that Turisan was staring at the couple's bound hands. He looked up at her, dark eyes intense. Eliani shifted her gaze, her heart racing uncomfortably.

Heléri bade Gemaron and Beryloni raise their joined hands high for all to see and make their personal pledges to each other. When they were finished, she turned to the Stonereach party and bade them bring forth the emblem of Beryloni's craft, a large distaff elaborately decorated with flowers and ribbons, to the dais. Beryloni was a weaver, a good one, and her family was justly proud of her skill. Her parents accepted the distaff and knelt, each holding an end of it just above the ground so that it separated Gemaron and Beryloni from Heléri.

"Beryloni, as you step away from Stonereach, you bring the gift of your craft to your new clan. Gemaron, as you welcome your lady into Steppegard, so you welcome her skill to the benefit of your people."

Eliani noticed Beryloni's mother brush away a tear. It was not always the female who left her clan to join her partner's, but more often than not it was so.

"Together you carry this gift from Stonereach to Steppegard as the symbol of your union. Let the step you now take be the first of a long journey of prosperity and happiness together. Come forward into your new life."

Heléri moved back, and together Beryloni and Gemaron stepped over the distaff. The minstrels at once burst into joyous music, and Heléri turned the couple to face the circle.

"Welcome, Gemaron and Beryloni of House Rhomironan!"

Eliani watched intently as Heléri clasped the couple's beribboned hands in her own, for this was the true crux of the ceremony. While the onlookers celebrated, Heléri's hands moved swiftly, unweaving and reweaving the ribbons. The tingle of khi in the air increased. In a few moments the weave had moved from the couple's hands to their forearms, covering them from wrist to elbow as would an archer's brace.

All the colors were present on each arm, their hands were again free, and the beautiful handfasting ribbon was now two ribbons, its shades and glints of silver visible in the weave on each arm, though Heléri had used no blade or tool and Eliani would have sworn nothing had been cut. The woven bands were secured not with knots but with magecraft, and would remain as a mark of the newly handfasted, never to come undone until the couple had reached their new home.

Eliani gave a small nod of satisfaction, glad to have seen the making of this bond, though an echo of heartache reminded her of Davhri's handfasting long before. Heléri, her work finished, glanced up at Eliani with a smile as the couple moved into the circle to lead the first dance.

"My lady, will you dance?"

A stab of dismay struck her as she turned to face Turisan. Of course, on such an occasion she would be expected to dance with him. To do otherwise would excite curiosity and undoubtedly displease her father. She managed to nod.

Turisan started to offer his arm, then turned the gesture into a sweeping bow, making it seem the most natural thing in the world for her to precede him into the circle for the dance. Gemaron and Beryloni already whirled around and around, hands clasped, laughing together. Eliani summoned a smile more gracious than she felt and raised her hand into the air to touch wrists, but Turisan struck a formal position with his own hand curving gracefully toward hers, separated by a handspan.

High-court style. Very formal, very elegant. Turisan's choosing to dance in this way made Eliani feel both annoyed and relieved. She concentrated on matching his style and releasing her resentment. It would be poor grace to hold the choice of high-court dancing against him, for she knew he had made it out of consideration for her.

I am a beast, she told herself. What a model of hospitality for my household and my clan! Our most honored guest is afraid even to speak to me, and thinks I consider a dance with him nothing short of torture.

She could feel his khi through the air between them as though they actually touched. She shivered.

There was much to admire in him—she was perfectly willing to admire him—she merely preferred to keep her thoughts to herself. She hoped he would understand this. To show her goodwill, she sought to begin a conversation.

"You dance with great elegance, my lord."

"As do you." Turisan smiled. "Someone once told me you were not graceful in gowns, but I see that it is untrue."

Eliani remembered their meeting by the Shades. She felt a blush creeping up her neck and glanced away toward the musicians, wondering when they would end her torment.

⌗

Turisan watched Eliani's dismay, frustrated that he had caused it. He would not have claimed a dance with her except that it was customary and expected, for she was the lady of the hall and he the ranking guest.

She tried to hide it, holding her head high and smiling politely, but her khi shimmered with distress.

Their dance was marked by stiff formality and inconsequent conversation. He did not approach her again but found himself watching her, a form of self-torture he seemed unable to resist.

She was not only graceful but beautiful in her flowing gown, its cool colors setting off the warmth of her hair. She moved among her guests and kin with all the graciousness that could be desired of a leader of state.

This lady was quite different from the wild thing in dusty leathers he had encountered—was it but four days ago?—and different still from the frightened girl who had fled from him at the Shades. Every time he thought he had begun to understand her, she showed a new face.

With the cool of evening approaching, the revelers moved indoors, filling Felisanin Hall with good spirits and laughter. Turisan joined them and feasted well, knowing he would be traveling hard over the next few days.

After more dances and many toasts, the handfasted couple departed and the hall grew quiet. Some sought their homes, and others settled into conversation over wine and sweet cakes. Turisan stayed until he felt his duty had been satisfied, then slipped away to prepare for his own departure.

He was forestalled by the young cousin of the house, who caught up with him in the hearthroom. His heart leapt with hope that Eliani had sent the boy after him.

"Your pardon, my lord. Lord Felisan desires a private word with you before you go. Will you follow me this way?"

Stifling his disappointment, Turisan accompanied the youth through a private passage that paralleled the hall and emerged directly into the governor's quarters. They entered the sitting room he had visited before, where Felisan stood waiting beside the fire.

"Ah, excellent. Thank you, Curunan."

The youth left, softly closing the door behind him. Turisan met the governor's gaze, thinking his green eyes were startlingly like Eliani's.

"I will not keep you long, Lord Turisan. I was much occupied this morning or I would have spoken with you then. I believe you should take this with you back to Glenhallow. Your father should see it for himself."

Felisan produced a small box, which he opened to show Turisan the severed kobalen ear lying in a bed of salt. Turisan remembered Eliani cutting it from the creature's head with a single stroke—their shared dread as they realized that the alben must have made the ring. He nodded gravely as he accepted the box.

"Yes. Thank you."

"I can give you a horse for the first part of your journey, and an escort to your border if you desire it."

"The horse I will gladly accept. I doubt the escort is necessary, though I thank you for offering it."

"There could be more kobalen in the forests."

"If so, I can evade them best alone." Turisan smiled. "Thank you again for your hospitality. My father did not exaggerate your kindness."

Felisan clasped arms with him, then drew him into a brief embrace. "In you I see him again, and all our old kinship is reawakened. I look forward most eagerly to our meeting at Glenhallow. Tell Jharan that if I could speak to him, he would tire of me before my arrival."

Turisan frowned in confusion. "Tell him what?"

Felisan smiled. "An old jest between us. In our youth we strove to acquire mindspeech together."

Turisan felt a shock, as if icy water had been dashed over him. "You did?"

"Yes, but it was all in vain, though we meditated for days on end and made many offerings to the ældar. I fear that gift may be lost to our kind at last."

The fire snapped. Turisan glanced over at it.

"Not quite lost." He had murmured the words half to himself, but when he looked up from the flames, he saw Felisan watching him. "L-Lord Rephanin is said to have the skill."

"Rephanin, yes. It will be interesting to meet him again." Felisan tilted his head. "Do you leave tonight or in the morning?"

"Tonight is best, I think. No reason to delay."

"The horse will be brought to your house at once, then, with provisions for your journey. Strength to the spirits who guard you, Turisan, and may they see you safely home."

"I thank you."

They left the room together, Felisan returning to the feast hall. Turisan caught the tapestry as it fell closed behind the governor and held it a little aside for a moment, searching the hall for Eliani.

She was standing by the vast hearth, firelight flickering in her hair as she talked with the two Steppegards who had stood witness to the handfasting. Turisan felt an urge to go to her. He might take formal leave of her, though what he truly wished to do was sweep her into his arms and carry her from the hall.

Did she know? Did she know what their fathers had prayed for? He doubted it, and guessed that to learn it from him would only make her angry.

More than ever he felt that he and Eliani were fated to be together. Their gift could be of enormous service to their people whether or not they faced war. He was so certain of it that he was willing to bind his very life to it, but how could he convince Eliani of his sincerity? How to assure her that she need not fear him? Heléri had said to give her time, and he trusted that lady's judgment better than his own.

He watched Eliani's eyes flash as she laughed at some

jest. Though he yearned to be near her, he remained where he was. If he approached her now, even merely to bid her farewell, it would chase the smiles from her face.

Not now, then, but he would see her again. She would come with her father to the Council in Glenhallow, and he would talk with her then. In the meantime, he would seek the right words to persuade her.

"Farewell, my lady. Spirits keep you safe."

Even as he let the tapestry fall, she glanced toward him, though his words had been a whisper. He waited, not daring to breathe, feeling the heat of her gaze through the cloth, hoping she would speak to him. A moment's stillness, then he sensed her turn away.

He closed his eyes. Not yet, then. Not yet, but soon.

He strode down the private passage and out beneath the stars, needing action. He would ride at once for Glenhallow and try not to count the days until the Council convened.

⁜

"Departed?"

Eliani stared in surprise at her father, who was straightening an untidy stack of papers. He carried the pages to a shelf, and she followed him.

"Why did you not tell me Lord Turisan was leaving? I would have gone with his escort."

"He chose to forgo the escort." Felisan sat down by the last embers of his fire. "Ah, I am tired!"

Eliani stared at him in disbelief. "You let him ride alone?"

"Turisan can look after himself, Eliani. He came here alone and on foot and came to no harm."

"That was before we knew kobalen had entered our woods!"

Eliani picked up a small log and poked the fire awake with it, then laid it on to burn. Yellow light flared, and she frowned at it, feeling restless.

"We should send a party to make certain he reaches the border safely."

"It is very late."

"There are some few yet talking in the hall. I will lead them myself."

"Eliani—"

"I will be back before morning."

In the feast hall she found Luruthin, two Steppegards, and Firthan, a cousin of her father. These four pledged to go with her and dispersed to make ready.

Eliani hurried to her chamber to strip off her finery and don her riding leathers. Perhaps she was being overcautious, but even a small possibility of Lord Turisan's coming to harm in Alpinon's woods was unthinkable. She would get no rest until she was assured he had crossed into Southfæld.

Into Southfæld and away from Alpinon. She smiled wryly as she pulled on her boots.

She met the others in the public circle and led them along the south road, then cut through the forest, retracing the path by which she had brought Turisan to Highstone. The full moon was westering, casting long tree shadows. They were nearing her old oak when at last she saw a lone mounted figure ahead.

Turisan had heard them. He turned, then halted and waited for them to come up.

"My lady?"

Though his words were formal, his gaze was intent. Eliani swallowed, suddenly nervous.

"I wished to be sure that you reached your border in safety, my lord."

"That is kind of you. I would not have put you to such trouble."

Eliani stared at him, wanting to say more, unable to find the words. He was leaving. She realized she did not know when she would meet him again.

Something in his face shifted, a warmth coming into his eyes. "Lady Eliani, will you walk a little way with me? I would speak—I would talk with you briefly."

A shiver crossed her shoulders. She shrugged it away. "Very well."

She dismounted and left her horse to graze. Turisan joined her, and they walked down the gentle slope while the others waited. Behind them the moonlight grew golden as the orb approached the mountains.

He did not offer his arm, but Eliani felt Turisan's presence almost as if they touched. Her skin tingled all along the side nearest him. At last he stopped and turned to face her, his voice low and soft.

"I hope I do not err by telling you this. Your coming here has given me heart. Do not answer now, but hear me and then think on this as long as you will."

He paused to draw a breath, his eyes near black in the fading moonlight. Eliani waited, wondering what arguments he would choose. He wanted her to accept the mindspeech, to yield her thoughts to him; that much she knew.

"I believe that our paths lie together, that we should use the gift we share to aid our people. I am willing to pledge my life to it, and to you."

Eliani took a step back, fear leaping in her heart. She opened her mouth, but Turisan stayed her with a gesture.

"Please—please hear me first." He lowered his voice to a near whisper. "I will do anything I must to assure you of my commitment. I will handfast with you if you wish it."

"Ah! No! Y-you speak without considering!"

"I have considered, my lady, and know my heart."

"But we are strangers!"

"We *were* strangers. Since that moment at the Shades, I feel I know you."

He smiled slightly, a small shift but enough to make her feel the wind at her back, the drop beneath her feet. Her body ached to accept him, to embrace him this moment, but she dreaded what would follow, and her kindred were nearby, waiting . . .

"I will not speak of our people or the service we could give them. You know what is at stake. Only let me say this: I swear by all the spirits of Southfæld that I will never hurt you, not if I can help it."

Eliani gazed at him, unable to sort a response from her jumbled feelings. A ray of dying moonlight lit the edge of his cheek and glinted in his fair hair. His face was controlled, the perfect courtier's. Only his eyes blazed with ardor as he bowed.

"I thank you for hearing me. Think on this as long as you will. You may send me your answer." He gazed intently into her eyes and lowered his voice. "Or you may tell me yourself."

Eliani glanced down at the forest floor. Panic cleaved her tongue to the roof of her mouth. He wished her to handfast? She, who had failed so miserably at a mere cup-bond? Surely he must realize how impossible was the suggestion. She heard him step away and looked up to see him waiting, ready to start back.

Slowly she set one foot before the other, and Turisan followed. In silence they returned to where the others waited. Did he think her foolish to have brought them? Yet she truly had been concerned.

She cared for him, she realized. More than mere desire, which she was well-practiced at ignoring. She wanted to believe his vision of the future they might share, to believe they could find happiness together, but she knew her own failings. She had sought such a partnership before, and it had ended in ruin.

When they reached the horses, Turisan swept a formal bow. "I thank you, lady, for the hospitality of your house. Alpinon is a fair land, and I hope to visit it again."

Eliani nodded, finding her voice. "You will be welcome whenever you return, Lord Turisan."

"I will send a guardian back with the horse."

"Have him turned loose at the edge of this wood, and he will find his way home."

They mounted and rode forward all together. Eliani glanced up as they passed beneath her oak, and a flash of memory made her halt. She stared up at the dark, twining limbs, a cold tingle running down her spine.

"Stay a moment."

She left her horse to climb the tree. At its top she looked up at the sky crowned with stars. The moon had gone, leaving the night deep dark.

From her treasure crook she claimed the scroll she had left there days before. She gazed at it a moment, then glanced skyward once more, wondering what spirits watched over her and in what strange ways they guided those who walked in the flesh-bound world.

Returning to the forest floor, she stepped toward Turisan's mount and handed the scroll up to him. He looked back at her as he accepted it, question in his eyes.

"That is what I was reading when I heard you come into the wood four days since."

He unrolled it and glanced at the text, then looked sharply up at her. " 'The Battle of Westgard.' "

Eliani nodded. A look of wonder crossed Turisan's face, then was gone as he schooled his features to disinterest. He was well trained, this lord of Southfæld's high court. He offered the scroll to her, but she shook her head.

"Keep it."

"Thank you."

He slipped it into his tunic, and the party rode on. At the edge of the South Wood she and the others halted, watching from beneath the boughs while Turisan rode on toward Midrange. He turned and raised a hand in farewell.

Eliani returned the gesture, knowing she certainly would see him again. She owed him an answer, and if she chose to decline, she would not add to his pain by doing so at a distance.

⁜

Luruthin rode back to Highstone in silence, paying scant attention to the others' conversation. He was watching Eliani, who seemed lost in thought.

He longed to know what the Greenglen had said to her. He sensed that their formal farewell had concealed stronger feelings, and not altogether happy ones.

In his heart he made a silent pledge. If Lord Turisan showed any sign of hurting Eliani, he would intervene. It would likely lose him even the reserved friendship she now gave him, but he could not bear to see her suffer further.

He had long cherished the hope that patience and loyalty would win her back to him. She had been so very young when they were close—too young, he now knew—and then Kelevon had turned her head.

Dashing, hot-blooded, and wild as the Steppes that were his home, Kelevon had dazzled Eliani with tales of his travels and brought tumult and discord to her house. Within two seasons he had tired of her. He had not broken his cup-bond that Luruthin knew, but he had violated its intent, flirting publicly with others, dishonoring Eliani. Spirits knew what else had passed between them in private. As far as Luruthin was concerned, Kelevon had broken the creed, for he surely had harmed Eliani.

For a full year after Kelevon's departure Eliani had scarcely smiled or laughed. She had abandoned her music, cut her hair short, and gone into Alpinon's Guard, spending more time on patrol than at home. Luruthin had found her pale, wounded silence more heartbreaking than her initial rejection of him in Kelevon's favor.

She was just beginning to recover her spirits, and now this Greenglen had ruffled them again. Another Kelevon she did not need. If Turisan showed the slightest sign of following that path, Luruthin would pay any price to prevent it.

⚜

It was well past midday when Turisan arrived at Hallowhall, the governor's palace in Glenhallow. Though covered with the dust of four days' riding, he made his way straight to his father, finding him in the audience chamber.

Hundreds could gather in this hall, but just then only two sat at its high table, a long piece of whitewood carved in an arc matching that of the chamber walls. Seated at the center of its curve were Lord Jharan and Lord Rephanin. Jharan wore one of the formal long tunics he commonly wore in the palace, the magelord a simply-cut robe of velvet the dark gold of tarnished bronze.

"Turisan!"

Lord Jharan rose and, abandoning his customary formality, embraced his son across the table. Turisan smiled, glad to feel the familiar comfort of his father's khi. When they parted, he made a slight bow to Rephanin.

"Lord Rephanin."

Rephanin nodded. Turisan had always been somewhat uncomfortable near the magelord; since his early youth he had carried the unsettling feeling that Rephanin was dangerous. It might have been the strangeness of Rephanin's foreign appearance—he had the black hair of an Ælvanen and still claimed allegiance to that clan though he had presided over Glenhallow's magehall for centuries. Unlike the blue eyes that were common to Ælvanen, his eyes were gray and piercing. Turisan had never been able to bear their gaze for long.

A mindspeaker, or so he claimed. Turisan wondered if he should ask Rephanin about mindspeech but was hesitant. Eliani would not thank him for mentioning it to another. Best to wait for her answer.

Jharan beckoned him to come around the table. "Come, join us. You look as if you just arrived."

"I did. I have—news to bring you."

Turisan glanced a silent question to his father, uncertain to what degree he should be candid in Rephanin's presence. With the slightest of nods, Lord Jharan gave him permission to speak freely.

Turisan opened his satchel. "Lord Felisan thought you should see this."

He withdrew the small box Felisan had given him, set it on the table before his father, and opened it, brushing the salt away from the desiccated kobalen ear within. Rephanin leaned forward to peer at it. Jharan's nostrils flared slightly.

"Well. That is something never before seen in Hallowhall."

"I have seen its like before. The ring, that is." Rephanin's deep voice echoed in the chamber despite the heavy tapestries on its walls. He glanced at Turisan, then at Jharan. "I know this work. If I may examine it more closely?"

Jharan nodded, and Rephanin picked up the kobalen

ear, brushing away grains of salt as he peered at the
tiny silver ring that pierced it. Turisan watched him,
waiting uneasily, conscious now as he had not been before of the many discomforts of long travel.

Rephanin turned the ear over, frowning as he ro-
tated the ring within it. "Yes. This is the craft of Farnathin. I saw his early work when we both dwelt in
Hollirued. He came there from Glenhallow to study
smithcraft."

Jharan tilted his head, frowning. "I have never
heard of him."

Rephanin glanced at him before replacing the ear in
its box. "He left long ago to join his kindred in
Fireshore."

Turisan felt a wave of dread. "Clan Darkshore."

"Yes. Darkshore."

Jharan drew himself up and reached forward to
close the box. Its lid fell shut with a small click.

"So this ring was made by alben."

"It was made by Farnathin. If he is yet in flesh, he
may well be alben."

Such statements were uncomfortably in conflict
with the concept that the alben were not ælven. An ar-
tisan who once had been ælven had become a member
of a separate race because of a war? Turisan wondered, not for the first time, what the spirits must
think of this attitude. Were there ældar who watched
over the alben, as there were for every other creature?
Were they different from the ældar of the ælven?

Jharan looked at Turisan, a shadow of concern in
his face. "Only one of them bore this mark?"

Turisan nodded. "It may have been their leader."

Jharan glanced down at the box before him. "Perhaps the alben are securing the loyalty of kobalen
leaders with gifts."

Rephanin shook his head. "I think there is more to it than that. Remember, 'preserve.'"

Turisan regarded him, then spoke quietly: "What if we brought you a kobalen to question? You could find the reason in its mind."

Gray eyes met his, narrowing. "And if the kobalen you select from the thousands that roam the western wastes happens to have no knowledge of such a ring? A futile effort."

Rephanin leaned against the high back of his chair, averting his gaze. Turisan was surprised, for it almost seemed that his suggestion had discomfited the magelord.

Jharan reached a hand toward the box, tapping it with a fingertip. "Is there any magecraft in the ring?"

"No. I would have sensed it. The workmanship is fine, but there is naught of magecraft."

Turisan felt a sudden weariness. He wished to leave, to get out of Rephanin's disturbing presence and out of his soiled riding leathers, to wash himself clean. He turned to his father.

"If you have no further need of me . . ."

"Yes, go. Thank you, Turisan. You and I will discuss this further when you are refreshed."

Turisan bowed to them both before retiring from the audience chamber. He had more to say to his father, much more, and a letter for him from Felisan, but they could wait until the two of them were alone.

As he made his way toward his chambers, he wondered how much to tell his father of Eliani. Thinking of her woke the yearning in his heart, and he touched the scroll still reposing in his leathers. He longed to speak to her, to cross the distance between them with a single thought. Though he was glad to be home, a part of him—a corner of his heart—remained in Alpinon.

✠

Eliani roamed the woodlands near Highstone under a starry sky, unable to rest body or mind. The air was chill, and she wore her cloak over her tunic and legs. Though this and the walking kept her flesh warm, she felt cold in her heart.

She had argued with herself for days, thinking over her past, pondering her future, and remembering again and again her last conversation with Turisan. She could no longer think, and she had reached no decision at all. She was numb.

Her aimless steps brought her to the bridge across the Asurindel. She walked out onto it, gazing at the tumbling river below. The distant thunder of the Shades reached up into her flesh through her feet, carried by the wooden bridge from the rock on which it rested. Darkwood, this bridge. Imported at great trouble from Fireshore. She crossed it to the north shore, following the path to the Shades.

She had kept away from them, hoping to forget her last visit there, but instead the memory haunted her. Perhaps looking at the falls, recalling that they were merely water and stone, would ease her discomfort.

She paused on the pebbled footpath, touching fingertips to the stone wall to steady herself, closing her eyes briefly. Even here she could smell the mist of the falls, feel its chill beginning to envelop her. Though she had loved the Shades since childhood, the sensations now evoked dread.

She feared Turisan, feared his gentleness, the dark eyes that called to her and made her ache to be held, the devotion he had offered. Eternal, eternal devotion. To be handfasted. Bound forever.

She could refuse him, refuse both handfasting and mindspeech, though it would make for awkwardness when they assumed the governance of their realms. Or she could resign that fate as well, cede it to Gharinan, who would be a competent governor, perhaps better than she. She could return to the Guard or retire to some distant holding, far to the north in the warm hills near the Steppe Wilds.

And be no more comfortable than she was now.

A part of her wanted to yield to Turisan, to let him overwhelm her, to drown herself in the physical pleasures she knew he could offer her. She had felt this way before. Kelevon had seemed wonderful at first, but that had changed after they had become lovers. All had changed, but not before she had made a pledge she soon came to regret.

She strode along the path to the Shades, taking care as she neared the falls and the footing became rocky and wet. Rounding the ridge that sheltered the path, she stepped onto the shore of the falls' wide pool.

Starlight painted the billowing mist in shades of silver and blue. White drifts floated among the old conces by the foot of the falls. Eliani felt the power of the crashing water ring through her flesh. She leaned her head back and closed her eyes, wishing the thunder would pound all her fears out of her.

What spirits watched her path? She had begged them for guidance in her meditations and never heard an answer. Did the æ ldar who watched over all ælven, the guardians of their race, see her plight? Was her distress worthy of the attention of such beings, or was it a mere trifling matter of the flesh-bound, not meriting their trouble?

She parted her lips and inhaled deeply, taking cold mist into her lungs, tasting a metallic tang of stone in the moisture. Dizzied, she opened her eyes.

A pale female figure stood beside the three conces. Eliani blinked moisture from her eyes, thinking at first that it was Heléri.

It was not, though the long hair was braided in two plaits as Heléri often wore hers. On a chill night in autumn Heléri would not have gone walking dressed only in pale gossamer, dressed only in . . .

Mist. The female's garments billowed and shimmered around her as she stood gazing at the conces.

Eliani's neck prickled. She began to breathe shallowly despite her efforts not to. Cold coursed through her limbs as instinct prompted her to run. She defied it and stood still, watching.

The female raised her head and turned to look at Eliani—or through her, rather—with eyes black and hollow. For a moment both were still, then the stranger turned away, leaving the conces and moving closer to the falls. At the edge of the pool she kept walking, crossing its agitated surface as lightly as if it were frozen over, disappearing at last into the surging whiteness where the cascade struck the pool.

Eliani stood trembling. She had never, in all her fifty years, seen a shade before.

She should tell Heléri. Her eldermother could explain what this meant. Eliani felt a sudden, urgent need to visit her at once. She turned, then a prickle of realization swept through her.

"Oh."

Glancing up at the sky, she saw the stars through wavering mist. She knew the spirits did not truly dwell among the stars, but still she thought of the sky as their home.

"I see. Thank you."

Her words were swallowed by the roar of the Shades. Turning her back on the falls and the vision they had given her, she hastened to Heléri's house.

Misani welcomed her in the hearthroom, and Heléri looked up from her place by the fire. She was weaving again, though she pushed her work aside at Eliani's entrance.

"I have missed you, child."

Eliani felt a tingle in her cheeks, knowing she had not visited in ten days or more. Usually she came more often.

"I needed to think. Forgive my absence."

"It was not a complaint. Come, sit here. You look chilled."

Eliani joined Heléri beside the fire, stretching her hands to the warmth. "I have been down to the Shades."

"Ah?"

Eliani glanced toward Misani, who was tidying the table where Heléri took her meals. Heléri followed her gaze.

"Some tea to warm you, my child?"

"Yes. Thank you."

Misani brought a cup, and Heléri poured from a ewer that sat warming on the hearth. Eliani fetched a fresh log to the fire and promised herself she would go when it was consumed, if not before. She sat in silence, watching flames lick the new wood.

A few moments later Misani took her leave. Eliani gave her a smile and a soft word of farewell. When she was gone, Eliani looked at the fire, where her log was now fully involved in flame and burning brightly, then glanced up at Heléri.

"I believe I saw a shade."

Heléri nodded as if waiting for her to continue. Eliani had not expected such a reaction.

"You do not seem surprised. Until tonight I did not believe they existed."

Heléri smiled. "Oh, they exist, though there are but

two at the falls, unless a third has formed. Tell me what you saw."

Eliani described the female figure who had seemed to gaze at her and then walked into the foot of the crashing water. Heléri listened, nodding.

"That would be Ghivahri, most likely. It sounds like her."

Eliani looked at her in surprise. "You know her name? Did you know the shades?"

"Oh, no." Heléri reached for the ewer on the hearth. "They crossed long before I came to Alpinon. I have seen two of them, though, and learned of them from my lord, Davharin."

Eliani felt a shiver run down her chest. "I had thought it was only a legend."

"Legends have origins."

Heléri poured tea for herself and filled Eliani's cup. All the scents and flavors of a summer orchard rose from the hot brew. Eliani sipped cautiously at it, then sat turning the cup in her hands.

"I thought perhaps my seeing her was the spirits' answer to my request for guidance. It seemed they were urging me to consult you."

Heléri set the ewer down by the fire. "Perhaps they were. If I can help you, I will gladly do so."

Eliani stared at the rosy tea in her cup. She did not know how to begin. At last she swallowed and drew a breath.

"Turisan wishes to be handfasted with me."

Immediately unable to sit still, she set her cup down and began to pace the room. Heléri watched her in silence, waiting patiently as she tried to shape her jumbled thoughts into coherence.

"I know I am not—that before, I was—" Eliani stopped, angry with herself, and faced Heléri. "Would it be a mistake?"

Heléri leaned toward her. "I cannot tell you that. What is your wish?"

"I—I do not know. I just thought perhaps, if we cannot escape each other, we may as well make it public."

Heléri laughed softly. "I have never before heard that given as a reason for handfasting." She leaned back in her chair, sipping her tea. "Do you dislike Turisan?"

"No." Eliani shook her head as she continued to pace. "No, of course not. He is—well, he is beautiful, he is everything desirable. Of course I would like to bed him, but that is not what I meant."

"It is not what I meant, either, Eliani."

Eliani stopped still, feeling helpless. "Tell me what I should do."

Heléri smiled softly. "Only your heart can tell you that."

"I think I cannot hear my heart any longer." Eliani came back to the hearth, sinking again into her chair. "I think I cannot trust it."

"One consideration is this. As Turisan is not of your clan, there is a better chance your pairing will bring forth a child, and though childbearing is a blessing, it is also a risk of your life."

Eliani sighed. "That did not happen with Kelevon, and he was a Steppegard."

"You were quite young then, and you did not share mindspeech with Kelevon. From what I have witnessed, that, too, increases the likelihood of conception."

Surprised, Eliani looked up at her. "I had not heard that."

A smile softened Heléri's face. "Mindspeech is rare enough that we know little about it. I can only tell you my own experience. I have known two other couples who shared the gift, both of whom were blessed with multiple children, as were Davharin and I."

Eliani's eyes widened. "Do you mean that you and Davharin shared mindspeech?"

"Yes."

"I never knew!"

"He returned to spirit centuries before you were born, child. Also, our gift is limited—much weaker than yours, I believe—so it never made its way into legend that I know of. It was quite helpful, though, in governing the realm."

Eliani gazed at her eldermother, marveling at this news, oddly comforted that Heléri had experienced mindspeech and so must understand her feelings. How intolerably intimate it was, yet Heléri had endured it and shared a long life with Davharin, bearing three children.

"Do you miss him?"

Heléri set aside her cup, leaning back as she gazed at the fire. "I miss his body occasionally. That is so unimportant, though, when compared with the soul. We speak together every day, so in that sense I do not miss him."

Eliani caught her breath. Heléri heard, and glanced at her, still smiling.

"That is part of the gift, Eliani. Many have doubts about the soul's continuance in spirit. I have none, for I know it to be true."

A hundred questions leapt to mind. Eliani blundered out the first.

"Why did you not go with him? I thought mindspeakers always crossed together, or nearly so."

Heléri's eyes closed briefly as a look almost of pain flitted across her face. "There are things I yet wish to accomplish here."

Eliani swallowed, chagrined. "Forgive me, Elder-mother."

Heléri shook her head and with a small laugh looked up at Eliani again. "I think the reason mind-speakers cross together is that those who first reach spirit urge their partners to follow. Apparently there is much less . . . heaviness . . . felt by those in spirit. Davharin begged me to join him at first, though he no longer does so. He respects my wishes."

Eliani gazed in awe at her. "You can speak to the spirit realm."

"No, I can speak to Davharin, who dwells in spirit. That is quite different."

"But he can answer your questions, can he not?"

"When he chooses."

Eliani felt excitement stirring in her heart. "He could tell you what it is like to be in spirit! Can he—can he tell you of the future?"

Heléri's smile widened. She reached for the ewer to pour herself more tea.

"Davharin warned me you would ask that. The future is not fixed, so he cannot predict it."

"But—can he tell what the consequences of a certain act would be?"

Heléri sipped her tea, then spoke gently. "Little better than you or I."

Eliani slumped back in her chair, disappointed. "Then it is a myth that we each have spirits watching over us."

"No. That is true."

"What help can they give us if they know no more than we?"

"I did not say that was the case." Heléri set her cup on her worktable, then leaned a little closer to Eliani. "Each soul makes a plan for its life before entering flesh. Those in spirit know of these plans and are their guardians, for when we come into flesh, we forget them. I do not perfectly understand all the ways in which spirit helps us, but I can tell you this much: when all seems dark and fearsome, they are beside us, lending us their strength."

Eliani looked into the fire, wishing for the comfort these words should have given her. Did her mother watch over her? She often had wondered but never sensed anything. She shook her head, half whispering.

"Why can we not tell?"

"We do not listen very well, and we have many distractions. Spirits do not often speak in words—those are a fleshly tool and require considerable effort for them to shape. Have you never had a sense of danger when contemplating some action of which you were uncertain?"

Eliani gazed back at her. "Yes."

"Often such feelings are from our friends in spirit. It is the easiest way they have to communicate to us."

"So my fears are not my own? They come from spirit?"

Heléri shook her head. "It is not so simple. Your fears are your own. It is when there is an extra sense of dread—a certainty—oh, I am not explaining it well."

Heléri rose and carried the ewer to the shelf by her larger table, where stood a basin. Eliani watched her, thinking she should be silent now. She should go. She had troubled her eldermother with enough questions.

After a moment Heléri returned to the hearth. She poked Eliani's log, which fell into two pieces. Sparks spat upward, then settled. Heléri leaned toward Eliani.

"We cannot easily discern when spirit is speaking to us. It feels much the same as our own thoughts. I can only urge you to listen carefully to your heart's guidance, for if you can hear the advice of your friends in spirit, you will hear it there."

Eliani rested her chin on her hands, staring glumly at the coals that were all that remained of her log. "I have never been a good listener. You are far better than I."

Heléri laughed softly. "I have had centuries of practice."

Eliani straightened in her chair, stretching tight muscles in her shoulders. "Well, thank you for listening to me tonight. Now I will leave you to your rest."

"Eliani."

She looked up. Heléri was watching her, the dark blue of her eyes close to black in the firelight.

"Davharin wishes me to tell you that you were correct. The shade's appearance was intended to bring you to me."

Eliani drew a breath. "The shades—are they spirits?"

"No. They are only shades. Echoes. There is a vast difference. Someday I will tell you about them, but now I have one question for you."

Heléri held out a hand. Eliani slowly placed her own in it, feeling the warm intensity of Heléri's khi.

"Do you want, with all your soul, to be handfasted with Turisan? For if you are considering it only because you think it right and not because you desire it, you are courting grief."

Swallowing, Eliani looked at the embers. "Turisan wants it in that way. I am afraid my feelings will be overwhelmed by his desire. He is—oh, he is like a flame! One of Fireshore's volcanoes! I am afraid he will consume me and there will be nothing left!"

"Ah."

"I am afraid I will lose myself like—like—"

Eliani's throat closed, and she caught back a sob. Heléri sighed and laid a hand on her shoulder.

"My poor child. Kelevon was very wrong for you. I was glad to see him go."

Eliani looked up, marveling at hearing even such mild censure from Heléri, who seemed never to speak ill of anyone. Her eldermother continued.

"I have always felt that it was he who failed you, Eliani. Do not fault yourself. It is time to let him go."

Eliani swallowed, trying to regain her composure. She sat up, straightening her shoulders.

"I let him go years ago."

"Not entirely. He haunts you like a shade; his shadow is in your eyes. You use your past pain as a shield, child, but you cannot shield yourself forever. You have a long life before you. Do not live it in fear. That is a lonesome road, and it is needless."

Eliani stared at Heléri, feeling utterly discomfited. She could form no answer, could not even rouse herself to anger, for Heléri's love was writ plainly in her gentle gaze and in the warmth of her khi.

"Enough." Heléri leaned forward to touch Eliani's face. "You are exhausted. Go and rest. You have time yet to consider all this. No need for haste."

Eliani nodded and slowly stood. She bent to kiss her eldermother's cheek, then fetched her cloak. Daylight was glowing softly through the windows. Bidding Heléri farewell, she walked out to face the dawn.

She felt close to tears, broken. She had thought herself recovered from her wretched bond with Kelevon, but the panic rising in her throat belied it. She did not see how she could ever be fit for a bond that would last a lifetime—and beyond.

Handfasting was the most solemn vow an ælven could make. For those who broke it, the customary atonement was to yield up their flesh and return to spirit, there to hope for better wisdom.

If she undertook this bond and failed again, she would make needful her own death. Would she cause Turisan's death as well? She tried to listen to her heart, to seek the whisper of some spirit friend, but all she sensed was her own dread.

✣ Hunt's Eve ✣

Shalár's pack reached Hunt's Eve at the end of the fifth night. A wide, dark grove deep within a forest of tall evergreens, Hunt's Eve lay at the feet of the Ebon Mountains, just south of the gap between the foothills and Blackheart. Beyond it the ground sloped gently down to the southern expanse of the high plains, the hunting grounds.

When Shalár had led her first small, desperate pack on their first hunt for kobalen centuries before, she had stopped here to shelter for a day and the next night had made her first catch. Ever since, she had made it her custom to rest here before embarking on a grand hunt.

A stream ran through the grove, and the dense woods, along with a shallow overhang of rock to the east, provided safe shelter from the sun's merciless rays. A short distance downstream was a copse of bitterthorn that Shalár and her folk had encouraged to spread into a large, nearly complete circle. It made an ideal holding place for the hunters' catch, for no creature could force its way through the vicious, stinging bitterthorn, not even the cunning kobalen.

Shalár halted her catamount beside the stream and dismounted, kneeling to drink the crisp cold water. Though the air held a chill of the coming winter, they would light no fires that might be seen or smelled by kobalen. Hunt's Eve was always dark save for the final night of the hunt.

The pack rested through the day. Just after dark, the hunt commenced. Shalár rode the catamount, its great paws padding softly on the forest earth, the fury in its mind contained by her will. Her hunters gathered behind her, silent, eyes sparking with eagerness. Through a screen of trees she could see the open plain, long grasses trembling in a light breeze, blue-white under starlight.

No kobalen were in sight. She raised her head, scenting the wind, seeking a whisper of heavy khi. She extended her awareness through the catamount's flesh to the ground and quested there for the weight of kobalen feet. None were close, but she thought she sensed that some were within a night's travel. She reached out farther, knowing that the cost to her strength would soon be relieved by fresh blood.

There. To the west, a small band moving slowly toward the ocean.

Shalár raised a hand. A moment's tense stillness, then she waved the pack forward and made the catamount leap out onto the plain. Like shadows, the hunters emerged behind her, flowing out of the trees and across the plain with no more sound than that of a breeze sighing in the grass.

Long legs ran swiftly over sand and rock, over grass and earth. The pack hungered; they would not rest now until they had caught their prey.

At length the taste of kobalen khi was palpable on the air. Shalár sensed a rising excitement in the hunters at her back. She led them on silently, swiftly.

A stream meandered across the plain, and a cluster of dark shapes farther down its path drew Shalár's attention. The kobalen, camped for the night. She sent a tiny tendril of khi toward them, delicately tasting their presence.

Two kobalen stood awake, watching. The others slept. It was the need for sleep that classed the kobalen among lesser creatures. Shalár's folk required rest but did not sink into unconsciousness each day.

She summoned her captains and gave them swift instructions. The hunters fanned out into a long line on either side of the stream, a thin shadow crossing the plain toward their prey. With a tendril of khi, Shalár took hold over the two kobalen guards, making them lie down and close their eyes. Her hunger sharpened with the effort.

When the center of the line came within a few rods of the camp, Shalár halted it, then signaled Yaras and Welir to lead the ends of the line forward to make a circle around the camp. Stealthily the hunters drew in around the place where their prey lay sprawled beside dying fires, closing ranks until they were shoulder to shoulder.

Eyes bright with hunger glinted starlight. Hands moved to the hilts of weapons, ready if needed, but it was not blades or arrows that would make this capture. Khi rose from the hunting pack like heat rippling up from a fire. Khi would be their chief weapon here.

In the kobalen camp, a youngling fussed. Its mother woke, reached out to bat at it with a heavy palm.

Shalár raised a hand. All the hunters paused, still and silent, waiting.

The kobalen female rolled over, grunting softly. She was still for a moment, then lifted her head, sniffing at the night air.

Stealth was at an end. Shalár clenched her fist, the signal for the capture.

The night air was suddenly awash with khi. The kobalen woke and voiced startled dismay as the hunters bore down upon them, overpowering their wills, seizing control of their feeble spirits. One or two had the strength to resist at first, to rise up and scramble through the camp, but there was nowhere to run, and the pack's khi quickly overwhelmed them.

They sank down again, defeated. Small whimpers were the only sounds left among the kobalen.

Shalár was near the limit of her strength. Hunger gnawed at her, threatening reason, threatening all. She must feed, but there was one thing she must do first or it would not be done at all.

She forced the catamount down and kept it there, dismounting carefully, dizzy with hunger. Walking among the kobalen who cowered at her feet, she sought among their minds for flickers of greater spirit, the possibility of understanding the worth of what she could offer them.

She found one: a large female cowering with its arms over its head. Shalár nudged it with a toe, and the creature leapt up, wielding an ebonglass knife in a desperate attack.

A roar of anger rose from the hunters even as Shalár seized the kobalen with her mind and its wrist with her hand. With her free hand she summoned Ciris, who hastened to her side and took control of the kobalen female.

"That one is to be reserved. None shall touch it."

Ciris raised an eyebrow. "As you will, Bright Lady."

She watched him lead the creature out of the circle. She was nearly spent. She looked over the kobalen on the ground before her. Difficult to see beyond the hunger, to see them as anything but food.

There! She turned to her right and stepped over a cowering creature, then had to steady herself. A few paces brought her to a male kobalen lying on its side, facing away from her. Not the largest in the band, not a dominant male, but his khi held the spark she sought.

She signaled to Ciris, who had followed close behind her. "This one as well. Set it aside with the other."

"Yes, Bright Lady."

His voice was tight with hunger. All the hunters were near desperation from the khi they were spending.

She ought to search the rest of the kobalen more closely, but she had no more strength left. Two would be enough to start. There would be more, perhaps, in the next catch.

She chose the largest in reach, a stocky male. Taking hold of its mind, she felt the khi of the hunters who had subdued it drop away. Their hunger pulsed in the air. What she wanted, what they all wanted, was to rip into their prey in a frenzy of gluttony.

That would be wasteful, though, and she would not permit waste. Others in Nightsand relied on them to share the bounty of the hunt.

Shalár made the creature stand up before her. Its fear shivered through the air around it, but it stood still in the grip of her control. Her nose wrinkled at the creature's rank smell. No matter.

She reached to her belt for her silver-hilted knife, mate to the one in the pens back in Nightsand. The blade glinted in the starlight as she set the point to the kobalen's throat, just beneath one ear. A careful slice, no more than a thumb's width, set the blood flowing.

Shalár had no cup. The hunt was not so dainty. She set her mouth to the kobalen's neck even as she felt her hunters inhale the ripe scent of its blood.

Khi, potent and weighty, filled her mouth along with the salt tang of blood. She swallowed, feeling strength flow down her throat into her belly. She drank deeply as her hunters waited, their anguish humming in her senses.

When she had taken enough to sustain her, she dug her thumb into the creature's neck near the cut to stem the flow and summoned Ciris to feed. His eyes burned with hunger as their gazes met, and Shalár felt a stirring of desire.

Later, perhaps. She took control of the two kobalen she had placed in his keeping and gave the feeder over to him. His hand brushed hers as he took over pressing against the vein in its throat, setting her flesh tingling.

Shalár stepped back, as dizzy with strength as she had been with weakness a few moments earlier. Colors around her seemed brighter even in their night-faded state. Every small sound was sharper, the smells of the plain and the hunters more intense though the stink of kobalen nearly overwhelmed them.

She renewed her grip on the catamount's mind, then moved her two kobalen prisoners to stand between its massive forelimbs. If for any reason she became distracted enough to lose control of them, the hungry cat would have its meal to hand, and the kobalen would not escape to warn others.

She selected another kobalen, made it stand, then beckoned to Welir. The captain strode forward eagerly, her face pinched with need. Shalár again took the first mouthful, out of ceremony now, though she still hungered and would take more when the others were fed. Handing the feeder over to Welir, she stepped back.

She gave to her captains. The captains gave to their hunters. The hunters would bring their catch back to Nightsand and receive due reward. It was what kept them all from becoming savages, rampaging across the wastes and feeding at will.

Shalár closed her eyes, remembering a time when Clan Darkshore had lived so. Those who had survived Westgard, who had fled across the mountains into the harsh Westerlands, had struggled merely to survive. Never again, she had vowed, so long as she walked in flesh.

The night was old by the time all were sated. Shalár fed again after the others all had taken their first share. When the feeders had been drained of khi and blood, the hunters began digging pits in which to dispose of the refuse. They would have burned it if there had been fuel in reach, but only grasses and scrub grew on the plain, and to set fire to the bodies without kindling would require more khi than she wished to spend.

Shalár glanced eastward. Far in the distance the Ebon Mountains loomed, dividing all the western lands from those of the ælven. Night was beginning to draw away from their peaks. Soon the sky would pale, and then the sun would throw its burning light across the plain. She must find shelter for her pack before then.

She turned to watch the diggers, gauging how long it would take for their work to be finished. The musty scent of turned earth muted the rank smell of kobalen and the even heavier odor of death.

At such a moment, Dareth would have ruminated over the possibility of kobalen possessing enduring souls and whether those they had just killed would confront them in the spirit realm. She was glad he was not here.

⚜

Several nights later, Shalár lay on her belly, gazing over a cliff's edge at the largest kobalen encampment she had yet seen. Full five hundred of the creatures, she judged. The heat from their fires reached her even here.

Her pack was much smaller now, for she had sent each night's catch back to Hunt's Eve in the care of a handful of hunters. Yaras had gone the first night and had been given command of Hunt's Eve until she returned.

The kobalen below were unaware of the hunters as yet. Their campsite was in a natural recess that curved into the cliff, a place that offered good shelter from the chill winds blowing down off the high plain.

Shalár quested gently toward the kobalen with khi, careful not to alert them of her presence. She sought more of the promising individuals she was collecting for her special purpose and sensed several in the large band below.

She glanced back at the pack, a short distance behind. Not quite forty remaining, too few to control the five hundred kobalen below, at least with certainty. She disliked letting any part of a band escape, for they would warn other kobalen of the hunt. Even though this hunt was nearly over, she preferred to keep absolute control of her prey. Kobalen had been known to retaliate against hunters who were careless enough to be caught.

She ran a thumb along her chin, her skin rough against the edge of her lip. If they made a good catch, this would be the last night of the hunt. She was better fed than she had been in decades, but she was also weary, ready to return to the Cliff Hollows and the softness of her bed.

Shalár caught Ciris's eye and signaled that they should withdraw. Silently they slid back from the cliff's edge until they could stand without being seen from below. The catamount lay listless. It raised its head at her approach, golden eyes—dull now, though reflecting a distant rage—silently watching.

Another reason for bringing the hunt to a close. The cat was well fed, but its spirit was broken. She would set it free in the mountains after returning to Nightsand, there to recover its vigor and doubtless to cherish a hatred of creatures that walked on two legs.

She turned to Ciris. "We take this band."

His dark eyes widened. "All?"

"All. A grand catch to end the grand hunt."

His chin rose, his eyes silently questioning. She felt the tingle of his desire in the air between them. She gave him no answer beyond a small smile and turned her head to look toward the kobalen camp.

"We must make the best use of each hunter. Have you any suggestions, Watcher?"

He looked toward the cliff's edge. "A distraction. Draw their attention while we move to cut off their escape."

"We have few enough in the pack as it is. I cannot spare any hunters to create a distraction."

Ciris met her gaze, a slow smile spreading on his lips and sparking a quiver of desire in her. "You need not."

⁜

Shalár descended the cliff carefully, slowly, making no sound. The rock was gritty to the touch, the ashen spew of some ancient volcano. Below her, twenty hunters waited out of sight.

Ciris was taking the rest of the pack down the cliff on the far side of the camp. At her signal the groups would come together to trap the kobalen.

She reached the base of the cliff and was welcomed silently by her hunters. She sent a thought probing toward the catamount, which she had left behind. It waited, wakeful and watchful.

She moved along the foot of the cliff toward the kobalen camp. Reaching a thrust of rock beyond which the dying firelight glimmered, she paused to let the hunters close up behind her and quested outward with a tiny finger of khi, searching for Ciris. He was there, his khi confident and smoldering. He was ready.

Shalár inhaled deeply, closing her eyes. She no longer addressed requests for aid to spirit or ældar. She was alone in the world. It was to herself that she looked for strength.

Shalár raised a hand to command readiness in the pack, then sent a stream of khi up to the clifftop. The catamount screamed.

Startled voices rose in the kobalen camp. She brought the catamount to the cliff's edge, made it show itself and give voice again. The cat's displeasure rang in its cry. Shalár signaled to her pack to move.

She stepped into the firelight, hastening across the open face of the recess with her hunters behind her. A second line came swiftly toward them, Ciris at its head. The kobalen, unaware, cowered and pointed toward the angry catamount.

One of the creatures flung a dart at the cat. It fell short, striking against the cliff below the cat's massive paws. Shalár sent the catamount back from the ledge. She did not want it wounded, and it had served its purpose. With a gesture she brought her hunters forward, closing off the front of the recess with a line of bodies.

Shalár raised one hand just above her head. The other held a throwing net ready to be flung. She stepped forward, and the pack followed.

A tall kobalen turned suddenly, its eyes wide. It cried out, and Shalár closed her fist.

Khi, piercing and bright, flew toward the kobalen camp. Many cowered, but their numbers were too great to subdue all at once. Shalár flung all her will toward them with a cry strangely like the catamount's and leapt forward.

Kobalen still stood, too many to count. The hunters were too close for the kobalen to use their darts, but they had wicked knives of ebonglass and a few spears, mostly in the hands of the ones who had been on watch.

To Shalár these defiant ones were bright spots of fire that must be smothered at once. Her thoughts were everywhere, pressing downward on a kobalen to her left, on two farther back in the recess, on one to the right with a spear raised.

She felt and heard Ciris voice his rage. All the hunters answered, keen voices skirling upward with the smoke of fires suddenly scattered by clumsy feet.

Shalár saw a spear thrust forward very close, nearly striking a hunter beside her. She cast her net to entangle its wielder and followed with a fierce thrust of khi. She felt more than saw the creature collapse.

Nets hissed through the air, and the kobalen bellowed in fear. A sharp cry rose to her right even as pain seared through the pack's khi. One of the hunters was wounded.

Shalár let his pain feed her rage and hurled redoubled khi at the kobalen. An agonized cry and the heavy smell of kobalen blood informed her that the creature that had struck a hunter had been slain. The pack would not tolerate the survival of a kobalen that had struck one of their own. She threw her last net, then drew her sword.

"Divide!"

In response, half the hunters stood back to spend all their strength in subduing the catch with khi. The rest took on those of the kobalen who still fought.

A black ax blade glinted toward Shalár in an arc,

swung by a kobalen female with desperation in its
eyes. Shalár turned the weapon aside with the flat of
her blade, then disarmed its wielder with a kick to the
wrist and sent it to the ground with a backhanded
blow to the head.

She was breathing hard now, and her strength was
dwindling. She must end it soon. The taste of blood on
the air lit her hunger.

The spear was back, catching at her leathers, causing the hunter beside her to cry out in alarm. Shalár
caught the shaft in her free hand and attacked the
kobalen who held it with both khi and her sword hilt,
a blow to the head.

The creature's legs buckled, and its grip on the spear
went slack. Shalár pulled the weapon free and sent it
spinning into the night behind her.

The catamount howled. She had let her grip on it
loosen, using the khi elsewhere. To get it back—

No. Too costly.

The cat screamed again, confused and elated at its
sudden release. Shalár made a frustrated growl in her
throat and aimed the flat of her sword at two more
kobalen before her. One dodged unexpectedly and
swept at her with a knife.

Reacting without thought, Shalár blocked with her
arm and felt the shock of a blow against her forearm.
Glancing down, she saw the black blade biting into
her leather brace.

She swung her sword down, across, up, cutting deep
into her attacker's arm as she lifted it away from her.
The knife, dislodged, fell to the ground. A moment
later the pain came.

Blood, sharp on the air. Hot blood, and she hungered so!

The catamount shrieked along with the pack. The
cat sounded near, too near. Shalár looked up and saw

it descending a tumble of rock at one side of the recess.

Kobalen coming at her. She freed her sword and this time used the blade to block. A glass knife shattered against it. Splinters flew. Shalár flinched, guarding her eyes.

The catamount leapt from a boulder onto the nearest kobalen, a smaller male. Claws sank into the creature's chest and shoulder. The kobalen's scream was cut off as the cat locked massive jaws on its throat, then tore it open with one powerful shake. Blood flew in an arc, pumping from the mangled flesh.

The kobalen cowering at the back of the recess screamed in terror. Those still fighting wavered.

Shalár summoned khi, drawing ruthlessly on the pack's remaining strength. Even as her hunters gasped, she flung their vitality against the kobalen.

The kobalen dropped their weapons. They fell to their knees.

Shalár released her pack and took hold of all the catch with the last of her strength. Those hunters who could do so lent their khi to the effort. She tightened her grip.

She made the resisters lie down on their faces. Some among them were clever ones—the ones she wanted to save—but she had no strength to search for them.

She strode forward, summoning the pack to follow with a gesture of her wounded arm. Her flesh ached in protest. She was too weary to wipe her sword and sheathe it, so she dropped it and drew her dagger.

Hunger tore at her gut, but she did not forget those behind her. Standing over the kobalen that had defied the pack, she glanced back at her hunters.

"Ten of you. Take one apiece."

Unable to wait any longer, she crouched and reached for the nearest kobalen. Her left hand was sticky with blood—her own—and her arm ached as she grasped the creature's scalp by the hair to pull up its head. The creature was unconscious; its good fortune. Shalár set her knife to its throat, then drank deeply, salt stinging her lips and the rich blood coating her parched tongue.

The catch shrieked in horror. She made certain the pack had them controlled, then ignored them.

She drank greedily, devouring the khi of her feeder even faster than she drained its veins. Bright pricks of relief in her awareness told her of the others who had started to feed. She breathed hard through her nose between swallows.

Her senses began to sharpen again. She became dimly aware of the frightened breathing of the catch and of the catamount calmly ripping bites of flesh from its kill. She snaked a tendril of khi around the cat's mind once more but let it feed.

When the edge was off her hunger enough that she could think again, she paused and summoned Ciris. He strode forward eagerly and knelt beside her, a strip of cloth in his hands.

She offered him the feeder. "Finish it."

Instead he cut the laces of her leather brace and wrapped the cloth around the long gash in her arm, tying it tightly to stem the bleeding. He looked up at her, his face wrought with hunger and concern. She had blood on her mouth—she could feel it—and suddenly she wanted to share it with Ciris.

With her free hand she caught the back of his neck and pulled him to her. She kissed him deeply and felt the fire of his response wash through her.

The pack's khi tensed with arousal. Those who were feeding paused.

Shalár pushed Ciris away.

"Feed."

His eyes were nearly mad with conflicting needs. His chest rose and fell with swift breaths, then with a snarl he turned to the feeder and took hold of it.

Shalár got to her feet, unsteady with the intensity of lust and hunger reeling through the pack's khi. She stepped away from Ciris.

There were wounded. At least two, perhaps more. She turned her attention to the pain she had shut from her senses and found it easily. One was nearby, breathing shallowly and silently enduring the bright anguish of a glass splinter lodged in a shoulder.

The other was feeble, dangerously weakened. Shalár sought that one first, stepping over fallen kobalen and a scattered tangle of nets and weapons as she crossed the fighting ground. She found him sprawled on his back, eyes open and staring at the stars, blood from a wound on his thigh soaking into the ground in a wide pool beneath him.

Shalár dropped to her knees beside him, laying a hand to his cheek. His eyes flickered but did not fix on her.

"Gæleph! Stay with us!"

She looked up at the pack, a staggered remnant of its former line. "Who has bandages? Bring them!"

Two came forward, Thanir and Ranad. Ranad stumbled, and Shalár recalled that this was his first hunt.

"Bind that wound."

Thanir took two long cloths from her pouch and went quickly to work. Shalár stood up and glanced over the kobalen lying nearby. She chose a large one and nudged it with a toe. It flinched.

She made it stand up and walk over to where Gæleph lay, then sit down behind Gæleph's head. She directed Ranad to lift the wounded hunter's shoulders and make the kobalen slide its folded legs beneath him. She took the kobalen's wrist and sliced it open, then pressed it to Gæleph's mouth.

It took a moment, then hunger seemed to wake Gæleph, and his eyes sharpened into a desperate frown. He sucked greedily at the blood, lunging, almost chewing at the creature's wrist. Ranad held the food to his mouth, a swallow betraying his own hunger.

Shalár brought another feeder over and gave it to Thanir, who had finished bandaging Gæleph's leg. She drank briefly, then passed the feeder to Ranad and took his place. Gæleph's strength was starting to return. Shalár would not lose him; she could sense his keenness to live. She breathed relief.

Turning her attention to the other wounded hunter, she now saw that it was Namir, who had fought beside her through most of the struggle. One of the first to feed had given his feeder to Namir and now was removing the glass splinter. Blood slid down Namir's shoulder as he pulled the wicked shard from her flesh.

Shalár winced and glanced at her own wound, saw the bandage dark with slowly oozing blood. Ebonglass knives were evilly sharp and made cuts that bled freely.

She went back to find her sword near where Ciris still fed. Kobalen blood had dried on the blade, a dark, sticky stain, gritty with dirt. She would have to clean it before sheathing it again.

She set it against the cliff wall. The catamount lay nearby, lazily picking over its mangled kobalen. It raised its great pale head to watch her pass. The fur around its jaws was dark with blood.

This had been a hard night's hunt, the hardest she could remember. She glanced skyward to judge how much darkness was left and was surprised to see that Saharis was still high and the fattening moon was just setting. Early yet, only half the night gone. She felt as if they had fought all through the darkness.

She must feed again. She had lost blood and spent khi lavishly. She was weak still, and needed strength to keep the catch under control.

Turning back to the ruined campsite, she reached for the kobalen lying nearest to her. It was dead, its blood wasted, drunk by the ungrateful earth.

A flash of anger went through her. Her hunger flared brightly again, and she strode to the next creature, a cowering female cradling a broken arm to its chest. Shalár seized its mind and knelt to it, opening a vein beneath its ear with a flick of her dagger. She fed, ignoring all but her hunger and her grip on the catch.

When her hunger abated, she raised her head and found Ciris beside her, patiently watching with dark eyes that were now warm where before they had been sharp with need. A breeze stirred his hair, silver against the star-scattered night.

Shalár thought of the danger of self-indulgence in this place, with a mere handful of hunters to control a large catch and the possibility of another kobalen band coming along at any moment. Thought of the journey they must make before dawn, taking their catch up the cliff and driving them to the nearest shelter, a wood that was some five leagues distant.

She smiled. Feeding was not the only act to which fear added spice.

She bent to her feeder once more, took a mouthful of blood, then shared it with Ciris in a kiss. His arms went around her in a strong embrace.

They were still for a moment, sharing relief that the hunt had succeeded, sharing a silent, growing elation.

At her movement he released her, and they both began pulling off their leathers.

She called one of the hunters over to take what was left of her feeder. No sense wasting it. She abandoned the creature and reached for Ciris.

The pack's khi rose in an eager, anxious hum. Those who were fed now turned to one another, seeking partners, frantic to couple. Those who were hungry left the line to take the feeders the others had deserted. Shalár gave her wordless approval of all in a rush of hot khi that swept through the pack even as Ciris thrust into her.

She took him deep, shivering with pleasure. A moaning rose from the pack, and ripples of delight washed through their khi. Shalár reserved a small, hard knot of her will to keep hold of the catch and the catamount and abandoned the rest to the rapture of coupling.

She felt echoes of Ciris's pleasure and changed how she moved to enhance them. Together they rolled over so that she could straddle him. She sank onto him, feeling him push against the knot of flesh within her, her second privacy that must open to him if she were to conceive. With each stroke she willed it to happen, willed her flesh to receive him, take him deeper inside her than any male had ever been.

She willed it, she wished it. She should have it, she who could control flesh more than any other, who could command hundreds if she chose! She should be able to command her own flesh to open to a mate and conceive. She beat herself against Ciris, howling her anguished desire to the night sky.

Others gave voice, and the catamount loosed a throaty yowl. Shalár felt the shimmer of someone's release wash through the pack, triggering others. She held off, still striving to open herself to Ciris.

He gave a grunt and pushed himself upright, thrusting hard into her, leaning on one hand while the other gripped her hips. She kissed him greedily, a storm of ecstasy singing through her khi as more of the others peaked.

Ciris gasped, and she felt the heat of his seed flood her, battering uselessly against her closed inner self. With a cry of frustration she let her flesh follow his into climax. A few more thrusts, then he lay back, spent.

Shalár drew a deep breath and let it out slowly as she lowered herself onto his chest. They lay still, their bodies throbbing.

She gave her attention to her surroundings long enough to reassert that the catch was still hers. Movement made her lift her head and glance back toward the mass of kobalen huddled against the cliff. Yes, many of them were coupling, their frenzy tinged with fear, their mating clumsy compared with the pack's.

She laughed softly. She had not seen that before; even the catch succumbing to her need. There would be a crop of young in the pens three seasons hence, she thought with a pang of senseless envy.

She turned back to Ciris and found him gazing up at her, his eyes tinged with regret. She kissed him to show she did not fault him, then rested her head on his shoulder.

Not his fault, nor hers. Perhaps some devious ældar had made their kind this way, able to breed only rarely. A cruel enough fate for the ælven but disastrous for Darkshore, who bore the added burden of their hunger.

Shalár wanted to stay there in Ciris's embrace, with the night breeze cooling her back. Instead she pulled away from him and stood up, looking toward the cliff. He reached out and caught her left wrist, gently turning her arm. A wide smear of blood had soaked through the bandage.

"Can you climb?"

"Would you carry me if I could not?"

"Yes, Bright Lady."

She smiled slightly and actually felt her cheek grow warm. "Luckily for you, I can climb."

She bent to pick up a piece of clothing, determined it was Ciris's, and dropped it across his legs. By the time she had dressed in her own clothes and leathers, the rest of the pack was stirring.

Now she took the time to look over the kobalen, and picked a few that seemed to have the wit she was seeking. She separated them from the others and charged Ranad with their special keeping, then selected a couple more.

She set the hunters to the task of sorting the captured kobalen from the dead and the dying feeders. Feeders that yet breathed were given the mercy stroke and added to the piles of dead. Kobalen spears, axes, and knives were first smashed, then thrown on the pyre. Shalár kept one of the knives for herself, a memento, to go with the scar she would bear.

Two of the spear staves were kept back to make a litter for Gæleph. He was strapped to it, swathed in cloaks, and carefully taken up the cliff, with ropes tied to the litter from above to protect it from falling. Shalár watched the pyres being set, then urged her pack up the cliff with their catch, eager to find shelter before dawn.

⁂

Three nights later the small core of Shalár's pack rejoined the rest of the hunters at Hunt's Eve. From the excitement in the pack's khi, Shalár knew they sensed what had happened after the final catch. They greeted the returning hunters, even the novices, with both deference and a display of sensual interest approaching outright courtship. Shalár watched with amusement as young Ranad received a warm welcome from Vethir, a veteran of more than ten hunts.

She made the catamount lie down, dismounted, and sent it slinking away to the ledge, then joined her captains. Welir took charge of the catch and herded them toward the bitterthorn copse, save for fifty that Shalár ordered to be kept back.

Ciris stood silent, his gaze hot on Shalár. She looked away from him to Yaras, whose hunger she could sense but who showed no impatience.

"Take me to the reserved kobalen."

Yaras led her toward the rock overhang, the hunters' daylight shelter. Near the southern end, opposite Shalár's resting place, three hunters stood guard over perhaps twenty kobalen clustered within a deep curve. The creatures had been talking, but at her approach they fell silent.

"Very good. I am glad you have kept them well apart."

Yaras glanced up. "They are for your household's private use?"

She smiled as they started back to the bonfire and the waiting feast. "No, for something else."

"I did not think they were the strongest you could have chosen."

"Not the strongest, no." She slowed her stride a little. "How fares Yalir?"

"She is well, thank you, Bright Lady." Pride in his daughter softened his voice. "She continues her study of the plants and herbs on the western slopes of the Ebons."

"Good. Let her know that if she finds anything of new significance, she should bring it to Nightsand. And Firan?"

He was silent for two paces before answering. "I tried to convince her to join this hunt. She preferred to stay on the farm. Putting up the harvest for winter."

Shalár nodded, watching him. "That is important."

"I had hoped . . ."

He halted, and Shalár stopped as well, waiting. He glanced at her with a rueful shrug.

"I always hope for another hunt like the one when Firan and I conceived Yalir. It is why I keep hunting."

"That is my hope for you as well."

Shalár held out her hand to him. He brought his up to meet it, and a small shock passed between them as their khi flared together in their palms. Shalár let her stirring desire flow out to him, and Yaras looked up, surprise in his face.

"Let us make haste. The others are waiting."

A small flush lit his cheeks, and he nodded, keeping silent. Their hands dropped apart, but the khi flowed even more strongly between them. Shalár felt his response, tinged with the urgency of his hunger, send a shiver along her flesh.

He was potent. He had conceived once and wished to do so again. Shalár inhaled, savoring his scent and the spice of his desire.

They reached the circle, and Shalár looked up at the moon. A bruise was beginning to show on the lower edge of the orb. She smiled, then drew her dagger and held it aloft.

"Hunters! I give you greeting beneath the blood moon!"

A hiss went through the pack—a shiver of indrawn breath. They drew closer.

"You have hunted well and made good catches. Tonight is your reward. Feast well and take your ease. Tomorrow eve we start for Nightsand."

Shalár chose a kobalen from the fifty under Welir's

control and made it stand before her. The creature shuddered with fear.

"Those who are not first to feed may kindle fires. Ciris, see to it that one is made for Gæleph."

Ciris nodded, frowning slightly. Shalár glanced at the moon, now rapidly going dark behind the world's shadow. Gazing over the eager faces of her pack, she raised her knife and took the first blood.

She handed the feeder to Ciris, gave feeders to Welir and Yaras, and saw to it that the rest were ready for the captains to share with their companies. The smell of blood hung heavy on the air as she made her way to where Yaras stood watching his company feed.

He looked up well before she reached him, and his eyes were hungry yet. He must have started his feeders and immediately given them away. His gaze burned into her, hunger and lust raising an answer in her flesh. Overhead, the moon went blood red as it fell fully into shadow. A low moan went up from somewhere in the pack.

Shalár wanted a feeder to share with Yaras, but there were none left. The bitterthorn copse was too far away, too much trouble. She wanted now, wanted here. Her hunger flared into anger, which burned away in the sudden rise of lust as she saw her feelings reflected in Yaras's eyes.

She reached out a hand and touched Yaras's face, the smooth, clean curve of his chin, past his ear into his hair. He had caught some of it back in a half braid, but the rest fell loose over his shoulders and down his back, soft and pale in the starlight, burnished by the ruddy moon. Shalár's fingers glided through it, then fell free.

She stepped closer, laid her hand on his shoulder, and leaned forward to kiss him. His khi enveloped her, bright with hunger, heavy with desire. He responded greedily to her kiss, and a tremor passed through the pack.

Someone made a small sound of surprise. Shalár looked up and saw Ciris taking hold of a feeder that a female of his company was using. He cut a second vein in the feeder's throat and latched on to it, sharp eyes urging the female to join him. She did, and the pack's khi pulsed hotter. As if freed by this, the others began to move, finding partners, changing feeders, some sharing as Ciris had demonstrated.

Shalár and Yaras tumbled to the ground together. His hands found their way beneath her tunic and danced over her breasts. She pulled it off, the cold air and his touch combining to bring her nipples painfully erect. His kiss warmed her, and she tugged at his leather legs. He reached down a hand to deal with them and then lay against her, his flesh warm on hers, his desire hot and hard.

She lay on her back, taking him in with a moan of pleasure that echoed through the pack. She opened her eyes to watch his face as he dug at her, a frown of urgency on his brow.

He felt good within her, strong and vital. She gripped his shoulders and pushed herself against him. He was there, right there, but her flesh would not yield.

"What did it feel like?"

He raised his head, mouth open as his body continued to strive, but seemed at a loss for explanation. She reached toward his khi, suggesting a more intimate contact.

"Give me the memory."

His eyes widened with momentary panic, then he closed them, seemed to struggle for a moment, and yielded. She felt him release his guard, opening his thoughts to her, trusting her and in that act becoming completely hers.

With a shiver of delight, she reached into his khi and sought for his remembrance of conception. He brought the moment forward and offered it to her: a hunt much like this one, a coupling much like this one, with the pack's passion triggered by her lust for Dareth on that occasion.

Shalár immersed herself in the memory, seeking every nuance of his flesh's sensation. A musky scent—Firan's—and her body moving beneath his, dancing in harmony with his, then suddenly opening like a flower—

With a cry Yaras peaked, taking Shalár with him in the depth of their shared khi. He arched his back as he drove at her. She twined her arm around his as they surged together, then gradually subsided.

They lay still but for the thundering of their hearts, their short, quick breaths slowly relaxing into longer, deeper ones. Yaras raised his head.

She found her voice, though it was rough. "You have taught me much more than I knew. This was well worthwhile."

Above, through dark branches, she could see the moon. A thin crescent of white gleamed along one side.

Yaras turned his head and suddenly tensed, a sharp inhalation accompanied by hunger flaring through his khi. A feeder lay not far from them, abandoned while those who had been using it grappled together. Shalár made it crawl over to them, urging Yaras to feed first. He twitched within her as he reached out and gripped the feeder's shoulder, turning it so that he could reach the cut on its neck.

She was so enwrapped with him that she tasted the blood for a moment. Gradually, as he fed and the sharpness of his hunger eased, she released Yaras and drew back from his mind.

She sent her khi lightly through the grove, noting

that most had fed or at least begun to feed. Those standing guard over the kobalen, in the copse and back at the overhang, were the last waiting, bright flares of hunger in the night. Soon their places would be taken by those who were sated, and the feast would ease to an end.

Yaras paused, turning to look at Shalár, then reaching to fumble among their scattered clothing. He found a knife and brought it across to make a second cut on the other side of the feeder's throat where it would be convenient to Shalár.

His gaze met hers as he set the knife aside. She smiled, then tucked her head into the curve of the feeder's throat and drank. A whisper of Yaras's khi caressed her as he bent to feed again.

⁜

Shalár stood before her reserved kobalen, her captains behind her. The kobalen watched her suspiciously as they cowered against the rock, silent though she knew they had been talking amongst themselves. Planning together. That was the sort of kobalen she had chosen to single out.

Behind her the quiet sounds of the pack moving about the grove echoed among the tall evergreens. The night was old now and they were preparing to leave, to travel at least a short distance before the sun forced them back into hiding.

Shalár looked over the kobalen with narrowed eyes. She addressed them in their own crude tongue.

"Your people are strong. Good hunters. I . . ."

She paused, frowning, for the kobalen had no word for "honor."

"I cheer for your strength."

The kobalen stood huddled together, watching her in wary silence. Some of them shivered despite the fine black fur covering their bodies. Fear, not cold.

"You are the wisest of your people. That is why you are here, apart from the others."

Shalár gestured toward the bitterthorn copse. Several of the kobalen glanced that way, then cringed closer together. Shalár picked out one to address: a wiry male with a hard, heavy brow, small but tough-looking.

"You are a leader of your folk."

The male kept its head lowered but glanced up at her. It spread its hands, palms down, in the kobalen gesture for "no."

Shalár placed her fist in her palm, the kobalen "yes." The male looked startled.

"Wise is sometimes more important than strong. Because you are wise, I bargain with you. I need good hunters to fight for me. You wise ones can convince others of your kind to join together. You . . ."

Again she paused, seeking a way to express her pledges. Their language had poor means for describing the future.

"Join me, fight for me, you have good reward."

The wiry male raised its head. "You hunt us for food. Why we fight for you? You promise reward, then kill."

Shalár fixed him with a glare. "We keep our promises."

The kobalen did not answer, though she saw mistrust in its eyes. The rest were silent, watching and waiting, content to have this one speak for them for now. Shalár continued.

"We not kill those who serve us. Fight for me, and you are safe from my hunters. Forever."

That word was of her own tongue. Those who lived a scant few decades had no need of such a word.

"Forever is today, next day, next day, all days. Safe forever."

Some of the kobalen muttered together. From their khi, she sensed their confusion. They had expected to be slain by her or die attempting escape.

The wiry one frowned. "You say you not hunt me. Even if you keep promise, other tall ones hunt me."

"No. I put my mark on you, and none of my people who sees it can hunt you. My promise is their promise."

She turned suddenly to her captains. "Yes? I put my mark on this one, you not drink from him. Yes?"

She knew they understood her. The kobalen's tongue was simple enough, and they had all hunted the creatures long enough to acquire the basics of their speech. First Yaras, then the others made the kobalen gesture of assent, placing a fist in the opposite palm.

A murmur went through the kobalen at seeing their hand-speech used by her folk. Shalár looked back at the wiry male.

"The other tall ones, the ones across the mountains. They not hunt me either?"

Shalár's lip curled. "I not speak for them. They are my enemies. They are the ones we fight. You fight them with us, you safe from our nets. Forever safe."

The kobalen frowned. It was too young by many generations to remember Midrange, but the story of the great fight with tall ones across the mountains might have been passed down.

Shalár opened a small pouch at her belt and shook from it a ring of bright gold, a little smaller than her smallest finger. It was open, with a sharp point on one end and a recess on the other to receive it. As a guard against forgery, she had instructed Farnath to inscribe it with tiny intricate script. No kobalen could work metal at all, so she knew they could never reproduce such a thing.

The first of the rings had been lost when Yaras's

small band was caught by the ælven. That had been but a test, and she counted it a success despite the loss.

She showed the ring to the kobalen male. It reached up to touch the shiny object, and Shalár pulled it back.

"I hang this from your ear, here." She touched her own earlobe. "None can remove it. This marks you as safe from our hunting. Forever."

"And then you take me away, make me fight for you, never free again."

Shalár's mouth twitched, but she resisted smiling. Astute, this kobalen. It would serve her purpose well.

"I not take you away. Everyone in your band who fights for me can wear my mark and be safe. Fight one big fight and win, then be free."

Shalár watched the kobalen turn away from her—an act of daring in itself—to consult with its fellows. Kobalen needed time to grasp new ideas. She waited for it to think through the concept of temporary service for lifelong immunity. If it were not for the prolific abundance with which the kobalen bred, she would not be able to make such an offer.

The male returned, accompanied by a somewhat smaller and heavier female. The latter looked at Shalár with challenging, frightened eyes, but it was the male who addressed her. It gestured to the small earring in her hand.

"I take this thing, what if some other take it from me?"

"It only protects the one that wears it. Some other could take it from you, but not to wear. Look."

Shalár slid the ends of the ring over the end of a leather strap and pressed them together until she felt the click of the ring closing. Then she cut the ring free of the strap and handed it to the kobalen, a bit of leather still clinging to it.

"Try to open it. You cannot."

The kobalen pulled at the ring, though its coarse fingers could get no hold. The female watched with interest, took the ring away from the male with a brief exchange of snarls, tried and failed to open it, and finally bit it. Shalár had anticipated this and had Farnath strengthen the gold with other metals. It did not yield.

"Once it is closed, it stays closed. It is no use to any but the one who wears it."

The male took the ring back, bit it as well, chewing off the leather, then spat the ring into its palm. "You put this in my ear, I bleed."

"A little, yes."

Shalár met the kobalen's accusing eyes. Yes, this one could think ahead. Excellent.

"Even if there is blood, you are safe with this mark on you. I not drink from you, my hunters not drink from you."

The kobalen stood staring down at the small golden ring in its palm. Finally it cast a glance at its fellows, then held out the closed ring to Shalár.

"Give. I fight for you."

"You must come to the hanging rock west of the big mountain pass, by the dark moon. If you fail, I hunt you down myself and drink your life."

The kobalen pounded its fist into its palm three times. "Give!"

Shalár permitted herself a small smile. She took another ring from her pouch and stepped toward the kobalen. The female stood by, nervously shifting from foot to foot. Shalár reached up to the male's left ear, slid the ring over the lobe, and pinched it shut.

The kobalen let out a grunt, and the smell of blood burst bright on the air. Shalár swallowed sudden hunger despite her recent feeding and stepped back, away from temptation.

The male reached up to its ear, feeling the ring. It grunted again, then turned to the female, which anxiously examined the ring. Shalár took advantage of their distraction to lick a smear of blood from her thumb. A mistake, for her hunger flared brighter.

She glanced at the rest of the kobalen. "Soon I hunt again. Any with my mark are safe. The rest . . ."

She let them imagine being hunted once more. The bold female ground its teeth, then spoke.

"Give me your mark. I fight for you under the dark moon."

Shalár reached into her pouch for another earring. The female took a sudden step toward her, making Shalár look up sharply.

"If you give mark to my young also!"

Shalár gazed at her narrowly. "If you fight well at the mountain pass, I mark your young. Not before."

The female swallowed, then gave a stiff nod. Shalár pinched the second ring through the female's ear. The kobalen winced but made no sound.

That was enough for the others. They began to clamor for Shalár's mark, pressing around her with no hint of order or restraint. She summoned Yaras with a glance and gave him a handful of the rings. Together they worked swiftly until each of her select kobalen wore one. The air was ripe with blood scent, making her ache with hunger even though her belly was full.

She stepped back, rejoining Welir and Ciris, who had watched silently. Putting a hand on either one's shoulder, she repeated her earlier command, this time to all the kobalen.

"Meet these captains at the hanging rock by dark moon."

Yaras, standing a little apart, looked up at her with startled question in his eyes. She ignored him.

"Bring others with you. All who fight at the mountain pass wear my mark."

Releasing Ciris and Welir, she stepped back, gesturing toward the nearest edge of the grove. Two of the hunters stood guard there, but she waved them away.

"Go now. Travel swift to hanging rock. Bring others. Go."

For a long moment the stunned kobalen did not move. Still suspecting a trick, she supposed. Shalár gestured again toward the plain, where the night was beginning to grow a shade less dark.

Finally the wiry male moved toward freedom. Watching Shalár all the way, he took three steps, then reached out toward the bold female, beckoning. With a wary glance at Shalár, the female joined the male, then both began to run.

Shalár did not move save to hold up a hand, preventing the nearby hunters from blocking the kobalen's escape. The rest of them flushed like a flock of mountain geese, running toward freedom as swiftly as their limbs would carry them. She heard their triumphant cry as they broke from the woods and ran across the open plain.

Shalár watched, grinning. Some would test her word, thinking no doubt that she would never know which of them fought at Midrange and which did not. They would learn their error when those who came to Midrange received a second, different earring. Two earrings or one of the second style would distinguish those who had fulfilled their promise. A single earring of the first design would become a mark for her vengeance.

She turned to her captains. "Ciris, Welir. If there is aught you need from Nightsand, I will send it here for you. Start now for Midrange. Watch the pass and report to me. Take five hunters from each of your companies to train as subcommanders and five more to carry messages back."

Ciris frowned. "Do we cross and watch the ælven roads?"

"No. Spend your time with the kobalen. As soon as they begin to arrive, teach them to act as companies and answer your commands. You will not feed from any that wear the ring."

Welir glanced sidelong at Ciris, then nodded. "We understand, Bright Lady."

"If none of them come to Midrange by the dark of the moon, wait five days and then commence hunting them down."

Ciris's lips parted in a smiling snarl. "Yes, Bright Lady."

"Go, then, while there is still dark. Travel swift and safe."

Shalár turned to Yaras, who stood mutely watching. She could feel his discontent.

"Yaras, you will take the catch to Nightsand."

He gave a small, stiff bow. "As you will, Bright Lady."

"Come, let us look them over."

She turned, leading him toward the bitterthorn copse and away from Ciris and Welir. He walked silently beside her for a few strides, then spoke in a low, tense voice.

"I may not serve you in battle?"

"I do not want all my watchers in the same place. There is a risk of organized attack by the kobalen, though I doubt even those clever ones will think of it."

He nodded, and she saw his throat move in a swallow. "Do you return to Nightsand as well?"

"For a short time. Then I will take my wretched cat back to its home territory and strike toward Fireshore. Irith should be returning by now. I want to know what he has learned."

"What care you for Fireshore when you are gathering armies at Midrange?"

Shalár paused, gazing at Yaras with a smile growing on her lips. "Fireshore is the prize. Midrange is merely a diversion. How would you like to lead our best hunters into Ghlanhras?"

✠ Highstone ✠

Eliani stood in her chamber before the curtained alcove that served as her tiring room, choosing what to take with her to Southfæld. She had continued restless, though many days had passed since Turisan had left Highstone.

Twenty-seven days. Her mind would not refrain from counting anew with each dawn. She pressed her lips together, fighting off the panic that arose when she thought of the dwindling number of days remaining before they were to meet again. The journey to Glenhallow would likely take ten, given the pace of the caravan. Felisan and Heléri would both be of the party, and neither cared for the sort of pace the Guard was accustomed to.

On a chair nearby were Eliani's saddle packs, and on the floor a small wooden chest with her new sword beside it. Her bedside lamp was the only light, flickering and casting giant shadows against the walls.

Her two best gowns were already in the chest, beneath spare tunics and legs suitable for wearing under her riding leathers. Misani had done it for her, as Eliani's lack of skill in the care of fine garments was famous within the circle of her household. In the saddle pack were the things she would need as the party traveled south.

She glanced at the leathers lying ready for her to don, her new ones, just delivered. They had been dyed a deep, rich blue, and a long belt of violet hue accompanied them. The sharp scent of the dyes filled her bedchamber.

She turned to her shelves, thinking to take something along with which to amuse herself. She would need distraction to stave off boredom.

She rejected a bound book of cradle tales and several scrolls of poetry. It was senseless, she knew, but she kept remembering how she had been reading of Westgard when she met Turisan and could not overcome a dread that if she read some other legend, it, too, would spring to life before her eyes.

Her gaze fell upon a clutter of gifts from her majority. Stepping over to the shelf that held them, she found the whitewood box and reed flute that Turisan had given her.

The box, which contained House Jharanin's magnificent brooch, she tossed into the chest. She should wear the brooch at Jharan's court, to demonstrate her gratitude.

She frowned at the flute for a long moment before picking it up. The reed was lightweight and satiny smooth beneath her fingers. Any sharp edges had long since been worn soft by handling. As she ran her hands along its length she felt a familiar tingling in her fingertips, and nearly dropped the flute as she recognized it.

Turisan. His khi was in this instrument. Embedded within it, engrained in it, as if through magecraft. Why had she not noticed it before?

Because he had given it to her *before*. Before the Shades. Before his khi had burned into her.

She closed her eyes, willing away a wave of fear. Some part of that fear—all of it, perhaps—was of Kelevon's making. She wished to be quit of it.

Taking a deep breath, she began hesitantly to explore the flute with her khi. Seldom did an object acquire such a strong impression of its owner's khi. Turisan must have made the flute, or at the very least spent days upon days handling it.

A feeling began to take form within her mind, of strength and gentleness, of depth and warmth, like the near-silent vibration of a flute's lowest note. She was about to raise the instrument to her lips to play when a knock fell upon her door.

Her eyes flew open, and with heart pounding she threw the flute into the open chest, where it clattered against the whitewood box.

"Who comes?"

"Your father. May I enter?"

Eliani picked up a scroll at random from her shelves. "Certainly."

The door opened, and her father came in. In a comfortable tunic and legs, with his hair caught back from his face in a half braid, he looked more his usual self than he had in the finery he had worn during all the fuss at Evennight. He smiled.

"Ah, good, you are packing. I came to remind you to bring your gift from House Jharanan. You should wear it in Glenhallow."

Eliani waved carelessly toward the chest. "I have it. I know Lord Jharan is very proud."

Felisan's face softened. "It is not so much pride as concern for appearances. He never expected to govern Southfæld and has always been anxious to uphold the dignity of the realm and of his clan."

Eliani looked up at her father in surprise. "Was he not Turon's nextkin?"

"Not before the Midrange War. He was a lesser scion of Greenglen, with seven others between him and Turon, but they all fell in the war, as did Turon himself."

Felisan's voice took on an unusually somber note. Eliani watched his gaze grow distant; he seemed lost in memory. She knew that the Midrange War had begun with a sudden invasion of kobalen through the pass, and that Felisan and Jharan had been involved in the fighting. They had scarcely had time to send messages to Glenhallow and Hollirued, calling for help, before the kobalen forced them to flee southward.

"Jharan might have fallen as well if we had not held out at Skyruach. There was a moment when we bade each other farewell in all earnestness."

Skyruach had been where they had stood against the kobalen, joined there by Turon and the Southfæld Guard to prevent the enemy from reaching Glenhallow. There had been some from the Alpinon Guard there as well, Eliani thought. She felt a sudden wish that she had paid better attention to these stories when she was a child. Her father had told them often enough, though not in recent years.

Felisan shook himself, and with a smile returned to his customary good humor. "We have greetings to look forward to on this journey, not farewells. I am eager to introduce you to Jharan."

"And I to meet him."

"He will love you instantly, I know." Felisan's smile widened with gleeful anticipation. "Well, I will leave you to your packing. We leave at dawn, so do not revel all the night."

He embraced her, then left. Turning back to the shelves, she scanned them once more. The little crystal kestral on its chain caught her eye. She reached for it, remembering a time before Kelevon had made her build a wall around her heart. Luruthin had been sweet to her.

She held up the chain, letting the bird dangle and glint in the candlelight. After a moment she stepped to the chest and picked up the whitewood box, gently laying the kestrel inside with her brooch and gazing at it.

The kestrel was not safe there. It would likely be battered against the massive brooch and shatter. She fetched a kerchief of violet silk and wrapped the tiny bird in it, then tucked it carefully beside the brooch and closed the box again, laying it in the chest next to Turisan's flute.

She picked up the flute, worried that her carelessness might have damaged it. She found it unharmed, and the tingle of Turisan's khi remained. She laid the flute among the softer things and covered it and the whitewood box with her better cloak. Perchance she would decline Turisan's offer to handfast. In that case, she would feel obliged to return his gift.

⌘

Luruthin watched Eliani fret, plainly impatient with the slow pace of Alpinon's delegation. It was a small party, only a handful of guardians to escort the two of them, her father, Curunan, and a slung chariot bearing Lady Heléri and her attendant, with a cart for baggage.

They had traveled for two days and only now were approaching Midrange, having first journeyed eastward to the trade road. The Silverwash was not yet in sight, but Midrange Peak was in view, its crest pale with fresh snow. Eliani fell back to join her father, who was riding beside Heléri's chariot. Luruthin heard him greet her.

"A pleasant day for riding, is it not? Just a hint of chill to keep one alert."

"Pleasant enough, but my mount wants to stretch her legs. Let me take Luruthin and two of the guardians and scout up to Midrange Pass. We may find signs of kobalen."

Luruthin looked over his shoulder and saw Felisan's

skeptical glance toward the pass. "There is new snow up there. It may not be passable."

"In that case we will return to report as much." Eliani's mount sidled, betraying her restless hand on the reins. "Let me ride up, Father."

"It is a full day's journey and more."

"We can be up and back by the time you reach the river."

"Four of you are too few. What if you should encounter kobalen?"

"Unlikely. They hate the cold."

"Then why scout the pass for them?"

Eliani bit her lip, flushing prettily. Felisan smiled, glancing at Luruthin before taking pity on his daughter.

"You chafe at our pace, I know. Very well, have your scout, but stop and inform Southfæld's outpost of your intention. Perhaps they will send a guardian or two along with you."

He glanced again at Luruthin, who took this to mean that Felisan trusted he would make certain Southfæld sent guardians. Luruthin nodded slightly.

"Thank you, Father!"

Eliani leaned from her saddle to throw an arm around her sire, then rode forward to accost Luruthin. They chose two guardians to take with them and made their farewells, then galloped ahead of the party.

By the time they neared the Silverwash, midday had passed, and Luruthin's stomach was grumbling. The river was obscured by a high bluff, but a greenleaf grove that followed its course could be seen farther to the south, still in leaf though burnished with red and gold.

Luruthin had not been this far south in some years, and his memories of the area were vague. This was

Southfæld, outside the range of Alpinon's patrols. He gazed at the high bluff that curved down from the mountains and shielded the river from view. Atop it, near its point, he saw a guardian cloaked in pale green.

Eliani left the road, leading her companions toward the wood. They soon found themselves ducking low branches and guarding their clothing from snagging on the dense undergrowth. At last they dismounted, leading the horses through the tangle until they reached a clearing. Luruthin smelled the river.

Two guardians met them as they neared the bluff. They were as like as kindred to the one he had spied on the cliff top: Greenglens both, pale-haired and dark-eyed. One greeted them with a small formal bow.

"I am Vanorin, captain of this post."

Eliani bowed in return. "Well met, Captain Vanorin. I am Eliani of Felisanin; this is Luruthin, theyn of Clerestone; these are Firthan and Hanusan. We come in advance of Alpinon's delegation to the Ælven Council. We wish to scout up to the pass."

Vanorin glanced toward the peaks. "There is little likelihood of seeing anything at this season."

"I wish to look for sign of kobalen. My kindred and I slew a small band not far from Highstone a short time since."

"You are only four."

"Four experienced guardians."

Vanorin glanced at Luruthin, who shook his head slightly. It was all he dared do, and when Eliani turned her head to look at him, he glanced away.

Vanorin's expression became guarded. "Forgive me, my lady, but I think four are too few for safety. The pass is treacherous at best and may well be deep in snow."

Luruthin ventured to speak. "Lord Felisan thought you might send a few guardians with us."

Vanorin's brows rose slightly. He answered thought-fully. "We are but twenty here, and six of our number are out on patrol. What would you seek up there?"

Eliani glanced toward the peak. "Answers."

"To what questions?"

"Why have the kobalen been so active this season? What was that band doing so deep in our woods?"

Why did an alben mark one of them? Luruthin knew Eliani was pondering that question as well.

Vanorin looked toward the peak, frowning, then turned to Eliani. "I will go with you, and bring three others."

His gaze shifted briefly to Luruthin, who nodded. Eliani, occupied in thanking the captain, did not notice.

Luruthin stroked his horse's neck. Four more guardians would protect Eliani on her excursion. It was the best that could be done, and Felisan must be satisfied.

Eliani soon had them in the saddle again. Luruthin watched as she rode ahead with Vanorin. He thought she looked more confident, less troubled than of late. Perhaps it was the excitement of travel. Despite having attained her majority, Eliani was in many ways still young.

They followed the Silverwash upward until its gorge steepened and narrowed to the point of being impass-able, whereupon the trail turned away from the river to wind along the mountainside. The higher they rode, the more barren were the greenleaf trees, gray branches amidst the darker evergreens.

Late in the day they reached the first significant drifts of snow on the trail and found in it the marks of kobalen. The tracks were old and had widened and softened in the cold sunshine, but their shape was still identifiable. Luruthin was glad to see that no kobalen had passed more recently.

The scout pushed forward through deepening snow-drifts that came near the tops of their horses' legs. The sky was clear, and a cold, light breeze blew in their faces from the west. With the sun nearing the peaks and the horses almost exhausted, Eliani reluctantly called a halt.

They dismounted, fed their animals, and made themselves as comfortable as they could among the rocks along the trail, a few of which protruded through the snow. Luruthin found a seat on one of these, dry at least, though cold.

They were now above the timberline, and what little life clung here was already asleep beneath the snow. Eliani smiled as she made her way toward Luruthin across the trampled snow, and his heart quickened. He made room for her on the rock.

She had brought a satchel of food and shared bread and cold meat with him. He passed her a skin filled with wine. She sipped at it, tipping back her head so that her hair brushed the back of her shoulders.

"Thank the spirits we have good weather." She glanced up at the peak. "Soon this pass will be impossible."

Luruthin nodded. "Impossible for the kobalen, too."

"I would not have expected them to cross it even now. They hate snow."

"They have crossed it before. In force."

"The Midrange War." Eliani looked at him, green eyes sharp with question. "Do you think that is their purpose? Another attack on Southfæld?"

"Why else would they be in the mountains at this season?"

She glanced up toward the pass, worry in her face. "But the season is exactly why they would not mount an attack. Why pursue a war on the eve of winter? Midrange began in spring and ended in high summer at Skyruach."

"Kobalen may not think so clearly."

"Will you fight? If there is another war?"

Her voice dropped as she met his gaze, and an image flashed into his thoughts: they were fighting in darkness against a numerous enemy, and he stood between Eliani and them, guarding her. He would do it, though his heart filled with dread.

"I will fight, if it comes to that."

She looked up toward the peak again and took another swallow of wine, then returned the skin. Luruthin capped it and set it aside. Wanting to reassure her, he offered a thought he did not believe.

"Perhaps there is some other reason that the kobalen are so active."

Eliani smiled wanly. "Maybe they have soiled every camping space west of the mountains and look to our lands for new ground."

Luruthin laughed. "I think not. The western wastes are vast."

"But the kobalen breed like rabbits." Eliani chewed a bite of bread. "It is a pity we have never learned why. Our numbers increase so slowly, we can never compete with them. Someday they may overrun all our lands."

"Surely not. They die like rabbits, too, remember."

Eliani made a sound of disgust. "They are vermin."

"Yet our ancestors made war against their own kin to protect them from harm."

She turned to face him, a sharp glint in her eye. "To protect them from cruelty. It is not quite the same thing. You and I have harmed plenty of kobalen."

"Yes." Luruthin looked westward, up toward the summit. "I have often been troubled by that. We strive to harm none, yet we are constantly in conflict with the kobalen."

"In our own defense! We do not attack them, nor seek to push westward beyond the mountains."

"We might do so if the land were more attractive. What if we dwelt in the wastes and they enjoyed the bounty of our realms? Maybe you are right, and it is our lands they want."

She tilted her head, green eyes narrowing. "You are their champion now?"

"No. I loathe them." Luruthin sighed, trying to capture a fleeting thought and put it into words. "I just want to understand why it was worth fighting the Bitter Wars to protect them."

Eliani gazed at him thoughtfully, considering the question. Her expression—open and intelligent—was one he had not seen in long years, and lit an instant fire in his heart. This was the Eliani he had loved and laughed with, many winters since. Luruthin kept still, afraid to shatter the moment, reaching out with all his senses to seek a taste of her khi in the living air.

At last Eliani shrugged. "The kobalen's protection was not the issue. The alben violated our creed, and when the Ælven Council ordered them to desist, they refused. When they turned their backs on the ælven creed, they ceased to be ælven. The kobalen were their victims, but it was the creed that was at issue."

"So we would have cast out the alben even if they had chosen some lesser creature to abuse? Horses, perhaps?"

Eliani's brow wrinkled, then she laughed. "I do not know. It is too philosophical a question for me." She glanced at the sun, which was edging toward the western peaks. "And it is time we pressed on. With luck we will reach the summit before nightfall."

She stood, tore the last bit of bread in half, and offered him a piece. Luruthin took it, thanking her with a nod, sorry their conversation had ended. He was no longer hungry, but he ate the bread as he watched Eliani walk away, not wanting to waste any gift from her, even the humblest. He took a last swallow of wine to clear his throat, and another to dull the ache in his heart, before rising to return to his horse.

⊕

Eliani glanced back at the straggling column, restraining her impatience to press ahead. They were near the summit, but it had taken longer than she had expected to reach. She had hoped not to camp in these heights.

She knew of a sheltered place on the western side of the pass, perhaps a league below the summit. Were she alone, she would reach it easily by nightfall, but not all of the horses were as hardy as her mountain-bred gelding. Eliani halted her horse, patted its neck, and waited for the scout to close up.

A sharp wind blew constantly from the west, swirling around the peaks and filling the air with gusts of stinging ice. The wind scoured snow away from the heights and piled it into deep drifts elsewhere.

Eliani noticed a conce protruding from the snow beside the trail. She did not know whose it was; some Southfælder. Lonely to die up here, even in clement weather, and the conce meant the death had not been peaceful.

Vaniron reached her, his horse's sides heaving, breath icing in the bright sunshine. The Greenglen's fair cheeks were wind-reddened, and his hair whipped in his face.

"You seem to know your way. Have you crossed this pass before?"

She shook her head. "Not in two decades. I recall a ledge some way below the summit on the western side. We might camp there tonight."

"I know the place. There was a fall of rock over the summer that blocked the trail above it, but if kobalen came through, they must have cleared it."

"Or climbed over it."

Eliani frowned. A blocked trail would pose a problem. They might have to clear it themselves to get to shelter. She glanced back toward the scout, then looked at Vanorin.

"I will ride ahead and see if the way is clear. Wait here until the others have come up, then bring them on."

Vaniron acknowledged this, pulling his hood up to protect his face from the wind. Eliani braced herself and turned into it, urging her horse forward through knee-deep snow.

The trail leveled as she reached the summit, curving along the shoulder of a craggy peak. Two others loomed overhead, bright against the blue sky. One bore on its side the headwaters of the Silverwash, here an icy trickle against dark stone, its first cascade frozen in its fall. Eliani remembered how the stream danced in summer, tried to warm herself with thoughts of better weather.

When the icefall was out of sight and the trail began to descend, she tightened her reins, holding her mount to a slow walk. She considered dismounting but found that as the slope steepened, the snow all but vanished except where the wind had driven it into crannies in the rocky western face of the mountains.

Not far ahead the trail rounded a ridge, and from there she should be able to see whether the way was clear below. She dismounted after all, listening to an inner prompting whose source she could not identify, something in the wind, perhaps. She remembered Heléri's advice to trust such feelings. Whether they were spirits' guidance or merely instinct, she could not tell.

Reins in hand, she reached the turn and paused, listening. No sound came to her save the wind's harsh breath. She laid the reins on the saddle, stepped forward, and looked down the westward trail.

The sun, still high above the flat horizon, glinted

harshly on the western cliffs, sharpening their edges. The trail below was clear of rock, but as her gaze followed it toward the camping place and beyond, she saw movement on the plain below, like the flickering of a firespear forest.

Eliani gasped and leapt backward, nearly tripping in her haste to get behind the ridge. She flattened her back against the rock and stood panting, her breath icing before her, each wisp caught away by the wind.

No forest, that. No greenleaf trees grew on the wind-scoured plains west of the Ebon Mountains. She had seen the glimmer of an army encampment.

She held still and sought to control her breathing, wishing there were some living thing in these heights through which she might expand her sense of what lay below. Air and rock were all she had. She scented the wind for a trace of kobalen nearby but detected none.

Laying a hand on the rock face of the ridge, she closed her eyes, feeling for a tremor of movement on the trail. Either there was none or her senses had been deadened by cold and wind. No khi, bright or dark, disturbed the thin air save that of her scout to the east and of their mounts. She drew a breath, left her horse, and dropped to her belly before edging around the turn.

The sight of the encampment was less a shock this time, but no less frightening. A smear of darkness sprawled out onto the plain, seeming to writhe with movement: the glimmer of spear points, their glass edges catching the late sun. That was what she first had seen.

Many kobalen were massed together below—hundreds, more than ten times the largest band she had ever heard of—far more than she had ever imagined seeing at once. As she watched, they rushed all at once to the south in a scattered, disorganized charge.

Eliani cupped her hands about her eyes, squinting to make out the leaders of the charge. There seemed to be none. The kobalen stopped and began to wander back to their starting place.

She shifted her gaze, taking in a vast scatter of rough camps and fire pits interspersed with the rubbish heaps that marked any place the kobalen dwelt. Judging from the size of these, the kobalen had not been there long. In fact, to the northwest across the wastes she saw what seemed to be a band of new arrivals approaching, some fifty or sixty strong.

She wasted no time trying to guess why the kobalen had chosen this remote and barren place for a winter camp. This was not their ordinary behavior. There was some game in the wastes but not enough to feed such a horde, at least not for long.

She crawled behind the ridge, then mounted her horse and returned through the pass. She saw Vanorin and Luruthin approaching at the head of the scout and signaled to them to halt, then rode forward to meet them.

"There are kobalen encamped on the wastes below. A large army."

She led the two of them to see for themselves. They all crouched on the trail overlooking the kobalen camp.

Luruthin frowned as he gazed at the masses of kobalen. "They could attack at any time. We must go back at once and inform Lord Felisan."

Vanorin nodded. "Southfæld must be warned as well."

"Yes."

With a shock, Eliani realized she had the means, perhaps, to warn Southfæld instantly. A slow dread poured through her veins.

She did not wish to use mindspeech to contact Turisan. She had not decided yet whether to commit to the use of their gift, and the mere thought of speaking to him now, of letting him into her thoughts, set her trembling. It would end any choice she had about her future, she knew. The next time they spoke, she would fall from the precipice, and be lost.

If she held off—if she sent Vanorin's folk galloping for Glenhallow instead—would she be placing her freedom above the safety of all Southfæld? She did not even know if she could speak to Turisan at this distance. The only way to know was to try.

She looked at Vanorin. "How long will it take you to get word to Glenhallow?"

"A message can be relayed along the guard posts in two days, three at most."

Two days, and another day to get down from the pass. If they traveled all night, they might reach the outpost by morning.

Eliani swallowed. "Let us go, then."

Chagrin smote her even as she got to her feet. She strode hard for the horses, fighting a silent battle within herself, every moment weighing on her conscience.

Surely the kobalen would not move in three days, not if they were still arriving, as the black column implied. She glanced skyward, seeing the fair weather now as a curse rather than a blessing. If only a storm would close the pass . . .

The ælven creed called for serving one's people. If her judgment proved wrong in this matter, lives could be lost—many lives, perhaps.

It would be so simple to pass the news to Turisan. No need to hasten the scout down the mountain again.

How much would three days' warning gain them, though? Time to raise a defense or even part of one? Would it matter at all?

It mattered. To her, if to no one else. She reached her

horse and swung into the saddle, calling out orders to the scout to return eastward.

She could not bring herself to speak to Turisan. Despising herself, she urged her fellow guardians down the mountain, hoping she was not risking their very lives.

✤ Nightsand ✤

The sky over Nightsand was hazy, a hint of rain in the damp air, the night Shalár brought her catch home. She rode the weary catamount, and Yaras walked beside it.

He had been her chosen at Hunt's Eve, but now they were returned to Nightsand. Dareth would be first with her here, always. Shalár felt a sharp impatience to see him, to give him the fresh, strong blood of a newly caught kobalen, to enjoy the strength it would give him.

She looked up toward the Cliff Hollows and saw him standing in the gallery with the draperies open behind him. He must see her and Yaras walking beside her. He was neither blind nor a fool, and he would know she had favored Yaras.

Well, he knew of all her couplings. She never hid them. She had too high a regard for Dareth to deceive him.

In silence, Shalár rode through the city and up the long, steep trail to the Cliff Hollows, then on it toward the pens. She reached the entrance to the pens and paused to dismount. The catamount had no fight in it; she left it lying beside the entrance, needing only a feather touch of khi to control it. Let the kobalen believe, if they would, that the cat would stand guard over them, ready to devour any that tried to escape.

None would escape the pens. None ever had.

Shalár turned the catch over to Nihlan, selecting a strong kobalen to take with her to the Cliff Hollows. When they had left the pens behind, the creature attempted to break free and would have flung itself from the cliff had she not instead forced it to its knees. She made it crawl the rocky path until she became impatient to be at home. When at last she let it rise again, the scent of its blood filled the air.

The guards at the entrance to the Cliff Hollows bowed in greeting, their khi flaring with sudden hunger. She swept past them and into the audience chamber, where she had seen Dareth standing.

He was there, tall, clad in gray, gazing out at Nightsand below. The city blazed with light, welcoming the return of the hunters.

"Dareth."

His head came up at the sound of her voice, though he did not turn at once. Shalár wavered between anger and concern that she had worn out his patience at last. She felt suddenly small and weary, wanted his arms around her.

No weakness. She drew herself up and strode toward him.

He turned at last and reached a hand up to brush against her cheek. "How strong you look."

"I have brought you a feeder."

His smile faded to a look of trouble. "Here?"

"Yes, here! Why not here? Do you think it shameful? It is time you embraced the truth of our survival, Dareth."

He winced as if her words had cut him. Shalár felt regret, but would not take them back.

She took his hand, felt the thinness of his khi against her flesh. He had not fed, perhaps not since she had left to hunt. She felt a flash of fear.

"Come."

She pulled him away from the gallery, across the chamber, toward her private rooms. He came, as reluctantly as the kobalen at first. She urged them both on, impatient now that his hunger had enhanced her own.

As they reached her bedchamber, she took his shoulders in her hands, leaning forward to kiss him. The kobalen tried feebly to escape her grasp. She bore it down instead, made it kneel, then lie on the cold stone floor. She pulled Dareth down with her onto the thick furs nearby and reached a hand to her knife.

Dareth's hunger flared. "Shall I find a cup?"

"No."

Shalár drew him close to the kobalen. Dareth's brow gathered into an anxious frown; his breaths came quick and short. She opened a vein behind the kobalen's ear with a flick of her blade, then bent to it and filled her mouth with the rich, khi-heavy blood.

Tossing the knife aside, she reached for Dareth, twining her arms around his neck and sharing with him as she had with others on the hunt. He shuddered, then seemed to come afire, embracing her tightly, deepening the kiss. Laughing, she pulled away from him and urged him to feed on the blood that was seeping, hot and vital, from the feeder's neck.

He was aflame with hunger now and needed no second invitation. While he bent to the feeder, she searched for her knife among the furs. She made a second cut for herself, wiped her knife and sheathed it, then curled around Dareth and abandoned herself to feeding.

Later, much later, after they had drained the feeder and coupled frantically and unsuccessfully on the floor beside it, Shalár rose and shed the few pieces of clothing she yet wore. Dareth's robe had been much easier to dispose of than her hunting leathers. He lay naked on the furs, sated, dreamily watching her, his smile tinged with sadness.

"I missed you."

Shalár knelt beside him. "And I you."

"So the hunt was successful."

"Very successful."

"I am glad."

She looked at him, admiring the line of his throat beneath the pale hair, watching the shadows at the back of his eyes. Glad of what? Glad she was back? Glad it was over?

"I have sent Ciris and Welir to gather an army of kobalen."

Dareth's brow creased, and he closed his eyes. "Another war? It will fail, just as before."

"No. This time I have a way to make the kobalen stand."

She told him how she had gathered the most sharp-witted kobalen from the hunt's catch, told him of the bargain she had made with them and how she planned to enforce it. Dareth listened in silence. She watched him, eager for a sign of his approval. He seemed only to sink deeper in concern.

"They need not defeat the ælven. They need only hold their attention long enough for us to recapture Fireshore."

At that Dareth raised his head and met her gaze. He said nothing, though his eyes told of hopelessness.

"We *can* win it back. Now is the time. We will never be stronger."

"And what of those who have dwelt there these many centuries?"

Shalár stood and went to a shelf for a pitcher of wine. She poured herself a glass, then glanced at Dareth, who shook his head.

"If they are wise, they will flee whence they came."

"And those who were born there in the meantime?"

Dareth's voice was quiet but unrelenting. Shalár took a mouthful of wine, savoring it before she swallowed.

"They may remain if they will give allegiance to Darkshore."

Dareth closed his eyes, shaking his head. Annoyed, Shalár tossed off the wine in her cup and poured more.

"Do you not wish to return to your home?"

He looked at her, a slight, sad smile touching his lips. "This is my home." He reached out to brush his fingers along her leg. "You are my home."

She sank down beside him again. "Fireshore is *my* home."

It was Darkshore's home, home to all of them, though they were beginning to forget it. Shalár clung fiercely to the memory of their true home, but others had begun to accept less. Nightsand had its pleasures. She felt a wave of despair at the thought that her folk might give up the fight for their rightful lands.

"I will take a force of hunters north within the season."

Dareth's throat moved in a swallow. He said nothing, made no sign of acknowledgment.

"Promise me you will feed while I am gone."

He gave a startled blink. His lips parted, then he looked away. Shalár moved closer.

"Dareth." She touched his face, frightened by the weariness in his eyes. "How can you have lost the desire to live?"

"I dislike the cost of living as we do."

"You liked it well enough just now."

He cast a resentful glance at her and sat up, moving away. The dead kobalen lay within arm's reach.

"Dare to tell me you did not enjoy it!"

"Yes, I enjoyed it. That does not change my belief that it is wrong."

"Wrong to survive in the only way we can? We have no choice, Dareth!"

He was silent. Cursing herself for falling into their ancient dispute, Shalár stood and went to her wardrobe, pulling out a robe. When she returned, Dareth had not moved. He sat watching her, his fair brow drawn into a frown.

Shalár moved toward him, fear, love, and anger warring in her heart. She knelt beside him, reached for him, wrapped herself around him. His body responded, sliding into her easily as his arms enfolded her. She clung to him, not moving, savoring the near completeness of their embrace. Only a little distance and they would be irrevocably joined, bonded in the making of a new life.

Shalár's heart leapt with hope. Would a child inspire Dareth to live on despite his misgivings? She needed no further reason to seek conception, yet here it was.

Moaning, she pushed herself against him. He pushed back gently. Slowly, gently, her silken robe caressing them both as they moved. No anxious rush. Perhaps this was the way. She reached for his khi, gathering it to her like petals of a fragile blossom scattered by the wind.

She whispered his name, feeling the heat of their coupling intensify. She arched her back, leaning into him with her hips.

"Come inside me, Dareth."

"Let me in." He pressed back.

She grasped at a shred of Yaras's memory, a moment's confusion of passion and swirling khi. Felt herself start to yield, then even as her heart leapt she was swept with a shuddering climax. She cried out in frustration and joy.

Dareth spilled himself into her. Shalár held him more tightly, savoring each hot pulse, hoping still to make her body do her will, though it was too late. They convulsed together, then slowly fell still.

"Close. So close."

His arms tightened around her. She felt him throb again inside her.

"Do not leave me before we have a child."

The air was heavy with his silence. At last he answered. "I will not leave while you are here."

He wished to keep her away from Fireshore. He would not succeed, but she acknowledged the reasoning behind his cruelty. She understood.

She wanted more, wanted his promise to feed, to live, to join her as the rightful governors of Fireshore. She knew it would be folly to make such demands. He had given her a promise, and it was not in Dareth's nature to promise less than he intended, so she knew she must be content with it.

She laid her head on his shoulder, closing her eyes for now to the toil that lay ahead. She must capture Fireshore swiftly if she was not to rule it alone.

⁜

The night was old by the time Shalár set out along the trail to the pens. She shivered in the cold and rubbed her arms through the sleeves of her tunic, wishing for her cloak. It was warmer here than on the plains but not so warm that she could forget the coming winter.

She must strike soon, while the nights were longest and the climate on the northern coast at its mildest. She needed every possible advantage.

She paused outside the chamber of the Greenglen female, who lay listless, curled against the wall. Shalár tasted her khi, found it dark with despair, heavy with anguish both mental and physical.

She frowned. Evidently her male guards had been too eager to obey her command that the Greenglens be bred. She should have foreseen the problem, with only one female among the new captives. She would have to remind the guards that the ælven captives were not to be damaged, and give Nihlan instructions that this female be left alone for a while.

Moving on, she found the cave in which the lone Steppegard was housed. He, too, lay with his back to the door. A plate of food sat uneaten beside his pallet. He did not move, even at the sound of her key in the lock. That desperate spirit was beginning to weaken.

Shalár stepped inside and pushed the door closed, hearing the bolt click into the lock behind her. She put the keys into an inner pocket of her tunic, then walked toward the Steppegard and nudged him in the back with her toe.

He heaved a sigh. "I am spent. Try another."

"Spent, my sweet? Then let us talk a while."

He turned his head at the sound of her voice, looking up at her in mingled fear and hope. His eyes were sunken with weariness, his curling hair tangled and dull. He looked less well than she had expected.

"Bright Lady." His voice was a hoarse whisper. "I thought you had forsaken me."

"I have been away."

"Have pity on me, lady. Let me go."

"Come now, you know better than that."

He struggled to raise himself, managed to sit up and lean against the wall. He seemed too weak for the short span of his imprisonment. Shalár glanced at the food, fearing he was deliberately starving himself. She picked up a dried apricot and held it to his mouth.

"Why have you not eaten?"

He made a face of disgust and turned his head away. "I cannot. I have tried. I am ill."

Shalár put the fruit aside and frowned, kneeling to look at him more closely. She caught his jaw in her hand and pulled his head up while exploring his khi. What she found surprised her.

"Oh." She released him. "Accept my commiserations."

He blinked at her. "What do you mean?"

She smiled wryly and sat beside him on the blanketed pallet. "You have started down a dark path. Sadly, there is no turning back."

He gazed at her in dull confusion. "What path?"

"The path of hunger. The path of my people, Steppegard. Your own clan will shun you if they see you again, not that they ever will."

Understanding crossed his face like a cold wind, wiping away what color was left in it. "I will never follow your path!"

"I gather the ælven still believe there is a choice? It grieves me to tell you there is none."

"No. No! It is unfair."

Shalár chuckled. "Quite."

She watched him, rethinking her plans for making him yield up what he knew. He would have to be tempted with blood, and before it would tempt him, he would have to learn that it was now his proper food. That could take time, and she had little to spare.

"Tell me what you know of Fireshore, and I will ease your pain."

He leaned his head back against the wall and closed his eyes. "I have told you all I know."

"No, my sweet, you have not."

Slowly, patiently, she questioned him, demanding details of every place he had seen in Fireshore in the last year. How many dwelt in Bitterfield? In Woodrun? In Blackland? How much darkwood was traded? How many hunters had the usurpers of Clan Sunriding, and how armed? How often did foreigners like himself visit each town? When was he last in Ghlanhras, and what was its condition then?

She kept at him until he slumped against the wall and his voice became a raw whisper. His answers seemed truthful, and some might be useful. When she judged he was near exhaustion, she asked the question she had kept in reserve.

"What is Alpinon to you?"

His brow tightened in a feeble frown. "Nothing."

"Untrue. You do not uphold the ælven creed, Steppegard."

His eyes opened as he turned his head toward her, a flash of spirit kindling in his glance. "Nor do you!"

"Not for many centuries."

He gazed at her hopelessly for a moment, then his head drooped in despair. She judged it time to offer an incentive.

She stood, leaving him there without a word. Going to the door, she let herself out and returned to Nihlan's antechamber.

"Hand me my chalice and knife."

Nihlan rose hastily and fetched them down from the shelf. "Shall I assist you, Bright Lady?"

"No need."

Shalár took the items, some dryleaf, and Nihlan's larger ring of keys, then went down the wide noisome passage to the pens where kobalen were kept. These large caves, a series of them, were accessed from the passage by short tunnels at intervals, each watched by a member of Darkshore's guard. Shalár went down the first, acknowledging the guard's salutation. She looked through the small grating set into the heavy darkwood door that secured the chamber.

Some fifty kobalen lay within, mostly sleeping. Shalár sought through their khi and found a strong one nearby. Taking hold of its mind, she made it stand

and come to the door. One or two others showed curiosity; she took their minds as well and stilled them.

She made the kobalen step out, then stand still while she locked the door again. She drew her knife across its throat and filled her chalice, stopped the flow of blood with a bit of dryleaf, and returned the kobalen to the pen. Carefully carrying the brimming cup, she returned the keys to Nihlan and sought the Steppegard once more.

There was much strength left in him—she must not forget that—but just now he was sorely depleted. The food she had brought, if he accepted it, would change that.

He lay in a heap on the pallet. She knelt beside him, setting her chalice nearby, and raised him to sit against the wall once more. His eyes watched her dully.

Shalár reached for her cup and held it before his face, close so that he could smell the blood within. The Steppegard frowned, then looked at her.

"Try it."

She moved the cup closer, held it to his lips. For a long moment he did not move, save the slight flare of his nostrils as he breathed, staring down at the fresh blood. At last he opened his lips and took a small sip.

He frowned at first, then swallowed and took a breath. Like a child trying a new food, he seemed to be deciding whether he cared for it.

Shalár waited, watching him. The smell of the blood was making her hungry, as was the Steppegard's distress. She should have taken some herself before bringing this to him.

Never mind. She could wait.

He shot her a resentful glance, then lowered his mouth to the cup again, taking a larger swallow, then another. His hand came up to grasp weakly at the stem. Shalár kept hold of it, tipping the chalice toward him as he drank, greedily now. He paused to breathe, and she pulled it back, his hand falling away. He had drunk nearly half.

He stared at her, blood on his lips, a look of wonder on his face. His gaze shifted to the cup and sharpened. He reached for it, but Shalár held it away.

"What is Alpinon to you?"

Anger filled his eyes even as fresh color flooded his sallow cheeks. Shalár stood up and stepped out of his reach. He was still weak but had taken enough to give him momentary strength.

"Tell me of Alpinon and you shall have the rest."

He stared at her resentfully, then collapsed against the wall. "I have not been there in decades. Last I knew there were some twelve hundreds in Highstone—"

"I know Highstone's condition, thank you. What does it mean to you?"

He let out a weary sigh. "Nothing, lady. There is nothing for me there. I have done all you required. For mercy's sake, let me go."

"Where?" Shalár stepped away from the wall, moved in front of him, crouched with the chalice in her hands. "Where would you go, Steppegard? Your people will not have you."

She watched his face sag with cold understanding. She had stopped trying to help the ælven who acquired the hunger in her keeping, but this one was more adaptable than most.

"You could have a place here. You could walk free under the stars."

He looked up, his gaze fixing first on the chalice then on her face. The golden-brown eyes stared at her coldly.

"At what cost?"

Shalár smiled. An idea was beginning to grow in her mind. This Steppegard might be very useful, after all.

"A small service you can do me. An errand. I will think on the details and tell you when I have decided."

As she began to stand, sudden panic flashed in his eyes and he lunged for the chalice. Shalár recoiled, but his hand caught at hers enough to tip the cup.

Blood spilled over her sleeve and across the stone floor. Shalár backed away from the Steppegard, who collapsed onto his hands and knees, staring at the spilled food.

Shalár licked the blood from her wrist, watching him as she caught her breath. "That was foolish, Steppegard. And wasteful. We cannot afford waste here."

A little blood was left in the cup. Shalár tossed it off while he watched in mute dismay. She gazed at him for a long moment, then turned to leave the chamber, alert for signs of another attack in his khi. There were none.

She locked the door behind her and looked in at him through the grate. He was still staring at the pool of blood slowly cooling on the floor. As she watched, he lowered his head to it and began to lick it up. Not with the desperation of the starving, but with the determination of the wise.

✤ Southfæld ✤

Luruthin rode beside Eliani as he had since Midrange, watching her in silent concern. She had grown more grave the closer they came to Glenhallow. He had given up trying to converse with her; it seemed only to annoy her.

The kobalen army's presence had thrown a pall of apprehension over all the party, and changed what had been a pleasant journey to an urgent one. Felisan had hastened them onward as fast as the animals could go without suffering harm, and they had reached the valley of Glenhallow in only nine days.

The city was visible as soon as they crossed the last ridge, shimmering golden in the distance. Their approach led them between meadows of dry grass through which twined the Silverwash, grown wide and lazy here.

Luruthin gazed in awe at Glenhallow. Highstone was a mere village in comparison with the sprawling, graceful curves of Southfæld's seat of government. Built of golden-hued stone, the city rested between two large hills at the feet of the Ebon Mountains. The chain was less wide here than in Alpinon, but its peaks were higher and more forbidding, a dramatic background for the golden city.

A river flowed down from the mountains, passing to the north of Glenhallow and then curving around its outer wall, winding southward to join the Silverwash. Arcing bridges spanned the lesser river, connecting the city with the river road.

They reached the confluence of rivers and turned westward. On a broad plain below the city's outer wall, troops of guardians were practicing, three hundred or more by his count. Luruthin wondered if they were on alert because of the kobalen at Midrange. He glanced at Eliani, who ordinarily would have taken an interest, but she seemed lost in thought.

They crossed the centermost bridge and continued on a wide road paved in golden stone. A large gate in the city's wall stood open, flanked by six guardians in Southfæld green. A tall Greenglen lady waited at the gate, dressed richly in silver-hued robes and mounted on a gray horse. As the delegation halted, she raised a hand in greeting.

"Welcome, Lord Felisan."

Felisan nodded. "Jhinani. Well met, my lady."

"Lord Jharan asked me to greet you and give you his apologies for not doing so himself. He is in conference with the Eastfæld delegation and will see you as soon as they have adjourned."

"Eastfæld arrived recently?"

"Yesterday. They had not yet heard of the kobalen massing at Midrange; that is what Jharan is discussing with them now. We are grateful to you for Lady Eliani's warning."

Her gaze shifted to Eliani, a delicate eyebrow rising in inquiry. Felisan made a gesture of presentation.

"This is my daughter, Lady Eliani, and these are my kindred Lady Heléri, Theyn Luruthin, and Curunan."

Jhinani nodded to them all. "Welcome to Glenhallow."

She turned her mount to lead them through a wide street lined with houses and guild halls. After some distance they came to a second gate through which they passed into the city's heart. Luruthin knew that the two walls together comprised the extent of Glenhallow's defenses; they had been built on Jharan's order after the Midrange War; before when the city had no defense at all, nor need of it.

With a grim smile, Luruthin reflected that Highstone was not much better protected. Only its difficult approach would deter attackers; it had no fortifications at all. Ælven cities were not designed with defense in consideration, for there had been no need before the Bitter Wars. Kobalen stayed away from larger settlements, ordinarily.

Within the inner wall Glenhallow formed a great half circle with its back against the foothills, curving streets crossed by wide avenues of golden stone. The main avenue sloped gently upward toward an immense public circle and a large building of the same stone, three-storied, with a central dome behind which rose a high tower. Luruthin stared in amazement at this structure as they reached the public circle.

Jhinani reined her mount to a halt. "Hallowhall, palace of the governors of Southfæld." Luruthin glanced at her and saw her smiling; probably she found his reaction amusing.

"What is the spire, my lady?"

"The Star Tower. It is reserved for honored guests."

"Who bides there now?"

She looked at him, her smile widening. "None, for we do not favor one realm above another at this Council gathering."

Jhinani led them across the public circle toward the palace. All of Highstone would have fit easily within the circle. They passed a statue at its center— a silvered falcon with wings upraised, taller than a horse—then crossed a wide greensward separating the circle from the buildings around it. It was planted with greenleaf trees that still bore a few leaves painted in autumn hues.

Attendants came to take their horses. The guardians went with them, leaving only Luruthin and the four from House Felisanin to follow Lady Jhinani into the palace, whose front was graced with arched colonnades. An entrance hall as big as Felisanin Hall gave into a huge round room beneath a sky-colored dome. Jhinani paused there.

"This is the great hall, where public assemblies are held."

She looked at Eliani, who was gazing at the floor. Luruthin sought to cover his cousin's inattention.

"It is magnificent. We have nothing like this in Alpinon."

Jhinani smiled, then led them to a wide staircase that rose to a gallery circling the chamber. Stone arches carved as trees surrounded it, their branches reaching upward to support the dome. From there they could see the great hall's floor, an elaborate mosaic medallion of leaves and vines in shades of green stone, polished and circled with a band of silver a handspan in width.

Luruthin felt overpowered by all this grandeur. Here was the difference in age and population between Southfæld and Alpinon; his homeland was young in years compared with this realm. Its artisans might be as talented as Southfæld's, but they were not as numerous, nor had they the resources for works of this scope.

He looked away from the chamber and found Lady Jhinani patiently waiting while her guests admired their surroundings. Noting his gaze, she smiled, dark eyes gentle and warm.

"This is your first visit to our city."

"Yes." Luruthin glanced toward Eliani, who still stared down at the floor below.

"If you are not overtired, I would be pleased to show you the fountain court. It is our most celebrated place."

"Ah, the fountains!" Lord Felisan nodded. "Yes, they are a wonder. Jharan has not yet added his own, I suppose?"

Jhinani's smile faded slightly. "Not yet."

"He has been building other things." Felisan glanced at his kin. "By all means, show us the fountains, though I think Lady Heléri might prefer to rest."

"The way runs past your allotted chambers. I will take you there first."

Jhinani led them out onto an arcade as broad as an avenue, bounded on the west by a colonnade of more carven trees between which the mountains seemed to loom suddenly larger. Drawn by the sound of running water, Luruthin stepped to the parapet and caught his breath at the sight below: a vast circular courtyard filled with the motion and glimmer of myriad fountains. Behind it a gigantic frieze of ornate trees had been carved into the mountainside, and by its golden hue Luruthin realized this must be where stone for the city had been quarried.

He hastened to rejoin the party, following Jhinani along the arcade and down a passage into the palace's interior. She showed them to a suite of rooms, high-ceilinged and richly appointed, where Lady Heléri chose to remain. Luruthin half expected Eliani to retire as well, but her father urged her to view the fountains, and she went along. They followed Jhinani down a long, curving stairway to the courtyard, where Luruthin hoped the fountains' beauty would lift Eliani's spirits.

⁜

Eliani walked a little way behind the others, listening as Jhinani told the history of each fountain, described their workings, named their creators and the governors who had commissioned them. All were lovely. Eliani admired them, but they were not enough to distract her from her worries.

At first she had been relieved that Turisan had not greeted them. Now she wondered if his absence signified displeasure. She knew she must face him soon.

And tell him what? She was no closer to a decision. Every time she tried to think about mindspeech, a storm of emotions swept away rationality. She had not even had the comfort of Heléri's counsel, for she had avoided private speech with her eldermother since returning from Midrange Pass, not wanting to face her disappointment.

Lady Jhinani's voice intruded on her musings. "This avenue is the newest addition to the court. It was commissioned by Lord Turon and is called the Whispering Walk."

Eliani looked up to find that the party had gathered in the center of the courtyard. Beside them was the entrance to what appeared to be a tunnel of water. Jhinani explained that it was made up of hundreds of tiny fountains on both sides of the walk, each sending a stream of water arching over the path, which ran from the center of the court to its south wall, a distance of some ten rods. At the far end Eliani saw that the path continued through a gate in the wall, out into the wooded land beyond.

Jhinani led them into the walk, and Eliani at once understood its name. The soft hush of flying water was a constant whisper that had an immediate calming effect. She felt disinclined to speak within the arching passage, and indeed, the voices of the others were muted by the gentle sound of the water.

She walked slowly, gazing up at the line where the narrow streams crossed overhead and formed a slight point in the arching roof. No drops fell upon her, but moisture hung in the air, active and energetic, akin to the sensation preceding a rainstorm in the woods.

Eliani breathed deeply of the calming air, not caring that she was falling behind the others. Her steps slowed and finally halted as she closed her eyes, reaching out with all her other senses. Ripples in the air—the footsteps of the others—slowly faded into the water's whisper.

Peace. Here was the peace she needed. A warmth seeped into her through the rippled khi of growing things within and without the courtyard, distorted by the moving water. Perhaps if she stood here long enough, the dancing air would wash away all her doubts.

"My lady?"

Eliani's eyes flew open. Her peace was at an end. Turisan stood a short distance away.

She turned to face him. Best get it over with. As her gaze fell upon his simple gray-green tunic and legs, his hair caught back from his face in a braid bound with green ribbon, she felt her heart leap anew at his beauty.

He gave a hesitant smile. "Forgive me. I meant not to startle you."

His eyes were warmer even than she remembered, though tinged with concern. Eliani did her best to return the smile, though she felt more awkward in his presence now than ever before. She grasped at the first thought that offered.

"The fountains are entrancing."

"Yes." He nodded, the smile widening briefly. "I am glad they please you. I am often drawn here, to think or merely to rest."

"They do seem very restful. And the intricacy of their workings is marvelous. Southfæld's artisans have immense talent."

"Thank you." Turisan bowed slightly, then looked

up, smiling. "Though I find I prefer the raw beauty of your Three Shades."

Eliani glanced away at the reminder of that night. She saw that the others had continued down the walk and were passing through the open gate into the gardens beyond.

"I hope you will pardon me for not being present to greet you upon your arrival. I thought perhaps we had best meet in private first, in case you wished to discuss Midrange Pass."

Ah. He would have it out now. Eliani turned and met his gaze squarely.

"You are displeased."

He looked startled, then seemed to understand. Disappointment flicked across his face.

"So you did not try."

He had not known, then. Eliani paced away restlessly.

"Go ahead, curse me for a fool and a coward. I cannot blame you for being angry. I am angry myself."

"I am not angry."

She spun around to glare at him. "No? You should be! What if the kobalen had followed us through the pass and attacked at once? It could have been disastrous!"

A troubled look came onto his face. "It is useless to regret what might have been. No harm was done, Eliani. Do not fault yourself."

His gentle words calmed her, though they did not ease her sense of failure. She turned away as if to follow the others, but instead stepped abruptly up to the wall of water.

Always in the past she had run from problems, run from feelings that disquieted her. Heléri's words returned to her. She had used her past pain as a shield. That solved nothing, and indeed it was a lonely path.

Watching the water rush past her eyes, she felt a faint mist on her face that suddenly reminded her of the Shades. Raising her palms toward the wall, she chanced to graze it with a fingertip. A splash of water fell across the walk, darkening the crushed rock underfoot; then the water wall healed itself as the fountain resumed its upward arc.

The soothing whisper wrapped about her, sparkling with a hint of Turisan that seemed to augment rather than disturb its restfulness. She turned her head to look at him, seeing patience in his gaze, and acceptance. She felt a surge of gratitude.

"Eliani! Come and see these orchards. They are . . ."

The running footsteps that accompanied the call faltered to a stop. Eliani looked down the path at Luruthin, who glanced from her to Turisan, his smile fading.

"Forgive me—"

"Yes, you should see the orchards." Turisan stepped forward, speaking with a diplomat's ease. "We are proud of our stonefruits especially. Some of the varieties are centuries old, descendants of cuttings brought from Eastfæld when Glenhallow was founded. Will you walk, my lady?"

Eliani looked at him and nodded, not trusting her voice. She smiled at Luruthin, hoping to ease the discomfort that was writ plainly on his face, and started down the walk between them, unsure whether she was glad of the interruption.

✠ Nightsand ✠

Shalár received Irith in her audience chamber upon his return from Fireshore. He paused briefly to glance at Dareth, then came forward to kneel before Shalár.

"Bright Lady."

"Welcome home, Watcher. Where have you been, and what saw you there?"

Irith looked up at her, triumph in his hard face. "I have been to Ghlanhras, Bright Lady."

"To Ghlanhras!" Shalár sat forward, eager for news of Fireshore's chief city. "Tell me!"

Irith leaned an arm across his knee and grinned. "We approached the city from the north. They do not watch that side. They have built a tall wall around all the city to keep out the forest and its creatures. All their guardians stand watch on the south side, where there is a gate."

A wall all around the city. Shalár frowned. That would make taking control of it more difficult.

"Did you go within the wall?"

"I did, Bright Lady. We watched from the forest for several nights and observed that parties of hunters often returned to the city at sunset with their game. I killed a small boar and slipped in with one of those parties, then hid myself in the city."

Shalár nodded, eager for more. Dareth strolled up

to the dais and stood beside her chair. Irith glanced at him, then continued.

"I traded my boar for a room in a lodge and spent five nights in the city's taverns, listening to gossip."

"You were not suspected?"

"I kept myself hooded and stayed out of plain view. I was taken for a Greenglen."

Shalár nodded. "What did you learn in the taverns?"

"There are not many folk in the city. The governor is planning a celebration for the Spirit Feast and another for Midwinter."

Shalár sat up straight in her chair. "The Spirit Feast falls during the Ælven Council."

Irith nodded. "I heard no mention of the Council."

Her heart leapt with delight. "They do not know."

"It seems not."

Shalár stood up, descended from the dais, and began to pace the chamber. She must take advantage of this. She must move on Fireshore as swiftly as possible. If only she were ready now, but it would be impossible to start for at least another twenty or thirty days.

She once had thought idly of sending her own message to the Council in Fireshore's name. Perhaps it could work.

Risky. Very risky, but possibly worth the hazard.

She stopped pacing and returned to the dais before which Irith waited. "Tell me everything you heard. Every insignificant bit of gossip. Leave nothing out."

He told her. Shalár sent for chairs and settled in to question Irith closely and at length about his stay in Ghlanhras.

The governor was Othanin. Irith had ventured near Darkwood Hall one evening and glimpsed him setting forth. Shalár demanded every detail of his appearance, his kindred, their homes. She made Irith tell her everything he had heard or observed about Clan Sunriding, the governing clan of Fireshore, formed in haste from a mélange of households that had volunteered to re-populate and govern Fireshore after the Bitter Wars.

"Sunriding still has no uniform appearance. I saw Sunridings who resembled Ælvanen, Stonereaches, Steppegards—"

"Steppegards."

Shalár stroked her upper lip, musing. She looked up at Irith.

"Go on. What about the wall? Why did they build it?"

Irith helped himself to more wine. "To keep out the forest and its creatures. I heard no other reason mentioned."

"Not to keep out the kobalen?"

"I suppose so, but . . ." Irith frowned, looking perplexed. "They have a terror of the wild lands, particularly between Ghlanhras and the coast. It seems almost greater than their fear of kobalen. Few of them will venture into the deepest woods. The hunters I saw were the only exception."

"They do not visit the ocean, then?"

"They have cut a wide road from the city to the shore east of Firethroat. That is the only way they will take to the ocean."

"They fear the forest."

Shalár frowned, pondering why. She remembered her own family's flight into that same forest centuries before. Ancient fear welled up within her, not of the woodlands but of the ælven warriors who had turned their wrath upon her people. She shook it away.

When she had exhausted Irith's knowledge of Fireshore, she turned to his hunters and questioned them about everything they had observed while waiting for him in the forest. At last she relented, bidding them all to return to their homes, but she stayed Irith with a hand on his arm.

"When you are rested, write down all you have told me and anything else you remember."

He looked mildly surprised but bowed. "As you will, Bright Lady. Do I then return to Fireshore?"

"Not yet."

She watched him go, then strode to the gallery to look out over Nightsand. Cold air smote her, moist and sharp, stinging her face. The night was aging, but she had one task yet to accomplish before retiring.

Dareth joined her. She glanced at him, then took his hand and stepped out onto the gallery, letting the drape fall behind them, shutting them off from the warmth of the Cliff Hollows. He stroked her hair.

"What are you thinking?"

"How best to use the tools that come to hand."

She watched the wind trouble the dark waters of the bay for a moment, then turned to look at Dareth. He was gazing at her, his face unreadable.

"Am I one of your tools?"

She caught him to her, kissed him fiercely. "No. Never think that."

He made no answer. She searched his face, kissed him once more, then pulled open the drape and led him inside.

"I have an errand in the pens. I will not be long."

She left him and hastened to the pens, not bothering to fetch her cloak. If she returned chilled, Dareth could warm her.

It had been some days since she had last seen the Steppegard and hence some days since he had fed, but she approached the door of his chamber with caution. He was on his feet and pacing, strength palpable in his khi even at a distance. He had taken advantage of the washing water she had sent, and looked in far better health save for the raging hunger she could see in his taut face. He caught sight of her and came to the door, lacing his fingers in the grating.

"Bright Lady. Give me my freedom."

His eyes shone darkly in the eternal night of the pens. Shalár tilted her head, watching him.

"What would that gain me?"

His hands tightened into fists around the grating. "I swear I will serve you, only let me free."

"Serve me? You would run the moment you were freed."

She took a step closer, observing his agitated state. He watched her with restless eyes.

"And where would you run? Across the Ebons, of course. But back to the Steppes? I think not." She smiled and paced a few steps to one side, aware of his gaze following her. "Not for long. Certainly not once your hair whitens, which it will within a year, by the way."

His glance shifted to his hair, which looked cleaner now, tumbling in curls to his shoulders, almost as wild as when she had first seen him. When he looked back at her, his intensity was diminished, replaced by confusion.

"What service can I perform for you? I will gladly earn my freedom."

Shalár resumed her leisurely pacing, her steps echoing softly down rock passages. It might do. She would not even mind losing control of him, as she certainly would, if she sent him all the way to Glenhallow.

Her plan was coalescing. She smiled and glanced back at the Steppegard.

"I will think on that and return when I am ready to discuss it with you. You may pass the time considering how to assure me that freeing you will be worth my while."

✠

"Bright Lady, Irith is waiting in your audience chamber."

Shalár smiled at Galir. "Thank you. Has the catamount been fed as I ordered?"

"Yes, lady. It was given a freshly killed buck."

"Excellent." Shalár glanced at the closed door of her bedchamber. "Put out my leathers and pack my gear for hunting."

Galir blinked. "Yes, Bright Lady. I had not heard there was to be another hunt."

"It is not a pack hunt."

She turned away, thinking over all she had pondered during a lazy day in bed with Dareth. His strength was improving, as was his lust, but still there had been time for musing. She had tried to think of every possible flaw in her plan and had become more and more convinced that it could work. Therefore, she must not delay.

Dareth would be displeased. There was no help for it; she could only hope to return to him swiftly, before he again fell subject to gloom.

Hurrying to the audience chamber, she shivered at the evening's chill and sent an attendant scurrying for hot wine. Irith was waiting, looking city-clean instead of hunt-worn. He held a curl of paper in his hand and offered it as he bowed at her approach.

"Bright Lady. I have written everything I can recall."

"Excellent. Thank you."

She took the pages, uncoiled them, and glanced through them, nodding. Irith had been thorough. It was a quality of his she liked.

The attendant returned with a tray bearing a steaming pitcher and two cups, which she placed on the table that had been brought in the previous night. Shalár took a cup of hot spiced wine and handed her Irith's pages.

"Have a fair copy made of this at once."

"Yes, Bright Lady."

Shalár took a chair at the table, inviting Irith to join her. "Did you visit any other towns in Fireshore? I failed to ask you before."

"No. We made straight for Ghlanhras, and afterward I thought you would want our news as swiftly as possible."

"You thought aright. Well done." Shalár took a swallow of the spiced wine, feeling it warm her all the way down her chest. "I hope you rested well yesterday."

"I did, my lady." He glanced up at her over his cup, a smile twisting his mouth. "Do you mean that is all the rest I am to have?"

She set down her cup. "I need to know of Westgard and of Bitterfield. The sooner the better."

Irith nodded and reached for the pitcher, offering to fill her cup before pouring more wine into his own. Shalár pushed it toward him.

"Am I to start tonight, or may I have a night to prepare?"

"You may have a night. I will be occupied for the next few nights myself."

Irith again looked curious, but she saw no need to enlighten him. She gazed past him at the ælven tapestry on the wall.

Dareth entered the chamber. She felt him even as she heard his step and turned toward him, smiling.

"Dareth. Join us."

She saw unhappiness in his face before his tight smile replaced it. That he should burn so with jealousy pleased a small, greedy part of her, but her wiser self regretted it. She reached for his hand and pressed her cup into it as he took a chair beside her.

Irith tossed off the wine in his own cup, then set it down on the table with a sharp clack of pottery on wood. "By your leave, Bright Lady, I have much to do this night if I am to return to Fireshore."

Shalár nodded, dismissing him. He cast a glance at Dareth before departing.

She watched Dareth take a long draught of wine, then took the cup from him, drank what was left in it, and filled it once more. His face was closed, his khi withdrawn. She sipped the wine and handed it back to him, taking his free hand in hers. Even touching thus, she could not read his khi.

"I must leave you for a little while. A few nights only."

"Going to Fireshore?" His voice was low with bitterness.

"No. Irith goes to Fireshore. I go west. I will take the catamount into the mountains and release it."

She felt relief flood through his khi, suddenly open to her again. She squeezed his hand. He pushed the cup away and brought both her hands to his lips, kissing them passionately.

"Forgive me."

"Hush."

She leaned close, looking up at him until at last he met her gaze. She had more to tell him, and he would not like it, but delaying would make it no easier for either of them.

"I will do the same with the Steppegard."

Dareth frowned. "What?"

"Take him into the mountains and release him."

"Why?"

"I have found a use for him. I think he will do as I wish in return for his freedom. I am sending him to the Ælven Council."

Dareth stared at her in incomprehension. "What good can that do?"

"He is to convince them he comes from Fireshore. He will enjoy that. He is deceitful by nature."

Shalár smiled, remembering the Steppegard's sullenness whenever she had made him talk of Alpinon. Yes, she expected he would enjoy deceiving the Council.

"Why do you wish them to be deceived?"

"So they will leave Fireshore alone."

"Oh."

Dareth let go her hands. After a moment he reached for the wine. Shalár watched him, breathed his khi. No longer jealous, but sad again. So sad.

"I will return as swiftly as I can to you."

"And then you will leave for Fireshore."

"Not for a while yet."

She felt him drawing away again, closing his heart. She dared not let him. Standing up, she pulled his hands.

"Come into the workroom."

Dareth looked up at her. She wanted him, needed him now. She wanted to reclaim him. She leaned forward and kissed him, ignoring the sound of a step from the corridor: the startled, muffled gasp of an attendant. She leaned her knee on Dareth's thigh and deepened the kiss. Not until he warmed to her did she pause to raise her head.

The attendant stood frozen, staring, dismayed. In her hands were two scrolls of paper.

"Thank you. Leave them on the table."

"Yes, Bright Lady." The attendant scurried forward, dropped the papers on the table, caught one as it started to roll away and replaced it, then fled.

Shalár turned back to Dareth. She leaned her forehead against his, feeling a hot wave of lust.

"Come into the workroom, my love."

His eyes reflected her desire as he slowly smiled. "Yes, Bright Lady."

⊹

Shalár stood outside the Steppegard's chamber, holding her chalice. It contained but a scant mouthful of food, all she dared give him, and that only to calm his hunger, which pounded at her even at this distance.

She herself was sated. She had drained a kobalen after sending a pitcher of its blood to the Cliff Hollows for Dareth and reserving this little for her captive. Strength flowed through her, and she knew she would need all of it this night.

The Steppegard appeared at the door to his chamber, drawn by the smell of the blood. Shalár brought it closer, saw him swallow.

"Yield to me and you shall have it."

He looked up in confusion, then stepped back. She reached out with her khi, slowly surrounding him, feeling the bright tang of his own khi, still foreign, still ælven.

"Yield."

She tightened her hold, demanding control of his flesh. His sharp glance told her he understood, but he did not yield at once. She pressed more strongly. The Steppegard shuddered, then closed his eyes. A moment later his resistance melted away.

"Good."

Shalár stepped to the door, unlocked it, and pushed it open. The Steppegard's hunger drove him to try for the chalice, but she kept him still, noting his surprise.

He submitted to being turned, having his hands brought behind him. Shalár set aside the chalice and bound his hands, then retrieved the cup and made him face her. His gaze stayed on the chalice.

She held it to his lips and slowly tipped it up. He drank greedily and uttered a grunt of protest when she moved to withdraw the empty cup. She tipped it again and let him lick as much as he could reach.

New strength coursed through his khi, and as she expected, he tried to break her hold. She kept it and bore down on him with increasing pressure as a warning not to try again. He winced but did not cry out.

Relenting, she turned from him and walked out of the chamber. He stood silent, watching her.

"Come."

She nudged him with khi. He took a startled step forward, then slowly emerged. She made him precede her down the corridor.

"Where are you taking me?"

"Away from here. Is that not enough?"

He asked no more questions, made no trouble as she paused to return her chalice and the keys to Nihlan's keeping. She caught the keeper's eye.

"Send fresh food to my steward every night."

"Yes, Bright Lady."

Shalár urged the Steppegard forward again, up the long sloping corridor to the cliff. As they emerged, he saw the sleeping catamount and recoiled.

"Be still."

She picked up her pack and slung it over her shoulders, then woke the catamount. It grumbled and yawned, stretching. The Steppegard drew back. Shalár mounted the cat, settled her pack more comfortably, then beckoned to her captive.

"Join me."

His eyes widened with fear. Shalár gave him an impatient nudge of khi, and he winced, then mounted the cat behind her, gingerly reaching a leg over its back. She had to steady him and considered unbinding his hands but decided to wait until they had left Nightsand. The city offered too many temptations for a daring captive. Though she had him in control, she did not want a struggle with him.

He was trembling, she realized. She laid a hand on his thigh to calm him.

"The cat will not harm you so long as I control it. I suggest that you not distract me from that task."

He nodded, and though his breathing remained quick, he seemed to relax somewhat. Shalár made the catamount start along the cliff toward the Hollows and the trail down to Nightsand. Its muscles rolled sinuously beneath her, and it growled a low protest at the weight of its burden. The Steppegard smelled of fear, and she knew the cat sensed it. Perhaps she should have made him unconscious and slung him over the animal's back, but it was too late now.

Her folk shrank from the catamount as it prowled through the streets to the shore. Shalár took the road through the canyon and left it when they emerged onto the high plains, striking westward toward the Ebons. Now she made the cat run, instructing the Steppegard to lean against her. He kept his balance, gripping the cat with his legs. The animal growled, scenting its home on the breeze.

Carrying two, the catamount tired quickly, and she had to let it walk from time to time. She did not wish to kill the beast, but she did not mind exhausting it, so she made it run as much as it could. By the time the sky was lightening, they had reached the foothills of the Ebons.

Shalár took them deep into a thick wood that spilled between two hills. A stream trickled among boulders that long ago had tumbled down the hillsides. Halting the catamount, she made the Steppegard get down first and sit beneath a tree. She felt fatigue tremble through his limbs and was careful in her own dismounting.

She unstrapped her pack from the cat, took out a wooden cup, and went to fill it from the stream, letting the cat drink a little farther down the slope. She drained the cup twice, then filled it again and carried it to the Steppegard.

Above the filter of the forest canopy the sky was growing light. Shalár glanced up at the spreading limbs of pine and decided they would be shelter enough. She stopped before her captive and stood regarding him.

He had his eyes closed, his head leaned back against the tree. She doubted he was comfortable, but he seemed resigned. He had neither protested nor attempted to escape during the long ride through the night.

"Drink."

She held the cup to his lips. He opened his eyes and complied, spilling a little of the water as he gulped it. Shalár set the empty cup down and took out her knife of ebonglass. The Steppegard's eyes flashed sudden fear.

"Sit forward."

She stepped behind him and cut the thong that tied his hands. He gave a small gasp of relief and leaned back again, rubbing his wrists.

"Thank you."

"You are not yet free."

He glanced up at her, then sighed. When she trusted he would not immediately attempt escape, she sat down against another tree a little distance away.

"May I have some more water?"

"There is the cup."

Shalár waved her knife toward it. The Steppegard slowly got to his feet and picked it up. She watched him go to the stream, drink his fill, then set the cup aside and splash water on his face.

She could feel his hunger, a dull pulse in his khi. She cast a searching thought through the woodlands, past the sheltering hills and down the plain, but sensed no prey. He stood up, weariness seeming to inform his every movement. For a moment he was still, then he took a step away, downstream.

Shalár frowned. The catamount uttered a low growl.
"You are not yet free."

He turned, gazed at her in a measuring way, then
bent to retrieve the cup and fill it again. He brought it
to her, crouching before her and offering the cup.

"Thank you." She took a sip and set it aside. "Make
yourself comfortable. We will rest here until nightfall."

He settled himself, sitting before her with ankles
crossed and his arms around his knees. "Where are we
going?"

"Across the Ebons."

His surprise was satisfactory. She could sense his
confusion as he pondered her motives. Also his confidence, which was returning swiftly. A struggle was
coming, one she would not relish. She narrowed her
eyes.

"I did not bring you here to slay you, but I will not
hesitate to do so."

"That would be wasteful, would it not?"

Shalár smiled slightly. "Indeed."

She studied him, noting the sinewy strength of his
limbs, gone just a little soft with inactivity. His hair as
yet showed no sign of whitening, which was fortu-
nate. He watched her with a hunter's patience.

"How am I to earn my freedom?"

Shalár's smile widened. She reached into her pack.

"You may begin by committing this to memory."

He caught the scroll she tossed at him, the copy of
Irith's recollections of Fireshore. With a questioning
glance at her, he unrolled it and began to read. A frown
grew on his brow, and he looked at her once more.

She nodded. "Learn every detail. Your life will de-
pend on it."

"You intend to administer an examination? It is a
severe tutor who slays her student for failure."

Shalár chuckled at his ironic tone. "I will leave the examination to others."

She pushed her pack behind her and settled herself more comfortably against the tree, then slid her knife into its sheath. Aware of his sudden attention, she brought the sheathed weapon to lie on her lap, a hand on its hilt. He went back to studying Irith's notes, and Shalár watched him lazily, waiting for the day to pass.

By late afternoon she had lost count of the times he had been through the pages, and the paper had begun to wear. So had the Steppegard's patience. He rolled the pages together and dropped them.

"I am hungry. May I hunt something for us to share?"

"There are no kobalen nearby."

"I did not mean kobalen."

Shalár raised an eyebrow. "You will find other foods less than satisfying. Do you not remember how you were sickened in the pens?"

He looked momentarily distressed, then shook it away with a frown. "But, fresh blood . . ."

Shalár shrugged. "You are welcome to try."

He looked toward the stream, his gaze unfocused as he searched the woodland's khi for prey. He stood up, glancing toward her. She let him feel her command of him, then allowed him to move away across the stream, toward some small creature hiding in the underbrush.

His prey, a rabbit, started as he drew near and bounded away through a patch of sunlight. Shalár sat upright, about to warn him, then decided against it. This was a lesson he must learn beyond forgetting, the sooner the better.

The Steppegard ran after the rabbit, straight into the sun. He cried out as the light struck him, and stumbled. Shalár winced in sympathy, for each instant it took him to escape the sunlight would cost him. Not as badly now, perhaps, as it eventually would, but badly enough so that he would not repeat the mistake.

He tumbled to his knees just beyond the sunlight and stayed, gasping, for a short while. Shalár felt pain ripple through his khi. She was sorry for that but knew it would convince him where her words of warning might not.

Slowly, unsteadily, he stood. Instead of returning as she'd expected, he moved on, following his prey. Shalár silently admitted grudging admiration as he stalked and caught the rabbit despite the agony of sun poisoning.

Determined, this one. Strong-willed. She must be very careful.

He returned, feet dragging, the lifeless rabbit dangling from one hand. He offered it to her.

She shook her head and watched while he dropped to his knees beside the stream and tore into the rabbit's flesh until he found blood. He sucked hungrily for a while, then raised his head.

His glance told her he knew she was right, and resented it. It also revealed his suffering. Shalár decided the lesson had been effective.

She stood and walked over to him, took the rabbit from his hands, and tossed it to the catamount. He made no protest, though he grimaced when she put a hand under his elbow to help him stand.

"Sunlight is poison to you now. Henceforth you are a night-bider."

She led him to the shadiest tree at hand and helped him sit beneath it. He muttered bitterly to himself.

"Why?"

"Why? Because fate is unkind."

Shalár knelt to search her pack for a small pot of balmleaf ointment she had brought against this need. She sat beside the Steppegard and gently spread the balm on his reddened face, throat, and hands where he had been touched by the sun. He winced but made no sound. When she had finished, she put away the ointment and took out a phial of powdered willow bark, then stirred some into the cup of water and made the Steppegard drink it.

He leaned against the tree and closed his eyes, breathing in short, sharp gulps. She watched him until he began to relax, then stood up to stretch her limbs.

He would need to rest for what remained of the day if he was to endure another night of travel. She hoped he would not need more than that. It was well that this had happened today, for the Steppegard must show no sign of sun poisoning when he arrived in Southfæld.

Shalár glanced toward the pool of sunlight that had hurt him, its beams slanting between trees, sparking motes of dust in the shadows. What creator would make such a deadly thing so pretty? What guardian spirit would suffer a race in its charge to be hurt so cruelly by a force that so filled the world?

She paced along the stream down to where the catamount lay idly chewing on the rabbit's remains. A glance at her captive told her the willow bark had brought him some ease.

Why? he had asked. Why, indeed? Clan Darkshore had pondered that question for many centuries. She doubted they would ever find an answer.

✤ Hallowhall ✤

Two days before the Council was to convene was the Feast of Crossed Spirits. Glenhallow was filled with quiet celebration, the day being given by custom to the remembrance of loved ones who had crossed the gray veil into spirit. Lord Jharan presided over a vast gathering in the public circle and asked Felisan to accompany him in the ceremony of greeting the ældar. Eliani had never seen so many people assembled together, most of them Greenglens. She found the sea of fair-haired folk unnerving, and escaped as soon as she could to pursue her private meditations.

She thought of her mother, as always. She spent much of the day in the fountain court, for she thought Belani would have liked that place. A wistful hope of hearing her mother's counsel clung to her, but the whispering water offered no insight.

In the evening, Jharan hosted a formal feast of welcome for the Council delegations. Hallowhall's feast hall was filled with long tables and made bright with candlelight and torchlight. Minstrels played softly from the high gallery, but all these comforts could not change the undertone of apprehension among the company. The talk turned ever and again to the possibility of war.

Eliani wore her best gown and her veil, bound with

a violet ribbon and caught at the shoulder with the
brooch given her by House Jharanin. She had neglected
to bring her new circlet, an omission for which she
had apologized profusely to her father. Felisan had
merely laughed and said she would be well served if
asked to care for the visitors' horses, but Eliani, feeling the need to atone, resolved to take note of all those
wearing circlets of state at the feast.

She looked to the head table, where Turisan sat
with his father and numerous Southfæld dignitaries.
He wore silver-woven robes and a large silver coronet
signifying his rank as governor-elect, and seemed to
her once again as one who dwelt in a realm far above
her.

Five other Greenglens besides Turisan and Jharan
wore circlets. Two Steppegards wore them over wildly
curling hair: a tall, stern-faced lady whom Felisan iden-
tified as Governor Pashani and a lord so like to her that
he must be her close kin, both in tunics of russet and
pine, elaborately embroidered.

Felisan wore a circlet of bronze set with crystals
from Clerestone. Heléri might have worn one as a former governor of Alpinon, but had chosen not to.

Several of the Ælvanen from Eastfæld wore multiple
interwoven bands of gold, including Lady Rheneri,
the governor's sister. She was present to represent her
brother at the Council, and to Eliani she seemed very
beautiful, tall and slender with dark hair spilling almost to the floor from beneath her circlet.

Nowhere in the hall did Eliani see the gray and orange of Clan Sunriding, governors of Fireshore. She
leaned toward her eldermother.

"Who is that Ælvanen lord who stares at us so?"

She nodded toward a tall black-haired lord whose
circlet was different from those of the other East-
fælders. It was of plain silver and bore at the brow a

small white stone. His robe was of white also, though golden threads glinted in its weave.

"That is Lord Rephanin. He is master of South-fæld's magehall."

"I had thought Lord Rephanin was a Greenglen."

"No. He came here from Eastfæld long ago."

Something in Heléri's tone made Eliani look at her, but she could read nothing unusual in her face. "Did you know him there?"

Heléri met her gaze, then slowly smiled. "Yes. We both studied magecraft at Hollirued."

Eliani nodded understanding, looking back at the magelord. "He seems rather stern."

Heléri made no answer, sipping her wine instead. Eliani saw Lord Rephanin start across the hall toward them and straightened in her chair, made nervous by the intensity of his gaze, which moved from Heléri to herself as he approached.

Her father rose from his chair. "Rephanin! How good to see you again after so many years."

"It is a pleasure to welcome you back to Glenhallow, Lord Felisan."

Rephanin's voice was deep and quiet, his eyes gray and penetrating. His glance fell on Heléri, and he bowed.

"Lady Heléri. I believe you have not visited the city before."

"No, she has not. Nor has my daughter, Lady Eliani." Felisan gestured toward Eliani.

The gray eyes turned to her, and Rephanin bowed again, then continued to gaze at her for a long moment, making her feel she was being studied. He tilted his head slightly.

"Has the Lady Eliani any interest in magecraft?"

Felisan laughed. "Not since she was a child listening to cradle tales. She would rather be hunting kobalen."

Feeling her cheeks prickle with color, Eliani answered Lord Rephanin. "I have not the aptitude, I fear."

"Nor the patience."

Heléri spoke over Felisan's chuckling. "Lady Eliani has been much occupied of late with service in Alpinon's Guard."

Lord Rephanin's gaze shifted to her, and one eyebrow rose slightly. Eliani wondered if he was speaking to Heléri in thought. She knew that was supposed to be his skill, and the idea that he might even speak to herself suddenly made Eliani uncomfortable. She gestured toward Luruthin beside her.

"My cousin Luruthin is also in our Guard and is theyn of Clerestone as well."

Lord Rephanin nodded greeting to Luruthin, gazing at him briefly before returning his attention to Heléri. "Welcome to you all. The Council will be enhanced by your presence."

He bowed, then moved away toward the head table. Beyond him Eliani saw Turisan watching, but his attention was called away from her gaze.

⊹

Turisan was at last able to slip away, though many of the guests remained talking in the hall long after the feast had concluded. He changed his robes for a comfortable tunic and legs, and went out in silver moonlight down to the fountain courtyard, carrying his lute with him.

Thoughts of his earlier conversation with Eliani followed him through the stone pathways, accompanied by the myriad voices of the fountains. This night they sounded mournful—his imagination, perhaps, inspired by the celebration of Crossed Spirits. He had lit candles for his mother and other loved ones now in spirit, but had found no peace.

He passed through the Whispering Walk and into

the wooded avenue beyond. Sitting on the low parapet that flanked the pathway, he rested his back against the courtyard wall. Its stones still yielded a shadow of warmth from the day's sun.

He settled the lute on his lap and lightly fingered a tune. The structure of the music pleased him, a fluid thing but with finite dimensions, easy to control in its defined complexity. No master musician, he played for pleasure and had little leisure for that, but his skill was sufficient to the demands of the piece.

It was an old ballad, a story of gallantry and reward, though he did not know the lyric. More important to him was its mood of quiet satisfaction, which made the muted sound of fountains behind him seem less sad. He played the song twice through, lingering on the final chords even as he became aware that he was not alone. A change in the khi of the garden set his pulse speeding.

Looking up, he saw Eliani standing nearby, watching him from just within the Whispering Walk. His heart gave a sharp thump as she stepped forward, her face dappled in tree shadows.

"Beautiful music, my lord."

"Thank you."

He set the lute down, leaning it in the corner where the parapet that was his seat met the courtyard's wall. Her presence set his nerves afire, and he had to restrain himself from standing and catching her in his arms.

She moved away from the Whispering Walk, and her khi sharpened in his awareness. He watched her, drinking in every small movement. A fleeting smile crossed her lips.

"That ballad is a favorite of my father's."

"Do you play?"

"A little. Not on the lute."

"We must play together sometime. If you did not bring an instrument—"

"I brought one. A flute."

Turisan fell silent. Her tone did not suggest eagerness to play music together.

Eliani crossed to the parapet and looked out over the orchards. He watched her for a few moments, then spoke.

"I am glad you chose to attend the Council."

"I understand Fireshore has sent no delegation."

"They may be on their way."

"We have kin there—Davhri, my father's sister. We have not heard from her in some years."

Turisan shifted on the stone wall. "My father has sent an armed party northward with a second message for Governor Othanin."

"That is well." Her gaze wandered the orchard as if seeking a friend or a memory. "I fear we may face war, and not just with kobalen."

Turisan let out a long breath. He thought she was right, and he wished to talk of something else. The words that came to mind—that she was beautiful in the shadowed night—seemed inappropriate. He contented himself with watching her, enjoying the lines of her throat and face, the drape of her cloak across her hip as she leaned against the half wall.

"Your trees still have their leaves."

"We are not as high here as in your mountain woods."

"Yet I feel winter's bite in the air. Or is it always so cool here at night?" She turned to look at him, eyes glinting in the starlight.

"It cools, but you are right that winter is in the air."

"Davhri wrote to me once that in Fireshore the heat may not let up for days and nights on end."

"You have never been there?"

"No. Have you?"

"No." Turisan rose and came to stand beside her,

gazing out over the orchard, savoring the hum of her khi in the air. "My visit to Highstone was the farthest north I have been. I liked Alpinon very well, perhaps because it is similar in many ways to this land."

"Well, you are welcome to visit whenever you please."

She had said something like that before. Turisan gazed at her, trying to read her face.

"Do you mean that you prefer me to remain a visitor? Is this a gentle way of refusing me?"

She glanced up, looking startled. "No, I—I have not decided."

Her manner implied that she did not wish to discuss it, but at least she denied a refusal. Turisan nodded and gazed at the trees, satisfied for the moment.

Into the uncomfortable silence Eliani spoke, her voice softer. "You must understand . . . I am very bad at such things. I only cup-bonded once, and it was disastrous."

"You have cup-bonded? I never dared to." Her look of surprise made him smile. "It would have raised hopes I had no intention of fulfilling, so I avoided it."

Eliani tilted her head. "Do you mean me to believe that of all the beautiful ladies in your father's court, none ever caught your fancy?"

"Many caught my fancy. None my heart."

She gave a wistful smile. "Not even for a year and a day?"

"Not until now." He stepped nearer. "If you would prefer a cup-bond—"

"No." She shook her head, her smile fading. "I will not cup-bond again."

He nodded understanding, pleased that she did not retreat from him. He was close enough to feel her warmth, taste a hint of her scent, hear her breath. Her khi shone in the air, tickling his awareness, making him yearn to touch her. She met his gaze, watching him with eyes large and seeming unafraid.

Slowly, gently, he bent to kiss her. His lips brushed hers, soft and sweet, then, as he sensed her welcome, again and more deeply. His heart thrilled as he closed his eyes, drinking in her scent, her taste, touch—emotion.

She wrenched away from the contact. Turisan winced at his error.

"Forgive me. I meant not to do that."

She let out a rough sigh, and after a moment spoke in a shaken voice. "I doubt you could help it."

He retreated to the wall, sitting down again and staring out at the trees, angry with himself. He heard her step past him and thought she had left, but a moment later she laid her hands on his shoulders from behind.

It startled him, but he kept still. She began to rub at the tension in his muscles, hands warm through the cloth of his tunic, her khi lightly meeting his. He closed his eyes, reveling in the pleasure of even this limited contact.

"It is not you, Turisan." Her voice was soft, almost a whisper. "I have been alone for a long while. I expected to remain alone. I took up the sword . . ."

He reached a hand over his shoulder to clasp her forearm through her sleeve. She permitted it, but he knew it would do him no good to reach for her in that way. He let go instead and turned to face her.

"Let me then speak to you as a fellow guardian. We are close to war, as you say, and will soon be called upon to serve our people. We will have need of every weapon within reach, every tool, every advantage. My lady—"

He checked himself, choosing his words carefully,

keeping his voice level. "I will accept any limits you impose, but I pray you, do not set aside this gift. Not now. Our people will need it."

She looked away, her face troubled. She took a step toward the wall, then restlessly to one side.

"I cannot talk of this now." Abruptly she turned and hastened through the archway into the Whispering Walk.

Well, Turisan thought, there is no more to say. I have laid all before her, and she must choose.

He picked up his lute and, laying it across his lap, caressed the silent strings. He had no heart for music now, and the fountains had returned to mourning.

⁂

The Ælven Council convened just after sunset on the first day of winter. The day had been occupied with more ceremonies and festivities, this time in honor of the season. Eliani was weary of formality by the time she and her kindred entered the council chamber.

Like the other public rooms at Hallowhall, this one was circular, though considerably smaller than the great hall. Hangings of Greenglen colors on its curving walls muted the voices of the councillors. The table was surrounded with dignitaries from all the ælven realms but one. Fireshore still had not arrived.

An attendant offered water with the golden petals of some flower floating in it, in tall cups of leaf-thin pottery that glowed with translucence in the torchlight. Accepting one with thanks, Eliani glanced toward where Turisan stood conversing with Eastfæld's councillor, Lady Rheneri.

As if he sensed her gaze, Turisan looked up at her. Eliani felt a small shock at the meeting of their eyes. She was intently, almost intolerably aware of him, had been since she had entered the chamber. It was as though her khi came afire in his presence. She looked away, sorry for having yet left him unanswered, but there was no mending that now.

When all the councillors had arrived, Jharan raised a hand in signal, and a deep chime sounded through the chamber. At its tone the voices stilled.

"My friends and kindred, welcome. I thank you for your attendance. We have matters of grave importance to discuss. Let us begin with the summoning."

Glenhallow's court herald stepped forward and announced Lord Jharan, Turisan, and Lord Berephan, warden of Southfæld's Guard. The Eastfæld herald then came forward, naming Lady Rheneri and several of her kindred who attended her. In her company was Lord Ehranan, who had been commander of Eastfæld's forces in the Midrange War. With no border touching the Ebon Mountains, Eastfæld was the only ælven realm that did not keep a standing guard, though Eliani had heard rumor that they had summoned their reserve forces to arms.

The delegation from the Steppe Wilds was summoned next, headed by the governor and her companion, who proved to be her son, Lord Parishan. Eliani looked away from his curling bronze hair, reminded too strongly of Kelevon.

Had representatives from Fireshore been present, they would have been summoned last, as theirs was the newest ælven realm. Instead, Alpinon was the last party to claim its place. They had brought no herald, so Felisan, Eliani, Heléri, and Luruthin were announced in decorous tones by Southfæld's herald. As they took their places at the curving table, the chime sounded again, and Lord Jharan bade the Council be seated.

"You all know our reasons for meeting. We have much to discuss; therefore, I will lose no time in raising what appears to be the most pressing of several urgent concerns. The western borders of Alpinon and Southfæld are threatened with war. We owe thanks to Lady Eliani of Felisanin for alerting us to the immediate danger of kobalen gathering west of Midrange Pass."

Eliani glanced down at the table before her, feeling she deserved no thanks. She sensed her cheeks beginning to color and reached for her water cup as Jharan spoke again.

"Lady Eliani, if you would, please describe what you saw at Midrange."

Governor Pashani stood up. "All honor to you, Lord Jharan, and to you, Lady Eliani, but should we not postpone until Fireshore can join the Council?"

"Every effort has been made to contact Fireshore. I have sent an armed party to them with a second summons. Until they return either with tidings or as escort to Fireshore's delegation, we must move forward."

Pashani glowered but resumed her seat. Lord Ehranan, the most experienced warrior in the room, leaned forward. He wore his black hair pulled back from his face in a hunter's braid, and his features looked stark above a pale gold tunic.

"Fireshore is far away. Assuming they have not yet sent out a delegation, by the time your envoy returns, we may already be at war."

An uncomfortable silence filled the chamber. Eliani gazed at her hands clasped before her on the table, her sense of dread increasing. A shadow approached— inexorable, inevitable. She glanced at Heléri, then at Turisan. Both were watching Ehranan.

Lady Rheneri turned to Jharan. "How long will it take the envoy to reach Fireshore?"

"Riding hard, thirty days at best."

"And as long again to return." Ehranan frowned. "Sixty days at the least before we have news. Past Midwinter."

Eliani thought of the swiftness with which kobalen raids could destroy whole villages and imagined the havoc the horde she had seen could wreak. What if a similar horde was already at work in Fireshore? If it was, and the news took the better part of a season to reach Glenhallow, what hope would there be of sending aid? Yet if aid was sent now and no threat existed, Southfæld's defenses would be weakened needlessly.

She had meant to hold silent in council, but the possible cost was too great. She knew she could not bear another burden of remorse such as that which had assailed her at Midrange Pass. Drawing a faltering breath, she spoke.

"We can have word in thirty days."

All eyes turned toward her, and she was struck with sudden awkwardness. She swallowed.

"I can ride to Fireshore and send back news . . ."

Courage failing, she looked to Turisan. He stood up swiftly, dark eyes blazing. Strangely, that calmed her rather than frightened her. The fire in his eyes was exhilaration. It burned for her.

He held her gaze, questioning, waiting. She gave a tiny nod, and Turisan's glance swept the room.

"Lady Eliani and I share mindspeech."

A burst of exclamation followed even as Eliani breathed a rough sigh. It was done. It was revealed. Her choice was made.

Jharan rose again, this time to demand quiet from the councillors. He directed a hard look at Turisan.

"You have not seen fit to mention this before?"

"We only recently discovered it."

Eliani watched Turisan stand firm before his father's frowning gaze, feeling more than willing to leave explanations to him. Coward yet again, she thought, and looked down at her hands. She realized she was clenching them together quite tightly, and tried to relax them.

"Have you tested it?" Jharan sounded half-angry, half-eager. "Can you speak across distance?"

"We do not know."

Eliani looked up, saw Turisan's slight smile as he glanced at her, and tried to smile back though her heart seemed to have sunk into her belly.

Lord Jharan turned his gaze on her, dark and intense, seeming to weigh her. He looked from her to Turisan.

"Well, we shall test it now. Lord Turisan, prepare yourself for riding. Skyruach should be far enough."

"My Lord Jharan." Heléri, who hitherto had been silent, stood. "Had not this test better be postponed until morning? If he is to ride, the horse will go faster and farther in daylight."

The governor's gaze flicked to her. His frown deepened slightly, but he nodded. "You are right, my lady. Turisan, you will ride at dawn." He glanced around the council table. "I need one to ride with him."

One breath passed, then Luruthin stood. "I will go."

Eliani turned her head to look at Luruthin and saw the hint of protectiveness in his gaze. She smiled, not so much from approval as from a knowledge that his instinct was futile. He could not preserve her, and at once she knew she needed no protection. Turisan would not harm her. She might yet manage to harm herself, but that would have to be risked.

The councillors had begun to murmur. Jharan silenced them, raising his hands.

"Gentles, in light of this news, I suggest we adjourn until morning. I will remain here to discuss Midrange with any who wish, though we shall make no decisions tonight."

The chime sounded, and the room filled at once with excited voices. Turisan, still standing, was surrounded instantly by Ælvanens and Greenglens. Only Rephanin remained seated, and even he was staring intently at Turisan.

Eliani was thankful that her kindred were around her, for she saw that the councillors nearby would have trapped her otherwise. Indeed, they called questions to her even as Heléri and Felisan swept her from the chamber with Luruthin close behind.

They hastened up the stairs and along the arcade to their suite, past the silvery whisper of the fountains below, into the privacy of Felisan's chamber. There her father caught Eliani by the shoulders, beaming with pride.

"My child! This is wondrous news!"

Eliani felt anything but wondrous. She hung her head. "Forgive me for not telling you at once."

"No matter, no matter."

Gently he took her chin in his hand, raising it. He was smiling with delight, though a slight frown dampened his joy as Eliani met his gaze.

"Does it trouble you, my daughter?"

Eliani opened her mouth, seeking words of explanation. Heléri spoke before she could form them.

"It changes everything. Imagine how much stronger it will make your alliance with Southfæld, how much more effective your defenses will be if you can communicate with Jharan from Highstone in the blink of an eye."

Eliani glanced at Heléri, wondering if her elder-mother meant merely to distract Felisan or sought to reassure her that she need not be near Turisan to use the gift. Indeed, it would be most effective if they remained apart.

That was no comfort. Whatever distance separated them, she knew that to touch in thought would bring them closer than she wished. She had, by revealing their gift, made that inevitable.

"Eliani." Her father's hands were warm upon her shoulders; his face, when she looked up to him, filled with tender concern. "Your kindred will always be here for you. You are safe, my child. And Turisan is as good as kin; he will protect you."

She shook her head, helpless to explain her fears. Her kin could not protect her from this. She was near to falling, or perhaps she already had fallen when she had let Turisan kiss her. Remembering it sent a shiver through her. She wanted him, and dreaded his touch.

Curunan took a decanter and a tray of goblets off a shelf and set them on the table. "That meeting was short. Are they all like that?"

Felisan chuckled, turning to him. "Well, Councils never accomplish much at their first sessions, but I believe this was the least effective I have seen. Scarcely begun before adjourned."

Heléri shook her head. "I disagree. Eliani and Turisan have made tonight's session one of the most important ever held."

Eliani stared at the fire, making no answer. She wished she were in Alpinon, on patrol, shivering in the snow, perhaps, but free of the terrible pressure she now felt.

⌖ The Ebon Mountains ⌖

Shalár paused to scramble on top of a high rock and look down the eastern slope of the mountain they had scaled. She had not been east of the Ebons since her people had been driven out of Fireshore. She could see the tree line, blessedly close, and far below a wisp of smoke rising from the woods.

She tensed at the sight, suddenly feeling dangerously exposed, and instinctively crouched against the rock. She knew of no ælven village so close to this crossing, though her watchers had told her of one a day's journey to the north.

A guard outpost? Travelers? The smoke was near the mountain road, she could see by the small gap in the trees. She frowned. She would have to go carefully.

"Please." The Steppegard leaned against a snow-strewn boulder. "Please, may we rest awhile?"

"We must get to the woods before dawn. It is not far."

She glanced at him, saw the shortness of his breaths, each puffing ice into the night. He was becoming a little too weak for her liking. She jumped down from the rock, landing softly in snow, and went to him. Taking hold of his arm, she sent a flow of warming khi through him.

"Come. When we reach the forest, you may rest."

He gazed at her, golden eyes pale in the twilight, surprise at her sharing khi with him writ on his face. Gently she urged him forward, and he complied.

They crossed a sloping snow-deep meadow, with occasional boulders thrusting up through the whiteness. Shalár regretted the marks their descent would leave, but there was little choice. By the time the ælven below took any notice, if they took notice, she hoped she would be far away.

She took the lead, easing the Steppegard's passage by breaking a path through the snow. The catamount snarled in anger as it followed them, so insane by this time that it no longer feared her at all. Only her hold on its khi kept it from attacking them.

She heard a surprised grunt from the Steppegard, turned to see him stumble to his knees in the snow. The catamount growled, and Shalár tightened her hold on it while she helped him to his feet. He was cold, very cold. She spent a little more khi on him and urged him onward.

"Only a little farther. Do you see?"

She directed his weary gaze toward the dark line of pine trees a short way below. He stared stupidly, then nodded.

There was no stopping when they reached the trees, though, for the snow was still deep. Shalár pressed on down the slope between pines, hoping to find a sheltered place where they might rest for the day. She steered southward, away from the smoke that she now smelled in taunting wisps on the air. Wood smoke, a fire built up anew from latent coals. Roasting meat.

Shalár paused, thinking. What ælven would be camped on this road in winter? No party of pleasure, no traders. A patrol, perhaps. Or a courier.

She frowned, misliking the direction of her thoughts. Instinct warned her to learn more.

Turning, she saw the Steppegard swaying where he stood. He was spent and could go no farther on his own. She put him up on the catamount's back and started forward again, this time heading toward the camp instead of away from it.

Her hunger was now a dull ache that stabbed with every step. She cast a searching thought wide through the woods, but there were no kobalen near. Soon she would resort to the transitory satisfaction of feeding on deer or bear. The catamount's khi was now unwholesome, but even that might tempt her as a last resort.

As she neared the camp, she moved with greater stealth. When she could hear the voices of the ælven, she made the catamount stop beside a copse of bare-branched saplings, leaving it and the Steppegard there in concealment while she ventured forward.

Slowly, slowly now, each step with a hunter's caution. Press a foot down upon the snow, make no sound.

She was close enough now to distinguish what the ælven were saying. She stopped behind a thick-trunked pine, spreading her khi through it and through its neighbors, the better to hear those around the campfire.

"Will we reach Heahrued today?"

"Tomorrow, more like."

"And then another ten days to the Steppes. I will be glad to be out of this snow."

Shalár thought the lilt of the male's voice had a hint of Southfæld in it, or perhaps Eastfæld. She closed her eyes, frowning in concentration.

"Nine days if we press, and we should." Another voice, male, a little lower than the first. "Remember, we must travel with all possible speed."

"Perhaps we can get fresh horses in the Steppes. That would speed us."

Horses! Shalár chided herself for a fool. She must be wearier than she had thought, not to notice.

She extended her khi through the woodlands, careful not to touch the ælven's khi lest she alert them to her presence. A short distance away she sensed where their horses—seven, all told—were grazing.

She made herself attend to the ælven's conversation. They were not a patrol, not if speed was important to them.

The woods were filled with a dim blue light that set a ghostly glow to the snowdrifts and woke shadows beneath the pines. Day was coming. She should leave here and seek shelter. She moved forward.

A glimpse of movement startled her into shrinking against a tree. She had seen a pale-haired, silver-cloaked form between the trees. The crackle of the campfire reached her ears, reminding her of how chilled she was.

"If we can get horses at Waymeet, then yes, but we must not go afield in search of them. Jharan stressed that we should reach Fireshore as soon as we possibly can."

Jharan! They were from Southfæld's governor. Shalár drew a sharp breath.

How could she take them? There were seven of them, and she was so weary with the Steppegard and the cat to control.

Her eyes narrowed. The cat.

She reached her thoughts back to where the catamount crouched and took a tighter hold on its khi. Slowly she brought it forward, letting it utter no sound. When it stood beside her, she pulled the Steppegard from its back and leaned him against a tree.

She paused to listen. The ælven still talked of horses. Shalár set her hand to the hilt of her kobalen dagger, then stepped away from the tree and started the catamount forward. She let it scent the ælven and their beasts, felt a growl building in its throat, and loosed it.

For a moment the cat's footfalls thudding on snow were all she heard; then it roared as it reached the ælven's camp. Startled shouting, the frightened shrieks of horses, an agonized scream.

Shalár started forward. The cat had killed and wanted to feed, but she would not let it do so. She paused to look through its eyes. A confused glimpse of a swinging sword that the cat dodged, then frightened ælven scrambling away as she sent it against them again.

Withdrawing enough to remember her own flesh, she staggered forward, drawing her knife. The camp was in an uproar, two ælven down and four others huddled together, preparing to fend off the cat.

One male had gone to the horses. Shalár circled the camp, following. The solitary ælven did not see her before she struck.

A slash to the back. The ælven screamed in surprise and fell to his knees. Shalár slashed again, grimacing. Slitting his throat would have been quicker, but she wanted this to look like the catamount's work. She managed a cut down one side of the throat, enough to set the blood flowing freely, splashing across the snow. She hissed at its sharp scent.

This one was finished. Hunger roared in her ears at the smell of his blood, but she turned away, left him bleeding into the snow and made for the camp where the four ælven were holding the cat at bay with drawn swords.

Shalár swept her knife across the back of a male's neck, then sliced at his neighbor before he could turn. The distraction made them lower their swords, and the cat leapt at them. Shalár stumbled back, evading a wildly swinging sword. The cat snarled, pinned a female, then tore her throat out.

Blood everywhere, spattered across the snow and the trees, its scent heavy on the breeze. The horses were shrieking in terror. She heard hoofbeats as one pulled free of its tether and galloped away down the road.

Shalár ducked another blow from the sword of the sole survivor. Releasing the cat, she turned all her will toward the ælven, wrapping her khi around his in a fierce grip. He looked shocked and for a moment dropped his guard.

It was all she needed. She parried his sword and stepped inside its reach, setting her knife to his throat, letting the black glass bite.

"Drop your blade!"

He stared at her, pale hair tangled across his face and his nostrils flaring with each short, sharp breath. The cat uttered a snarling grunt and commenced devouring the flesh of the female it had killed.

The ælven's frightened eyes darted around the camp and widened with the realization that all his companions were slain. He let go his sword, which fell into the snow with a muted thump.

"Good. Turn around."

Shalár stepped back as he obeyed her. The catamount growled, then sank its teeth into the shoulder of its prize and dragged the corpse away toward a thicket of gray bushes. Shalár caught hold of the ælven's long hunter's braid and laid her knife along his throat again.

"On your knees."

He sank down in the trampled, bloodied snow. Shalár stood over him, pondering what to do next. She was dizzy and out of breath. She let go his hair and laid her hand on his shoulder, beginning to draw on his khi.

The ælven gasped and sagged forward a little. Shalár tightened her grip on him. His khi gave her strength, though by now she needed more than just khi.

"Where are you going?"

"T-to Fireshore."

"Why?"

"A message. For Governor Othanin."

"From?"

"Governor Jharan."

Movement in the woods drew her attention. The Steppegard was staggering toward the camp. Shalár felt a stab of panic as she realized she had lost control of him as well as the cat, but he was too weak to be a threat or even to escape.

He seemed to know it. He came to a halt beside a nearby pine, blinking as he leaned heavily against it. Shalár kept her gaze on him.

"Who carries the message?"

The ælven turned his head, then pointed toward one of the dead. "Korian."

Shalár looked at the Steppegard and jerked her head toward the corpse. "Find it."

Slowly the Steppegard pushed away from the tree, swayed a little, then came forward and dropped to his knees beside the dead ælven. He searched and a moment later held up a sealed parchment. It shook with the trembling of his hand.

Shalár nudged her captive. "Any other messages or copies of this?"

"No."

She shifted her grip on the knife, preparing to kill the ælven, but hesitated. The Steppegard, still on his knees, no longer watched her. He was looking at the corpse before him. He started to bend toward it.

"No."

He looked up, nearly snarling. The golden eyes flashed with raging hunger. Her own hunger flared in response.

She cast a glance around the camp. Nearby she saw a length of narrow cord lying coiled upon a rock.

"Bring me that snare."

The Steppegard stared at her angrily, then slowly retrieved the cord. He brought it to her and gave her the parchment as well. She tucked the message into her leathers, then sheathed her knife and bound the ælven's hands behind him with the snare.

Rarely had she done this. Even though she had renounced their creed long ago, she did not like to feed upon the ælven, who were, after all, her kin, deny it all they might.

She had no choice, however. She was nearly spent and must feed now.

She came around to stand before her captive, who looked up at her with fearful eyes. A fair-faced Greenglen. She would remember him. She owed him that much, as kindred.

She glanced at the Steppegard. "Kneel there."

He moved beside the ælven, who turned his head to watch him. While the ælven was thus distracted, Shalár swiftly stepped forward and opened the vein of his throat, then bent to the wound and fed even as he cried out in pain and alarm.

The first mouthful burned through her like sunfire, hot and so rich that it stung. She held the knife to his throat so that he would not struggle, reinforcing the threat with a grip on his khi as she drank deep of his life. She felt herself reviving, blossoming with strength. Every sound, from the shifting of snow on the branches overhead to the panicked shifting of the ælven's horses, became sharper and brighter.

She paused, raising her head to breathe the cold air. She had the strength now to dull her captive's senses, and out of pity she did so. He breathed, but as in a trance, eyes far away, as were his thoughts, no doubt.

The Steppegard was watching her in taut anxiety. She took hold of his khi again, letting him feel her grip.

He flinched a little but continued to stare at her, mute and demanding. She smiled slightly and with her knife made a second cut on the ælven's throat, a downward claw stroke. She watched the Steppegard bend to it, watched him swallow with desperate urgency, then returned to her own feeding.

Sometime later she felt the ælven's spirit depart, felt the sudden absence of his khi from the blood she was consuming. She continued a little longer, until drawing from the corpse became an effort. Letting go, she raised her head and watched the Steppegard until he, too, gave up.

He sat back on his heels and looked at her, flushed with strength, eyes aglow. Now, if ever, he would take his chance and try to escape. Shalár braced herself, watching him warily.

"Bright Lady."

His voice was hoarse with emotion. Shalár gripped her knife's hilt harder.

His eyes traveled her form. She sensed a different hunger in his khi, a different need. So strong! She shivered, tried to mute the sensation of his rising desire. He might yet attack her, might yet try to overpower her.

Watching him, she set the tip of her knife to its sheath and slowly pushed it in. The Steppegard's gaze followed her hand, then returned to her face. He swallowed.

Shalár stood up. "Come here."

He obeyed, stepping over the ælven on whom they had fed. Glancing around the camp, she saw where someone had bedded down, blankets still covering a pile of brush. She led the Steppegard to it.

He threw off his cloak and pulled off his tunic, then reached for her leathers. Startled, Shalár bore down sharply on his khi, causing him to grunt in surprise. He meant no harm to her; she could feel that now. Relenting, she let him undress her, let him cover her on the cold blanket, let him drive into her. She had the strength now to stop him in a heart's beat, but there was no need.

He was good. So much better this way than bound and helpless. She should use this chance to try for a child, but before she could focus on the memories Yaras had shared with her, the Steppegard brought her to ecstasy. She pounded a fist against the snow and drove at him, feeling him flood her with seed, feeling his urgency ebb. They lay still for a moment; then Shalár softly laughed.

"Very good, Steppegard."

He raised his head, the golden eyes that regarded her bright once more. "Ælven blood is so much better. Why do you even bother with kobalen?"

She raised her head, anger rising in her heart. "Because it is wrong. Understand, Steppegard, this is not our way. Today we had no choice but to feed upon ælven blood, but it is not our way."

"But you care nothing for the creed."

"That does not make me a savage. They are our kindred. Even the kobalen do not feed upon their kin."

He was silent. She had the sense that she had not convinced him, but it mattered not. She controlled him; he would do as she bade.

They caught two of the ælven's horses and rode south until dawn drove them to seek cover. For Shalár, it required almost as much effort as controlling the catamount, since horses were terrified of her kind. Fortunately, the Steppegard had skill with the animals, and it seemed the hunger had not yet made him fearsome to them, so she had only her own mount to control.

She looked at the Steppegard, appraising his appearance with a critical eye. She had given him the fresh clothes she had brought for him: a tunic, legs, and cloak of Fireshore make, with a sash of Clan Sunriding's orange and gray, all from her carefully hoarded store. He would pass as an envoy, she thought. He must.

He had wanted to wear one of the Greenglens' swords as well, but that she would not permit. She had grieved to leave them all behind—seven swords of Southfæld make, a priceless treasure—but whoever discovered the slain Southfæld party must have no cause to suspect that any other than the catamount had killed them.

She turned to him. "How goes the darkwood harvest, Councillor?"

He glanced at her, eyes narrowing. "Well enough, though we have need of new saw blades for harvesting. The wood wears them too quickly, and our bladesmiths have all left Ghlanhras. I hope to speak with Glenhallow's smiths about commissioning some blades."

Shalár nodded her approval. He spoke naturally enough, though the words were almost exactly as Irith had written from a conversation he had overheard in Ghlanhras. Shalár had taken Irith's notes back from the Steppegard, not wishing them to be found on his person in case he was searched.

"Why this charade, Bright Lady?"

"My reasons need not concern you. Be aware, however, that if you fail to carry it through, I will hunt you down."

He grimaced. "There is no need to threaten me. I will carry it through."

"Remember to inform them upon your arrival that you are a night-bider. A little haughtiness will serve you well."

"That I can manage."

"I doubt it not." She looked at him, permitting herself a smile. "When you are finished there, come back to Nightsand."

"Why in the name of all spirits would I do that?"
His golden eyes flashed with sudden resentment.

"I will give you a house in the city and a position of
honor in my guard if you desire it. A home, Steppegard. It is the only home for you now."

He fell silent, and she did not press him further. He
was wise enough to know he had no better choice.
East of the Ebons, he would always be in danger of
discovery.

She would treat him well when he came home to
Nightsand. His strength would be a boon to Clan
Darkshore. He would sire children, she hoped, though
not upon her. She would not couple with him again, for
it was with Dareth that she wished to conceive.

⌗

Some few nights brought them to Midrange, where
they left the protection of Alpinon's woodlands the moment the sun set and rode cross-country into the
foothills of Midrange Peak. There they unsaddled their
horses and dumped the tack into a crevasse. The Steppegard wanted to keep his mount, but Shalár would not
risk its being recognized. She turned both animals loose
and sent him to approach the outpost on foot.

She stood in the shelter of the woods, following the
Steppegard through his khi more than by sight. She
could just see the glint of firelight at the ælven's camp
below. This would be the moment that determined his
chance of success in Glenhallow.

She extended her awareness through the ranks of
trees and the small creatures of the woods to listen to
the ælven even as she kept a wisp of khi around the
Steppegard. She felt his anxiety but no great danger
yet.

She could hear the ælven's voices, though it was hard
to distinguish their words through the blurred awareness of trees and small beasts. She smelled horses and

fire. She sensed feelings from the ælven more easily than hearing their speech, and so it was their sudden surprise that told her they had noticed the Steppegard's approach.

She tensed even as she felt the Steppegard's tautness rise. Giving nearly all of her awareness to the effort, she looked through the Steppegard's eyes and saw glimpses of woodland, firelight, tall Greenglens much like those they had slain in Alpinon. Questions were asked, and the Steppegard answered too swiftly for her to follow at this distance, though she understood the guarded curiosity they represented. The effort was costing her khi, but she spent it willingly.

The Steppegard's khi sparked with anticipation. He was trying to convince them of his urgency. Suddenly they were moving, clasping arms. She felt the shock of the Steppegard's contact with ælven khi. She had warned him to avoid that when he could, for his khi might betray him. It seemed not to have done so, however. Before long she sensed the looming shape of a horse, then the motion of riding.

Shalár withdrew from the Steppegard's khi, leaving only a small tendril of contact. He had convinced the Greenglens and talked them out of a mount.

Relieved, she brought her awareness back to her surroundings. Midrange Pass was too exposed, but there were lesser trails over these peaks, accessible to a solitary walker. The ælven at the outpost were too few to guard every rocky way.

She struck for a landmark crag that Yaras had described to her, anxious to be west of the Ebons again. She wanted to observe Ciris's progress with the gathering kobalen, wanted then to be home again in Nightsand, preparing her hunters to be warriors. Despite these concerns, she found her thoughts running southward with the Steppegard.

She was taking a great risk, letting him go. He might turn on her, betray her intentions to the ælven, though it would bring him little advantage. She had taken care to let him know nothing of her plans for Fireshore, but the exposure of his charade would certainly be enough to arouse suspicion.

She paused, turning to gaze toward the road. In her heart, she knew he would carry out her plan. They were alike in some ways.

"Ride swiftly, Steppegard."

She stood still, listening, her breath icing in the chill of coming winter. She closed her eyes, shifting her attention to him, feeling his anticipation, his strength of will. Oh, yes, he would carry through.

She smiled and sent a pulse of khi after him to show him she was not weakening. Then she released him and turned westward.

⚜ Glenhallow ⚜

Well before sunrise, Turisan donned his riding
leathers. He had spent much of the night in the council
chamber, talking with Ehranan, his father, and several
others of the possible unfolding of a second Midrange
War. Afterward he had walked in the fountain court for
a time, trying to find peace, but even when he had retired, he could not rest.

His heart was filled with tumult. His thoughts
leaped ahead to the moment when he would speak to
Eliani from Skyruach—touch her thoughts with her
full permission—a moment he desired with a passion
strangely intense.

She had agreed to this test, and to send a message
from Fireshore, and that was all. He knew he must not
expect more, yet what he expected and what he desired were wildly different.

He went out to the stable courtyard, where a great
number of attendants, far more than were needed to
prepare two horses for a day's journey, seemed to have
found occupation. Turisan saw the gray gelding he cur-
rently favored saddled and waiting, along with a lively
roan from his father's string. Water skins and satchels
of food had been tied to the saddles.

Luruthin joined him, dressed for riding, his hair

caught back in a hunter's braid adorned with hawk's feathers. Turisan summoned a friendly smile.

"Thank you, Theyn Luruthin, for taking part in this journey." He offered an arm, but the Stonereach stood aloof, merely nodding.

Very well. Perhaps that was best. There was more than one test underway.

Luruthin was kin to Eliani; thus, it was natural that he should be protective of her. Turisan began to wonder if there might be more to his reserve than that.

They mounted and rode out of the stable yard along the broad way that led to the public circle. Even there, folk stood waiting to watch their departure, but the crowd that milled in the public circle was far larger. They commenced cheering as the two riders approached.

Turisan saw a banner of Ælvanen white and gold, borne by Eastfæld's herald, near the falcon statue at the circle's center. Beneath it stood a small group of councillors. With a glance at Luruthin, Turisan guided his horse up to them.

Lady Rheneri greeted them, holding two beribboned parchments in her hands. She held up a hand, and the crowd fell silent.

"Good morrow to you, Lord Turisan, Theyn Luruthin. On behalf of the Council, we wish you good speed and safe riding."

Turisan bowed in his saddle. "Thank you, my lady."

Rheneri smiled, then stepped toward the roan. "Theyn Luruthin, I give these missives into your keeping. When you reach Skyruach, hand them over to Lord Turisan."

Luruthin reached down to accept the messages. Ribbons of blue and violet, of silver and green, fluttered in the cool of morning. He tucked the parchments into his leathers.

Ehranan stepped up beside Turisan's horse and gazed up at him for a long moment. "I was at Westgard. I wish you success this day."

Turisan nodded gravely. "I thank you."

A breeze caught at Eastfæld's colors and tossed them above the heads of the councillors even as the sun's first rays broke over the horizon. Turisan glanced at Luruthin, then turned his horse eastward.

As they rode from the circle, the crowd began another rippling cheer. Turisan wondered if Eliani could hear it. He resisted an urge to glance back at Hallowhall. The Council would continue in session this day, and Jharan, if he knew his father at all, would be keeping a close eye on Lady Eliani.

When they were beyond the gates, he gave his horse a loose rein, and the gray led the roan in a gallop that carried them across the bridge and all the way to the Silverwash before they slowed. He glanced at Luruthin, whose eyes were lit with the pleasure of the run, and the Stonereach gave a reluctant smile. Turisan smiled back and sat at ease in the saddle, letting the horses set their own pace as they started northward along the river road.

"May I ask you a question, Lord Turisan?"

Glancing up, Turisan found his companion's green eyes watching him rather intently. He nodded. "Of course."

"When did you and Eliani discover you shared mindspeech?"

Turisan reached down to stroke his horse's neck. He had been relieved that this issue had not been raised in the Council. Now it seemed he had not escaped it, after all. He met Luruthin's gaze. "During my visit to Alpinon."

A small frown creased the other's brow. "And you have not yet tested it across distance?"

The question stung—an overreaction, Turisan knew. He drew a deep breath and phrased his answer carefully. "Lady Eliani had not decided whether she was willing to make use of the gift."

"Ah."

Feeling suddenly impatient, Turisan quickened their pace, leaving little leisure for further conversation. Even riding swiftly, it was past midday when they reached the broad valley where Skyruach loomed, a great black rock towering at the foot of a long slope.

They crossed a stream and paused to let their horses drink, then followed the watercourse uphill toward Skyruach. They began to pass conces, a scattered few at first, then more thickly strewn until the horses had to weave their way among them. At the foot of Skyruach they dismounted and left the horses to graze beside the stream, which formed a small pool at the base of the rock tower before running down the valley to join the Silverwash. Conces stood thick here, silent reminders of those who had perished in the fighting.

They both drank from their water skins, then began to ascend the great rock. Dark, heavy boulders had calved away in places, impeding the steep, narrow path to the top. The way passed near a gigantic conce that had been carved in relief into the very rock of Skyruach to memorialize Turon's army. Luruthin paused to read some of the many names carved upon it.

The exercise felt good after more than half a day in the saddle even though Turisan's thighs complained at the unaccustomed work. He was warm by the time they emerged onto the flat, roughly even surface of Skyruach. A brisk breeze out of the mountains caught at his hair, cooling him. He strolled north along the barren stone, gazing toward the peaks of Midrange Pass just visible in the distance.

Luruthin bent down to pick up a dart head of ebonglass, once razor-sharp, now weathered smooth by centuries of wind and rain. He turned it over in his hand, then looked up at Turisan.

Placing the dart head back on the rock, he straightened, reached into his tunic, and produced the sealed messages Lady Rheneri had given him. The ribbons fluttered in the breeze, blue and violet, pale green and silver.

Turisan's heart gave a sharp thump. He took the parchments—such fragile things, but they meant so much—and noted that the colors of the ribbons went well together. Stonereach and Greenglen. His heart quickened as he thought of them twining in larger, longer ribbons. Too sweet, that dream. He would be grateful for far less. With a wry half smile at Luruthin, he broke the first seal.

⸙

Eliani sat beside her father in the council chamber, trying to attend to the discussion. The topic had shifted from the probability of war at Midrange to the logistics of a general muster, and apart from giving the numbers of guardians Alpinon could contribute, Eliani had little to say. Her temples were beginning to ache, and she was tempted to lay her head on the council table, but imagining Lord Jharan's reaction quickly cured her.

Heléri was seated beside her, which she found a comfort. Lord Rephanin was also present, and Eliani had noticed him watching her intently more than once. She avoided meeting his gaze.

Eliani?

It was soft, it was gentle. Feather-light, Turisan's touch calmed her after her initial surprise.

She closed her eyes in acceptance. She had held herself so tightly to herself for so long that it took her a moment to relax, as if opening her cloak to a sudden ray of sun in the midst of winter.

I am here.

A wave of joy washed over her; his feeling, not hers, but she let it envelop her. It decreased a moment later as if pulled back, though not diminished.

Are you ready to write?

Eliani opened her eyes. Ehranan was speaking, detailing the forces that would be needed to defend Midrange Pass. She drew a page toward her and dipped her pen.

Yes.

Lord Felisan writes thus—

Eliani wrote "Felisan" at the top of the page and took down the words her father had sent with Luruthin:

> *My heart rejoices at your wondrous news.*
> *This gift comes to us in good season.*
> *May it bring you great joy.*
> *The falcon and the kestrel are well matched.*

That is very like my father. Eliani smiled as she completed writing the final line, and felt color rising to her cheek.

And on a separate page, Lord Jharan writes,

Eliani set the first message aside, noticing as she did so that Heléri was gazing at her. She gave her elder-mother a small smile, then took a fresh page and wrote "Jharan" at its top. The Southfæld governor's message was longer:

> *To Lady Eliani and Lord Turisan,*
> *Greeting—*
>
> *Should your gift prove true it will be a great boon to our people. All ælven realms will honor you for the service you offer, which will be a ray of light in advance of the coming darkness. May it*

guide us through storm to a new place of peace. As the bards have written, "All blessings to the singers of the silent spirit, eternal joy rewards their dark and lonely toil."

And that is most unlike my father, or rather, it is like him in that it contains a number of tricks.

Eliani frowned, reviewing what she had written. *Tricks?*

It is not in his usual style and includes errors. The verse he quotes is of the Lay of Lore, which our bards preserve by oral tradition, so it has never been written. He has also misquoted the verse. A further test, I must assume.

Eliani drew a breath and set down her pen. *I think we may conclude success.*

Turisan made no immediate answer. She sensed a vague regret, a breath of cool breeze, a glimpse of dizzying height.

Thank you, my lady.

She gazed at the two pages before her. *You owe me no thanks. If I had not been so stubborn, you would not have had to ride out today. I—I apologize.*

A flood of warmth threatened to overcome her. *Never apologize! Never feel regret. I have imposed on you against your wishes; it is I who should apologize. Forgive me!*

Eliani gave a soft laugh. Turisan's tenderness enfolded her, touching her to the core. It elated her and frightened her both. She felt dangerously adrift, yet she knew without doubt that she was safe.

Turisan?

She sensed his attention, again caught the brief impression of wind across a black cliff top. She felt as if she, too, stood at the edge of a precipice.

She took two breaths and closed her eyes, swallowing.

My answer is yes.

She sensed his sudden alertness, his wordless query. She swallowed.

I will be handfasted with you.

A stillness drew her attention back to the council chamber even as his elation filled her mind. All the councillors were watching her in varying degrees of doubt, and Lord Rephanin was staring at her with unpleasant intensity.

⚜

I must go!

Abruptly Eliani's mind closed to him, but Turisan's heart had no room for disappointment. She had agreed!

His soul thundered with joy. Opening his eyes, he strode to the edge of the rock, gazed southward in the direction of Glenhallow, flung his arms wide, and gave a wordless cry of triumph.

"I take it the test was successful."

Turning, he saw Luruthin watching him with a wry expression. Half-wild with happiness, Turisan could not begin to form an explanation.

He looked down at the pages in his hand and laughed softly, then folded them and slipped them into his leathers. Striding back along the tower to the head of the trail, he glanced over his shoulder, grinning at Luruthin.

"Let us ride."

⚜

Eliani rose from her chair, unnerved by the intense gazes of the councillors. She picked up the two pages she had written, handed one to her father beside her with a small smile, and carried the other to Lord Jharan. As she returned to her seat, her father met her with a beaming face.

"Word for word."

Lord Jharan looked up from the page in his hand, then let it drop to the table. "Word for word."

A murmur rose within the chamber. Eliani stood behind her chair, held by Lord Jharan's intent gaze. She sensed Rephanin's eyes upon her as well, and others.

Lord Jharan bowed. "I felicitate you, Lady Eliani."

She looked down at the table and noticed a stray drop of ink. How careless of her.

"Do you hold by your offer to ride to Fireshore?"

"Yes."

He gave a single nod. "We shall make arrangements for your departure tomorrow morning, then. Forty guardians will accompany you—if you think that number sufficient, Lord Felisan?"

Her father raised his eyebrows and glanced her way with a smile. "More than sufficient. I would send only ten. Fireshore is not our enemy, after all."

"Twenty guardians, then." Jharan nodded to an attendant, who hastened away. Another attendant stepped forward to speak softly with the governor.

Eliani quietly resumed her seat, then leaned toward Heléri. "I want to talk with you."

Heléri nodded, her gaze on Lord Jharan. The governor of Southfæld swept a glance around the chamber, then spoke.

"My lords, my ladies, it is well past midday. Let us pause for a time. Refreshment awaits those who wish it in the feast hall."

The chime was rung, and the councillors arose from their seats. Several came to offer their congratulations to Eliani. More gazed at her sidelong or murmured together out of her hearing.

She stood up, glancing at Heléri, who nodded and moved toward the outer door. Lord Rephanin swept up to them, blocking their way.

"Did you have any difficulty hearing the message?" His voice was sharp, his gaze challenging.

Eliani was annoyed but kept calm. "No. It was as if Lord Turisan stood before me."

Rephanin seemed not to like her answer. He made no move to step aside. "Five leagues is nothing compared with the distance to Fireshore."

"Let be for now, Rephanin."

He shot a glance at Heléri then, to Eliani's surprise, stepped aside. With one long, narrow look at Eliani, he turned and passed into the feast hall.

Eliani gave her eldermother a grateful look. Heléri smiled back.

"Shall we retire to my chamber? Or are you hungry?"

Eliani shook her head. "Not hungry."

She led the way out to the arcade. Heléri followed, drawing her veil over her face against the daylight.

Lady Heléri's chamber was as dark as draperies could make it, save for the fire burning low on the hearth. Every window had been shrouded, and the door covered with a heavy tapestry. Heléri kindled lanterns on the table and in sconces, then moved to the fireside and sat in a wide, low chair.

Still standing, Eliani gazed at her eldermother. She felt rather stunned.

"I have agreed to be handfasted."

Heléri raised her eyebrows, then smiled. "I wish you all happiness, my child."

"Is it a mistake?"

"Dear child. That I cannot tell you."

Eliani felt her heart filling with conflicting feelings. She let them spill out as she paced the room.

"He is so far above me. He is much more experienced, and knows everything about the high court and about governance. I will be expected to live up to him!"

"You are heir to the governorship of Alpinon. It is not so unequal a match."

Eliani gave a short laugh. "If I had spent more time learning from my father instead of riding with the Guard—I am not fit for much within palace walls."

She paused, realizing with the words that handfasting would mean leaving her clan, aligning with Greenglen. She could not ask Turisan to renounce his position and come to Alpinon; Southfæld was much more important. She would have to leave Stonereach. Leave Highstone. She frowned.

"You are fitter than you know. Turisan has chosen wisely. He is devoted to you, as even you must know by now, Eliani. I think you need not fear him."

"I do not." She turned to look at Heléri. "I do not fear him. I fear my own failure."

"You must not have felt so when you agreed. What is different now?"

Eliani struggled to remember the clarity of that moment. "I—it felt right. I knew it was right."

She came to sit beside Heléri and stared into the fire. There was much she did not know of Turisan, it was true. Much for them to learn of each other. Remembering the calm she had felt as he spoke to her from Skyruach, she understood now that what had made her agree to be handfasted was that steadiness, that clarity and gentleness, that was his touch in thought.

She could no longer deny her desire for him, which seemed to increase with each passing moment. Desire alone, however, was not enough for a successful match, as she well knew.

A sharp knocking on the door to Heléri's chamber startled Eliani. She rose at the sound, glancing at her eldermother as an imperative voice came through the door.

"Heléri, I would speak with you."

It sounded like Lord Rephanin's voice. Eliani took a step toward the door, but Heléri stayed her with a gesture. She watched her eldermother rise and draw a breath as if to calm herself, then slowly walk to the door and open it.

Rephanin stood in the corridor, his eyes dark in the shadow of his hood. "I congratulate you on finding a mindspeaker, my lady. I suppose you knew of her potential when you brought her here? You might have informed me."

Heléri's brows drew together. She pushed wide the door, stepping back and gesturing to him to enter.

"You are mistaken. I did not bring her here." She glanced toward Eliani.

Rephanin's gaze followed hers, and he looked briefly startled. It seemed he had not known Eliani was there. He stepped in and closed the door, shutting out the daylight, then put back his hood and gazed at Eliani with an intensity she now found familiar, if still uncomfortable. When he moved toward her, she put up her chin, watching him warily.

"Look at her. Hardly more than a child." Rephanin's gaze shifted to Heléri. "Turisan is not the best choice to guide her."

"They will find their way."

Rephanin shook his head. "Two children in the dark. We cannot afford it in these times."

Eliani began to feel insulted, and decided it was time she took part in this discussion. She stepped toward Rephanin.

"We are both experienced in the guardian arts, if that is what you mean, my lord."

Rephanin turned gray eyes on her, a wry smile curving his lips. "Guardians are expendable. I meant that your gift needs shaping, my lady. You do not even know its limits. Suppose you find them tomorrow as you gallop northward? What then?"

Eliani felt dismayed, for she had not considered that possibility. She was spared having to answer by Heléri's gentle voice.

"I do not think that will be the case, Rephanin. Their gift is as powerful as any I have witnessed."

This seemed to anger the magelord. He stared at Eliani, his expression hungry.

"Such a gift deserves experienced guidance."

"They shall have it."

Rephanin looked at Heléri. "Yours?"

"And yours, if you will offer it. Should we speak privately of this?"

Rephanin seemed to take this as a challenge, for his eyes narrowed as he stared at Heléri. To Eliani's surprise, it was he who looked away. Heléri's voice was gentle as she spoke.

"They discovered their gift in Alpinon, Rephanin. Just after Evennight. I learned of it afterward."

The magelord froze at her words, and a look of grief fleeted across his face. He cast one glance at Eliani— almost desperate, she thought—then strode to the door and went out without another word.

Heléri sighed. "You must pardon him, Eliani. He is not himself."

"But why is he angry with me?"

Eliani turned her back on the door and went to stir the fire, catching up an iron poker more elaborate than any such tool had a right to be and plunging it into the coals. Heléri joined her at the hearth, resuming her seat.

"Not angry. Envious. He has long coveted a gift such as yours."

Astonished, Eliani turned to look at her. "He *is* a mindspeaker! Turisan said he can speak to anyone!"

"Anyone in his presence. Though he did not speak to me just now. Did he—"

"No, thank the spirits!" Eliani stabbed the poker into the fire's heart, raising sparks.

Heléri sat watching quietly for some moments. Having relieved her feelings, Eliani put aside the poker and returned to her chair to sit glowering at the flames. Heléri turned to her.

"Rephanin can speak to anyone in his presence, but only while they remain in his presence. He cannot speak across distance, nor even through closed doors. Distance speech is the gift he craves, and I am afraid that your finding it has vexed him."

"He may have my share and welcome!"

Heléri met Eliani's gaze, plainly amused. Eliani reluctantly smiled back. She had not meant it, she silently acknowledged. For all her protests, she would not now relinquish her gift, even if it were possible.

⁂

Glenhallow lay before the two returning riders, its golden walls pale in the light of a rising moon. Turisan gazed at them, feeling less exhilarated than he had when they had left Skyruach. The long ride back had given him ample time for doubt, and he worried that Eliani might change her mind.

An agreement to make a pledge was not the pledge itself, and where handfastings were concerned, the creed's stricture of keeping faith was held not to be in effect until the actual handfasting was performed. Eliani could, without need for atonement or even explanation, withdraw at any time before the ceremony, and he feared she might do so.

He had sent no questing thoughts toward her as he rode. Now, as they let their horses take an easy pace across the center bridge, he ventured to break silence.

Eliani? We are approaching the city gates.

We await you in the public circle.

The circle?

Jharan has decreed that you be given formal welcome.

Turisan winced. *My father.*

Amusement rippled through her khi, making him abandon the apology it had been his first instinct to offer. He felt a swell of love for her, so strong he feared it would be expressed in his khi. He glanced toward Luruthin, who seemed absorbed in his own thoughts.

The outer gate was opened to them by a contingent of guardians. The street between the two walls was lined with folk, many bearing torches and lanterns, and the inner gate, too, was tended by guardians. As the ornately worked barriers swung open, Turisan saw that the crowd was much thicker along the main avenue. Blessings and good wishes blended into one long, happy cheer.

An escort of guardians preceded him and Luruthin up the avenue. A horn sounded as the riders reached the public circle's east side. Attendants came forward to take the horses, and as Turisan dismounted, he traded a glance with Luruthin, who looked rather overwhelmed. Turisan himself had not seen such a gathering that he could remember.

Two lines of guardians held clear a passage from the avenue to the circle's center, where all the Council stood gathered beneath pennons fluttering by torchlight in a crisp evening breeze. Turisan could see Eliani waiting there with Jharan and Felisan at the base of the falcon. His heart beat faster at the thought of being near her. He wished all these hundreds of wellwishers elsewhere.

A second horn sounded as he and Luruthin arrived in the center of the circle. Without pausing, Turisan drew the folded pages from his tunic—ribbons dangling loose from the seals—and walked straight to Eliani to place them in her hands.

The ghost of a smile that crossed her lips was reward enough. She looked up at him, and as their gazes met, a cheer broke forth from the assembled crowd.

The horn pierced through the noise, calling stridently for attention. Jharan stepped forward and bowed to his son.

"Welcome, Lord Turisan. You and Lady Eliani have given us new hope today. May your gift serve us well in these direful times."

He offered his arm and clasped Turisan's tightly, then turned to Luruthin, thanking him for his part in the day's test. He kept his remarks short, to Turisan's immense relief. In a few moments the guardians opened a new path eastward into the palace, and Jharan indicated that his son should lead the Council in.

Turisan turned to Eliani, bowed gravely, and offered his arm. She laid her hand on it, causing a delicious prickling of khi to climb up to his shoulder as he led her toward the palace to the accompaniment of cheers.

May I have a private word with you, my lady?

You are.

I mean, may I see you privately?

He sensed her hesitation. *Lady Jhinani has arranged a reception in your honor.*

In our *honor.*

He turned his head to look at her, saw a slight flush wash into her cheek. He had no wish to embarrass her in the midst of this crush of folk.

Afterward, perhaps?

All right. Yes, we must discuss tomorrow.

As they passed through Hallowhall's entrance, a new crowd greeted them. The heads of all Glenhallow's notable clans, visiting dignitaries from elsewhere in Southfæld, and it seemed every foreigner who had traveled to the Council were gathered in the great hall. They crowded around, each wanting to express good wishes. Talking with them was tiresome, and Turisan was anxious lest Eliani be overwhelmed by it, but she bore it patiently. She had kind words for each new person she met, and her thanks were sincere, even the hundredth time she expressed them.

This was Felisan's daughter, the confident lady he had seen in Highstone at Evennight. Turisan felt proud of her, the more because he knew that she, like he, disliked this sort of occasion.

Once the feasting has commenced, we can escape.

But not yet.

He followed Eliani's gaze and saw Jhinani approaching, dressed in formal robes glinting with silver. She smiled as she offered both hands to Turisan. She had stood as a mother to him after her sister had crossed, and it was a mother's pride that shone in her eyes now. She squeezed his hands, then released one and offered it to Eliani.

"Welcome, Lord Turisan, Lady Eliani! Congratulations on your success!"

Turisan nodded, and Eliani murmured her thanks. Jhinani looked past them, smiling.

"And Theyn Luruthin. You will be remembered for your part in this day's events."

Eliani stepped aside, allowing Luruthin to come forward. He bowed.

"I thank you, though my part was small and will not be remembered long."

"Oh, no! It is already being wrought into song!"

Luruthin blinked. "Song?"

Felisan stepped up beside him. "In golden chords, Cousin! You three will live in legend. Talinan the bard is here and has already composed seven verses. I have heard them. 'The riders twain to Skyruach made them haste, Lord Turisan and Luruthin the bold—' "

Luruthin looked dismayed. "Oh, no!"

"It is a most excellent ballad! Jhinani, I have spoken with Talinan, and he is willing to sing what is finished tonight."

Jhinani smiled. "By all means. Invite him to go to the gallery. Our minstrels will accompany him if he desires it."

"He is already with them." Felisan nodded toward the gallery above, where two musicians were playing while the rest had their heads together in animated discussion.

Jhinani glanced toward them, then turned back to Turisan and Eliani. "A fitting tribute, I am sure. Tonight we celebrate what you have accomplished this day and the promise of your gift for the future!"

She raised a hand, and the tall doors into the feast hall swung open. The crowd surged toward it, sweeping them along. Turisan and Eliani were separated quickly, much to his annoyance. Surrounded by well-wishers, they could scarcely move.

Turisan began to edge his way toward the back of the hall, hoping to break free. He kept his eye on Eliani while he answered questions and accepted praises. She was being pressed toward the banquet table, which was laden with the elegant art of Hallowhall's kitchens.

There is a door behind you, just the other side of the table. If you move toward the honey cakes, you may be able to slip through it.

Ah, I see it. Shall I bring you a cake?

Her playfulness gave him sudden hope. If she could tease him, she must be comfortable enough with him. He hungered not for cakes but for the sweetness of her lips.

Follow the corridor to your right, and you will reach the arcade. I will meet you there.

He made his own way toward a different door and before long was able to excuse himself and withdraw. Breathing a sigh of relief, he hastened to the arcade.

Luruthin was there ahead of him, talking with Felisan. The tone of his voice was earnest.

"She should not go with only Greenglens to escort her. I could accompany her."

Felisan smiled. "That is good of you, Luruthin, but she will not be with only Greenglens. Ten of our guard will join her in Highstone, and ten of Jharan's will return to Midrange."

"But she should have kindred along, not just guardians! She—"

Luruthin broke off catching sight of Turisan. He came forward.

"You are talking of Eliani?"

Felisan nodded. "Yes, of her departure for Fireshore tomorrow."

Turisan winced inwardly. He had forgotten Eliani's volunteering to ride to Fireshore, the pledge that had set off all this day's events. He was to bid her farewell so soon! Eliani joined them, glancing at Turisan. Luruthin turned to her.

"Eliani, I offer to accompany you to Fireshore. I, too, would be glad to see Davhri."

Eliani glanced from him to Turisan and back. "That is kind of you . . ."

A slight frown creased Felisan's brow. "That would leave only two of us representing Alpinon in the Council."

Luruthin turned to him. "The Steppes have only two councillors."

"Ah, but Pashani counts for at least two herself!"

Felisan grinned, but Luruthin, it seemed, did not appreciate the jest. He turned his gaze to Eliani again, eyes filled with anxious hope.

"I would be honored to accompany you, Cousin."

With sinking dismay, Turisan realized that Luruthin had strong hopes of Eliani or perhaps had been her lover already. He had known they were close, but Luruthin's khi sang with more than unfulfilled hope. A stab of anger smote Turisan, but he schooled his face to show nothing and controlled his own khi as he spoke.

Eliani, what is your wish?

She blinked but did not look at him. *I wish that my cousin's feelings may not be hurt.*

Turisan swallowed, then drew a breath and addressed Felisan. "It would be well for Lady Eliani to be accompanied by her kin. The journey will be long."

Luruthin looked at him, his expression astonished. Felisan's was thoughtful as he nodded.

"It is Eliani's choice, I think."

Eliani looked at Luruthin and smiled. "You would be welcome, Cousin."

"Thank you. I thank you." Luruthin looked at Turisan, uncertainty in his gaze. "I will retire, then, to rest and make ready. Good night."

"Good night, bold Luruthin!" Felisan chuckled as Luruthin departed, then turned to Turisan and Eliani, his smile softening. "That reminds me, I wish to hear that ballad! Do you join me?"

Eliani shook her head. "I have had enough of feasting for tonight."

"Aye. You did not even get near the table."

"I was near it."

Felisan regarded her, an eyebrow climbing slightly, then glanced at Turisan. "Well, you will wish to rest as well, no doubt, and Turisan here would probably enjoy a bath. Good night to you both, and good rest."

He turned away, humming as he returned to the feast hall, leaving them alone. Turisan looked at Eliani and noticed she was wearing the simple blue gown he first had seen in Highstone. He had a sudden memory of her treading on its hem beside the Three Shades, and felt a swell of affection. Conscious of the possibility that others might seek respite on the arcade, Turisan offered his arm.

"Will you walk, my lady?"

She laid her arm lightly atop his. More formal, more distant. Perhaps her cousin's offer had given her doubt. He knew not how to fight it.

He led her down to the fountain court and to the Whispering Walk. The arcade's chilly mist surrounded them, and moonlight turned the flying streams overhead to liquid silver.

Their steps slowed, then stopped. Eliani turned to face him, a smile hovering on her lips.

Suddenly he wished he *had* taken off his riding gear. Felisan had been right; he needed bathing. Never had he tried to woo a maiden while wearing all the dirt of a day's hard riding. Never had the wooing meant so much to him.

Eliani was no gently bred court flower, though. She would care nothing for the dirt if she wanted to be wooed. *If* she wanted it.

He took a step toward her. "I have never felt such joy as I did today at Skyruach."

His voice came out hoarse, which surprised him. She glanced down, the smile fleeting across her lips. He saw in the infinitesimal tensing of her shoulders the answer to his concern. His heart sank, though he would not let her see his disappointment.

"You are hesitant. I understand. This day has been—"

"Why are you always so reasonable?"

She stared at him, green eyes demanding an answer. Thrown off guard, he gave a soft laugh and glanced at the silvery wall of water beside them.

"My father is deeply devoted to the creed and taught me to be the same. Always to serve others, never to be selfish or do harm. I suppose it has made me overcautious—"

"Turisan."

He met her gaze. "Yes?"

"Be selfish for once." Her eyes narrowed slightly, and she tilted her head. "I want to see how it looks on you."

He drew a breath. "Very well."

Two steps closed the distance between them. He caught an arm around her waist and pulled her against him, kissing her hungrily.

Her khi was like mead on her lips, honey-sweet. He savored it and after a moment felt her respond. His heart began to thunder in his chest as her arms slid around him.

Ah, yes. The joy he had felt that afternoon returned, overwhelming him, banishing all thought. He raised his head to gaze at his love.

"I thought you were afraid of me. I am glad to be mistaken."

Her green eyes glistened with tears as she looked up at him, a slight frown creasing her brow. "Not of you. I am afraid of hurting you. Of doing something to destroy this."

He kissed her again, more urgently, losing himself in her mind this time as well as in her flesh. She permitted it, and his elation soared as their khi blended. He sensed the stab of fear in her, the worry she spoke of, and dismissed it.

This cannot be destroyed.

He reached deep into her, wanting to touch every part of her khi, wanting to feel her throughout himself. Everything they had shared before was as nothing to the closeness they now both sought.

Sparks of fear still flashed within her. He accepted them, as he accepted everything of her. She burned into his very soul.

On the edge of awareness he sensed a change, a shift in the fountain's note, a new shape in the air of the garden. Though the moving water interfered with his acuity, he knew someone else was present.

Withdrawing swiftly from the sweet tenderness that dwelt within Eliani, he spun dizzily back into himself. It was a moment before he felt steady enough to open his eyes and look toward the court end of the walk.

Someone walking past, a pair of females, heads together, talking. Turisan swallowed. The reception had spilled onto the arcade and into the gardens. This was no longer a safe trysting place. He sighed and glanced at his attire.

"I should get out of these leathers."

Eliani smiled. "You must be weary."

He wanted to take her in his arms again and prove how much strength he yet had. Instead, he offered her his arm.

"May I escort you to your chambers?"

She nodded, though he sensed slight disappointment from her. Her hand on his arm lit a fire through him, and he had to refrain from reaching for her in thought, lest he lose all sense of their surroundings as he led her down the walk.

She gave a small sigh. "I suppose I should try to rest if I am to ride tomorrow."

"I offer to go in your stead."

She laughed. "I wondered how long it would take you. Thank you, but it makes more sense for me to go, particularly with the uncertainty about Fireshore's situation. I have kin there, my father's sister, Davhri. I can make a visit to her my excuse for entering the realm, if an excuse is needed."

He began to reconsider his decision to keep apart from her this night. If this was their only chance before she departed . . .

"Here they are!" cried an excited voice as they stepped out of the walk into the fountain court.

"Turisan! Lord Turisan!"

"Hail the mindspeakers!"

As they were surrounded again by well-wishers, Turisan cast a rueful glance toward Eliani. She gave a small shrug of resignation and turned to greet their eager admirers.

✤ Hallowhall ✤

"Hail, Lady Eliani of Felisanin. On behalf of the Council I bid you carry this message to the governor of Fireshore."

Lord Jharan held out a parchment sealed with the ribbons of all the realms attending the Council, so that there was scarcely any paper to be seen beneath them. Stifling a laugh, Eliani gravely bowed her head and bent down from the saddle to accept it.

"Ride swiftly, lady, and send us word as soon as you have it."

"I shall."

A cool breeze tossed the councillors' banners. Again the circle was crowded with well-wishers, and all the Council had come to bid her farewell.

She turned to Turisan, who stood smiling up at her. She felt the warmth of him, suddenly brilliant in her mind.

Spirits watch over your path, my love, and guide you safely back.

Thank you.

Eliani.

Her name in his thought was a caress, filled with longing. She felt him reach for her and closed her eyes, turning her head away even as she returned his wordless embrace. This was too strange and too intimate an indulgence in a public place. She withdrew, but leaned down to clasp his arm, a gesture for the benefit of those looking on.

"Farewell, Lord Turisan."

"Farewell, my lady."

Even the khi sharing of an arm clasp, muted by comparison with mindspeech, was almost too intense. She released him and turned her mount toward the city gates.

Luruthin fell in beside her as she left the circle, and Vanorin on her other side. The guard captain she had met at Midrange had volunteered for the honor of riding with her to Fireshore, as had an embarrassing number of others, and Jharan had allowed her to select those who would go. She had chosen Vanorin to command her escort because she knew him somewhat better than the rest.

Cheering followed her down the avenue, and she felt her cheeks begin to redden. If this sort of noise awaited her every time she showed her face in Glenhallow, she would inform Turisan that she intended to withdraw to the highest peak she could find and live as a hermit.

A child darted forward from the crowd, his hands full of golden cup-shaped flowers. Eliani's heart jumped as he came near her horse's hooves, but his mother snatched him up, then lifted him onto her shoulders so that he could offer his flowers to Eliani. She caught them, calling her thanks as her mount continued forward. The cheering grew louder.

Eliani raised the flowers to her face, inhaling their spicy-sweet scent. She was not familiar with this bloom but had smelled the fragrance before.

Can you smell this?

She took deep breaths, closing her eyes as she tried to share the impression with Turisan. The effort made her a little dizzy.

Honeycup. A favorite of our gardeners, though the bloom will be nearly finished by now. Where did you find it?

A child just gave me some.

Ah. The last fruits of his family's garden, no doubt.

Eliani glanced back, but the child and his mother had vanished into the throng. She tucked the flowers into a strap on her leathers, where she could bend her head to smell them.

I am at the gates now.

She sensed his warm farewell, returned it, then let go, withdrawing her thoughts to herself again. Though the crowd still cheered, her heart seemed wrapped in sudden silence.

So soon, to have become accustomed to his constant touch. It still frightened her, though she wanted it again, wanted it always. In some ways he was yet a stranger.

She turned her gaze ahead as she and her escort passed through Glenhallow's gates. She would search her heart as she rode and discard all the old fears, so that when she passed these portals again she would be free to embrace her new life.

⚜

Luruthin watched Eliani covertly as they rode, wondering each moment whether she was speaking with Turisan. The Greenglen was all courtesy so far. He hoped this journey would give Eliani time to accustom herself to this gift without the pressure of Turisan's evident admiration.

It was well after sunset when the party turned away from the road, following a creek up into a small valley nestled in the arms of the mountains. Vanorin led them to a campsite that bore subtle signs of prior use, in a sheltered arm of the foothills, with a stand of willows for a windbreak, grazing for horses, and a stream nearby. Luruthin had just turned his horse out to graze when Eliani joined him.

"Walk with me, Cousin. I have something to tell you."

She led him downstream, away from the others. When they were well past the horses, she paused and for a moment stood gazing eastward toward the road and the Silverwash.

"Turisan has asked me to be handfasted with him."

All the world seemed to stand still. Luruthin scarcely dared breathe, his mind trying to deny what he had heard. Eliani looked at him, her expression apologetic.

"I—have agreed."

He stared at her even as she turned to look again at the river. She did not seem joyful. He swallowed, trying to command his voice.

"W-why?"

She gave a soft laugh and closed her eyes. "Because it is inevitable."

"I thought . . . you have not . . ."

"I am sorry if this hurts you."

He put out his hands as if warding off a blow. She turned to look at him, her eyes filled with worry. He drew a breath and chose his words carefully.

"You have not hurt me. If I am disappointed, that is my own concern."

"I thought your feelings had changed long ago."

He gave a sharp laugh. "Ah, Eliani. You never could see what lay at your feet."

He took a step away, toward the camp. Heard Vanorin call out a command to one of the guardians.

He should have known that Turisan would waste no time. What amazed him was that the Greenglen had induced Eliani, who had been so evasive since her regrettable cup-bond, to agree to handfast.

He turned to look at her. "Eliani, are you sure?"

She smiled wistfully. "Sometimes. When he speaks to me, I am sure."

He gazed back, suddenly seeing a stranger. She had moved into a world he did not know.

"Your gift has taken you from us. It will carry you far above us all, into the realm of legend."

Eliani looked down at her dusty boots. "It is a mixed blessing."

"I can see that."

He strode a few steps westward, struggling in his heart. Eliani should not suffer because of his disappointed hopes. As her friend, her kindred, and one who cared for her, he should strive to lighten her burdens, not increase them.

The sun was going golden, sinking toward the Ebons. He was reminded of the previous day, when he had stood atop Skyruach with Turisan. Only a day ago.

He cleared his throat. "I do not know what message you gave him after he read the notes from Jharan and Felisan, but the look on his face was unutterable joy." He drew a deep breath, trying to keep his voice steady as he turned back to her. "I w-wish you great happiness, Eliani, and I think you shall have it."

She made a small dismayed sound, then ran two steps toward him and caught him in a tight hug. Startled, he stood frozen for a moment, then brought up his arms to hold her—lightly, ever so lightly, in case she wished to pull away.

He closed his eyes, inhaling. She smelled of new leather, but beneath was her own familiar scent.

"Thank you." Her voice was muffled against his chest.

Luruthin swallowed, blinking fiercely. He would not grieve, not until he was alone.

When he dared to speak again, he stepped back, suggesting that they rejoin the others. Eliani agreed, and they returned to the camp, where golden flames were leaping up into the twilight as the party gathered to share the evening meal.

The food was luxurious for trail fare, having been sent by Hallowhall's kitchens, but Luruthin had no appetite. He took some cheese and part of a loaf of soft bread and sat near the fire. Vanorin joined him and offered a small flask. Luruthin sipped from it, savoring mead laced with sunfruit.

"Thank you. A fine brew."

Vanorin smiled. "My mother's."

"She could win prizes with that."

"She has."

Luruthin nodded, unsurprised. He tore off a piece of bread but could not bring himself to eat it. Instead he stared into the fire, thinking of Eliani. She seemed content, but so had she been with Kelevon at first.

No, she had been blindly smitten with Kelevon. She showed no sign of that now. She was a little older and a good deal wiser. As long as Turisan did right by her, she would be happy.

He glanced around, looking for her, but she was not in sight. Gone into the woods, perhaps, to seek a private place to speak with Turisan.

Vanorin offered the mead again, and Luruthin accepted gratefully, taking a larger swallow. A nighthawk's cry made Vanorin sit up, suddenly alert. A second brought him to his feet.

"What is it?"

"Our sentry. Someone is on the road."

Stuffing his uneaten bread and cheese into his pouch, Luruthin followed Vanorin up the nearest slope to a crag that afforded a view of the road. A female Greenglen met them and silently pointed out a solitary rider approaching from the north, traveling swiftly. He was not by looks a Greenglen and probably not a guardian, riding alone and at night.

Where was Eliani? The thought became suddenly urgent, though this single rider could be no threat to her. Luruthin cast a frowning glance back toward the camp.

Vanorin caught his eye and jerked his head downhill, indicating that they should return. Luruthin followed him, keeping silent until they were back beneath the willows.

"A courier, perhaps?"

"Perhaps."

"Will you hail him?"

Vanorin nodded. "I will offer him the hospitality of our camp and hope for his news."

Eliani came toward them as they reached the clearing, to Luruthin's relief. She had her cloak wrapped about her and gave Vanorin an anxious look.

"What is it?"

"A rider on the road. I go to meet him."

"I will join you."

"That is not necessary, my l—"

"I did not ask if it was necessary."

She brushed between Vanorin and Luruthin on her way to the horses. Luruthin met Vanorin's gaze and smiled in spite of himself.

"She has better days."

Vanorin made no reply, though his face was eloquent. By silent consent, they both followed Eliani down the slope.

They caught their horses and bridled them, not bothering with saddles for the short ride down to the road. By the time they reached it, the rider had come around the bend of the foothills. The horse slowed to a trot as the rider saw them.

Luruthin and Vanorin placed themselves on either side of Eliani. They waited for the rider to reach them, Luruthin noting his appearance as he came closer.

His clothing was of fine make, with a cloak of rich satin, more a court garment than one fit for traveling and somewhat light for early winter. Boots of fine suede, hair in a wild, curling tangle, he had to be a Steppegard.

Luruthin frowned as the stranger brought his horse to a walk and raised a hand in greeting. What was a Steppegard doing here alone? Some messenger from Governor Pashani's court? Had kobalen appeared on their border as well?

His heart began to sink. This could not be good news. He stared at the rider's face, thinking it familiar. Not until a grin flashed across it did he realize he knew this Steppegard. At the same instant he heard Eliani draw a sharp breath beside him.

"Kelevon!"

⊹

Eliani's heart roiled with dismay. She had hoped never to meet Kelevon again. Failing that, she had hoped that more than two decades would have enabled her to meet him calmly, but the sight of his laughing face framed with wild curls at once took her back to Highstone.

To a Midsummer's night when he first had entranced her. To the bewildering year of passion and sorrow that had followed.

Eliani?

Not now.

Is something—

Not now!

Kelevon's eyes were guarded as he bowed low over his saddle, his smile somewhat fixed. "Eliani. I am delighted to meet you again."

Vanorin turned his head. "You know this fellow, my lady?"

He was staring at her. They all were staring at her. Eliani felt her cheeks flaming.

"What are you doing here, Kelevon?"

"Governor Othanin sent me with his apologies for being unable to attend the Council."

She was astonished. "You come from Fireshore?"

He bowed again and threw back his cloak to reveal the sash of gray and orange he wore across one shoulder: Clan Sunriding's colors. Eliani remembered how they had flashed in the sunlight in Davhri's handfasting ribbons, the orange hot amidst the cool gray, blue, and violet.

"Then . . ."

She looked at Vanorin. He met her glance, then turned to address Kelevon.

"Will you come to our camp and share our evening meal? We would learn your news of Fireshore."

Kelevon's smile widened, and his eyelids drooped lazily over his golden eyes. "Thank you, but I must make haste to Glenhallow. I prefer to travel at night."

"Did you meet the couriers Lord Jharan sent to Fireshore?"

Kelevon's gaze shifted to the Southfæld captain. "A party of some six or seven? Korian and the others? Yes, I met them in Alpinon. They continued on, being charged to deliver their message to Governor Othanin and not to me."

He looked at Eliani expectantly. They were all waiting for her to say something, when all she wanted to do was flee as far as she could get from Kelevon and all the disturbing memories the sight of him had roused. She swallowed.

"Come to our camp for a little while. We must talk."

Kelevon's mouth curved in a slow smile, a smile she

knew, a smile whose taste she remembered. "Very well, since it is your wish."

Eliani turned toward the camp. Her horse, perhaps sensing her mood, started to run, and she had to rein it in. Luruthin brought his mount up beside hers.

"I do not trust him."

She glanced at him, a wry laugh escaping her. "Nor do I, Cousin."

Luruthin's frown deepened. He moved closer and spoke in nearly a whisper. "He does not honor the creed."

"We have no cause to doubt him." She glanced over her shoulder at Kelevon. "No recent cause."

"Why would Othanin send a single courier to the Council instead of a delegation? It is an insult!"

"Perhaps some crisis prevented Othanin from attending. We must hear what Kelevon has to say."

They reached the camp and dismounted. Vanorin summoned some of his guardians to see to the horses while he led their guest to the fire. He must have signaled the others to withdraw, for those around the fire arose and left at their approach. Eliani found herself alone with Kelevon, Luruthin, and Vanorin.

She sat and pulled her cloak tightly closed, though she was warm enough. Kelevon, watching her, smiled.

"Allow me to congratulate you, Lady Eliani."

"For what?" Eliani glanced at him, somewhat alarmed. How much did he know of her?

He looked mildly surprised. "On being confirmed in your majority. Should I congratulate you for something else?"

She looked away, staring into the fire. Vanorin approached with a platter of carved meat, sparing her from answering. Vanorin offered the platter to Kelevon. "Would you have some?"

"Thank you, but no."

A slight curl of disdain turned Kelevon's mouth. Eliani remembered that expression as well. Her stomach seized tighter.

"Why does Governor Othanin not attend the Council?"

"Pressing matters prevented him from attending."

Luruthin leaned forward. "What pressing matters?"

Eliani tried to catch his eye and frown him down, but he was intent on Kelevon. In his turn, Kelevon regarded Luruthin with narrowed eyes and a slight smile.

"I cannot say. I am sure the governor's letter explains all."

"You carry a letter?"

"For Governor Jharan."

Eliani frowned, blinking as she looked back at the fire. She must tell Turisan of this development. Jharan should know that word finally had come from Fireshore.

She must speak to Turisan. She felt frozen, numb.

"So if you are finished with your questions, I should continue my journey. I had hoped to make Glenhallow tonight."

She turned her head to look at him. "You did not used to be a night-bider."

He smiled back. "I find that it agrees with me. I much prefer night to day. Something to do with starlight, perhaps."

Eliani looked away, remembering a soft summer evening they had spent together in a meadow near Highstone. Kelevon had made her laugh with outlandish stories about figures he imagined in the stars—no true constellations, but creatures of his own fancy—and they had made love, over and over.

She squeezed her eyes shut, trying to banish the

memory. That was over, gone. Kelevon was not her lover, would never be her lover again. She must think of him only as Fireshore's envoy.

Abruptly she stood and glanced at Vanorin. "Please excuse me. I need a few moments."

Vanorin nodded. Thank the spirits for his calm understanding, she thought as she looked at Luruthin, who plainly seethed with hostility toward Kelevon. Kelevon seemed amused by it, but she knew only too well how Kelevon's mood could suddenly change.

"I will return shortly. Please wait."

Kelevon shrugged and gave a nod of agreement. She strode away, pulling her cloak close about her as if it could protect her from all harm. Uphill, into the woods, which soon became more dense and jumbled with small bushes. Finding a boulder bathed in starlight, she climbed onto it and sat gazing at the sliver of a moon, trying to calm herself. At last she closed her eyes.

Turisan.

Eliani! I have been waiting—are you all right?

Yes. We have news.

News?

A rider has come from Fireshore.

A moment's silence followed. She could sense his amazement, though it seemed muted. She realized that this was because she was holding herself closed, not sharing all of herself with him. She had done the same when they first had found the gift.

This is good news! I must tell my father.

Yes, please do. I need to know whether he wishes me to ride on or return.

He is in the feast hall. It will not take me long to reach him.

Eliani waited, huddled in her cloak. A cool night breeze kissed her cheek, and she shivered. She did not want to think about Kelevon, so she distracted herself

with thoughts of the feast hall at Hallowhall. She
pitied the poor bard who was composing a grand ballad about her and Turisan. His song might now end
rather abruptly, if her great deed was to announce
Fireshore's arrival a day's ride from Glenhallow.

*Eliani? We are in private now, in the governor's
chamber. My father asks why Fireshore sent only one
rider.*

He says Governor Othanin was unable to come or
to send a delegation. He claims to have a letter of explanation for Jharan.

Is he a member of Othanin's house?

He is not even from Fireshore. He is a Steppegard.

*How do you know? A Sunriding could look like a
Steppegard.*

Eliani winced. She had not wanted to talk about her
acquaintance with Kelevon.

I have met him before.

A moment's silence followed. She would have to explain this tangle to Turisan, but not now. Not like this.

You know him. Do you think him trustworthy?

I do not know.

That alone was condemnation. To imply that an ælven did not uphold the creed was the highest of in-
sults, and Eliani hesitated to impugn even Kelevon so.
She could only answer honestly, though. She did not
know whether to trust him. She hoped for guidance
from Jharan.

Shall I ride on?

She could continue to Fireshore and be free of
Kelevon's company, though only the spirits knew what
he would say of her in Glenhallow. She liked neither
choice.

*No. Jharan asks you to accompany the courier to
Glenhallow. Stay . . .*

Eliani waited, wondering what Jharan was saying.

Perhaps he would give her a new message to take to Fireshore.

My father suggests that you request permission to read the letter and convey its contents to us.

Eliani frowned. *He will refuse. The letter is not sent to me.*

The others in your party will confirm that you are a mindspeaker. It is worth attempting.

You will have the letter by morning in any case. He is—a night-bider and wishes to ride now.

Jharan asks that you try. The sooner Othanin's explanation is known, the sooner the Council can respond.

Very well, I will try.

She got to her feet, stiff from sitting on the cold rock after a hard day's riding. As she walked back toward the firelight glinting through the trees, she tried to compose a gracious request to read the letter that had been entrusted to her former lover. She could not even begin.

Vanorin heard her approach and turned to glance at her. Sitting by the fire, he and the others might have looked companionable to one who did not know better, but Eliani saw the tension in each of them as they looked up at her.

"Kelevon, I have just consulted with Lord Jharan."

Kelevon glanced around. "He is here?"

"No."

His brow creased as he looked up at her. It made her heart jump with fright, remembering what that expression had signaled in the past.

Vanorin broke the silence. "Lady Eliani is a mindspeaker."

"A mindspeaker?" Kelevon laughed, then looked at Luruthin, who solemnly nodded.

"My partner is Lord Turisan, Jharan's son."

A myriad of feelings seemed to cross Kelevon's face. He glanced away for a moment as if musing.

"A mindspeaker. Truly?"

"Yes. Lord Jharan has asked me to request that you give me the letter you carry for him. I will read it and convey its contents to him through Turisan."

Kelevon's eyes narrowed. "I was charged to place it in Jharan's hands."

"Do you question Lady Eliani's honesty?"

Luruthin's voice was quiet but full of challenge. Kelevon glanced at him, then looked at Eliani with a smile.

"No, but I am just—amazed! I had not heard of this."

"It was revealed only two days ago."

Kelevon gazed at her, still smiling, his eyelids drooping lazily. "Our own Eliani a mindspeaker. All the world will be pleased to learn of this."

Eliani shifted her stance, growing impatient. "Will you give me the letter?"

Kelevon's smile widened. "Of course."

He reached into his silken tunic and withdrew a parchment sealed with orange and gray ribbons. Standing up, he bowed gallantly and held it out to her.

Eliani accepted it and glanced at Lord Jharan's name written on the outside of the parchment. The hand was tall and spidery—Othanin's hand, she presumed, though she had never seen it before. She sat down, arranging her cloak comfortably about her, and broke the seal.

Turisan? I have the letter.

Excellent!

She willed herself to open a little more to Turisan, enough to convey the words to him as she read them. Even that raised panic in her, though she did her best to ignore it and turned her attention to the letter. It covered only a single page, all in the same thin hand.

> To Lord Jharan, Governor of Southfæld, greetings from the Governor of Fireshore
>
> I have received your message bidding me to attend Council in Glenhallow. Alas, to my great regret I am unable at this time to comply. Matters here require all my attention at present, however, I have good news to share with you—there are no kobalen threatening our borders. We see few of them here, though winter may draw them north to our warmer climes. Should we have any news of this nature to share with you, rest assured I will send it at once.
>
> Fireshore has no standing guard, so I have no support to offer you against the increased activity of kobalen. My ardent hope is that they will be no threat to you or to our good neighbors. If I should prove mistaken in this hope, I will of course send to you whatever help it is in my power to give. Our numbers are yet small, but let it not be said that Fireshore failed to contribute to the destiny of all ælven realms.
>
> I send you this word with my good servant, to whom I hope you will extend the hospitality for which Glenhallow is so justly famous. Pray believe me to be,
>
> Yours in service to Fireshore,
> Othanin

Eliani frowned as she folded the parchment, feeling dissatisfied. She fingered the ribbons, noting that one was a trifle frayed.

That is all?

Yes.

Does the courier know what matters are so important as to keep Othanin away from Council?

I think not, but if you wish, I will ask again.

Do.

She looked at Kelevon. He was sitting with his arms clasped loosely over one knee, watching her in apparent fascination.

"What keeps Governor Othanin so busy of late?"

He shrugged. "I am not privy to matters of governance, so I really cannot say. I know there has been difficulty with the darkwood harvest this year."

Eliani frowned. That seemed insufficient to warrant the governor's absenting himself from Council, but she shared Kelevon's comment with Turisan.

What shall I do?

Turisan was silent for a moment, consulting with his father and the Council. Eliani waited, resigned to spending the night in discomfort whatever Jharan decided. She began to long more than ever for the solitude of that mountain peak.

Bring the courier to Glenhallow.

Very well.

Eliani?

Yes?

Turisan hesitated. Eliani could sense his fear of angering her. It was as if all they had built together had been smashed, and they were back to their initial awkwardness. She hated it but did not know how to cure it.

You seem upset. Can I be of help?

She drew a breath and carefully let it out. *Not now. I will explain when I see you in Glenhallow.*

Very well. I . . . Spirits guard you.

Thank you.

She felt him withdraw, became aware that she was

staring into the fire. The others were silently watching her.

Spirits help me. I cannot see my path.

She stirred and handed the letter back to Kelevon. "Lord Jharan wishes to meet you. We will ride with you to Glenhallow."

"Excellent!" Kelevon returned the letter to his tunic and stood up, casting a sly glance at Luruthin. "We have so much to talk about."

Eliani rose, as did the others. Vanorin and the guardians set about dousing the fires, breaking their newly made camp. Eliani fetched her packs and bow and joined Luruthin and Kelevon with the horses. Vanorin was there, tightening the girth on her saddle.

"Thank you, Captain. Thank you for all your service."

Vanorin gave a nod, smiling slightly. "It is an honor to serve you, lady."

Eliani gave a sudden bark of laughter. "But not a pleasure."

She laughed again at his silence, and saw an answering glint of humor in his eye. She liked Vanorin, she decided. She turned to her horse, her body protesting with weariness as she hauled herself into the saddle once more. She cared little that she would be riding through the night. After this evening's events, she would have had no rest even on the softest bed in Hallowhall.

⚜ Hallowhall ⚜

"My deepest concern is that Othanin was unclear in his reasons for not attending this Council."

Turisan had not seen his father look so stern since he had brought him the kobalen's ear. The Council, hastily summoned, looked equally grave as Jharan's gaze swept across them.

"Have any of you knowledge of matters in Fireshore that might have required him to remain there?"

The councillors exchanged glances and murmured, but no one came forward. Jharan's brow tightened.

"I have not met Othanin, though we have corresponded in the past. Do any of you here know him?"

Governor Pashani stood, a wine goblet from the feast hall in her hand. "I met him when I visited Ghlanhras some while ago. He is a dull sort."

The councillors laughed, and Pashani waved her goblet. "Well, he declined my invitation to ride to the coast, even when I offered him the best mare in my string!"

Ehranan rose and bowed to Pashani, his powerful form oddly graceful in the double-woven gold robe he wore. "Your pardon, my lady, my lord Jharan. Gentles, I think we must ask ourselves whether it is possible that Clan Sunriding has gone the way of Clan Darkshore."

A stunned silence filled the chamber, followed by an outburst of protest. Ehranan held up his hands.

"Hear me. I have given this matter long thought, and I do not like raising it. The truth is, however, that casting Darkshore out of our favor did not resolve the question of why they broke the creed."

Pashani came to her feet again, slapping a hand on the table. "They broke the creed because of their foul and twisted cruelty!"

Ehranan turned to her, his chiseled face stern though his voice was calm. "They claimed they had no choice, and the Council never heard their explanation."

"There could be no explanation! They drank the blood of kobalen for their own amusement!" Pashani's golden eyes flashed as she faced Ehranan. "Mark me, I have no love for kobalen—nasty, vicious creatures— but it cannot be denied that they are intelligent beyond any other breed save ourselves! We drive them out of our lands, we slay them if need be, but what Darkshore did to them was beyond cruel and shamed the very name of ælven!"

"Gentles, please!" Jharan held out his hands for peace. "Lady Pashani, you are right in upholding the decision of past Councils, and I know that you know better than any of us what the alben have done to the kobalen. I would hear Ehranan's theory, though."

Pashani sat down again, frowning. Ehranan nodded thanks to Jharan.

"I was young at the time of Westgard, newly armed and hastily trained for the wars. I felt then as you do now, Lady Pashani. Yet in the centuries since, I have pondered why the Bitter Wars had to be fought. I made a point of seeking out all of the councillors from that time who were still in flesh and asking them what they remembered of the deliberations. One who has since crossed told me something that is not in any history I have found. He told me that Clan Darkshore claimed a change had come upon them."

A murmur went around the chamber. Turisan sat forward in his chair, intent upon Ehranan's words.

"Some of Darkshore's members became afflicted with a hunger that could only be slaked by the blood of kobalen, or—beg pardon, Lady Pashani—of other ælven."

A gasp went up from the councillors, and Turisan also sucked in a breath. This he had not heard.

"That cannot be true!"

Ehranan nodded grimly. "Other ælven. It happened only once that I heard of, and the offender later yielded his life in atonement. Not only did this hunger afflict them, but they became unable to tolerate daylight. It went beyond a preference for night. The sun's light actually did them harm. You all know that the alben shun the sun."

The councillors murmured. Jharan gestured for silence, and Ehranan continued.

"All this speaks to me of some ailment of the flesh. What I now wonder is, could this be a sickness, and could Clan Sunriding be at risk of suffering the same fate?"

Turisan sat back, stunned by the implications of Ehranan's suggestion. He wished Eliani were there.

Pashani stood again, glaring at Ehranan. "The alben are a separate race."

"We have called them so, but in truth they are separate only because we have imposed separation upon them."

Angry voices rose again. This time Jharan let the councillors vent their outrage and dismay.

Turisan leaned toward him. "Could this sickness

Ehranan suggests have changed the alben so that they truly are a different race?"

"Possibly."

"I wonder if healers have ever tried to counter it."

Jharan turned a direct look on him. "That is a salient question."

He stood up and reclaimed the attention of the councillors, begging them to take their seats again. The chamber quieted.

"Lord Ehranan, Lord Turisan has raised a question in regard to your theory. If the alben suffer a sickness, have healers ever tried to cure it?"

"I know of no such attempt. None of the councillors I questioned ever referred to them as suffering a sickness; that is my own surmise."

Heléri spoke into the silence that followed this remark. "If it is a sickness and can be healed, then it is possible the Bitter Wars were needless."

Pashani's fist hit the table, rattling her goblet. "No! The alben had to be stopped!"

Heléri did not flinch. "We cannot change the Bitter Wars, but we can perhaps prevent another."

Pashani glared at her. "How?"

"By crying truce with the alben and offering them our help to fight this sickness, as we should have done from the first."

Ehranan's face darkened with doubt. "We are beyond making peace with them, I think."

Felisan stood up, staring at Jharan with a dark frown. "This theory implies that the courier now riding south with my daughter could be afflicted with this sickness."

Turisan felt a jolt of alarm, then shook his head. "No. She said he was a Steppegard, not a Sunriding."

"A Steppegard?" Pashani let out a crack of laughter

and leaned back in her chair. "Playing courier for Fireshore's governor? I think not."

"She seemed quite certain. She said she knew him."

Felisan turned to regard him. "As far as I am aware, she knows only two Steppegards. One was recently handfasted to a cousin of ours, as you witnessed, Lord Turisan. The other we have not heard from in many years. Did she give his name?"

"No."

Turisan's misgiving increased, for Felisan seemed as unhappy about this Steppegard as had Eliani. All the anxiety he had felt before his ride to Skyruach had returned.

Rephanin's deep voice rang forth. "Your pardon, Lord Felisan."

Turisan glanced up at the magelord, who had risen in his place at the council table. Rephanin's gray gaze flicked his way, then returned to Felisan.

"I do not like to increase your concern for your daughter, but I must point out that this Steppegard, whoever he is, must have resided in Fireshore for some time if Governor Othanin entrusted him with a message for Lord Jharan. If Fireshore is indeed the source of some affliction, it is possible that he is affected."

Turisan leaned toward his father. "I will speak to her and ask his name."

His father's hand on his arm stayed him. He met Jharan's gaze even as he felt the eyes of all the Council upon him.

"Ask her to inquire of him whether there is sickness in Fireshore. Only that. Suggest no details."

Turisan nodded. With a glance at Rephanin, he closed his eyes.

Eliani?

He felt her startlement, the jolt of alarm as she nearly

lost her balance. He sensed swift movement, a hint of wind and dust.

I—we are riding.

Can you slow your pace for a moment? I have a question to ask you on behalf of the Council.

Very well.

He kept his eyes closed as he waited, aware of the councillors murmuring. He almost wished he had stepped out of the chamber for this, but as a simple question or two would take mere moments, he had not thought it worth the trouble.

We have halted. What is your question?

We have been discussing Othanin's letter and trying to understand the reason he chose not to attend the Council. Would you ask his courier if there is sickness in Fireshore?

Sickness?

Yes.

I will ask.

Turisan drew a deep breath, trying to relax as he waited. He kept his eyes closed, but small sounds in the room distracted him: whispering voices, a chair shifting, the click of someone's goblet against the table.

He says there is no sickness there beyond what is usual.

Do you trust his answer?

A moment passed. *He seems sincere.*

Turisan gripped his hands together. He did not want Eliani to think he mistrusted her.

Who is he, Eliani?

Her pause was much longer this time. Turisan felt his pulse throbbing in his temples. He was frowning, he knew.

His name is Kelevon.

It meant nothing to him. He tried to swallow, but his mouth was dry.

Thank you.

Ask Heléri to tell you who he is.

I will. Thank you, my heart.

Turisan.

Yes?

He looked up as if she were before him and for a moment was distracted by Rephanin's face across the room. The magelord was watching him intently. He glanced away.

I will speak to you when we halt to rest the horses.

Yes, do.

He felt her touch slip away and was suddenly lonely. He raised his head and glanced around the chamber, unsurprised to find that everyone was watching him.

A cup of water stood on the table before his father. Turisan reached for it and took a sip before addressing the Council.

"The courier claims there is no unusual sickness in Fireshore. His name is Kelevon."

"Kelevon!" Pashani laughed aloud. "Othanin made Kelevon his courier? He must be duller than I thought!"

Jharan regarded her. "What do you know of this Kelevon?"

"Well, he knows his horses. He would not be my choice for a courier, though. He is . . . not the most reliable soul."

Turisan glanced at Lord Felisan, who was staring at the table before him, frowning. Kelevon was not the one who had handfasted lately in Highstone. He must be the other Felisan had mentioned.

"Would this Kelevon falsely deny sickness in Fireshore?"

The very question was outrageous, but Pashani seemed to take no offense on the part of her clan brother. She merely looked a little grave and tilted her head in thought.

"That would surprise me. I have not known him to tell untruth."

Jharan turned to Ehranan. "Then we may hope that your theory is unfounded, Lord Ehranan."

Ehranan acknowledged this with a slight bow. "I will be glad to learn that is so. We have not learned it yet, however."

"No." Jharan glanced around the chamber. "Gentles, there seems to be no more we can decide until we have seen Kelevon and questioned him ourselves. I suggest we adjourn until his arrival."

He waited a moment and, when no one objected, signaled for the chime to be rung. As its tone echoed through the chamber, the councillors stood and began to talk. Few moved to depart, but among those who did were Heléri and Felisan.

Turisan hastened after them, catching up with them just inside the doorway. "Lady Heléri, may I beg the favor of a word with you?"

Dark blue eyes gazed at him steadily. "Of course. Will you accompany us?"

"Thank you."

He walked with them to their suite on the upper arcade, past braziers that had been lit against the evening's chill. The fires gave light and warmth but no reassurance.

Felisan was unusually silent. Heléri appeared calm as she always did, but even she seemed troubled. She did not smile, nor speak until Felisan paused beside his chamber door.

"Will you join us, Felisan? Lord Turisan, you have no objection?"

Turisan glanced from her gentle face to Felisan's rather somber one. "Lady Eliani bade me ask you to explain who Kelevon is."

Felisan met his gaze, his frown deepening. "Then you do not need me. I will only bluster away and hinder Heléri's good sense." He laid a hand on Turisan's arm. "You need not be concerned about Kelevon."

Surprised at this gesture, Turisan watched him go into his chamber. Heléri led him to her own room at the end of the corridor. She invited him in, going to the hearth, where she laid fresh wood on the fire and hung a small kettle over it.

Making tea. Turisan smiled, comforted by this simple act. Heléri had a soothing way about her.

She beckoned to him. "Come, sit with me."

He sighed as he relaxed into a chair. Heléri brought out a tray bearing cups, a ewer, a bowl, and several small jars, which she set upon the table between them. She picked up a jar, opened it, and sprinkled a few dried leaves into the bowl, then closed it and reached for another.

"Kelevon is a horse trader, or was when he first came to Highstone. He and Eliani fell in love when she was very young."

Turisan felt cold understanding wash through him. He nodded.

"I see."

"Too young, I thought, but Felisan saw how much she cared for Kelevon and gave his approval to their cup-bonding."

So this was the ruinous cup-bond Eliani had spoken of. It was Kelevon who had made her so shy of sharing her heart. Turisan frowned, wishing now that he had not let Eliani ride north, that he had gone in her stead.

Heléri opened a third jar, smelled its contents, then

seemed to change her mind and put it back. She lifted the bowl, stirred the mixture of leaves therein, and reached for another of the jars.

"Eliani's affection was more enduring than Kelevon's, or so it seemed to me. Before the year was half spent, he became . . . inattentive. He left to take a herd of horses to the plains farms in Eastfæld and returned the next season with a party of friends who wanted to see Highstone, including a number of females."

Heléri gave a small sigh as she stirred the herbs with her fingers. "Eliani was—well, she has never been patient, and Kelevon's temper is uneven at best. He admitted no violation of his pledge, nor did any come forward to accuse him, but from then on their bond was increasingly troubled."

Heléri shook a few dried blue flower petals into her hand from a small glass bottle, then scattered them into the bowl. From another she added petals of a golden hue; still bright though the petals were dry.

"Honeycup."

Heléri glanced up at him, smiling. "Yes. I have found a number of interesting herbs in the markets here. I hope you do not mind my trying them out."

"Not at all."

He watched her stir the herbs, raise the bowl to her face to smell them, and give a nod of approval. She set the bowl down and checked the kettle, which had not yet boiled. Sitting back in her chair, she met Turisan's gaze.

"Eliani felt betrayed by Kelevon, but she also seemed convinced that she was somehow responsible for the failure of his love."

Turisan frowned. "How could she be responsible?"

"I know not. I suspect he may have told her so."

The kettle spat, and Heléri leaned forward to take it off the fire. She set it on the hearth, emptied the herbs from her bowl into the ewer, then poured hot water over them. Fragrant steam rose, laced with the sweet scent of honeycup. Turisan closed his eyes, remembering Eliani's touching him with that aroma. Only that morning it had been, yet he felt as if they had been separated for an age.

"However she reached it, she never lost that conviction and never trusted herself to love again."

Turisan swallowed and opened his eyes. He looked into the fire and nodded his understanding.

Heléri gentled her voice. "Until recently."

Hope was remarkably painful, Turisan realized with surprise. He leaned forward, resting his elbows on his knees and clasping his hands between them. The fire flickered and danced, and he stared at it until Heléri roused him, offering him a steaming cup. He took it, nodding his thanks, and sipped the sweet scents of summer.

"You have a gift for this."

"Thank you."

He leaned back, the cup warming his hands, and met her gaze. "There is nothing I can do, is there?"

"About Kelevon? No." Heléri sipped her tea. "It may be a blessing that he has returned. She is now wise enough to see his flaws."

"Does she still love him?"

"I cannot tell you. I agree with Felisan, however. He need not concern you. The gift you and Eliani share is far greater than the shadow of a cup-bond that failed long ago."

He thought this was true, but it gave him no comfort. He saw now that Eliani, having been hurt in a bond of her own choosing, might easily resent being trapped in a bond she had not sought. He silently resolved anew never to force his presence on her. He feared he might have pressed her too much already.

He closed his eyes, remembering the kisses they had shared. They might never be so close again.

Turisan?

He started, spilling tea on his sleeve. Heléri looked inquiringly at him.

"Eliani."

"Ah. Will you excuse me?"

Without waiting for his answer, she stood up, carrying her tray of herbs away. Turisan set his cup down on the table and brushed at his sleeve.

I am here.

We have stopped at Skyruach.

I am with Heléri.

Oh.

Silence stretched between them. He wanted to reach for her, to embrace her in the only way possible at this distance. He held back.

Has she told you?

Yes.

I was going to explain to you in person when I returned.

I understand.

You are not angry?

He felt a warmth of love flood him and smiled. *I do not think I am able to be angry with you.*

She seemed to withdraw a little. *You should be. I make mistakes.*

We all do.

He sensed her restlessness, a feeling that took him back to Highstone and the Three Shades. He wished he knew how to reassure her.

Luruthin and I were lovers also. Before Kelevon.

Her bluntness made him smile. She seemed to wish to confess all her past. He would not bore her with a recital of his own dalliances, for they meant less than nothing.

I thought you might have been. He still cares for you.

*I know. It is my fault. I failed to be clear with him.
Now he is unhappy.*

Eliani—

*I do not like causing pain to those I love. I do it far
too often.*

He wanted to take her in his arms and kiss away all
her worries. She would have let him, he knew, if she
were there. Instead, leagues of doubt lay between them.

I have faith in you.

He felt a ripple of emotion from her, so quickly
damped that he could not tell what it was. He waited.

I should go.

Very well. I will see you when you return.

Yes.

He wanted to tell her he would think of her every
moment until then. He wanted to warn her against
Kelevon, but that would be folly. He could not win her
trust by trying to bind her to him. He had to let her
find her own path.

Spirits guard you, Eliani.

And you.

She slipped away. Turisan let his breath out slowly,
then reached for his tea.

Heléri returned and warmed both their cups from
the ewer. "I hope all is well."

"She wanted to know if I had talked with you."

"Ah."

Turisan watched Heléri sip her tea, searching for a
trace of Eliani in her features. They were very unalike,
but if there was a resemblance, it was in the determination of her chin. He smiled.

"Thank you, Lady Heléri. I am in your debt."

"We shall soon all be in your debt. Yours and Eliani's."

He gave a small shrug. "Perhaps not. Fireshore has
sent word at last."

"There will be other calls upon you."

He met her gaze, thinking of the kobalen at Midrange. Yes, there would be other occasions for the mindspeakers to serve their people. With some surprise he realized that he no longer doubted Eliani's willingness to serve in that way. She had accepted their gift as her fate. He knew it with certainty.

The rest was still in question. Kelevon's return might have destroyed his own chance of happiness with Eliani. Or it might, as Heléri had suggested, enable Eliani to resolve her feelings at last.

⁜

By the time Eliani's party reached Glenhallow again, dawn was spreading pale fingers into the sky. Kelevon wore a constant frown and gave clipped answers to Eliani's occasional attempts at conversation. Eliani was actually glad to see a small crowd of well-wishers gathered at the outer gate.

Turisan? We are arrived.

Welcome.

Should we go to the circle?

No, ride straight to the palace stables. My father made no announcement of your return, though it is known. The Council will be summoned when you have had time to refresh yourselves.

Eliani glanced at Kelevon. *Good. Our courier is in a sullen mood.*

Why so?

The sun is near rising, and he is a night-bider.

She sensed sudden dismay from Turisan, a breath's length, no longer, before it vanished. He had hidden it quickly, but not before she felt it.

What is it?

Nothing. Bring him to the great hall. My father and I will meet you there.

Very well.

She looked back eastward. The sun was not up yet, but golden streamers were rising into the sky. She saw Kelevon draw the hood of his cloak forward to shade his face and was reminded of Heléri, who went veiled whenever she was abroad in daylight because the sun hurt her eyes.

Maybe it was so for Kelevon as well, though she did not remember his being troubled thus in the past. He had changed, perhaps. So had she.

She urged her weary mount to a trot and hastened to the stables, sparing smiles and waves for the scattered crowd that greeted her return to Glenhallow. In the stable yard, she slid to the ground with a small grunt of weariness and gave her reins to the groom who approached.

"Coddle them. They have been ridden hard."

"Yes, my lady."

She slung her packs over her shoulder and looked around the yard. Kelevon had stepped already into the passage that led up to the palace. She joined him in the archway, pausing to wait for Luruthin, who was talking with Vanorin.

Kelevon moved a little deeper into the passage. "You are well loved here."

Eliani shrugged. "It is the mindspeech. They do not know me."

"Not many do. I am not certain I ever did."

The gentleness of his tone surprised her. She glanced at him and saw regret in his face.

"Eliani . . . I believe I owe you an apology."

Within the shade of his hood his golden eyes glowed, sparking memories both fair and painful. She felt confused, not knowing if he meant to apologize for rushing them to Glenhallow or for something else.

Before she could ask, Luruthin joined them, some-what breathless.

"Pardon my delay. I think my horse has thrown a splint."

Kelevon's eyes snapped to glare at him. Eliani turned and started up the passage.

"Come. Lord Jharan is waiting for us."

She led them to the great hall at the palace's center. She had not been there at dawn before, and the sight of sunlight streaming through high windows to strike the murals on the west side of the gallery, lighting them in shades of green and gold, made her pause in admiration. Beside her, Kelevon drew his hood farther forward.

Jharan and Turisan stood talking quietly in the center of the hall. Eliani approached them, and Jharan turned, smiling in greeting.

"Welcome back, Lady Eliani, Theyn Luruthin." His gaze moved to Kelevon.

Eliani swept a brief bow. "Governor Jharan, this is Kelevon, who has come from Governor Othanin in Fireshore."

"Welcome, Kelevon, and thank you for your service. We are glad to hear from Fireshore at last."

Kelevon bowed and handed Jharan the letter Eliani had read. Jharan glanced at it, then indicated Turisan.

"This is Lord Turisan."

Eliani saw Kelevon's eyes narrow as he bowed again. Turisan acknowledged him with a nod, watching him intently. Jharan addressed Kelevon. "You must be weary. Allow me to show you the rooms we have pre-pared for you."

Kelevon hesitated. "You need not have troubled. A lodging in the city will suit me."

Jharan smiled. "That is the purpose of a palace, to

accommodate visitors of state. Come, I have much to ask you."

Jharan led Kelevon away toward the south wing, ascending the curved stairs to the gallery. Silence hung in the air for a moment, then Luruthin coughed.

"I suppose I should retire."

Turisan turned to him. "A meal has been sent to your chambers. To yours also, my lady."

"Thank you."

"The Council will be summoned later in the morning."

Eliani nodded. She felt awkward, embarrassed. Hallowhall's roof was vast, but not vast enough for her to be comfortable sharing it with so many lovers, former and would-be. Suddenly she wanted only to be alone.

"Bid you both good morning."

She strode toward the stairs after Jharan and Kelevon. In her chamber she found a covered tray on the table by the hearth, and a bathing tub placed nearby, with ewers of steaming water and a pile of soft towels on a low table beside it. Calling silent blessings down upon Jhinani, Eliani sighed and began to unfasten her leathers.

A handful of withered flowers scattered about her feet: the goldencup—no, honeycup—that the child had given her the previous morning. She knelt to pick up one of the blooms, fingering its wilted stem. The petals were still bright, but they were only a shadow of what they had been. How fair, and how quickly faded. Like all her love affairs.

Eliani's chest tightened. She had expected to have leisure for reflection on her journey to Fireshore. Now she was back where she had been a day earlier, with the added confusion of Kelevon's presence. She felt as if she could not breathe.

She undressed and emptied the ewers into the bath, forgoing the slender, flower-shaped phial of scented salts. She hissed as she stepped into the hot water and immersed her aching body.

A day and a night in the saddle, and she was already a mess of aches and stiffness. Glenhallow had made her soft. She regretted returning, not having the journey ahead. She was not made for the idleness of living in a palace. This place, with its perfumes and promenades, was too seductive.

As was Turisan. He wanted her and would soon seek consummation with her. Eliani swallowed as she rubbed her sore muscles in the water's heat. She wanted him also, but not in her present troubled state of mind. She would only hurt him, as she had hurt every male she had touched.

What now? She closed her eyes, fighting panic. She had agreed to handfast, and now there was nothing to delay it. She was not ready.

She scrubbed her body, focusing on the flesh and trying not to think about Turisan or Kelevon or any of the questions that circled round and round in her mind. She washed her hair, using a pot of mildly scented soap that the attendant had left for her, and submerged herself to rinse it out.

Underwater her hair floated free, soft against her fingers. It reminded her of a time she and Kelevon had gone to the hot springs above Highstone and drifted together in the warm water, making love with aching slowness. It had lasted all night and had ended with a crashing peak she still vividly remembered. Her flesh tingled even now.

She came up from the water abruptly, shook her head, and wiped at her stinging eyes. Rising from the bath with a great sloshing, she stepped out and wrapped herself in a towel. She used another to rub vigorously at her wet hair, then sat in a chair by the hearth, basking in the fire's warmth.

Why can I not be free of Kelevon?

Because it never ended, whispered a small voice within her. The thought coursed through her like the deep vibration of a summoning chime.

It was true. Her life had ceased in one way with Kelevon's departure, and she had tried to let that corner of her heart die, but here it was, pumping out blood anew through an unhealed wound.

She closed her eyes. She had tried for two decades to avoid hurting a lover by the simple plan of having none, but even that had failed. Abstaining from involvement had not served the purpose. She must change tactics.

She must face Kelevon.

Impatient to act on the decision, she left the hearth, towels sliding to the floor as she strode across the chamber to where her trunk, still packed, sat against the wall. She opened it and pulled out the first garment she found—her blue gown—and pulled it over her head. Its loose fit seemed too informal for the Council, so she added a violet kirtle sewn with crystals from Clerestone, then dug out a pair of slippers. Donning these, she fetched her comb from her satchel and returned to the hearth while she untangled her damp hair.

She would have to find Kelevon's chambers. She wondered if the governor was still closeted with him.

She combed her hair until it was nearly dry, then threw her cloak about her shoulders and left her chambers, striding out to the arcade. The fountains below were still shaded by the palace, though the sun was well up. Drifts of chill mist occasionally reached the upper arcade. Eliani paced its length slowly, hoping for some sign of where she might find Kelevon.

A chime rang, deep and sonorous. The Council was being summoned.

Eliani glanced back toward the center of the palace, surprised and a bit irritated, for she had expected to be given more time to rest. She would have to talk with Kelevon later. He might already be in the council chamber. She reluctantly turned back.

Eliani? May I have a private word with you before the Council?

Yes, all right.

Shall I come to you?

To her chambers—no. Altogether too private. She turned to the nearest staircase and hurried down it.

I am in the gardens.

She reached the fountain court and paced its paths aimlessly. A sharp breeze whipped cold spray around her and chilled her ears beneath her damp hair. She drew her cloak tighter.

She found herself drifting toward a far corner of the court where the sun was spilling down the high wall. She sat on a bench beside a series of curving pools that poured into one another in a gentle cascade, mimicking a stream but with a much slower pace. Closing her eyes against the sun's glare, she turned her face to the light.

"Eliani?"

Startled, she blinked and shaded her eyes with a hand. Turisan stood before her, wearing a formal tunic, his hair caught back in a half braid. He looked very like Jharan, she thought inconsequentially. He looked troubled.

"There is something I wish to tell you before the Council meets."

Eliani nodded. With a gesture she invited him to sit beside her. Her cloak fell open as she moved, and Turisan smiled as he joined her on the bench.

"I like that gown. It always looks well on you."

Elinani smiled back but pulled her cloak close again. She felt chilled despite the warm sunshine.

"What did you wish to tell me?"

His face became grave again. "Yesterday in Council, Ehranan put forth a disturbing theory. He believes the alben may suffer a sickness that they acquired in Fireshore."

"Sickness?"

"Yes. He believes it to be the cause of their misdeeds, their hunger for blood, their hatred of the sun. Eliani, he suggested that it might even now afflict Clan Sunriding."

Fear gripped her heart. Davhri, her father's sister, was a Sunriding.

"No. We would surely have heard—they would have told us—"

"Would they? After what happened to Darkshore?"

She met his gaze, saw deep concern in his eyes. Her heart sank.

Turisan continued quietly. "If he is right, then it is possible that Kelevon is affected."

"Kelevon!"

He nodded. "I wished you to know my concern."

Eliani stared at the graveled walk beneath their feet. Turisan wished her to believe that Kelevon was afflicted with a sickness—the sickness of the alben.

"No. He is perfectly well."

"He shuns the daylight."

She felt a flash of annoyance. "So does Heléri! Is she sick as well?"

"Eliani—"

She jumped up from the bench and began to pace. "This is too much conjecture. Ehranan may be right, or partially right, but until we are sure of that, we can make no assumptions." She halted before Turisan, glaring a challenge. "Kelevon showed no sign of being unwell."

"I did not mean to anger you."

"I am not angry!"

He drew a breath, then said nothing, instead pressing his lips together. A small frown creased his brow.

I know you and Kelevon were once very close.

Turisan—

Such feelings might make it hard for you to be objective.

I would rather not talk of this now.

I am concerned for your safety.

She inhaled and stopped herself on the edge of a cutting reply, hastily turning away instead. It was all she could do not to stride away from him.

So it began. Even with Turisan—gentle, patient Turisan, whom without doubt she loved—she could not keep from strife.

The pools before her silently flowed on, the last of them at ground level, grown with reeds and lotus, though no blooms just now. She wondered where the water went from there. It seemed still, but could not be or it would have flooded the path.

She breathed deeply, willing herself to be calm. After a moment she turned and saw Turisan watching her, his dark eyes filled with worry. How she longed for his touch, for the smell of him, the taste of him.

Turisan, I need to be alone.

His face was momentarily stricken; then he glanced down, and the neutrality of the courtier fell into place. He stood up.

Very well.

He stepped toward her. Despite herself she flinched, and he hesitated before gently laying his hands on her shoulders. He kissed her brow, a feather's brush of *khi* tingling over her face, then stepped back and with another fleeting smile turned and walked away.

She watched him go, unable to move or speak. The summoning chime rang again. Council was called.

She glanced once more at the pool by her feet, suddenly remembering the shade she had seen back home. They were portents of ill, some said. Slowly, numbly, she turned away and walked back into the palace.

✤ Hallowhall ✤

Evening could not come too soon for Eliani. She spent all day in Council, trying to attend to the discussions, but was too distracted by thoughts of Kelevon. Turisan was carefully inattentive, which rather than soothing her, filled her with frustration. She wanted to speak to him but refrained for fear that they would only argue.

When the Council recessed for the evening meal, she escaped at once to the arcade and sought out Kelevon's chamber. She had asked a palace attendant to show it to her earlier, and now that the sun had set, it would not be rude to call upon him.

Kelevon answered her knock and opened the door wide to her. He wore the same formal clothes, though he appeared to have bathed. His bronze hair curled richly about his face and shoulders.

Eliani nodded in greeting. "I came to ask if you would join me for the evening meal."

For a moment his face looked strained, then he smiled. "Thank you, but I would prefer a walk. I understand there are fair gardens here."

"Yes, the fountain court. Shall I show you?"

His smile softened. "Please."

She waited while he fetched his cloak, then led him

along the arcade and down the stairs to the court. He stood a moment at the foot of the stairs.

"All this water. Do you not find it disturbing?"

"I dwell near the Three Shades."

"Ah, yes."

They strolled through the court, and Eliani dredged up bits of what little she remembered about the fountains. She could recall some of the points of construction, a few of the names of governors who had commissioned various works, and none of the fountains' creators.

"Jhinani can tell you much more. I fear I did not pay close attention when I arrived."

"Jhinani is Jharan's lady?"

"No, his lady has crossed. Jhinani is her sister. She is hostess here at Hallowhall."

Kelevon nodded absently, looking around the court. He glanced at her with an apologetic smile.

"I fear I do not find this very restful. Are there no other gardens?"

"Orchards. This way."

She led him through the Whispering Walk, telling him its name and that Turon had commissioned it but making no other comment. Walking down the length of arching water made her think of Turisan. She found herself frowning and realized as she stepped through the archway into the orchards beyond the wall that she had been holding her breath.

Kelevon let out a satisfied sigh. "Ah, this is better. Where does this path lead?"

Eliani gazed along the graveled pathway that cut along the hillside beside a low stone wall, dividing the orchards. Dusk lay heavy beneath the trees to either side, making the orchards seem darker than the gardens had been. A few early stars glinted among branches that were mostly bare.

"I have never been its length. To the edge of the orchards, I am certain. It may continue beyond."

Kelevon started forward, his gaze rising to the mountain peaks above the orchards. Eliani followed, offering occasional comments. She had not attended well to Jhinani here, either, but remembered that the upper orchards were the oldest, where the prized stonefruits grew. In the lower orchards were apples and some few varieties of fruit brought from realms to the north, including a sprawling hedge of berry brambles that had grown from a single plant Felisan had brought long before.

She stepped over the wall to walk alongside the hedge, out of habit searching for berries beneath the leaves though she knew it was long past the season. Just the familiar tangle of the boughs, the smell of the bushes and their khi, comforted her with thoughts of home.

"Careful. You would not want to snag that pretty gown."

Eliani turned to face Kelevon, who had followed her into the orchard. His easy smile faded a little as their gazes met.

"Kelevon . . ."

"Yes?"

"What were you apologizing for this morning?"

Sadness flicked across his face. "For everything, I suppose."

"We never—" Eliani took a breath, frightened of creating another disaster. She would not run, though. Not this time. "Our cup-bond did not end satisfactorily."

He laughed softly. "No."

"I want to make peace with you."

"That sounds as if we were at war."

"Were we not?"

"I never meant to be."

He strolled a pace or two away, leaned against a tree, and gazed at her. His golden eyes were the same as they had been on that long-ago midsummer night, so rare and beautiful that they stirred her.

"I never cup-bonded again."

Eliani swallowed. "Nor did I."

"Perhaps such as we are not made for it."

She was silent. Turisan leapt into her thoughts, and she wondered yet again if she was making a mistake to bind herself to him.

"You were so young then." Kelevon left the tree and came toward her, smiling. "I think you may be even more beautiful now."

She stiffened. "I did not come to you seeking compliments."

He stopped a pace away from her. His curling hair draped his face as he gazed down at her.

"No? What did you come for, then?"

Eliani swallowed, feeling her heart begin to thump painfully. He was very near. She could smell him, half-familiar, half-strange.

"Eliani." He reached up to stroke her cheek. His khi felt odd, almost stinging. She stepped back.

"No." It came out a strangled whisper.

"I still care for you. When I was—alone and lonely, I thought of you. I always sought news of you, and when I knew you had reached your majority, I realized that I missed you."

"No, Kelevon. It is over." She was startled at how strong her voice sounded.

"We could begin again." His eyes half shut as he bent toward her, laying a hand on her shoulder.

"No!"

Eliani pulled away, stumbling into the berry hedge. Wicked thorns caught at her gown and tore a gash in the back of her hand as she freed herself. She gave a small cry of frustration and raised her injured hand to her mouth.

"Clumsy fool!" She rubbed at a tear in her gown, then froze as she glanced at Kelevon.

He was staring at her with frightening intensity. His face wore a look of—desire? Hunger?

"I am all right." She lowered her hand, hoping to cool his mood. "It is only a scratch."

Kelevon said nothing. His gaze followed her bleeding hand. His breathing was quick and shallow, nostrils flaring, his face taut with need.

"Kelevon?"

Golden eyes flicked to her face, then back to her hand. With a sudden lunge he seized her hand and hauled it up, fastening his lips to it in a hungry kiss.

"Kelevon, no!"

Eliani pulled, but he would not let go. At last she wrenched her hand free and stumbled away, almost falling into the brambles again.

"What are you—"

He stood staring at her, panting now, his face drawn into a scowl. Her blood was on his lips.

Eliani felt as if the ground had dropped away beneath her. Turisan's words of caution returned to her, the suspicions she had dismissed in anger. She caught a horrified breath.

"You are one of them!"

With a wordless snarl he lunged for her again. She twisted free and half ran, half stumbled down the hillside, away from the brambles and Kelevon.

Regaining her balance, she faced him, blinking rapidly as she tried to move into the stance of a guardian. This was difficult given that she was unarmed, with her gown tangling about her legs and her unbraided hair flying into her eyes.

Kelevon stood between her and the path. His face

changed, eyes narrowing as the frown shifted into a mirthless grin.

"You have learned a trick or two since I left you."

Eliani tried to calm her breathing. She might run, but she suspected she could not escape Kelevon. He had chased her down many times before, although then she had wanted to be caught.

She glanced around the orchard, searching for anything she could use in her defense, but the keepers of Hallowhall's grounds were too efficient. Not a limb, not even a twig, lay beneath the well-tended trees. She kicked off her slippers to better her footing, hoping the keepers were as efficient about clearing rocks from the fields.

"Kelevon, do not do this!"

She stepped sideways, north toward Hallowhall, keeping a gnarled apple tree between herself and Kelevon. He countered her movement.

"Why not? You are a danger to me now, and I am hungry."

"You said you still cared for me!"

"Oh, I do. I shall remember you fondly. You are as delicious as ever."

She gave a sound of disgust and darted to the next tree northward. Kelevon followed, keeping between her and the path. He made another attempt to catch her, but she skipped back from his reach. He laughed.

Eliani realized she was gasping, not from fatigue but from fear. She had fought kobalen and hunted catamount, had contested in games with fellow guardians, but never had she fought another ælven for her life.

Alben, not ælven, she corrected grimly. An ælven would not do this. She felt a pang of grief for the Kelevon she had once loved. This was not he.

He lunged for her again, and this time she saw the flash of a knife in his hand. She fell back and struck his wrist away with one hand while she caught a fistful of his silken tunic with the other, pulling him down with her. He gave a surprised grunt as she planted a foot in his gut and threw him over her head and down the slope.

She rolled onto her hands and knees, uttering a curse as her gown hampered her. Kelevon was getting to his feet. He still had the knife.

Eliani stood, catching up her skirt and stuffing it into her kirtle, baring her legs to the chill evening breeze. She felt her flesh prickle with the cold even as Kelevon leered.

"Ah, I knew you still wanted me, sweetheart!"

She forced out a scornful laugh, though her heart was pounding with fear. "Keep deluding yourself. It is most amusing."

Anger flashed in his eyes, replaced a moment later by a cunning smile. "You have not changed so much, after all."

He strode toward her. Oh, for a tall tree! But these apples and stonefruits grew low and densely branched. Still, the one beside her might serve.

Before Kelevon was within arm's reach she leapt up onto a branch and caught the next higher, turning as she swung around it and aiming her feet at Kelevon's back, hoping to knock him down. Twigs whipped at her legs. He was too quick for her, evading most of the blow. He swiped at her ankles with the knife, missing by a hairbreadth.

Eliani let go the branch and landed uphill from Kelevon, turning to face him as she did so. She glanced toward the path, but it was still a good five rods away.

She swallowed. Kelevon had never been a guardian, she reminded herself. She had some advantages yet.

She took a step backward. His eyes glinted as he followed, a hunter's pleasure in pursuit.

Good, she thought, and suddenly leapt forward, lowering her head toward his midsection and launching all her weight downhill toward him. He reacted belatedly, bringing up the knife. She caught his wrist in both her hands and pushed it away, catching his cloak as she passed him and yanking it.

He let out a cry of pain but did not fall, though she heard the knife thud to the ground. Kelevon's hands went to his throat, and the cloak went limp. She dropped it as he grabbed at her, and suddenly they were grappling, struggling together as they often had, but with no laughter this time.

She jabbed an elbow at his gut. He twisted and caught a hand in her hair, wrenching her head back and pinning her against him, trapping one of her arms. Fear hammered in her chest as she tried to get at him with her free hand. She landed a blow on his shoulder blade, but he only laughed.

"Do not fight!" He tugged at her hair as he did so. "It will go harder for you if you do."

She was gasping for breath. Her scalp felt on fire, and fear roiled in her belly. Kelevon raised his head to grin at her, then kissed her throat. Blind panic flashed through her.

Turisan!

Eliani!

She sensed a glimpse of the feast hall, bright with candles. Turisan's sudden alarm filled her.

Help me!

Where are you?

The orchards, in the orchards!

I am coming!

Kelevon's teeth closed on her throat, crushing her

flesh. She grabbed at his hair and pulled a fistful of curls as hard as she could. He gave a cry of angry surprise, his hold loosening enough for her to twist free, though she lost some of her own hair as she did so.

She scrambled away from him, looking around wildly for the blade he had dropped. Saw a glint of metal and dove for it, even as he came after her again.

Dirt and dry grass ground into her bare knees. She scrabbled for the knife's hilt, found it just as Kelevon landed on her legs, knocking her sprawling.

She tried to roll over, but he was on top of her, weighing her down, trying to force her legs apart. She struggled up onto one elbow and thrust under her arm with the knife, stabbing at whatever she could reach. The thud of the blade catching in flesh and Kelevon's shout of pain told her she had succeeded.

She threw him off, rolling onto her back as she did so, then getting to her feet. Kelevon caught at her ankle and tried to pull her down again, but a swipe of the knife at his wrists made him loose her. She stumbled backward downhill, gasping for breath.

She was terrified, horrified, aghast. She wanted to flee, trusting that the knife would make him hesitant to pursue, but she knew she could not let him go.

Kelevon knew that she and Turisan were mindspeakers. If he took that fact back to the alben, they would lose much of their advantage.

She stared at him, blinking rapidly. Her hair was in her eyes, and she tossed her head to try to get it away. Her throat ached dully and her scalp burned where he had torn out her hair. She was shaking.

Kelevon, on his knees, brought a bloodied hand away from his wounded shoulder. He looked up at her, furious.

"You shall regret that."

He stood and came toward her. Eliani saw her death in his pale eyes.

Turisan!

I am here! Where are you?

Apples, near the berry hedge. Hurry!

She backed away, ducking her head beneath a low branch of an apple tree. Darting sideways, she put its trunk between her and Kelevon.

He strode toward her. "Enough of this game."

He lunged left, then shifted to the right even as she dodged that way. Tricked by a feint! She was furious.

His hand caught her wrist, twisting it down, then behind her. She felt her fingers losing their grip on the knife's hilt.

He thrust her against the tree, pressing himself against her. The knife's edge bit into her back. She aimed a knee at his groin but missed. He caught her leg and pushed it wide.

Lust, hunger, and rage burned in his eyes. She knew his intent, felt her heart pound with terror. He fumbled one-handed at his clothing, and in that moment's distraction she reached her free hand behind her back and took the knife in it, cutting a finger on the blade. She shoved against him, got the hilt clear of the tree trunk, and brought the knife to his throat.

Kelevon stopped. Eliani pressed the blade's tip against his flesh.

"Back away."

He grabbed for the knife but she whipped it aside, leaving a tiny cut on his neck and a slash on his hand. She darted away from the tree, stepped behind him, and caught his hair again. She pulled his head back and laid the knife to his throat.

"On your knees."

"Eliani. My sweet—"

"I am not your sweetheart. On your knees!"

Slowly he obeyed. Eliani pressed the blade hard against his throat. She probably was hurting him. She did not care.

Footsteps running. She glanced up at the path, blinking.

"Eliani!"

Turisan ran down the hill toward her, all pale in the starlight, silver glinting from his tunic and his hair flying loose. She gave a sob of relief as he stopped to stare at her and Kelevon.

"You were right." She was gasping. "He is—he is alben."

"Spirits walking!"

"Help me bind him."

Turisan looked confounded for a moment, then reached for the sash of Sunriding colors that Kelevon wore. Eliani planted a foot between Kelevon's shoulders and pushed him onto his face in the dirt, letting go of his hair. She kept her foot on his back and pressed the knife's point against his throat to keep him still while Turisan bound his hands behind him with the sash.

Turisan stood up, dark eyes filled with concern. "You are bleeding."

Eliani straightened and glanced wearily at her hands, both bloodied. Her gown was smeared with dirt, as were her legs and feet, and her skinned knees oozed blood. She still clutched the knife and felt no inclination to let go of it. She tugged at her gown with her other hand, trying to free it from the kirtle to cover herself.

Turisan stepped forward to help her, gently pulling her skirt loose and letting it fall around her ankles. His eyes rose to meet her gaze, worried and loving. She flung her arms around him, and he gasped as he embraced her tightly.

I am ruining your tunic.

I have many others. Too many.

Turisan.

She opened her heart to him, felt his warmth flood her soul. She wanted to lose herself in him but was conscious of Kelevon at their feet.

Not now.

She pulled back, dizzy and trembling. Kelevon stirred. She nudged him with her foot.

"Get up."

He rolled onto his side and struggled to his knees. Turisan took his arm and helped him stand, earning only a dark glance from Kelevon for his trouble. Eliani gestured with the knife for Kelevon to precede them, and he trudged up the hillside to the path with Eliani and Turisan close behind.

Are you all right?

Yes. Just a few cuts.

What happened?

She told him briefly. He listened without comment, casting concerned glances at her.

Others met them as they followed the path back toward the palace. Councillors and guardians spilled into the orchards from the fountain court, and Jharan hurried forward with Felisan close behind. Eliani let Turisan explain, keeping a wary eye on Kelevon, who stared at the ground, defeated but unrepentant.

Jharan's face grew stern. He turned to two of the guardians. "Take him to the garrison. Place him under heavy guard."

"Take this." Eliani handed Kelevon's knife to one of the guardians. She wanted nothing of his.

"My child."

She looked up at her father and gave him a weak smile as he caught her in his arms. "I am all right."

"Oh, my child!"

The guardians led Kelevon away while Eliani and the others returned to Hallowhall. As they passed through the Whispering Walk, she reached for Turisan's hand, not caring who saw or remarked on it. His khi was a glow of comfort against her battered palm.

Her father waited for her at the foot of the stairs to the upper arcade. Luruthin was with him, she saw. She had not noticed his presence before.

Turisan hesitated, his grip on her hand loosening. *Shall I leave you with your kindred?*

She squeezed his hand tighter. *Stay with me.*

He needed no more urging. Eliani climbed the stairs between Turisan and her father, weariness nearly overwhelming her now that danger was past.

Heléri met them on the upper arcade and led them all into her chamber. The males kindled lanterns and drew chairs up to the hearth while Heléri summoned Misani and spoke quietly with her. Misani nodded and left the chamber. Heléri made Eliani sit by the fire and prepared to tend her wounds.

"What happened, child?"

"I was just saying good-bye to Kelevon."

Turisan gave a cough of laughter. The others were silent for a moment, then Felisan laughed aloud.

"Take heed of how she says good-bye, Turisan!"

"I shall."

Luruthin looked from Turisan to her. "I was not in time to see it, but I hope one of you gave him the thrashing he has long deserved."

"Eliani did." Turisan grinned at her. "I merely bound his wrists after she had subdued him."

Eliani shook her head, repressing a shudder. "If you had not come then, I think he would have had the better of me."

Heléri took Eliani's right hand in hers and applied a cloth soaked in warm, herb-scented water to the jagged wound made by the berry thorns. Despite her gentleness, Eliani flinched.

"Kelevon did this?" Heléri asked.

"No. I backed into the brambles. It was this that set him off, though."

Feeling easier in the company of her family, she recounted her fight with Kelevon. Heléri continued to wash her hands, then rubbed a pungent salve into the cuts. Instantly the pain cooled.

"Ah, that feels good. What is it?"

"Balmleaf and lavender."

"May I have some for my knees?"

"Of course. Tell me again, child. You say Kelevon fed from this wound?"

"Tried to. Started to, yes, until I pushed him off."

Heléri glanced at Felisan. Eliani watched her father's face grow grim. She recalled Turisan's attempt to warn her, his concern that Kelevon might carry the sickness Ehranan had surmised. Her heart sank.

Oh, spirits.

Turisan rose from his chair and came to stand beside her, laying a hand on her shoulder and gripping it tightly. *I share your fate.*

But if—

Have I not yet convinced you that I do not want to live without you?

She looked up at him. His face was calm but grave. She could not help smiling.

You look like your father.

I can be every bit as annoying as he.

Eliani chuckled, then glanced at the others, conscious of their concern. It was wrong to speak privately with Turisan before them. She did not wish to be rude to her kin.

Heléri took Eliani's torn hand between both of her own and closed her eyes. The sudden heat of her khi made Eliani catch her breath. After a few moments, the warmth faded and Heléri opened her eyes.

"I can sense nothing amiss. We should visit the Healers Hall. They will want to examine Kelevon as well."

Heléri glanced at Turisan, who nodded. She returned her gaze to Eliani and gently squeezed her hand.

"Do not be frightened, child. Remember who watches over you."

Eliani gave a weak smile. "You, my eldermother."

"And your own mother. And many others."

Turisan's hand squeezed her shoulder. "Lady Heléri, I have a boon to ask of you. How long do you think it might take you to weave a handfasting ribbon?"

Heléri gazed up at him, a smile slowly growing on her lips. She glanced at Eliani, then without a word stood up and went to the shelves set into the chamber wall. From among her possessions resting there she took up a long, slender box of whitewood carved with twining willow leaves, which she brought back and laid upon Eliani's lap.

Eliani looked at her in surprise, then lifted the lid from the box. Inside reposed a ribbon, folded many times, the visible span of which showed images of stars, woodlands, fountains, rivers, and golden fires-pear trees.

Elaini gave a little cry, letting the box's lid fall as she caught up the ribbon. It tingled against her palms and cascaded in coils to the floor as she explored its length. Her name and Turisan's shone out in golden script, along with blessings and many beautiful images of both their lands, all entwined with the blue and violet of Stonereach, the pale green and silver of Greenglen.

Turisan knelt beside her and caught a span of the ribbon in his hands. "When did you begin it?"

"The night you told me you shared mindspeech."

He laughed softly. "You knew better than we."

"You had many questions to ponder. I saw this one thing clearly, though I did not know how soon it would come to pass."

"Oh, Eldermother, thank you!" Eliani reached up to catch Heléri's hands, loops of ribbon spilling from her lap. "It is beautiful!"

Turisan nodded. "Most beautiful. A rare gift."

Felisan came forward to admire the ribbon. "You shall have to think about when you wish to use it."

Eliani looked up at him, then at Turisan. "Tonight."

Turisan smiled. "It need not be tonight."

"Yes, it must, because I want your ribbon on my arm when I start again for Fireshore."

Felisan frowned. "Fireshore?"

Eliani looked from him to Heléri to Turisan, watching their smiles fade. "Kelevon deceived us."

"We do not know that."

Eliani shook her head impatiently. "Why did he come here if not to deceive us? Why would he risk discovery? That letter was sent by the alben! Father, you yourself doubted its authenticity."

"So I did." He looked aggrieved. "Kelevon must be questioned."

Turisan glanced up at him. "If I know my father, he is already doing so."

"I doubt Kelevon will cooperate." Eliani felt her anger returning but shook it off. "We are back to where we were before he arrived. I must go to Fireshore at once."

"Eliani—"

"We have already lost two days."

She gazed earnestly at Turisan, hoping he would understand. His face was taut with concern.

"She is right."

Luruthin raised his head. He had been silent until

now, brooding as he gazed at the fire, but now he looked at Eliani.

"I will ride with you if you still wish it, Cousin."

Turisan glanced at him sharply, then shook his head. "I will go."

Eliani reached for his hand. "Jharan needs you here. And if—if the alben do suffer a sickness, I am already at risk."

Turisan's brows drew together in a frown. Eliani pressed his hand tightly.

"Let us be handfasted tonight."

He sighed and gave a rueful smile. "I would like nothing better, but I fear my father will object. He will want a large celebration with dignitaries from every ælven realm—"

"If the dignitaries who are here for the Council do not satisfy him, he may have his celebration after Eliani returns." Heléri smiled. "That will not be so very long."

"I will handle Jharan." Felisan turned to Luruthin, who sat staring at his hands clasped between his knees. "Luruthin, you will stand with me for Stonereach."

Luruthin looked up, startled. Eliani thought he seemed alarmed and shook her head.

"You need not."

Her father shrugged. "It is Luruthin or Curunan. Or one of the guardians. Heléri will be presiding."

Luruthin managed a laugh. "One of the escort to stand for her while her own kin declines? That would not look very well, I think." His face became serious. "I will be honored to assist in the ceremony."

Felisan clapped him on the shoulder.

"We had best prepare, then. Come, help me do away with Jharan's objections. In truth, I fear him less than I fear Jhinani. She will no doubt be surprised at this addition to the evening's agenda."

Eliani rose to walk with them to the door, leaving the ribbon behind on her chair. With a strange, breathless feeling, she realized what she had set in motion. She was going to be handfasted this night.

When her father and Luruthin had gone, she turned back and looked at Turisan. He stood watching her, softly smiling. She wanted to run into his arms but was conscious of Heléri's presence. She glanced down at her soiled gown.

"I suppose I ought to bathe and change. Again."

Heléri began to gather up the handfasting ribbon. "I asked Misani to have a bath brought to your chamber. You had better change your clothes as well, Turisan."

"Yes." He turned to help Heléri, picking up the whitewood box Eliani had abandoned. "Thank you, Lady Heléri. We all assumed you would perform the ceremony, but if . . ."

She paused to smile at him. "Of course I will perform it. Nothing would give me greater joy."

Eliani joined them in folding the ribbon and returning it to its box. Her hand brushed against Turisan's, and she glanced up at him. He smiled.

Keep that gown.

It is ruined!

I am fond of it. Make me a kerchief from it.

If you had ever seen my needlework, you would not ask that.

His eyes glinted with silent laughter. *I shall treasure your needlework.*

Eliani felt her heart fill with joy. Suddenly self-conscious, she bent to fold the last of the ribbon and lay it carefully in the box. Heléri closed it and took it from Turisan's hands.

"Go, now, children. Make you ready."

Eliani stood up and caught Heléri in a hug. "Thank you, Eldermother."

"You are welcome. Hurry now."

Eliani and Turisan left together, pausing in the corridor outside Eliani's chamber. Torchlight glinted warmly in Turisan's pale hair, but the air was chill. Eliani shivered, and Turisan caught her close for a moment.

I am the luckiest soul walking in flesh.

Eliani leaned her head on his shoulder and pressed her eyes closed, feeling a shadow of her old fear. *Say that in a year and a day.*

I will say it every day of my life.

He held her at arm's length, gazing into her eyes, his dark eyes filled with love. Eliani felt her fear fly away, caught on a breeze of cold fountain mist. She smiled as he bent to kiss her. A moment's tenderness, then they said a silent farewell as they parted.

⁂

Turisan hastened to his chambers, his soul filled with gladness, though it was mitigated by sorrow that he must part with Eliani the next day. He shook off that regret. Tonight was theirs. In a short time they would be joined forever. His heart beat faster at the thought.

In his chambers he found Pheran, a youth he favored as his personal attendant because he made the least fuss of any of the palace folk, awaiting him. Jharan or Jhinani must have sent him.

"All happiness to you, my lord!"

Turisan nodded. "Thank you."

"I took the liberty of laying out a robe for you."

Pheran led him to his tiring room, and Turisan saw that Pheran's usual understanding of his taste had failed him. The youth held up a robe of silver weave heavily crusted with peridots and lined in brocaded silk. It had been a gift from Jharan, and Turisan had worn it once to please his father, but it was as uncomfortable as it was beautiful.

"No. My lady has no such rich attire. Find something like the tunic I took to Alpinon. The same, if you like."

Disappointment showed in Pheran's dark eyes. "So simple as that?"

"Yes."

Turisan picked up a comb and turned away. He stripped off his court clothes, frowning as he noticed the blood smeared on the back of the tunic: Eliani's blood, from her poor wounded hands.

"This one, my lord?"

Turisan turned to see Pheran holding up a long tunic of double-woven silver and soft green, its pattern of leaves and tiny silver flowers. It was a little grander than he liked but much better than Pheran's first choice, and there was no time to spare.

"Yes, all right. Some plain green legs to go with it. Hurry now."

Turisan changed into the tunic and donned the legs that Pheran fetched, then combed out his hair and caught two strands back from his face. Pheran braided them with a third at the back, tying it all off with a silver ribbon. Knowing his father would want him to show token of his rank, Turisan took out the fillet he had worn in Highstone at the handfasting of Eliani's cousin. Pheran removed it from his hands.

"Forgive me, my lord, but Lord Jharan told me you were not to wear aught but this." He proffered the larger coronet set with a single pale green stone that Turisan customarily wore on state occasions.

"I had rather not."

Pheran's brow creased with concern. Turisan had to laugh, and relented.

"All right. Neither of us wants to endure my father's wrath."

Looking relieved, Pheran set the coronet on Turisan's head, and they both turned to the mirror to observe its effect. The green stone gleamed in the torchlight, and the tunic's silver threads glinted golden, like Turisan's pale hair spilling over his shoulders. It would do.

On impulse, Turisan pressed the smaller fillet into Pheran's hands as they left the tiring room. "Take this to my lady. Tell her it is my gift. Go on, I am ready."

Pheran hurried out. Turisan drew a deep breath, then followed him. The handfasting would likely take place in one of the public rooms, a smaller one, he hoped.

He was not to enjoy such fortune. He found his father waiting in the corridor outside the northern entrance to the great hall.

Jharan, wearing his coronet of state and a long robe of brocade in many shades of green embroidered all over with silver and ornamented with white and green gems, took in Turisan's attire with a look of silent resignation. He then broke into a smile and embraced him.

"I am most happy for you, my son."

"Thank you, Father. Thank you for honoring our wishes."

"Hm. Felisan gave me to understand I had little choice."

Lady Jhinani joined them, dressed in a fine gown of silver-gray adorned with pearls over a dress of pale green silk. She carried two long ribbons, one of sage the other of silver, which she handed to Jharan.

Turisan welcomed her with a smile. "Do you stand for me, Jhinani? I am glad."

Jhinani smiled. "It is my honor and my pleasure. I wish you great happiness."

Thank you for the gift, my lord.

Starting, Turisan smiled even as he met his father's gaze. Jharan raised an eyebrow.

You are welcome.

Eliani's thought-touch still thrilled him whenever he

felt it. He said no more, not wanting to offend those with whom he stood.

At last the door before them opened, and the murmur inside the great hall died to a hush. Jharan signaled his color bearer, who carried the Greenglen pennant on a long staff, to precede them into the hall.

Music rang out as they entered, a fanfare of twin trumpets from the gallery above. Turisan saw the councillors ranged along the raised dais at the west side of the circular hall, where ordinarily Jharan sat as he held audience. The hall was filled with the kindred and entourages of all the councillors and with many ranking citizens of Glenhallow. Despite the short notice they had come in force, wearing their finest to honor the occasion.

As the Greenglen party entered from the north, the Stonereach colors were carried in from the south, and Turisan glimpsed Eliani beyond her kindred. He had guessed aright; she wore the same gown of blue and violet silks she had worn in Highstone. Probably it was her best.

She looked well in it. The rich colors set her skin aglow. She wore the fillet he had sent, silver bright against her warm auburn hair. She glanced up and smiled at him, and his spirits soared.

The hall fell silent as Heléri came forward to the top of the steps, holding aloft the handfasting ribbon. Turisan gazed at it, marveling anew at its beauty.

"Councillors, gentles, noble folk of Greenglen and Stonereach and all other clans represented here, witness now the handfasting of these two souls before you, who are a bright hope to our people in these troubled times. Who stands forth for Greenglen?"

The herald droned a lengthy list of Jharan's titles, followed by Jhinani's, then for Stonereach an equally impressive catalog of Felisan's and Luruthin's honors.

Turisan paid no heed, having eyes only for Eliani as they met in front of Heléri. He reached out a hand, and she laid hers in it.

At once Heléri grasped both their hands and drew them forward. Startled, Turisan sensed a tingle in his hand that he thought came from the ribbon draped over Heléri's arms.

"Turisan and Eliani, you stand before this gathering to be handfasted according to the ancient custom, never again to part in flesh or in spirit. If this is not your choice, now is the time to withdraw."

Turisan knew a moment's dread. He kept his eyes on Heléri's face and his mind free of thought. He did not want to coerce Eliani at all, and this was her last chance to retreat from the unbreakable pledge.

All was silent for the space of a breath, then Eliani said, "I choose to be handfasted to Turisan of House Jharanin, never to part again."

Turisan inhaled and dared to look at his lady, who was smiling softly. He swallowed.

"I choose to be handfasted to Eliani of House Felisanin, never to part again."

Even as he spoke, he realized that he was trembling. Eliani's fingers slid between his, and he gripped her hand tighter.

"Then be bound together by your kindred before these witnesses."

Lord Luruthin stepped forward bearing a ribbon of sapphire blue. His gaze moved from Eliani to Turisan, who saw resignation in his green eyes. Laying the ribbon across their clasped hands, he spoke in a quiet but clear voice.

"I bind you together under Stonereach."

He took a step back, holding the ends of the ribbon, and did not look again at either of them but gazed at

Lady Jhinani as she came forward with the ribbon of pale sage.

This she laid over the blue, speaking the words of binding, and Lord Felisan followed it with the violet ribbon. Lord Jharan paused, the silver ribbon in his hands, and looked each of them in the eye before binding them with it.

Heléri stepped forward. "I bind you together in heart, body, and spirit." She laid the handfasting ribbon over all the others, and the tingle Turisan had sensed earlier returned tenfold.

He looked at Eliani. *Do you feel that?*

Yes.

Heléri began to weave all the ribbons, taking and handing them with the others as she spoke of Greenglen and Stonereach. Turisan did not follow her words. He was feeling light-headed and conscious of every move of the handfasting ribbon.

Now his father held it, and his hopes for the future of Southfæld ran down it; now Luruthin accepted a strand from Heléri, seeming surprised to sense the power in the silken weave. Felisan's laughter, Jhinani's kindness flowed through the ribbon, streams of khi blending into a bond that shimmered brightest whenever Heléri touched it.

Turisan's and Eliani's hands were entrapped in a gleaming tapestry through which the handfasting ribbon showed in glimpses: here a star, there a firespear, a fountain, the Three Shades. The ribbons twined down their arms, their kindred's khi glowing in the weave.

"May those in spirit as well as those in flesh extend their blessings over Turisan and Eliani, who from this day forth shall be as one."

The weaving ceased. The ribbons' ends hung glimmering in the torchlight. Heléri smiled at Turisan and

Eliani, then gently lifted their joined hands, drawing them to face each other.

"Raise your hands for all to see and make your pledges now before these witnesses."

Pledges!

Eliani's look of dismay smote him. They had not discussed pledges; there had not been time.

Turisan drew a long breath and spoke the words that came to him. "I pledge you my eternal loyalty. My heart is already yours; my hand I give to you before our kindred here gathered. I am yours and yours alone from this day forward."

Eliani gave him a wavering smile. "I pledge you my trust. I give you my heart and hand before these witnesses. I am yours and yours alone from this day forward."

Heléri gave a slight nod. "Know all here present that these two are now one. Bring forth the emblem of this lady's craft."

Turisan's gaze was drawn to Luruthin, who stepped forward bearing the sword that Felisan had given his daughter upon her majority. The sight brought Turisan's mind back to the threatening war and all that it might mean. Eliani was a guardian before all, or so her clan presented her this day. Theirs would be a union forged in strife. Already he rued the coming dawn that would separate them.

Luruthin's gaze brushed Turisan's as he knelt. Gently the Stonereach lowered the blade before the couple until Lord Felisan caught its tip in a piece of violet velvet just above the marble floor.

Heléri was speaking again, ceremonial words. He half heard them, but his thoughts were all on Eliani.

"The step you now take is the first of your journey together. May it bring you great joy and peace. Come forward into your new life."

Eliani smiled at him. Together they stepped over the sword. As their feet touched the floor beyond, a shock went through him and through their joined hands, strong enough to make him catch his breath.

His awareness of Eliani deepened as the tingling of the ribbon spread along his arm and through his whole body. He set his other foot down and looked at her, feeling unsteady. Heléri's voice recalled him even as her hands turned him and Eliani to face the hall.

"Welcome, Turisan and Eliani of House Jharanin!"

Still dizzy, Turisan blinked and tried to catch his breath as the hall roared with cheers and sudden music from the gallery. Spots of glowing light ranged over the dome above. At first Turisan thought they were illusions, but they remained steady when he moved his head.

Eliani turned her head toward him. *Do you see them?*

Yes—what are they?

Spirits, I think.

Spirits?

Turisan had no time to ponder it, for Heléri drew their bound hands to her and began the reweaving of the ribbons. Her hands moved too swiftly for him to follow in his giddy state, but as she worked, his head began to clear and he was able to look at Eliani without losing himself in her gaze. The tingle of the ribbon subsided to a low, steady glow on the edge of his awareness, a pleasant feeling, almost as if the ribbons now woven onto his forearm were merely a bit heavy.

Suddenly it was done: the ends of the ribbon had vanished into the weave, which was firm about his arm and felt as if it would not loosen. Eliani's arm bore a matching band, and her hand squeezed his as she looked up at him.

The music resolved from fanfares into a dance of

celebration. Turisan glanced up to see the guests
drawing back from the center of the hall, opening a
space and revealing the central mosaic of leaves within
a silver circle. The spots of light above had vanished,
but his euphoria remained. He looked at his lady.

Shall we?

Her smile was her answer. He led her down from the
dais, and as one they crossed into the circle and began
to dance.

⊹

Luruthin stood apart from the cluster of councillors
who gossiped as they watched Turisan and Eliani
move gracefully through the figures of the dance. He
knew it was unwise to stay and yet was unable to tear
himself away.

"A handsome couple, even leaving all else aside."

Turning, he saw Lady Jhinani smiling at him, soft
brown eyes warm in the candlelight. "Do you care to
join the dance?"

He bowed at once and offered her his arm, chagrined at his lapse of courtesy. "Of course, my lady.
Forgive me. I would have remembered in another moment."

"No need to apologize. If you do not wish to dance,
I will not be offended."

Luruthin summoned all his reserves of graciousness
and matched her smile. "By no means. I claim a dance
with you as my privilege."

He led her onto the floor. He had performed this
dance—an old one, traditional at joyful celebrations—
often enough that he had no need to concentrate on
its figures, but glimpses of Eliani distracted him. He
strove to ignore her and devote his attention to his
partner.

Jhinani was a graceful dancer. He told her so, then
complimented her gown, admiring the richness of the

cloth and the embroiderer's skill. When that topic failed, he sought for another, but Jhinani forestalled him.

"So many people in this room. Would you mind if we stepped outside for a moment?"

The floor had become crowded with dancing couples, so their departure would occasion no remark. Luruthin nodded assent and led Jhinani out to the arcade, sighing with relief as they left the crowded hall for the crisp cool of night.

Jhinani crossed to the balustrade that separated the arcade from the fountain court, and Luruthin joined her there. He still had not found a subject for conversation, but she seemed not to expect it. They stood companionably, silent, listening to the hush of falling water. After a moment she glanced at him and nodded toward the courtyard.

"Shall we walk?"

Luruthin smiled. "Yes."

He followed her out among the fountains, feeling his tension ease as they wandered slowly through the court. He had not realized how rigidly he had been holding himself.

Breathing deeply of the damp air, he sought to relax, though not completely. He could not afford that yet. He would need time and privacy for that, and the spirits knew when he would get them. Not soon, for in the morning he would depart with Eliani for the north and must maintain a guard on his feelings.

He noticed an increase of moisture in the air and realized that he had been following Jhinani blindly and that she had led him into the Whispering Walk. He stopped and stood blinking foolishly as she walked on, remembering how he had intruded upon Turisan and Eliani's privacy here. Suddenly his resolution seemed to dissolve, and he felt on the verge of grief.

Eliani. Lost to him for all time, now. Still present but forever out of reach. He had been a fool not to purge her from his heart years ago.

Jhinani's touch on his arm made him start. He looked up and saw concern on her face.

"You are trembling. I should not have brought you out into this chill."

Luruthin sought words of denial, but his voice would not obey him. Jhinani's hand brushed his cheek, then rested on his shoulder. Her khi was warm and as gentle as her smile. He had first sensed it through the ribbons during the handfasting ceremony.

"I know where there is a fire. A quiet room, a cup of wine, perhaps. Will you come?"

He gazed into her dark eyes, seeing further invitation there. A fresher, simpler, and more urgent yearning awoke in him, promising forgetfulness, at least for a time. He nodded, his voice emerging in a harsh whisper.

"Yes."

✤ The Star Tower ✤

Eliani and Turisan finished the dance at the foot of the dais just as the music concluded. Before she could catch her breath, folk crowded around them, offering congratulations. Turisan introduced an elder of the city and of his father's house, but before he could name the next well-wisher, Lord Felisan strode up to them and laid a hand on either one's shoulder.

"A word with you both, if you please."

It was spoken as a command and seemed so unlike her father that Eliani had to stifle a startled laugh. He ushered them into a small chamber at the back of the dais, nodding graciously to the well-wishers as he shut the door upon them.

Felisan smiled. "You will be here all night if you express your thanks to every soul who wishes you happiness."

Turisan laughed. "Ah, I thought this might be a rescue. Thank you!"

Felisan stepped to the back of the little chamber, beckoning to them to follow. "Whoever designed this palace was quite ingenious, I find. They have placed a door here through which one might slip away from an assembly such as this. I suggest you use it before Jharan drags you into the feast hall."

Eliani bit her lip. "I would not wish to offend him."

Her father shook his head, a glint of roguery in his eye. "We shall toast you in your absence. Go along, now, and great joy to you." He shepherded them out through the door, smiling conspiratorially as he closed it.

Finding herself in a torchlit hallway alone with Turisan, Eliani felt her heart quicken. She looked up to see him softly smiling at her. She placed her hand in his and felt an echo of the dizzy sensation that had carried them through the handfasting ceremony.

He led her down the corridor, away from the public rooms of the palace. At the foot of a stair leading to the upper floor he paused, and Eliani realized he was wondering whether to go to his chamber or hers.

At that moment an attendant stepped out of the adjoining corridor, a slender youth, fair-haired and brown-eyed, his features still sharp-edged like a young colt's. Eliani recognized him as the one who had brought her Turisan's gift of the circlet she wore.

"My lord and lady, good evening. I am to guide you to your chamber if you are ready to retire?"

Turisan gave him a suspicious glance. "Pheran—"

"This way."

The attendant smiled, then moved past them and started up the stair. Turisan glanced at Eliani, and they followed. At the upper floor Pheran turned back toward the heart of the palace. Eliani thought he would lead them to the gallery above the great hall, but he turned away to another stair, much smaller and winding upward in broad, curving steps.

Ah. I know where he is taking us.

Turisan's hand squeezed hers, and Eliani suffered herself to be led up the short stair, then along a curving corridor to a second, much longer stair. By the time they had emerged into an antechamber, she had lost all sense of direction.

The golden stone of the anteroom's walls glowed in soft candlelight. A small fire burned brightly in what Eliani assumed was a welcoming hearth, and on the opposite wall tall vases of white winter lilies flanked a wide door. Pheran opened the door and led them up yet another stair, this one short and straight.

Eliani caught her breath as they emerged into a chamber that was circular and open to the night, with balustrades rather than walls and pillars—carved into the shape of living trees, like those of Hallowhall's great dome and arcades—at intervals framing the views. Overhead a few bright stars glinted between the carven branches.

Four great fireplaces roared with fires burning brightly against the night's chill, and heavy tapestries were caught back at the pillars, ready to be let down to block cold breezes. In the center of the chamber a large bed was draped in lighter tapestry.

Feeling shy of a sudden, Eliani walked to the balustrade at the west, looking out at the starlit sky above the dark bulk of the mountains. Far below, she heard the whispering of water in the fountain court and saw the fountains as pale, dancing shadows. She leaned against a pillar and drew a deep breath of crisp air.

Magnificent.

The Star Tower. One of my favorite places.

Eliani smiled at Turisan as he joined her. Beyond him she saw Misani come into the chamber bearing a tray of wine and small cakes, which she set upon a low table by one of the fireplaces.

"Many blessings, my lady, my lord. Lady Heléri sends you her good wishes."

Eliani turned to her. "Thank you, and please convey my thanks to Lady Heléri for sparing you to me."

Misani nodded, smiling, and walked over to the eastern side of the chamber, where Pheran was engaged in lowering the tapestries. She took his arm and drew him toward the stair. "Good evening, my lord and lady."

Pheran gave a start of surprise but quickly recovered. "Yes, good evening." He made a stately bow, then accompanied Misani out.

When the soft closing of the door below reached them, Turisan turned to her, eyes bright in the firelight. Eliani gazed at him, trying to memorize every line of his face, to take in all the details of his form, in the hope that his image would replace all other memories.

His tunic of sumptuous cloth, silver-woven in intricate design, quietly proclaimed his realm's rich culture. He had taken off his coronet, she noted, so that the handfasting ribbon on his left arm remained the brightest thing about his person. It glinted in the firelight as he took a step closer.

"Are you hungry?"

Eliani shook her head, then reached out her hand. He took it, kissed it gently, then turned it and pressed a second kiss into her palm, sending a shiver through her. He glanced up at her.

"Cold?"

She shook her head. It was not cold that made her tremble but a tingling awareness of him. Every part of her was afire with anticipation.

His eyes flashed in response, and the gentleness left him as he kissed her. She closed her eyes and, when she could breathe again, inhaled his scent, warm and slightly musky. A tremor ran through her with the next, deeper kiss, but it was not caused by cold, nor fear. This she did not fear. This she knew how to enjoy, though it had been long since she had permitted it.

With surprise she realized that Turisan was holding back his thought—refraining from mindspeech—touching her only with hands and lips. Running her fingers from his shoulders up the back of his neck and into his soft, flowing hair, she reached out her mind to his and was overwhelmed by his desire.

The double embrace, mind and body, had a dizzying effect as sparks of sensation passed between them: his hand on her cheek, both the warmth of the cheek and the cool hand at once, scents and tastes and touch blending into storm. They embraced the confusion of sensation and beyond it found a place where balance returned.

No words passed between them; no thoughts as formed as that. She suspected she might be able to move his body with her own will, but there was no need for that, because they were in complete accord. Together they explored pure physical sensation, enjoying not only each touch but the ripples of pleasure it awakened, reflected back and forth until they began to lose sense of who was touching, who was feeling.

Eliani emerged again as Turisan moved away, only to catch her off her feet and carry her without pause to the bed. She pushed aside its drapery to let them through, and he laid her down among the soft pillows, then stood gazing at her, dark eyes afire and chest swelling with the depth of his breathing.

Her sash had come untied and been left behind somewhere. She pulled off her overdress of Stonereach blue and sat in her violet silk, reaching up a hand to him, smiling. Taking it in his own, he sat beside her and bent to kiss her throat.

She gasped, remembering Kelevon's teeth closing on her flesh. Turisan drew back, eyes alarmed, filled with questions.

Gripping his hand, she fought the instinct to withdraw and instead opened the memory to him. She felt first his anger, then his understanding, regret, sympathy. He reached up to brush his fingers against her throat. Even that light touch made her flinch; she would have a bruise there by morning.

He gathered both her hands in his and pressed his lips into her palms. *I will never hurt you, my love.*

With a small gasp, she felt sudden tears rise to her eyes. Turisan kissed them away with infinite tenderness, careful not to touch her bruised throat. His kisses started them spiraling together again.

Hands moved, touching flesh, discarding garments, all the while trading kisses and feather touches of the mind that lengthened and deepened into unity of thought. At last it was skin alone save for the handfasting ribbons that bound their arms—somehow their sleeves had come free without disturbing Heléri's handiwork—and in their state of mutual awareness the ribbons sensed touch almost as would skin, sending shivers through them at each caress.

Their joining was filled with amazement as each shared what the other felt, the strangeness of sensing pleasure in a part one's own body did not have quickly giving way to elation at knowing instantly how to magnify their mutual pleasure. As their bond deepened, they left words, then individual thought behind and gasped with delight at each new sensation.

When they caught and followed a particular stimulation, lending it focus through double awareness, it led to higher levels of ecstasy than either had ever known. They danced, perfectly in harmony, pursuing pure physical joy, transported by echoes and reverberations of sensuality.

At last this frenzy reached its peak, and they sank

back together, amazed and delighted, slowly returning to their separate selves. They had but one thought.

This night will pass too quickly.

⁜

Shalár reached the bay just as the eastern star was beginning to fade. She hastened to the city, black sand hissing beneath her feet and a warm breeze giving her comfort. It had been cold at Midrange, and the Wastes were never pleasant. She was glad to be back, anxious to resume her preparations for reclaiming Fireshore.

Ciris and Welir had the kobalen well in hand. Unless the snows came early, they would be ready to cross the mountains at her bidding. Her plans were unfolding as she had hoped.

She climbed the steep path to the Cliff Hollows and smiled as she reached the ledge. Four guards in Darkshore colors saluted her. She nodded to them and went in, hastening through the public rooms to her private quarters. In the corridor she met Galir, who was carrying a covered tray. He stopped upon seeing her, looking startled.

"Bright Lady! You are returned!"

"Just now. Where is Dareth?"

"I-in your chambers, Bright Lady."

Shalár lifted the cloth that covered his tray. The smell of fresh kobalen blood drifted up from her goblet, which stood full upon the tray. She looked at Galir.

"You are taking this to him?"

Galir ducked his head. "I have just brought it away, Bright Lady. At his bidding." He glanced up at her nervously. "We have taken him fresh food every day, as you desired."

Shalár stood still for a moment, gazing at the cup, her heart turning cold. She took the goblet from the tray without a word and strode back to her private chambers.

"Dareth?"

She unslung her pack from her shoulder and left it on the floor. The front chamber was empty, the hearth cold. She walked through to her bedchamber.

Dareth lay upon her bed, propped up by pillows, a scatter of scrolls across his lap. He had been reading, but perhaps not for some while. His eyes were closed, hands lying limp. He was deathly pale.

"Dareth!"

Shalár hurried to him, pushing more scrolls off a table beside the bed to set the goblet on it. She caught Dareth's hand in hers, felt the feathery thread of his weakened khi in it, so thin it was almost beyond detection.

"Dareth. No."

She touched his face. Cold—so cold—but not quite devoid of life. His eyes opened, and he smiled dreamily.

"Shalári. Good, you have returned."

"Why have you done this?" Her throat was tight with grief, and angry tears escaped her eyes. "Why, Dareth? I did not go to Fireshore!"

"But you will. I cannot support it, Shalári. Forgive me."

His words stabbed at her heart. She clutched his hand and stroked his face, searching his eyes for a hint of what might stir his interest.

"You promised to give me a child!"

"I have failed to keep that promise. I will atone."

"No!"

She wanted to shake him but feared doing him harm. She seized the goblet and held it to his lips.

"Drink!"

He turned his head away, frowning as he closed his eyes. Shalár caught her breath on a sob.

"Please, Dareth. I beg you, do not leave me!"

He was silent, his lips pressed tightly together. Despairing, she pushed the goblet onto the table again, slopping a little of its contents onto a scroll.

From habit she picked the page up and brushed away the blood, seeking to preserve the scroll, for good parchment was not easy to make. It was old, a copy from her archives of a poem that had been written many centuries ago in Eastfæld.

She glanced at some of the others and saw that they were all similar works: old ballads, lays, histories. Dareth had been seeking something in the distant past.

The scroll in her hands was "Creed of the Ælven," a poem whose first stave every ælven child learned by heart almost from the cradle. She remembered her mother teaching it to her in Darkwood Hall. It had been written by the great bard Vahlari on commission from the first governor, Arithan, who had codified the creed by which the ælven lived.

Shalár was tempted to crumple the page. She had not known a copy of this poem was in her archives.

"It is a beautiful verse, is it not?"

She looked at Dareth, who lay gazing at her once more, softly smiling. His tranquillity drained all the rage from her.

"So many of these old songs are beautiful. We should ensure that they are remembered."

"Do that for me." She had no wish for it, but she would encourage anything that might keep him with her. "You know much more than I of such things. Do not let your wisdom be lost."

"I am too tired." He sighed. "Forgive me. Some

younger soul will have to take on the task. I am sure you will find someone."

"Dareth—"

"Kiss me now."

Weeping, she let the scroll fall to the floor and leaned over Dareth's wasted form. She pushed his pale hair back from his brow and kissed it, her lips trembling against his cold flesh.

"Stay with me."

"Spirits be with you."

"That is an ælven expression."

Her response, her rejection of his words, had been automatic. She felt a stab of regret, though Dareth only smiled again.

"But we *are* ælven, Shalári."

Dread rose to tighten her throat, along with arguments and denials, but she dared utter none of them. His smile frightened her.

She kissed him, trying to wake him with her passion, trying to send her own will into him. He yielded too easily, like a gauzy curtain might yield to the wind, no barrier to its force. When she sat up again, he smiled once more, then closed his eyes.

She felt his spirit fly, escaping her grasp, leaving behind the flesh that he no longer cared to sustain. Leaving her to struggle on without him.

Leaning her head against his silent chest, she wept. Her only friend, who bettered her simply by being, gone. She had never felt so alone.

Later, much later, a tiny sound disturbed her. She sat up abruptly and wiped at her face, though her tears had long since dried.

It was Galir. "Forgive me, Bright Lady. Nihlan wishes to know if you require anything of her before sunrise."

"No."

Turning her head, she saw Galir leaving the chamber. "Stay."

"My lady?"

Shalár waved a hand at the scrolls scattered about the chamber. "Pick all these up."

"Yes, my lady. What shall I do with them?"

Shalár stood up, glancing at Dareth's silent face. She would look no more at that husk. He was not there.

She took up the goblet and drank deeply of its contents. The blood had cooled but still flooded her with new strength, though it could not fill the hollowness within her. She emptied it, then set it down.

"Burn them."

She strode out of the chamber, treading heedlessly on the old songs of the ælven. She had no energy to waste on such follies. Reclaiming Fireshore was all she cared for now. The living souls of Darkshore were her duty, and she would give to their preservation all the passion she had left.

⁜

Luruthin rolled onto his back, pleasantly disoriented. He could not remember where he was, but he was warm, and the scents around him were rich though unfamiliar. Spices of Southfæld, he thought. That was right; he was in Southfæld.

Memory returned in a rush, bringing him fully alert. He opened his eyes to see soft firelight glinting off long tresses of honey-gold hair spread across his forearm. Honey, not russet.

His initial dismay was replaced by remembrance of how he had come to be here, in Lady Jhinani's private chamber. She had taken pity on him, but had not made him feel pitiable. He closed his eyes again, inhaling her scent, feeling her khi as a gentle glow enfolding him. He breathed a sigh of gratitude.

Jhinani turned to face him, smiling as she nestled

her head into a silken pillow. He smiled back and reached up to caress her cheek.

"Thank you."

She glanced aside, her lashes veiling her eyes. "That was you making love to her." She reclaimed his gaze, her dark eyes wide in the chamber's dimness. "Now make love to me."

Luruthin drew a long breath. Certainly he owed her at least that much. He swallowed the apology he knew she did not want and carried her hand to his lips, then began slowly to kiss the length of her arm.

She rolled onto her back, smiling as she closed her eyes. He kissed her deeply, then gently all over her face, throat, and shoulders. She let out a soft moan as he moved on, taking his time, exploring all of her body with his hands and dropping kisses like flower petals on her trembling flesh.

Now, instead of thinking solely about Eliani, he could not help comparing Jhinani's beauty with hers. The lady of Greenglen was rounder, soft and warm in her curves, with a sweet gentleness that hid strength and passion.

He kissed her to the point of elation and, finding his flesh inspired anew by her pleasure, entered her, intending to complement her ecstasy with his own. Moving slowly, he sought to sustain her delight. Their lips met and kissed warmly, deeply.

Everything about her was warm, her khi a golden haze in his awareness now. He drew it close and offered his own in return. She sighed, and he felt her acceptance, felt it in his khi and in her flesh, which yielded to him unexpectedly.

A shudder went through him as her body opened to him, drew him in deeper, deeper than he had ever been before. Astonishment filled him, along with a rising elation. He lifted his head and gazed into her eyes, feeling her khi pour through him, her flesh close around him in a tight embrace.

His wonder was reflected in her face. Neither spoke. There was no need. Luruthin understood what was happening though he had never experienced it—nor expected to—and surely she understood as well. He searched her eyes for any sign of doubt and was glad to see none.

Their khi flowed together, blending in a closeness as new to him as their physical union. It sang through him, imprinting Jhinani's essence forever on his soul. Then his body left his control, and he had no thought but awareness of his seed flooding her in waves of ecstasy.

As his passion ebbed, he sensed an unfamiliar presence, a glow akin to Jhinani's khi yet different, brighter, more powerful than any he had experienced. From this presence came a flood of warmth, happiness, gratitude.

Greetings, and my thanks to you, Mother and Father.

The voice rang through his being like music and sunlight together. Was this what the mindspeakers felt? If so, he could understand the impossibility of resisting the gift.

Luruthin opened his eyes and gazed at Jhinani, dropped an unsteady kiss onto her lips, and was rewarded by her smile. They had gone from near strangers to a bond that would never be broken, for now they were three.

⌖

Eliani and Turisan awoke as one, roused by sunlight striking the Star Tower. During the night they had closed all the tapestries, trapping the fires' ebbing heat within the chamber, but now the daylight passed in through the tower's latticework crown, throwing soft tree-branch shadows across the draperies of the bed.

Turisan closed his eyes, shutting out the confusion

of two vantages, reveling in his awareness of Eliani, still deeply intimate as he watched the growing dawn through her eyes. He knew that he was himself, and that he was on the verge of being her as well, and this pleased him.

They were profoundly rested in a way he never could have put into words. Just as their passion had multiplied, so their repose deepened with their union. He cherished every moment, dreading the coming separation.

She responded by clasping him more tightly. Despite this, their minds drew apart as each remembered tasks that must be completed before Eliani's departure. The world and their duties in it intruded on their thoughts, and soon would intrude on their privacy.

Sighing in unison, they released each other, though they clung together in thought, finding a level of closeness just short of confusion. He gazed at her, wanting to kiss her and knowing it would throw them back into heated passion. She smiled and slid to the edge of the bed, finding violet silk and twining it haphazardly about herself before drawing aside the bed's drapery.

Newly built fires crackled softly, defying the dawn's chill. Wraps had been laid out for them. Eliani reached for one, let her silk fall, and put it on. Turisan felt its soft thickness.

He got up and donned the other, and together they moved to sit before one of the hearths. Muted light, blue and crossed with the shadows of carved stone branches, filtered down to quarrel with the golden-orange glow of the fire.

Turisan took her hand, their beribboned arms lying together, sparkling in their awareness like the prickling of blood returning to a chilled limb. He formed a wordless thought—that Heléri had made a more powerful bond than he had imagined possible—and Eliani silently agreed. They remained sitting thus until they heard the cautious opening of the door below and the tread of their attendants on the stair.

"Good morrow, my lord and lady."

Misani's gentle voice struck them as a stone shattering glass. With a gasp they dropped hands and hastily drew apart in thought—regretfully, but both knew it was necessary if they were to interact with others.

Eliani managed a smile for Misani, who brought forward a tray with two steaming cups and a plate of sweet bread and cured meat. Behind her Pheran emerged from the stair with his arms full of clothes. Eliani saw her own blue riding leathers among them and felt a sharp pang of sadness. She hid it from the attendants but could not hide it from Turisan, who had felt it as strongly as she.

That her feelings could hurt him had not occurred to her, and she turned a look of silent apology toward him. He smiled, shaking it away, and held out a piece of bread.

Eat. You will need your strength.

She had eaten little the previous day and, finding that she was now ravenous, attacked the meal with gusto. Turisan ate more sparingly, watching her with an amused smile. He guarded her from his deeper feeling, not wishing to cause her grief with the heartache that was growing in him. Sharing that pain would serve neither of them.

When the meal was eaten, there was no more to do but allow the attendants to dress them. Pheran had brought a formal robe for Turisan but had been wise enough to choose a plain one of pale sage with only a narrow border of silver leaves.

"Yes, that will do." Turisan found it strange to be speaking aloud.

When Pheran offered the state coronet, he shook his

head, and the youth set the ornament aside without further comment than a small, resigned smile. Instead he picked up a cloak—again, the simplest choice available in Turisan's wardrobe, his Southfæld guardian's cloak—and held it up for him.

Turisan gazed at the garment for a moment, then took it from Pheran's hands, nodding his thanks. He carried it across the chamber to where Heléri's attendant was close-braiding Eliani's hair to keep it out of her eyes, it being too short for an effective hunter's braid.

The Stonereach attendant glanced up at Turisan, finished the braid, and moved away. Eliani turned to him, dressed in riding leathers over soft tunic and breeches, much as he first had seen her, though not so dusty. The memory drew a smile from him.

He laid the cloak around her shoulders. It was heavy-woven for warmth and mage-blessed for protection, sage green with a silvery lining and a clasp of silver falcons' heads that he fastened at her throat. He felt her surprise as she looked down at the garment.

My new colors.

He glanced up and saw that the attendants had withdrawn, so he drew her to him and held her tightly, wrapping his love around her along with the cloak. He kissed her long and gently, then drew back.

There were no more words. Words would only carry pain. Each knew what was in the other's heart. The gift that had united them so deeply would best serve their people through their separation.

Turisan had not fully realized the bitter irony of this until now. He rejected the thought and offered Eliani his arm. She laid hers upon it, and together they descended from the tower to embrace their fate.

❖

"Shall I ask to be excused from the Fireshore expedition?"

Luruthin gazed at Jhinani in the soft haven of her bed. Their bodies had remained joined for most of the night, but as dawn had crept around the tapestries at her window, they had separated. Her khi still tingled through him, along with a faint sense of their child's presence.

She smiled and stroked his hair. "That is kind, but no need. What could you do besides bear me company?"

"Oh . . . pamper you into a state of insensible bliss?"

Jhinani laughed. "There are plenty here who will wish to do that." Her hand found his, and her expression grew thoughtful. "I think your cousin will have greater need of you. And you will not be away for long."

"Sixty days at the very least."

"That is less than a season." She smiled at him. "Nothing important will happen in that time. I often serve in the healing hall, and you may believe that my colleagues there will take exquisite care of me."

Luruthin felt warmth fill his heart. Jhinani was so generous. She gave so freely, without ostentation or demand, out of sheer kindness as far as he knew. He could grow to love her deeply, he was certain. Most likely he would, for he intended to share their child's upbringing as much as possible.

"I should have known you were a healer. You have healed me."

She smiled and moved into his embrace. He kissed her, then froze at a sound in the outer chamber of her suite.

Jhinani raised her head, listening, then turned to him with a gesture for silence and softly kissed him before leaving the bed. He watched her don a silvery silken wrap that flowed like water over the curves of her body as she walked out of the room. With a sigh he lay back, listening to the murmur of voices from the other room.

In a few moments Jhinani returned, carrying a small tray of tea and fruit. "It was Suliri, my attendant. I have sent her away, but I fear you must not stay. The Council is gathering to bid you and Eliani farewell."

Luruthin sat up, letting the silken bedclothes fall away as he realized with a start that he had made no preparations for his journey northward. Jhinani sat on the edge of the bed, offering the tray to him.

"Here, have some of this. There is only one cup, I fear."

He glanced up at her, laughing softly as he reached for the tea. "One cup is all we need for a bonding."

Her head turned sharply toward him. "Do you wish to cup-bond?"

He paused with the tea halfway to his mouth, caught off guard by the intensity of her tone. "It was a jest—"

"I know it was, but . . ."

She looked away. Luruthin watched her for a moment, then put the tea back on the tray and gently took it from her, setting it aside before gathering her hands into his.

"What were you going to say?"

Jhinani shook her head. "A foolish thought. Never mind."

He leaned forward, laid his cheek against hers, and whispered into her ear. "Do you wish to cup-bond?"

Merely speaking the words set his heart racing. He knew at once that it was his wish whether or not it was hers. He had no lover back in Alpinon, so to make such a pledge would be no hardship. Indeed, he wanted to claim Jhinani, he realized with sudden fierceness. He wanted her to be his alone for the year of a cup-bond—the year that would end in the birth of their child—if not for longer.

She gave a slight laugh. "It would make little difference for my part. I will care to keep no other company for this year, but that need not affect you." Her hand went to her belly where his seed had so lately taken hold.

He looked into her eyes, trying to read her wishes. He sensed that this was a gift he could give her, one that would mean a great deal to her. He solemnly kissed both her hands.

"I would be honored to bond with you for a year and a day." Or forever, he thought a bit wildly.

Her shy smile was his reward. "Truly?"

"Truly."

He reclaimed the teacup and wrapped her hands around the tall, slim vessel, covering them with his own. The tea's warmth seeped through the pottery, radiating between their fingers.

"Lady Jhinani, I pledge myself to you alone for this day and for a year of tomorrows."

He drew the cup to his lips and sipped, laughing inwardly at the thought of a cup-bond made with tea. Usually wine was used, and some degree of ceremony employed, but that was the couple's choice. A pledge was a pledge, whether made privately or before witnesses, and the creed required that it be honored.

Jhinani repeated the vow and sipped the tea, and for a moment they stayed so, warmth spreading through their hands as they gazed at each other. Carefully, so as not to spill the hot beverage, Luruthin leaned forward to kiss his lady over the cup. The pledge sealed, his patience with the tea was ended and he took it away from her, putting tea, tray, and all on a table out of the way before gathering her into his arms.

"You must not stay."

"I know."

He kissed her, sliding his arms inside her silken garment, clasping her warm flesh to him and trying to put a season's worth of passion into the embrace. Finally he let her go; standing up so that he would not be tempted to reach for her again, he looked about the floor in search of his clothing.

⚜

A roar of cheering greeted Turisan and Eliani as they stepped from Hallowhall's doorway into the public circle. He had thought no greater crowd could fit within the circle than those he had seen in recent days, but he had been mistaken. The circle and all the avenues leading up to it were packed tight with folk, and had there not been a double line of the Southfæld Guard holding them back, he and Eliani never would have been able to walk to the center of the circle where the Council awaited them.

Pennants stirred in the early breeze—sage and silver, blue and violet, white and gold—all the colors of the ælven governing clans save one. Clan Sunriding was still absent.

Jharan held up a hand for silence and began wishing Eliani a formal farewell on the Council's behalf. The words did not catch in Turisan's mind. He was more strongly aware of Eliani, her hand gripping him tightly, her khi awash with apprehension and also with desire. Still desire, though they had coupled again and again through the night. He ached for her even now.

Jharan finished his praises and embraced Eliani, as did her father. The Council all clasped hands with her in turn, then Turisan accompanied her to her horse. Laying his hands on her shoulders, he kissed her. The crowd cheered wildly, and Eliani glanced up at him, eyes dancing with wicked mirth.

Shall we give them a greater thrill?

He chuckled. *Best not. It would shatter my father's dignity.*

Hm.

She hefted herself into the saddle with ease. Her face resumed the sternness he had seen in Alpinon when they had discovered kobalen in the South Wood. She was girding herself for the journey, arming herself against loneliness with her old protective shell, though her gaze when she looked upon him was lit with love. He smiled up at her, hiding his heartache.

Speak to me often as you ride. If we are limited by distance, we must know as soon as possible.

Her green eyes flashed fire. *I will speak to you from the edge of the world.*

He stepped back, giving her room to turn the horse and join her cousin, who was waiting a little distance away. Turisan glanced at Luruthin, thinking his position pitiable, but the Stonereach appeared calm and even welcomed Eliani with a smile that seemed perfectly easy as her mount came up beside his. Rather a change from the previous day, but Turisan had no time to ponder it. Eliani was leaving.

Led by Vanorin, who carried a lance pennanted with sage and silver, the small cavalcade started forward. A horn sounded as they left the circle, and a slow roar began among the onlookers—a cheer of sorts, but with a mournful note that swelled and echoed from the surrounding mountains.

Stay with me. Eliani did not look back, but her voice pleaded.

I am here.

He watched her pass down Glenhallow's main avenue toward the city gates, followed by the twenty guardians of her escort. The crowd that parted to let them pass closed behind them and shuffled along in their wake, calling out blessings and good wishes.

Turisan remained standing in the circle until he no longer could see Eliani, though he knew precisely where she was. He knew the moment she passed the city's inner gate, then the outer, then when she crossed the bridge on the road to the Silverwash. He stood gazing eastward, the morning light harsh in his unseeing eyes, as she met the river road and turned north. He knew when the mounted party picked up the trot, then let their horses stretch into a lope.

"Lord Turisan?"

Startled, Turisan turned his head and saw Lady Heléri beside him. She was veiled against the sun, but through the dark violet he saw her smile.

"Such a bright morning. I fear I am unused to this much daylight. Will you escort me back to the palace?"

He subdued a stab of impatience. She was right, of course. Why should he stand here all morning, uselessly watching an empty road?

The crowd was dispersing, he realized. Some few remained in and about the circle, talking and glancing at him with wondering eyes.

Turisan bowed to Heléri and was surprised to find it difficult to straighten himself, as though moving had disturbed the heartache he hoped to keep at bay and it now threatened to overwhelm him. With an effort he controlled himself and offered her his arm, then walked with her toward Hallowhall. He saw his father ahead of them, talking with Felisan and Ehranan as they returned to the palace.

We have passed out of sight of the city.

Turisan swallowed. *Spirits guard you, my love. Tell me when you reach Skyruach.*

Will you be resting?

I believe the Council is reconvening, and I had best be present.

He paused and with a rueful smile added another thought. *Your eldermother is urging me not to behave like an idiot.*

Her laughter glittered in his mind, falling as rain on the desert and instantly lifting his mood. *Heed her, love. She is always right.*